everyday a monday

EVERYDAY A MONDAY

STEPHEN BARNES

Copyright © 2020 Stephen Barnes

The moral right of the author has been asserted.

Apart from any fair dealing for the purposes of research or private study, or criticism or review, as permitted under the Copyright, Designs and Patents Act 1988, this publication may only be reproduced, stored or transmitted, in any form or by any means, with the prior permission in writing of the publishers, or in the case of reprographic reproduction in accordance with the terms of licences issued by the Copyright Licensing Agency. Enquiries concerning reproduction outside those terms should be sent to the publishers.

This is a work of fiction. Names, characters, businesses, places, events and incidents are either the products of the author's imagination or used in a fictitious manner. Any resemblance to actual persons, living or dead, or actual events is purely coincidental.

Matador
9 Priory Business Park,
Wistow Road, Kibworth Beauchamp,
Leicestershire. LE8 0RX
Tel: 0116 279 2299
Email: books@troubador.co.uk
Web: www.troubador.co.uk/matador
Twitter: @matadorbooks

ISBN 978 1 83859 551 7

British Library Cataloguing in Publication Data.
A catalogue record for this book is available from the British Library.

Typeset in 11pt Adobe Garamound by Troubador Publishing Ltd, Leicester, UK

Matador is an imprint of Troubador Publishing Ltd

For my wife Christine
1947–2004

PART ONE

1968–

Chapter I

The ocean spray rose in white plumes from the destroyer's flared bow and was carried on the Atlantic wind to bite into the exposed flesh of the watch keepers standing on the open bridge.

'Bridge... Captain.' The barking voice sounded metallic and hollow as it echoed in the small, grey speaker.

The Officer of the Watch took the binoculars from his eyes and moved his right hand to pick up the rubber encased microphone. He depressed the raised spine on the handle to speak.

'Bridge.'

'Is the Navigator there?' The tone was urgent and the Sub-Lieutenant shot a glance towards the chart table tucked away in the forward section of the bridge. The tall figure of the Navigator was bent over the chart but on hearing his title turned to face the young Officer of the Watch.

'Yes Sir, he's here.' Both men's eyes met and their eyebrows raised in anticipation of what was coming next. The Captain continued;

'Don't bother him, just ask if we are in the area yet?' The Navigator nodded his head and walked from beneath the metal canopy that protected the chart table from the North Atlantic weather. He raised his right leg and hoisted himself up onto the exposed compass platform. The message was passed and the Captain began issuing orders in short, staccato bursts;

'Close up the extra lookouts, reduce speed to twelve knots and remain on this course until advised by me to alter.' The orders were acknowledged and the Sub-Lieutenant breathed easier when the intercom went dead. He had only been in the ship for three weeks and its commanding officer was still, and would probably remain, an awesome figure. However, on board a warship there is a hierarchy and he in turn felt better when addressing one of the most junior in that established order.

'Bosun's Mate. Pipe for the lookouts to close up.' Within moments the sound of heavy footsteps on the bridge ladder heralded the arrival of the extra pairs of eyes to be used in the search that was about to begin.

The Navigator stood silent while the lookouts were briefed and assigned their sectors of observation.

'Do you think we'll find them sir?' The young officer asked as the sailors moved out of earshot. The man he was addressing was only a few years older than himself but boasted the two and a half stripes of a Lieutenant Commander and the title of Squadron Navigator.

Peter Wells was a high flyer in the Royal Navy. As one of the youngest officers ever to be selected for the Long Navigation Course and the youngest officer of his rank he was destined for the top. His manner was formal without being aloof.

'Your guess is as good as mine Paul. A forty foot yacht in the middle of all this.' He raised his left arm as if the gesture confirmed his statement about the vastness of the white capped ocean. 'They may have taken to a raft by now. We're going to need a lot of luck.'

The Officer of the Watch slowly shook his head from side to side and drew a deep breath of the cold sea air. The Navigator returned to the chart table.

'We did get a position before contact was lost so let's keep our fingers crossed.' He tried to inject a note of optimism into his voice.

Through sore and tired eyes Peter Wells stared at the white chart and focused on the pencil point that indicated the ship's estimated position. 'Estimated', the word echoed in his troubled mind. He had told the Captain the ship was in position. How could he be sure? For the past thirty six hours they had been steaming under billowing grey clouds that obscured anything above the horizon. The biting wind that tore at the surface of the sea appeared ineffectual in moving the mantle from the sky overhead. To get a fix on the chart was impossible. They had been running on dead reckoning and it was only dead reckoning that told the navigator that the ship was now in position.

'Are you happy, pilot?'

The gruff voice of the Captain startled Peter and caused his heart to pound under the layers of wet weather clothing. It was not the barking tone the Captain always adopted, but the fact he had read his

Navigator's thoughts that caused Peter's discomfort. He had been so engrossed in his calculations he had not heard the Captain come onto the bridge. He swallowed hard, composed his expression and turned to face his commanding officer.

'I'm confident, Sir. It is all on DR but I have calculated the errors and believe us to be in the right place.'

The Captain's eyes squinted inside lined sockets. He tucked a white towel around his neck and inside the collar of his heavy duffle coat.

'I'm sure you are right, Peter.' He replied and pulled himself up onto the high wooden chair that was positioned on the port side of the bridge.

Thinking it may be seen as a sign of uncertainty Peter did not return to the chart table. Instead, he climbed up onto the compass platform and scanned the ocean through powerful binoculars.

The search continued throughout the day and into the night. In the darkness signal lanterns were trained on the flattening sea. With the night came the rain. The brilliant white beams of light highlighted the water droplets as they fell and ricocheted off the black surface of the waves. No light penetrated the wall of cloud and the Navigator had gone below with doubt eating away inside of him.

'No luck then Peter?' The Torpedo Officer said as the Navigator entered the crowded wardroom. It was dinner time and the ship's officers who were not on watch were seated around the long mahogany table. The Torpedo Officer had turned towards the door, a sympathetic, almost brotherly expression on his lined face. He was older than his fellow officers. He had joined the Navy before the Second World War and had risen to commissioned rank through years of hard work, study and dedication. It had not been easy, especially the studying. He was not naturally academic. Perhaps that was why he respected the Navigator. A man almost half his age but already one rank higher. A man to whom everything appeared to come so easily and who accepted this with charm and equanimity. Although, now he could see the worry in the young officer's face. The Navigator shook his head when he spoke;

'We are locked in solid and it's raining now. At least the sea has moderated.' He walked over to the table and took his seat beside the older man.

'Do we know how many people are in the yacht?' Another voice joined the conversation. It was the Engineer, who added apologetically; 'I've been tied up below with the starboard propeller shaft. It has been playing up since the skipper asked for full power to get us here.'

At the end of the table the First Lieutenant pushed the soup bowl away from him and wiped the traces of the liquid from his red beard.

'The signal said two adults and three children. The youngest is a boy of three. A family.'

They ate in silence, each man visualizing the terror out in the dark night, and, when the plates were cleared away more than one went back with the food hardly touched.

Following the meal Peter went to his cabin. He did not want to get into a conversation about the search and his part in it. He had told the Captain they were in the correct position and he did not want to hear anything that might raise doubts in his mind.

In the quiet of his cabin Peter sat down at the grey metal bureau that functioned as both a writing desk and a chest of drawers. He sat staring at the empty desktop and then reached into one compartment that was set along the right hand side. He did not know what guided his hand. He had almost forgotten the photograph was there. Slowly he brought it out of the darkness and into the cabin's bright light. The face of a young woman, full of love and pride, looked back at him. A fringe of bobbed, blond hair framed her wide and sparkling blue eyes that glowed with joy. She held a baby to her rounded cheek and Peter felt an emptiness deep within as he looked into both their faces. While his eyes stared at the photograph his mind focused on images from the past. He recalled the day of the wedding. The grandeur of the ceremony, the archway of drawn swords formed by naval colleagues, the love they felt for one another, the brief honeymoon in France and then, the recriminations.

'Angela.' The thought of her name caused him to screw his eyes tightly shut as if to erase the picture of her innocent face and those pleading blue eyes. She could not, or would not, understand why he had to leave her for months on end. She never forgave him for not being there at the birth of their son. She would not accept that he was a naval officer and that sacrifices had to be made if he was to get as far and as fast as he could in the service. His eyes then looked on the tiny face of his baby son. 'Sacrifices to be made.' The words echoed in his saddened mind. 'How old would he be now? Nearly six, or was it seven?' He had been taken away in such a fast and orderly manner that Peter had felt powerless to fight back.

The Navigator now wanted to stop these thoughts that tortured his mind and broke his heart. However, as if to torment him his memory conjured up pictures of that final argument. His ship had returned to Portsmouth after a ten month deployment to the Far East. They had exchanged loving letters. Letters expressing feelings that can only be written by people kept apart by great distance and time. Expressions of what should have been bore little resemblance to reality. Angela had been there to meet the ship but he had kept her waiting for an hour while he reported to the Staff Operations ashore. It was the final straw. One hour after the ship had docked his marriage was over. Through streaming tears Angela said how she had tried but could not accept the secondary role he had given her. 'You can have your life... your Navy!' She had cried and stormed from the ship.

The news of the separation was good scandal in wardrooms throughout the fleet, but the stigma of divorce did not affect his selection to the Long Navigation Course and promotion soon thereafter. Losing his family had hurt him, but he would not admit to having lost everything. He was a very successful Naval Officer and an excellent Navigator.

His ego restored he replaced the photographs back into a pile of old correspondence and rose from his chair. He would go to the bridge before turning in for the night.

'Wake up Sir...excuse me Sir. We have a contact.' The excited voice of the Bosun's Mate roused the Navigator from a troubled sleep. He soon realised what was being said.

'What time is it?' He asked.
'Zero five twenty, Sir.'
'Is it visual or radar?'
'Radar Sir. Very faint.'
'What's the weather like?'
'It's stopped raining but the wind had increased to force six.' Peter pulled on his foul weather gear.
'Tell the Officer of the Watch I am on my way.'

As the Navigator stepped from the hatch and onto the open bridge he noticed the Captain had got there before him. Peter knew the Captain would have been called first but still he resolved to get ready quicker next time.

The Officer of the Watch had his face buried in the rubber cover that shielded the amber glow of the radar screen from the light of day. The Captain was perched in his chair with his binoculars pressed hard against his eyes.

'Is it still there Mr. Mays?' The Captain called over the biting wind.

'Affirmative Sir. Range is closing.'

'I can't see a bloody thing.' The Captain swore and dropped the glasses so they hung from the strap around his neck.

Minutes passed with each man in turn looking out at the wind tossed sea through binoculars that quickly became smeared with flying salt spray. Then the call came.

'Bridge... Port Lookout.' All eyes turned toward the junior sailor as Lieutenant Mays responded,

'Bridge.'

'Red three zero. Wreckage. Far.'

As if choreographed all binoculars were raised to their respective eyes and turned on the bearing.

'He's got bloody good eyesight,' muttered the Captain to no one in particular. The racing wind streaked the wave tops with white tracks of foam. 'Have you got anything Pilot?' This was the first acknowledgement the Captain had given to the presence of his navigator. Peter felt a failure when he had to answer no. Anticipating the Captain's next question Lieutenant Mays looked at the radar screen.

'The contact is on the bearing Sir.'

'Increase speed to eighteen knots.' The Captain's voice betrayed his excitement. He was on the scent and closing in on his quarry. 'Get the sickbay prepared. Lookout! Do you still have the contact?' The sailor confirmed that he had and indicated the bearing with his arm.

'I see it sir!' Peter held his elation in check and continued, 'twenty degrees on the port bow and halfway to the horizon. It looks like wreckage all right.' There was silence on the bridge as each man retreated into his thoughts.

The destroyer's razor like bow sliced through the oncoming waves and left a white scar of turbulence in its wake.

'I've got it now, sir.' The Officer of the watch exclaimed and checked the compass bearing. 'Bearing two two zero.'

'Steer two two zero. The Captain ordered and then added impatiently, 'I still can't see a bloody thing.'

Time passed with only the sound of the wind whistling in the radio aerials and the rush of the sea down the ship's sleek sides to mark its passage.

'Got it!' The Captain cried triumphantly. 'Bring us down to ten knots and take us alongside Mr. Mays.'

The wreckage was strung out in a long ribbon of destruction along the wave tops. Panels of splintered wood floated alongside half submerged boxes and waterlogged bedding.

The ship slowed so that it wallowed in the rolling sea. The destroyer's upper deck became crowded with silent sailors staring into the water's inky blackness.

'Oh my God...' The exclamation came from a sailor standing on the Bofor deck below the bridge. In the lee of the ship the surface of the sea was calm and flotsam passed slowly on the tide down the destroyer's flank. Among the evidence of destruction and floating just below the surface of the waves, like a macabre image of childhood, a vivid yellow teddy bear, its glass eyes staring lifelessly, looked out from its dark and watery grave. Under its haunting spell the ship and all those in it were held as surely as it was held in the ocean's grip.

Beneath an overcast sky the pale dawn had given way to a grey, clear morning. As if satisfied with its part in the destruction of the man-made craft the wind died away. It was the combination of a more calm sea and the slow speed of the ship that enabled the port lookout to make his next sighting.

'Bridge... Port Lookout. Contact. Fine on the port bow. Far.' All eyes looked at him before turning toward the new bearing. The Officer of the Watch moved back to the radar screen. The Captain ordered an increase in speed and a small cloud of black smoke billowed from the funnel. The destroyer gathered headway and eyes strained to find the object that the ship's sharp eyed look out had reported.

As he scanned the sea the Navigator could not erase the picture of the waterlogged teddy bear from his mind. He tried closing his eyes but that did not work. The child's companion was more than evidence of a recent tragedy. It became the symbol of a more personal loss. A separation of father and son that was as final as death itself. It was the price he had paid for success and would continue to pay for the rest of his life. In that instant he wondered if it had been worth it.

The harsh reality of the question brought him out of his personal inquisition. He massaged his tired eyes with the fingers of his right hand and took a deep breath of cold morning air. Returning his attention to the search he thought he saw a flash of colour rise on a wave and then disappear. He concentrated his vision and waited to see if it would appear again. Seconds passed. He tightened his grip on the frame of the glasses. Foam streaked waves rose, moved over the surface of the sea and then disappeared in rolling troughs. Peter saw it again. The bright orange canopy standing out in sharp relief against the sombre backdrop of the dark ocean.

'It's a raft, Sir.' He reported.

The Captain nodded and without taking his binoculars from his eyes acknowledged the sighting. They had found the needle in the haystack but elation was not the immediate reaction. As the bow of the warship bore down there was no sign of life from the tiny raft.

'You have the ship.' The Captain addressed Lieutenant Mays, letting him know that it would be his task to retrieve the raft. He then turned to the Navigator. 'You get down there Peter.'

The First Lieutenant was standing in the port waist talking to the Chief Bosun's Mate and issuing instructions to the sailors whose job it was to secure the raft when it came alongside. The bearded face of the ship's second in command turned as Peter came up to him. Neither officer spoke.

As the engines of the two and a half thousand ton destroyer were put astern the twin propellers bit into the water. White foam churned in her wake. The ship gradually lost headway and the engines were stopped. The orange canopy of the raft rode on the wave tops as it drifted down the destroyer's side. It drew amidships and two divers jumped into the water. With waves washing over their heads they attached lines to the raft. Back on board sailors pulled on the ropes until the small craft was held tight against the ship's hull. There was still no life from inside the canopy. The First Lieutenant motioned to one of the divers to raise the ventilation flap.

Peter drew close to the rail and looked down as the diver hauled himself onto the raft's rounded side and lifted the orange fabric. The only sound to be heard was that of water passing between the ship and the rubber side of the raft. Up on the bridge the Captain leaned over the side and anxiously followed the actions of the diver. Steadying himself against the uncertain movement of the small craft the black suited swimmer threw back the flap with his left hand.

'Thank God…' The tired voice of a man came from inside. 'Thank God.' He repeated as realisation of his rescue sparked renewed energy in his tired and vomit encrusted body. He rose to his knees and began shaking the lifeless forms around him. 'Wake up, wake up.' His voice became loud and hysterical. 'We've been found… bless you… bless you.'

On board the destroyer men began to shake hands and laugh. The small head of a child appeared in the opening and a cheer erupted that carried along the upper deck. The red, bristling face of the First Lieutenant was cut by a broad white smile and his eyes betrayed his emotions. He turned to the Navigator and took both Peter's hands in his own.

'Well done Peter. Bloody marvelous.'

Peter Wells looked down at the exhausted, bewildered and relieved faces in the raft and then at the raft itself.

'If it had not been for the strips of radar reflective tape sewn onto the fabric of the canopy they may never have been found.' He thought. Then he saw the father lift a small boy into the waiting arms of a sailor and he felt as if his heart was being torn from his chest. His eyes became moist and he felt pride in the First Lieutenant's words. He knew then that he had been right all along. Right about everything. He was a Naval Officer and a Navigator. He would continue to be the best at both.

Chapter 2

'Why did I agree to come here? I knew it would only be the Navy!' Carol addressed these bored remarks to Jane, a friend who had a vested interest in being there. For Jane it was the opportunity to meet a Royal Marine Lieutenant she had seen at a previous party. On that occasion he had left early denying her an introduction. She vowed it would not happen again.

To Carol, the evening was a non-event and she was not surprised. To her a naval party was predictably boring. Living in a naval area nullified the romantic image of a handsome male cutting a dashing figure in a blue uniform. Not only did she find the company uninspiring she resented having to get dressed up in an evening gown. After the jeans and loose fitting jumpers she was used to wearing the long, figure hugging gown felt very confining. She looked down at the roundness of her breasts forced upwards by the underwired bra, and then across to the young Lieutenant.

'What do you think he's like in bed?' Carol asked, as interest finally found her. Jane's face turned red with embarrassment.

'What are you trying to do? He could have heard you. Do you always have to be so basic?'

Very quickly annoyance turned to resignation. Jane knew her friend was not trying to wreck her plan, but simply voicing her thoughts.

Although now living with her parent's Carol had spent eighteen months in London. The experience, coupled with her rebellious and unconventional spirit, led her to adopt her own rules in life. Rules that had taken her into two very stormy relationships. The first, with a married export executive whose wife soon discovered that her husband's trips were not all abroad; and secondly, with an out of work musician of whom she grew tired of supporting.

Carol returned to Portsmouth and tried to settle back into life in a provincial city. She had her old friends with whom she socialised. She even cultivated a brief but passionate affair with the manager of the insurance office in which she worked. Nothing seemed to last. Life lacked meaning and direction. She had her horse riding, to which she was devoted since her first time on horseback at the age of five, but that was a solitary pastime. She did not like the 'horsey types' who frequented the stables, and, for a young woman of twenty, a solitary pursuit was not the way she planned to spend her life.

The party she was now attending was held to commemorate Nelson's victory at Trafalgar. She used the event as one means of staying in the mainstream of life. Although uninspired by the prospect of socialising with the Navy, Carol knew that the food would be delicious and the alcohol unlimited. While sipping her drink she pondered as to why all naval officers looked the same and what the Navy did to transform so many individuals into blue tailored clones?

Carol looked round at the women with them and marvelled that they should want to get involved in a life that allotted them a place in a hierarchy alongside their men.

As the evening wore on the party moved into a lower gear. Jane succeeded in meeting the Lieutenant of Marines and they were involved in a close embrace on the dimly lit dance floor. Carol decided she could safely leave her to take care of herself.

'Going so soon?'

As she passed the bar the words halted her retreat. She looked round to see the face that belonged to the sensuous voice and stared into the charcoal grey eyes of Peter Wells. Her body became hot and her heart felt as if it had stopped in her breast. Her thoughts became confused. She now wanted to stay but could not think quickly enough to make it happen.

'Yes, it's getting late and I have work tomorrow. It's been a lovely evening.'

'You are tactful but not very honest.' Peter replied. 'I've been watching you for some time and you didn't look like a lady who was enjoying herself. It's not too late. Why don't you stay and have one for the road? The champagne is still in good supply and I think we owe it to the memory of Nelson not to give up on this evening without a fight.' He was smiling broadly and Carol breathed easier. She wondered how she had missed seeing him.

The first drink was followed by another and then they danced. They could feel the attraction as their bodies moved as one. Even when the music stopped and other couples had left the dance floor, they remained together.

A tap on her shoulder startled Carol as she clung to Peter, thinking of how wonderful it was to be held by him.

'Carol, I'm leaving. Stuart is giving me a lift home. Do you want to come?'

Carol looked at her friend and thought about what an actress she was. 'If I say yes she will not speak to me for a week, probably two. If I say no it looks like I am throwing myself at this man. Well, I might as well find out what he plans to do.'

Carol half turned her head to Jane, being careful to ensure that a questioning and provocative eye could be directed at Peter.

'I'll be alright. I'll get a taxi.'

Peter sensed the feeling behind the gesture more than the gesture itself and was not slow to respond;

'I will see that Carol gets home safely.' He placed his arm around her waist and they bid the couple good night.

'Time for another dance. It's a shame to miss the slow ones.' Peter guided Carol back towards the centre of the dance floor. 'I hope I haven't kept you here under false pretenses.' He spoke softly into Carol's ear while changing the position of his hands to bring their bodies closer together. 'I don't have a car and will have to ask you to share my taxi. I live on board and will drop you off on my way to the dockyard.'

'Oh no!' Carol's mind recoiled. 'He lives on a ship and hasn't even got a car.'

'If you are around next Saturday you can come house hunting with me. I'm going to look over one of the new flats on the Lee-on-the-Solent sea front. It's about time I moved out of the wardroom and got a place of my own again. You will be able to give me your opinion. I can use all the help I can get.' Carol's lips parted in a disarming smile.

'I would love to go with you, but I don't know how much help I'll be.' She replied and wondered what he meant about having his own place, again.

The crowd thinned and the shutters were erected behind the bar. Peter asked the hall porter to telephone for a taxi while he and Carol waited in the lobby trying to make conversation. In the bright light of the wardroom's entrance words did not come so easily.

'I'm off to sea tomorrow, but will be back on Friday afternoon. I will call you then, if that's all right?' Peter turned awkwardly formal.

The voice of the Hall Porter saved them from any further embarrassed pauses.

Peter opened the car door for Carol and then moved in beside her. He went to give the driver the directions and then realised he did not know Carol's address. She took over and told the driver who smiled knowingly into the rear view mirror.

'Let me take that down for future reference.' Peter took out his orange navigator's notebook that travelled with him everywhere. 'By the way, what is your telephone number?'

It was not a long drive to Carol's home and they

arrived far quicker than either passenger had hoped. Peter asked the driver to wait and escorted Carol to her front door.

'I would invite you in for coffee but my parents would only hear us come in and then time us until you left. They are very concerned that I'll make them grandparents before they are 'in-laws.' Thank you for a lovely evening.'

Peter bent forward and gave Carol a kiss on the cheek. He would later question his lack of drive, arguing to himself with masculine frustration, 'you never know what they expect'.

'I'll ring you Friday at seven.' He called as he opened the door of the taxi. The cab headed for the dockyard and Peter was alone with his thoughts. He analysed the whole evening. 'She was lovely, but, young. Probably ten years his junior. A daunting prospect for a man who had been out of circulation for so long.' The uncertainty played on his mind, but he was sure that he wanted to see her again.

The taxi arrived at the gates to the naval dockyard and was beckoned through by the Ministry of Defence policeman on duty. The car finally came to a halt alongside the brow of HMS Lysander. Peter got out, paid the driver and smartly strode on board.

He was home again. As he made his way to his cabin he continued to consider the evening, and, Carol. He was impressed. He had never met a girl quite like her. She appeared to be a very confident young woman and he liked that. He was surprised that he did. 'Like poles' were not supposed to attract. Then he thought about what really drew him to her. He wanted her with an urgency that kept sleep at bay. For the first time in nearly two years he wished his situation was different. He wished he had a place of his own where he and Carol might be at that very moment. Thoughts like these tormented him, so he fought them. It was only their first meeting. She would never have spent the night with him. What about her parents? They wouldn't have stood for it. There again, she was independent. She would have expected more than a peck on the cheek. 'Blast! Why don't they lay down rules for these things?' He said aloud and turned on his side in the hard bunk and forced further thoughts from his mind.

'Just when you get things organised the ship sails.' These words from far off times now returned to haunt Peter Wells. One of his friends from his Midshipman days would ruefully say the maxim every time he left port. Peter always laughed at the ritual and told his friend to seek more stable employment.

On that Monday morning, as Lysander steamed out of harbour, Peter scanned the houses of Old Portsmouth to see if he could make out the one where Carol lived.

'Don't be a fool. Get on with your job.' He told himself.

'What did he mean about having a place of his own again?' This question tormented Carol and she was determined to learn more. She prayed he would contact her and so give her the opportunity. For Carol, the week passed very slowly.

The same could not be said for Peter Wells. 'Cat and mouse' exercises with a submarine off Portland and NATO exercises in the Channel kept his week fully occupied both day and night. By the time Friday came around he had all but forgotten his promised telephone call and it took a reminder from one of his fellow officers to jog his memory.

'Why do I always crack the duty on the first night in harbour?' Complained the Gunnery Officer, as he poured himself a cup of coffee from the polished silver urn behind the wardroom door. Peter barely heard the grumbling as he concentrated on the signals just handed to him by the Duty Radio Operator.

'Haven't you got a date tonight Peter?' The Gunnery Officer then asked.

'What's that? Good God! You're right. What time is it?' Peter looked at the wardroom clock. 'Eighteen thirty. Thank heavens!' Hurriedly he signed the signal log and handed it back to the waiting R.O. The sailor turned and left the wardroom with Peter close on his heels. He called back over his shoulder. 'Don't any of you use the phone at 1900? I'll be right back.'

Peter went to his cabin, had a shower, changed into casual clothes and was back in the wardroom by five to seven. He went straight to the telephone and, in an effort to gain more privacy, turned his back on the other officers who were gathering for dinner. He lifted the receiver and dialed the number written in his notepad. The phone was ringing on the other end of the line.

Carol had been guarding the telephone since five o'clock. She did not know whether she loved this naval officer, but she was not going to miss the opportunity of finding out. The phone rang and although she was sitting right next to it, let it ring four times.

'Hello.' Peter hesitated at the sound of his own voice. He was already feeling out of his depth. 'Is that Carol? This is Peter Wells.'

'Yes, hello Peter.' Carol replied and said no more. Even she was not sure how to handle this conversation and was more confused when Peter asked her out to dinner.

'On Friday night I usually go down to the tennis club.' Off guard she said the first thing that came into her mind. It was the truth, but it was not what she wanted to say. 'At least it sounded as if she had more than one iron in the fire and was not just waiting for him to call.' She thought. Never let them think they can take you for granted was Carol Adison's philosophy on men. She composed herself and replied. 'I would love to have dinner with you.'

'Excellent'. Peter was relieved. 'I'll call for you in an hour.' He then hesitated; 'is an hour all right?'

'Perfect.' Carol lied. She knew she needed more time than that.

While she got ready Carol thought about the night ahead. She had a lot to learn about this man. Just how she was going to do it occupied her thoughts as she soaped herself in the bath. She hoped he had a car. Living at home meant that privacy was at a minimum and if he did not have a car how would they ever get to be alone? This thought agitated her in an immediate way. From the moment she first saw him she was attracted by his masculinity. During the past week she had imagined what it would be like to make love to him. To feel his hard body against her, to take and be taken by him.

'Carol, there's a taxi outside.' Her mother's voice broke the sensual spell.

'No car. That can't be helped.' Carol told herself as she made a final check of her appearance in her bedroom mirror.

The doorbell rang and Carol's father opened the door to reveal a small, portly, middle aged man who announced that he was a taxi driver with a message for a Miss Carol Adison. As she came down the stairs Carol saw the driver hand a buff coloured envelope to her father.

'What is it? What is that?' Carol pointed to the envelope in her father's hand. He was not given the chance to answer. Carol flew from the staircase to her father's side, tore the envelope from his hands, ripped it open and let the shredded paper fall to the floor. She read the enclosed note with mounting fury and frustration.

Dear Carol,
A SUBMISS Exercise has been called. We sail immediately. The crew has been recalled. I could not telephone. I hope that you understand. I will call you when I return.
Best Regards.
Peter Wells

'Damn, damn, damn!' Carol was enraged. She paced up and down the hall and all the time she ranted and tore at the paper. 'Bloody Navy! Damn and blast them all!'

With her fury spent she slumped into an armchair and gazed at the crumpled remains of the letter lying in her hands.

'Bugger it!' She said and was immediately chastised by her mother for swearing. Carol was passed caring. She was not a girl whose spirit was easily extinguished. She soon came to realise that one broken date was not the end of the world. She was dressed to go out, it was still early and the tennis club did not liven up until later. The evening could still be salvaged.

Chapter 3

'Finished with main engines.' Peter passed the order to the wheelhouse signifying that the ship was once again secured alongside in harbour. It was seven o'clock on Monday evening and the whole ship's company had experienced a very tiring long weekend. No one felt more exhausted than the navigator. It felt to Peter that he had not been off the bridge for more than a few hours in the last three days. 'Bed. I must get some sleep.' He told himself as he tidied his chart table. He placed his navigation instruments in their respective cases, put them under his arm and left the bridge. As he walked to his cabin he wrestled with the dilemma that, until now, he had not time to worry about. He had told Carol he would telephone as soon as the ship returned, but now, after Friday night's fiasco, he was unsure of the reception he would get, and, he was too tired to handle any aggravation. For a man so sure of himself in his career, he was very uncertain when it came to this young lady. He resented his own timidity and formed an ambivalent attitude to Carol that fluctuated between his desire to see her again and his fear that she would cause him untold worries. 'Perhaps it would be better to let it die.' He told himself, but was not convinced. On the short walk to his cabin he continued to debate the issue and finally came to a decision. He would stay on board tonight and put off any contact with Carol until another day. He was annoyed with himself for taking the easy option. These were the first emotional thoughts to trouble Peter Well's ordered mind for a very long time.

As he sat eating and chatting with the other officers remaining on board that night, Peter felt drawn to the telephone. With the passing minutes he wanted more and more to pick up the telephone and hear Carol's voice. When finally he got up to leave he made straight for it. A voice within cautioned him not to be a fool. 'What if she hangs up?' He stopped, turned on his heels and left the wardroom for the sanctuary of his cabin.

Carol's weekend had been a disaster. On that Friday night nothing could move her out of her black mood. Her broken date hurt her more than she wished to acknowledge. No one knew the reason behind her short temper but all knew well enough to stay clear. Saturday was little better and Sunday was the longest day she had ever lived through. Every time the telephone rang she waited to hear her mother say that it was for her. She would not admit her infatuation by answering the calls herself. By Monday morning Carol was not so aloof. She was certain Peter's ship had returned. She worked through the morning trying to concentrate on the typewriter keys that her fingers touched but her eyes hardly saw. When lunchtime came around she raced from the building to the nearest news stand and bought a copy of the local paper. She turned to the shipping movements and tried to remember the name of Peter's ship. She looked down the names of those arriving that day but none looked familiar. She swore under her breath and stuffed the newspaper in an already overcrowded rubbish bin.

The first thing Tuesday morning Peter contacted the estate agent and arranged to view the flat, he had told Carol about, at six thirty that evening. The timing was right. They could carry on to a restaurant afterwards. He tried to think of a suitable place but nothing came to mind. As he went to ask the more social members of the wardroom the realisation came to him that he had been out of the game for far too long.

Fortified by a couple of Gins and Tonic at lunch time Peter telephoned Carol's home. He knew she would be at work and was hoping to get the number from her mother. It was not difficult. Like most mothers Mrs. Adison was only too pleased to help her daughter find a husband that she thought was suitable. Armed with the number Peter now wondered whether he had the nerve to talk to Carol directly. He ordered his third drink from the wardroom bar steward while he gathered his thoughts. He removed the notepad from his pocket and jotted down the points he wanted to make. His drink arrived. He took a sip, looked at what he had written, formulated what he was going to say and then dialed the number.

The telephone on her desk rang as Carol was about to leave for lunch. 'Blast!' She thought. 'I should have gone while the going was good.' She had remained behind to type up an urgent report and now regretted not having left with the other girls. She was looking forward to a break and this phone call was another threat to her lunch hour. She thought about letting it ring but the piercing note of each ring sounded louder than the one before, compelling her to answer.

'There's a Peter Wells to speak to you Carol.'

The decision had been taken out of her hands as the voice of the receptionist called from the outer office. The full meaning of the message took a little longer to register. 'He was on the other end of the line. How had he got her number? What was she going to say?' Carol took a deep breath and picked up the telephone.

'Hello Peter, it is lovely to hear from you.'

One outcome of the past few days was that Carol had decided to stop pretending. She knew she wanted to see him and that was all that mattered. The conversation was at times confused and often stilted but their feelings were plain. Halfway through Peter discarded his notes.

Having arranged to call for Carol that evening Peter said goodbye. He had one more telephone call to make and that was to a car hire company close to the dockyard. He was not going to be without a secure base from which to conduct the evening. After an apartment, a car was to be his next purchase. These were changing times for Peter Wells.

Peter collected the car and arrived outside Carol's front door at precisely five thirty. The years in the Navy had made him a servant to time. He was soon to learn that Carol did not share his respect for the hands of a clock.

'Time waits for no man, but all must wait for Carol I'm afraid.' Her father said as he offered Peter a sherry and a seat. 'You must not be offended. She has always been bad where time keeping is concerned.'

Peter glanced at his watch and thought of the appointment with the estate agent. He worked out when he would have to leave Carol's house in order to arrive at the flat on time. It was while he was making this calculation that Carol entered the room. Peter sensed her presence and looked toward the door. It was almost a reflex action, but, when his brain registered what his eyes were looking at, he took a second and lingering look.

'Beautiful.' He murmured, as if there was no one else in the room except for him and this girl. He got to his feet and walked toward her. 'You look lovely.' He then paused, 'I am sorry about last Friday.' He had told himself he would not bring this subject up again, but, standing there, face to face, he could think of nothing else to say. It seemed the only common ground they had. Carol too did not want to open old wounds and quickly stopped him.

'Let's not talk about it. It's great to see you again.'

There followed one of those awful pauses where no one knows what to say next and Peter took the opportunity for them to make their exit. He said goodbye to Carol's father, who had discreetly moved to the other end of the lounge room. Peter opened the front door and escorted Carol to the car. Her heart gave a jump when she realised it was not a taxi waiting. She had not thought he would get a car. Things were definitely looking up.

Peter opened the car door and Carol passed close to him to take her place in the passenger seat. He could smell the fragrance of her perfume and the freshness of her body, and he felt himself becoming aroused. It was an excitement he had not felt for a very long time and he revelled in the rekindled sensation. As he took his position behind the steering wheel he explained that the car was only hired but he intended to buy a car as soon as the flat was finalised. He then looked at his watch.

'We have twenty five minutes to make the appointment. I don't think we're going to make it.' As the words were said he realised it no longer worried him. All he cared about was having this girl beside him. He barely knew her and already she was influencing his life. It scared him, but he did not want to stop it, and he did not want to think about it too deeply. As they drove through the streets of the city, now congested with rush hour traffic, Peter explained the exercise that had ruined their weekend. Carol wanted to let the subject drop but was happy just to sit by his side and listen to him talk. She had never felt like this before and was determined not to let the feeling go.

'Sorry for the delay.' Peter apologised to the estate agent, but said no more. He was not used to apologising, especially for not being punctual.

The estate agent, a young man who appeared to Peter to be too glib by half, showed them around the property. He even pointed out that, 'Mrs. Wells' would like the convenience and layout of the kitchen. Peter and Carol smiled at each other but did not bother to correct the mistake. When they finally came to the master bedroom, with its panoramic views across the Solent, the young man kept silent, judging that the room would sell itself. He was right. While Peter and Carol stood looking over the dark waters to the lights of the Isle of Wight, they could feel the bond that was drawing them closer. Even the young salesman sensed the emotional force and left the couple to be alone. Carol was the first to break the silence,

'It's fantastic, Peter. The whole flat is a dream. You will be very happy here.'

'It does have a good feel to it,' he replied and turned away from the sea to face her. 'I'm sure I'll be happy here.' He looked into Carol's eyes as he moved toward her, 'and I will not forget who helped me choose my new home.' He reached out his arms, drew Carol to him and kissed her lips. His body trembled as he held her, he had not intended to make his move so soon, but, the feeling was just too great. Their kiss was long and tender and when it was over they remained with arms about each other, staring into the other's eyes.

Carol was momentarily shocked by the embrace, it was unexpected, but not unwanted. She returned his kiss and hoped it would never end. She was happy, contented, thrilled and aroused all at the same time, she was in love. They held hands as they left the room and rejoined the agent in the more impersonal surroundings of the lounge room.

'I will have it.' Peter announced. 'I will instruct my solicitor first thing in the morning.'

'I wish they were all this easy,' the young estate agent

thought as he tried hard not to stare at Carol's figure confined erotically in a black mini skirt that promised all yet revealed nothing.

The young man closed the front door behind them and they bid him goodbye.

'Now that I am a man of property again we must celebrate.' Peter said, as he opened the car door. Without realising it he had said the word that aroused Carol's curiosity to the point where it almost matched her desire.

The restaurant was intimate, the dinner delicious and the wine removed the inhibitions that form barriers between new lovers. Carol felt the time was right to ask the question that had been plaguing her mind since the party.

'Peter,' she said his name with a quizzical, apprehensive tone in her voice. 'What did you mean when you said that you were a man of property again?'

The question stunned him. He had not had to explain his marriage and divorce to any one for a long time and the thought of it brought back visions of failure and guilt. He went silent and stared into his wine glass. Carol saw his expression change and instantly regretted the question.

Peter thought. 'It had been a lovely evening, why had she brought up the past?' While he sat, looking into the depth of his wine glass he came to realise that his marriage, and more importantly, his divorce, was now behind him. He had been asked a simple question by a girl for whom he felt a deep affection, she deserved an answer. He looked up and began to relate the story of his marriage, and, as he spoke so his conscience eased. It was as if a weight was being lifted from him with every word that was spoken. Carol listened in silence. Having proposed the question she did not have to do more. She always suspected Peter had been married before. She also hoped that it was not true, she was young, in love and wanted to be the first and only woman in his life.

Peter finished his story a happier man. He felt free, liberated from his past and now able to try again with love and to find happiness. He saw his new life in the face of the pretty woman sitting opposite him. He had finally acknowledged he was in love and now could not understand why Carol had become so quiet. He ordered coffee and liqueurs but for reasons he did not understand, something had been lost.

Carol could not help herself. She knew she was being unreasonable. She was not a child, but this was different. Peter should have been hers and hers alone. For the rest of the evening this thought played on her mind and what started out so beautifully ended with formality and confused emotions.

Peter drove Carol home, never tiring in his efforts to rekindle the feelings he knew had been within her earlier that evening. He talked and she did answer, but, the conversation had lost the animation that had held him spell bound. He did not understand what had brought about this change but knew now that he could not live without her. He had to win her back.

At Carol's front door he gave her a gentle kiss and said he would call the next day. She returned the kiss but without the passion that marked their first embrace. She hated herself and could not help it. She was hurt and could not fight back. Once inside the sanctuary of her home she slumped to the floor and wept.

Early the following day Peter arranged for flowers to be sent and Carol arrived home from work to find the bouquet lying in the kitchen sink. She smiled to see such beautiful flowers so unceremoniously placed. She knew her mother must have been eager to put them out in vases but feared her daughter's wrath if they were touched. 'I am a bitch.' She thought as she smelled the bouquet of the reddest rose. She read the card and felt close to tears once again.

Carol had done a lot of thinking since last night. She realised that life was never as expected and that her disappointment at Peter's divorce paled into insignificance next to the love she felt for him. At the sound of tearing Cellophane Carol's mother was by her side.

'They are beautiful,' she said. 'May I put them out for you?' Carol nodded her head, smiled, kissed her mother on the cheek and left the kitchen to run upstairs. Over her shoulder she called back,

'If the phone rings it will be for me.'

The flowers marked the beginning of a love affair that deepened with the passing months. Peter moved into his flat, but soon found that sea views were not enough. He asked Carol to live with him. It was a move which did not impress her parents, but which Carol was more than willing to make.

The first five months of their life together were full

of love and laughter. Peter never knew such happiness and Carol never believed that living with a man could be as wonderful as it was with him. They built a life in their flat that did not let the world outside encroach on their happiness. However, it was a joy born of love not reason. Carol never believed she could love a man whose career took him away from her. To love Peter was easy, it was beautiful. For those first months he was never away. His ship was in dockyard hands and every night he came home to her.

For Peter it was a life he had never known. A life away from the Navy. His love for Carol consumed him and without the challenge of an operational ship he was content to let his passions rule. For those first few months he relented in his striving to be first. His work was not demanding and he did not care. He had momentarily forgotten the Navy and what it meant to him. However, the Navy had not forgotten Lieutenant-Commander Peter Wells RN.

Chapter 4

'Peter, may I see you for a moment?' The Captain stood in the wardroom doorway and motioned for Peter to follow. Peter rose from his chair and followed him into his cabin that was situated just along the passageway. 'Sit down, Peter. I have some good news for you.' Peter did as he was bid and then looked at the piece of paper the Captain handed to him. 'You are going on the next Dagger 'N' course. It will be held in May. Congratulations. I know you've been waiting for this.'

Peter sat quietly for a moment. He had been hoping for this course ever since he decided to become a navigation specialist. It was the ultimate qualification and the passport to a Commander's 'brass hat.'

For the past few months he thought very little about the service, or his career. Now, all that was to change. He was on the way up again. He thanked the Captain, whose recommendation would have helped to win him a place on the course, and left the cabin. His mind was buzzing with the news and plans he must now make. 'I must get studying, barely two months to prepare and I haven't been to sea for so long. If I top this one I have got it made.' The fire of ambition was once again rekindled. Peter's mind was filled with thoughts of success and promotion.

That night he arrived home late and preoccupied with the plans he had made that day. Carol could not fail to notice the change. She became worried. For the first time he had come home late to her and did not even apologise. She could sense that whatever had happened that day was to change their life forever. His news confirmed her worst fears.

In order to gain some practical experience and counter the time spent ashore Peter had arranged to go aboard one of the squadron destroyers until his own ship was ready for sea. 'He had volunteered to leave home, to leave her.' Carol was both saddened and outraged.

'But why, Peter?' She cried. 'The course is a long time away. Why leave now? I thought you were the expert. What do you need practice for?'

He tried to explain that this was his big chance and anything he could do to ensure his success, he would do.

'Please understand Carol.' He took her hand and looked into her moistening eyes. 'I am a naval officer, and a very successful one. I have been given the chance to make a real name for myself. I must take it.'

Carol was quick to react,

'I suppose I should have expected this. I broke my own rule.' Carol's voice was hard, she was hurt and trying to fight back.

'Please don't talk like that.' Peter begged. 'I love you and nothing will ever change that.' He reached out his arms and she came to him crying.

The weeks preceding the course were very full ones for the Navigator, not only was he preparing for the Long Navigation Course, but, his ship was out of the dockyard and undergoing sea trials. He revelled in the work and especially enjoyed being at sea. 'This is what it's all about,' he thought as he stood on the bridge and watched the forecastle rise and fall as the bow sliced its way through the dark sea. He looked around him and felt secure.

Carol felt her future threatened. She saw Peter drifting away from her. He stayed away from the flat for greater periods of time and when he was there his nose was always buried in the pile of textbooks that were his constant companions. She hated the Navy more vehemently with every passing day. She grew angry with Peter for allowing himself to be taken away from her. Eventually, it all proved too much and she could stand her supporting role no longer.

Two days before Peter was due to start the course at HMS Grenville Carol walked out. She always said that once a person left home, they could never go back. Now, she had nowhere else to go. Peter had been so preoccupied with his work he had not recognised the signs. When Carol finally made her move he was too bewildered to fight. 'It is happening all over again.' He thought. He told her that he loved her and that she was making a mistake, but, even to him his words sounded insincere and somehow unreal. What mattered most was, the course. He could not let anything distract him from that.

It was a demanding three weeks and yet from the beginning

Peter knew he would succeed. He had mentally prepared himself to think of nothing but navigation. However, as the course progressed his mind wandered. He thought of Carol and the time they spent together. He even telephoned her but there was no reply. He was relieved when those extracurricular thoughts did not impair his performance in his work. Although, he did search his soul and ask what price he had paid for success? He did not believe that he lost more than he gained, that would be ridiculous. He had come first in the most difficult test a navigator can undertake. He would soon receive confirmation of his posting as Navigating Officer to the aircraft carrier, HMS Sovereign. Such a job surely meant he was moving up the ladder and the elusive 'brass hat' of a senior officer was not far away.

Carol returned home and hated it. Jane was engaged to the Royal Marine Lieutenant and looking forward to a mid-summer wedding.

'More fool her!' Carol told herself, in yet another attempt to convince her doubting heart that life with a serviceman was doomed to heartache. As much as she tried, the memory of Peter Wells would not leave her. She was missing him and hurting all the more because she would not admit it to herself. She had not accepted the telephone calls he made soon after their separation, and, now inwardly punished herself for being so stubborn. She had lost him, she had given him up, and she wanted him back.

Chapter 5

The wind almost took Peter's cap as he stepped out of the taxi. He put his left hand to his head and pulled the black peak further down over his face. As he did so he looked up at what was to be his new home and mistress for the next two years. The grey sides of the aircraft carrier loomed above the dockside wall and dominated its physical surroundings and the thoughts of her new Navigator.

The taxi driver removed Peter's cases from the boot of his brand new Ford Zephyr. He was careful not to damage the paint work. However, once they were clear of the shining chrome bumper he deposited them heavily, and with a magnificent sigh, onto the concrete wharf. He held out his hand for the fare and tip. A sum that guaranteed that his love of new cars would always be satisfied.

Peter climbed the brow, saluted and introduced himself to the quartermaster. It was Sunday afternoon and everything was quiet on board. The Leading Seaman saluted the new Navigator and dispatched the Bosun's Mate to retrieve the bags.

'Welcome aboard, Sir.' The Quartermaster said as he lowered his right hand from the salute. 'I'll pipe for the Officer of the Day. He is doing his rounds at present.'

'More like the officer is in the wardroom with a cup of coffee and reading Sunday papers.' Peter mused and looked at the sailor's left arm. Two good conduct stripes. He was dealing with a professional and one who looked after his officer. 'A good sign.' Thought Peter, who was looking for anything that might make him feel more at ease in that monstrous ship.

The Officer of the Day arrived soon after the pipe was made. He was a young Sub-Lieutenant who was discreetly trying to catch his breath. A sure sign that Peter was right about the officer's whereabouts prior to his arrival on the quarterdeck.

Peter was led across the quarterdeck and through a hatch that took him into the officers' living accommodation. He felt overawed by the sheer size of the ship. He walked along the passageways lined with cabins and recalled the legend of Theseus and the Minotaur. He wondered if, like the Greek hero, he too would need a length of string to find his way out of this labyrinth.

The afternoon was spent settling in. This was his new home. The flat was on the market, he would never live there again. It was the symbol of another emotional failure. While he unpacked his belongings his mind kept repeating over and over again that this was where he belonged. These grey metal bulkheads and the varnished wooden fitments were his home. He was a fool to ever think otherwise. Only rarely did thoughts of Carol intrude on his mind, for it was only rarely that he would drop his guard and remember how things used to be.

The wardroom was an imposing sight. The main fore and aft passageway separated the dining area from the anteroom. This was where the ship's officers came to relax. To unwind and enjoy the company of fellow officers away from the harassment of the ship's company, and even, the Captain. As Peter entered his stomach muscles tightened. He looked around the large room. Being Sunday there were not many officers on board. Those that were tended to be the older men with no home to go to, or the duty officers, who would rather be at home than trapped on board on a Sunday afternoon. Two junior lieutenants looked over from the bar. It was closed, but, they stood there anyway, savouring the atmosphere. After a cursory look at the intruder they returned to their conversation. The rest of the occupants were encamped, either singly or in silent pairs, behind large newspapers. 'What am I doing here?' Thought Peter. 'Is this what I studied so hard for?' He felt a momentary panic overtake him. Never before had he felt an alien in his own ship. Quickly, he regained control and stifled his disquieting thoughts.

'You must be Lieutenant-Commander Wells.' A booming voice that seemed to come out of nowhere shattered the tomb like quality of the wardroom. Peter jumped visibly and looked to see a very large figure in white overalls coming towards him with his right hand outstretched. 'Welcome aboard, I am John Hinton, Senior Engineer. Excuse the rig, I am off to work miracles on number two boiler. I never get away with overalls in here during the week, even if they shone like the star over Bethlehem.' The Engineer's voice dropped as he mentioned the dress regulations. A sign of deference to the rules of the mess and life aboard an aircraft carrier. 'We heard you were coming, but didn't expect you until tomorrow. Nobody joins this ship early. You must be a small ship man.' These questions and statements were fired at Peter and were not meant to receive a reply. 'Well, must be off and get my hands dirty. See you for dinner.' The white clad figure turned away and disappeared around the bulkhead and Peter was alone once again. He too turned and left the wardroom.

The remainder of the afternoon was spent touring the ship. On his way to the bridge he stopped on the flat expanse of the flight deck and looked about him. 'What a monster,' he mused and shook his head in concerned amazement as he considered getting the ship out into the channel and through the narrow harbour entrance. Putting these thoughts behind him he walked across the flat deck and into the towering island that housed the operational nerve centre of the great ship. He climbed the ladders that took him to the bridge. Once there all doubt was replaced by confident anticipation. As he looked out from his high vantage point at his own ship and the other grey hulls secured alongside the dockyard wall he felt a strengthening of his commitment to himself, the ship and the Royal Navy.

That night Peter had a drink at the wardroom bar and ate dinner with John Hinton.

'Your appointment surprised us Peter. We were expecting a Commander. What happened? Is there a shortage of Commander 'N's, or are you some kind of whiz kid?'

'I like to think so.' Peter replied and the Senior Engineer knew he had just received an answer to both questions.

At 0800 on Monday morning Peter was lined up with the other ship's officers on the after end of the flight deck. The White Ensign was being hoisted and the whole dockyard was at a standstill as each ship observed this long standing tradition. The Royal Marine bugler sounded the carry on and Peter turned to see Captain Harlow.

Sovereign's Captain was a midget of a man who appeared to be consumed by his own gold braid. His eyes glared from under the gold embossed peak of his cap. Peter approached his new commanding officer, stopped two paces from the diminutive, yet imposing, figure, saluted and introduced himself.

'Good to have you aboard Lieutenant-Commander Wells.' The voice came from the depths of the man in a low growl. 'Come and see me at 0900 in my cabin.'

'Aye aye, sir.' Barked Peter, caught up in the regimented aura of this little man.

At 0900 Peter stood outside the Captain's cabin, cap in hand and feeling apprehensive about his first private meeting with his Commanding Officer. He knew that the working relationship between the Navigator and the Captain was critical to the effective and efficient running of the ship. It was a bonus if the two men could also respect and even like each other. Peter knocked on the heavy wooden door, emblazoned with a brass plaque that imposingly told all, who lived within.

'Enter!' The voice bellowed from inside.

Peter entered and found the Captain looking smaller than ever behind a vast mahogany desk.

'Take a seat Peter.'

'Had he heard correctly? Had he just been addressed by his Christian name?' In any other ship in which he served Peter would not have given a second thought to being addressed by his Captain in such a manner. However, in this ship, it came as a shock.

'I expected a Commander as my navigator.' The Captain quickly went on. 'You come highly recommended. I trust you will live up to your reputation.' This was said as more of a command than an expectation. 'As you know Peter, this command is the key to my flag. That is what I want and I will not allow anything, or anyone, jeopardize my chance. You might think that I should not be telling you this, but, you would be wrong. You Peter, probably more than any of my officers, can be instrumental in my achieving my goal. Like you, I am new to this ship. We both have this commission to enhance our careers.' The Captain sat back in his chair. His point had been made. Both men knew where they stood; although, Peter was amazed to be told so openly, the expectations of his commanding officer. Amazement soon gave way to gratitude. He was now in his Captain's confidence and together they would succeed. 'Any questions for me?' Harlow asked. There followed a discussion of the ship's programme for the coming year. It was routine enough, but Peter knew that with this Captain it would not be dull.

'It was a beautiful wedding, Jane.' Carol managed to get the bride away from the other guests. 'I wish you all the happiness in the world.' Carol said the cliché but felt the meaning in her heart. Since breaking up with Peter she had come to appreciate the benefits of being loved by just one man. She had always been very casual about marriage and fidelity. The past months with no one except casual acquaintances and well-meaning parents had given her time to think. Her life with Peter now crowded her mind. Where had they gone wrong? She knew the answer, but could not stop herself from asking the question. They had been so happy and even now she would smile at the memory of him loving her, caring for her. Then happiness would turn to regret, and recrimination. Conflicting thoughts of love and anger would rise up, sweep away her happiness and take the smile from her lips as the sea takes a child's castle from the shore, leaving nothing but a hollow image of what used to be there.

Carol, along with the bride's mother and countless other ladies, had cried throughout the wedding ceremony. She hid her eyes behind a white lace handkerchief and scolded herself for her emotions. For the first time her heart was touched by a wedding ceremony and her tears would have been rivers of joy if the man she loved was not the one she had already lost.

'You must come and see us when we return from honeymoon and I have managed to turn the married quarter from a cell block into some kind of home.' Jane clasped her friend's hands as she spoke.

'You will have to be quick,' Carol replied. 'I am off to

Australia in five weeks.' Jane let go of Carol's hands and put her own up to her face.

'What!' She exclaimed, loud enough for those around her to stop their own conversations and tune into the two friends. 'Why didn't you tell me earlier?'

Carol looked at Jane long and meaningfully. It was an unspoken answer that the bride soon understood.

'You're right. I have been pretty preoccupied.' She smiled happily and then as fast as it appeared the smile vanished. 'But why? Why Australia?'

'Why not?' Replied Carol. 'What have I got to keep me here? I'm young, unattached, living at home, why shouldn't I go to Australia?'

'Because you haven't done anything wrong.' Jane paused. 'You only go to Australia if you are convicted, and you haven't even been caught yet. It's the other side of the world.' By this stage Jane was almost breathless.

Carol could not understand her reaction. 'What had Australia ever done to her?' She wondered. However, the answer was not to come at that time. Jane's new husband reclaimed her. Bride and groom left the reception under a cloud of pink and white confetti that they would be removing from their clothes and the inner recesses of their bodies for days to come.

Chapter 6

Carol's pace quickened as she neared the boarding gate. She knew that until she was sitting in that aircraft seat freedom would not be hers.

The past weeks had been a living hell. Her mother would not accept that her daughter was leaving home again, let alone going to Australia.

'You need to settle down my girl. Stay at home with your father and me where we can keep an eye on you. We should never have let you go to London. Lord knows what you got up to while you were there. You can forget Australia. I don't know where you get your ideas from, I really don't.'

Carol allowed her mother this victory, and many others, in the weeks leading up to her departure. Although there were times when even Carol had second thoughts. The idea of travelling alone to the other side of the world did worry her. She might have even given up her dream if her mother's attacks had not been so persistent. As it was, those attacks only served to steel her resolve. She would show her parents that she could lead her own life. She was a woman, not a little girl to be protected and controlled.

As her departure drew nearer the atmosphere at home became intolerable. Carol hardly spoke at all for fear that the mere sound of her voice would ignite the seething inferno of fear, anger and frustration that her mother had become. Any opportunity to escape from this explosive situation was welcome, and although dinner in the company of a newlywed friend was not the most exciting of social engagements, it did provide a few hours respite.

Jane had returned from honeymoon and, having transformed the bleak naval flat into a home, invited her friend round for a meal and a chat. It was over coffee that Carol broached the subject of Australia. Up until that moment Jane had been lost in her own world of weddings and honeymoons and Carol had not wanted to appear self centred by introducing a topic that excluded her friend's happy state. In particular, Carol wanted to learn why Jane had spoken so vehemently against the country during their last meeting. What followed was a family history of black sheep and recriminations. To allay the blame from the shoulders of individuals the whole continent was burdened with the family guilt.

It transpired that at the end of World War Two, rather than return to the family business, Jane's uncle decided to remain in Australia. As the only male heir to the printing company that had been in the family for two generations, 'Uncle Jack' was needed to secure the future of the firm. Instead, he disregarded the wishes of his family and headed off into the outback of New South Wales, in search of his own fortune. The 'prodigal' never returned to England and the mantle of treason never left him. Jane grew up with a loathing for the country that had caused her family so much anguish. She could not hate the uncle she never met and who, from the time of her birth, sent gifts and exciting letters from the other side of the world. Why he favoured her she never knew. She could not ask him and her family would not speak of it.

Uncle Jack was now the owner of a struggling cattle property in the northern part of New South Wales and Jane suggested Carol should visit him. It would be somewhere to head for she argued. Carol knew that such a meeting would provide a vicarious fulfillment for Jane, and she also knew that it was a good idea. She had been worried about being a total stranger in a foreign land.

The next day Carol found an old Atlas that was lying in the attic. She turned to the maps of Australia and found New South Wales. Finding the town of Walcha, the town nearest Jack's property, was not so easy. She checked the index and confirmed that it was on the page somewhere. A closer inspection revealed a black dot on the page and the name she was looking for. Her heart sank. It was in the middle of nowhere. She recalled Jane saying that it was about three hundred miles away from Sydney. What concerned Carol even more than the distance was that there appeared to be nothing in between.

Carol went ahead with her plans. She wrote and

received a reply welcoming her visit. Her mother was pleased to know her daughter had someone to go to. Carol did not show her the atlas. Her father was not so easily fooled, but had no desire to return to the hostility of the past weeks. All he would say was, 'Don't do anything foolish.'

Chapter 7

What began as a great adventure was becoming a boring and seemingly endless ordeal. The aircraft landed, exchanged passengers, re-fuelled, re-catered and took off in a treadmill like cycle. The names of the transit stops had appeared romantic when spoken by the travel agent, but, in reality, every minute spent in a transit lounge seemed to add an hour on to the journey.

Hong Kong was the last stop before Sydney. When the pilot announced that they would be landing in fifty minutes Carol welcomed the news. The end of the ordeal was in sight. The oriental name that appeared so exciting at the beginning of the trip was now just one more hurdle to be taken before normal life could be resumed away from an aircraft seat.

The aeroplane flew low over the crowded tenements of Kowloon, its wing tips appearing to barely clear the roof tops. Hong Kong Island was lit up like a fairyland. The lights on its craggy back were challenged in their brilliance by those on the flotilla of ships that dotted the waters of the harbour.

The aircraft descended rapidly and Carol's muscles tightened as she felt the downward angle and heard the pitch of the engines change. She was alarmed still further when she saw water, first outside her own window and then outside the windows on the other side of the cabin. She held her breath and closed her eyes as the wheels touched the runway and the aircraft lurched from side to side as if gripped and shaken by a giant hand. The engines roared as they were put into reverse thrust and the aircraft rapidly slowed its headlong race toward the end of the runway and the water beyond.

When the noise subsided and the forward motion eased Carol opened her eyes and released the grip on the armrest of the seat. She gave an audible sigh and looked round for confirmation that all the faces she had grown accustomed to seeing, were still there. Not only were they there, most of them were already on their feet retrieving their luggage from the racks above their heads. It was a strange feeling but Carol took strength from the activity around her. Man was regaining the initiative and control was being wrested from the hollow, metal shell and the people who worked within it. The cabin staff were helpful enough but Carol could not get out of her mind that this was their environment and they exercised control over all who entered their world.

'Transit passengers may leave the aircraft during this stop in Hong Kong.' The message came over the public address system and Carol wasted no time in taking advantage of a few minutes of freedom. Twenty hours of sitting, eating, talking to fellow passengers, and trying to sleep in unnatural positions was taking its toll.

The glamour of international air travel was conceding ground to its attendant horrors.

As Carol browsed round the duty free shops she concluded that every transit lounge looked the same. She then had a thought. She had not bought any cigarettes or alcohol and remembered Jane saying that her uncle, 'had a liking for both'.

It was as if every passenger from every aircraft in Hong Kong had the same idea at the same time. The duty free shop was a heaving mass of bodies with arms that stretched, grabbed and jabbed as the individual in charge of each fought for their entitlement. Carol stood outside and considered whether the prize was worth the effort.

'What the hell.' She muttered to herself and moved toward the fray.

'Pardon, you talking to me?'

A deep Australian drawl made Carol stop and look over her left shoulder. She focused first on a yellow tee shirt that stretched tightly around a well-muscled chest. She then noticed the tanned skin of the arms and looked up. She felt her eyes widen.

'Sorry.' She said distractedly. 'I was talking to myself. I'm worried about getting through that crowd.'

'No worries. You stick with me.' He told her and strode towards the door. 'Here, take my hand.' It was more a command than an invitation and Carol obeyed without hesitation. Together they entered the maelstrom. 'What do you want to buy?' His deep voice cut through the din.

'Cigarettes and Scotch.' She shouted back.

'Right.' He answered and set about cutting a path

through the bodies that stood in his way. It was so easy. Before she knew it Carol was standing in front of the cigarette counter.

'What Scotch do you want?' The Australian enquired. He was standing close by her now and she could sense his presence.

'Oh, I don't know.' Carol shook her head.

'Okay, I'll get you one. You stay here. Don't move.' Carol had her orders and watched as he maneuvered through the crowd, until he was no longer visible, except for the yellow mane of his hair.

She turned to the counter, chose a carton of cigarettes and then turned back to scan the crowd. She caught sight of the yellow tee shirt and then saw his grinning face as he came toward her through the lines of people.

'Is this okay?' He held up a bottle.

'Fine.' Replied Carol. 'I've got my cigarettes.' She held up the carrier bag with the cigarettes inside.

'Great. Let's get out of this mad house.' He once again took Carol's hand. It seemed so natural she did not object. They made their way to the door.

'Glad to be out of there.' The relief was apparent in Carol's voice.

'Too right.' Agreed her saviour. 'By the way, my name's Phil.'

'Hello, I'm Carol. Thanks for your help.'

'No worries. Where are you heading?'

'Australia, Sydney.' Carol answered.

'No kidding. So am I. That's where I'm from.' He could not hide his eagerness to find out more, but, the call to re-board the aircraft meant that Carol had to go.

'That's my flight. Thanks again for your help.' 'Shot down before I have even got started,' she thought as she said goodbye.

'Not so fast. I'm on that flight. Perhaps I'll see you on the plane? Right now I've got to get some aftershave. See you later.' With those words he was off, side stepping the crowd like a rugby player.

Carol re-boarded the aircraft, nodding to the faces she recognised and noticing the empty seats. A lot of people had left the flight in Hong Kong. 'Perhaps I can stretch out for the rest of the trip.' She thought. The cabin address system soon quashed that idea.

'Would all transit passengers please return to the seats marked on their boarding card as the empty seats have been allocated to passengers joining the flight here in Hong Kong. Thank you.'

Those joining passengers soon started to arrive. Carol looked towards the door, studying each face as it entered, looking for the only one that interested her.

There he was. She watched the steward at the door point down the cabin. He was walking towards her and Carol watched his face break into a smile when he saw her. He stopped at the end of her row. He looked at his boarding card and then the number on the hat rack.

'Is this 22C?' He pointed to the aisle seat. His smile lit up his whole face. 'It must be fate.' He said, placing a leather jacket in the locker and then sitting down.

The hours that had dragged with boredom now passed too quickly. Conversation that had meant no more than a means of passing time now brought two people together. Where before Carol had only listened with her ears and a vaguely interested mind to the conversation of her fellow passengers, she now attended with her heart. Theirs became more than just a social intercourse. It was a sexual exploration by means of language.

Phil Sewell had left school and entered university only to find that he could no longer sustain the academic discipline.

'There is more to life than can be found in books.' He said and Carol judged that he had dropped out. Like her he had had enough and was seeking an alternative to the socially acceptable way of life, ordered by parents and expected by friends. At least, that is how Carol saw his situation and it was comforting to meet someone with ideas akin to her own, especially there, thousands of miles from the security of all things she held familiar. It therefore came as a shock when Phil explained that by leaving his studies he was committing himself to two years National Service in the Army, with the prospect of spending one of those in the paddy fields and jungles of Vietnam. She could not believe that he was actually looking forward to joining up and fighting for his country.

'Someone has to stop them.' He said as he tried to explain his willingness to risk his life in the conflict against an enemy he saw as threatening the democracy of all South East Asia.

Carol could not accept his arguments. It was not that she held strong views about the war, she had never really given it much thought. What Carol could not accept was the commitment with which the young man spoke. 'Why did everyone know where they were going?' She asked herself in frustrated rage. 'Did they know where they were going? Phil might be going to his death. Did he really want to do that?' Carol's thoughts were in turmoil and her whole body felt on edge as she tried to justify her own actions in a life that was characterised by retreat from one transient situation after another. While Phil talked about his new life Carol's thoughts turned to a time in her own life when she knew another dedicated service man. 'Why didn't she ever get a break?' She asked herself and fought to return her attention to what Phil was saying. The hours passed quickly and despite the niggling feeling of inadequacy Phil had wrought in her, Carol found herself becoming very attracted to this young Australian.

He had noticed Carol's withdrawal when he spoke of his, and his country's involvement in the Vietnam War. He had no wish to bore such a pretty travelling companion and so dropped the subject in order to concentrate on her.

'Where are you going to stay while you're in Sydney?' He asked. It was a leading question, but, he only had a few hours to learn as much about her as possible. Carol was only too willing to answer.

'I thought I would stay in a hotel for a few days and then take the train up to Walcha.' Carol explained that she was going to stay with an uncle of a friend and after that, she did not know. Phil thought he had learned enough and moved on to expound the virtues of his country. Carol found his unbridled nationalism both galling and admirable.

The subject of Carol's accommodation was next

raised as the aircraft was beginning its descent into Sydney's Kingsford Smith Airport. After nine hours of getting to know her Phil thought he could ask the question, and he knew that he was running out of time. The aircraft banked and through the windows on both sides of the cabin could be seen the blue Pacific Ocean and the golden beaches of the Sydney coastline.

'I live just down there.' Phil said as he leaned across and pointed out of the window. 'Maroubra, right by the beach, it's great.' He sat back in his seat but continued to look through the window. By doing so he could also watch Carol's expression. 'She's a real beaut,' he thought and took a deep breath. 'Would you like to stay at my place for a few days?' He asked. The words were carried on his exhaled breath. Carol turned her head so sharply that he felt compelled to defend himself. 'No funny business, promise. I just thought you would be lonely in a hotel room.'

Carol was not shocked by the suggestion. Her manner reflected amazement not indignation. She knew it was a good idea, but, how was she to accept without appearing too eager?

'I couldn't possibly do it Phil. Thanks for the offer, it was very kind.' The ball was back in his court.

'What are you afraid of? It's a big house. My grandfather left it to me. You will have your own room and, like I said, I won't try anything on.' He looked to see if she was weakening. 'I'll get a taxi at the airport and we'll be home in ten minutes. No worries. You don't want to get ripped off in a hotel. What do you say?'

The runway extended out into the bay and as the

wheels touched down it appeared as if the boats on the water would collide with the lumbering bulk of the slowing aeroplane. Carol looked out at a lone figure water skiing and then a fleet of brightly coloured sailing boats caught her eye. 'Paradise,' she thought and then looked back at Phil.

'Okay. You're on.'

The bright morning sunlight made Carol shield her eyes as she came through the automatic doors and out onto Australian soil. Excitement welled up in her. Here she was on the other side of the world. She knew nobody, and nobody knew her. She could start a new life on her own terms, and when she saw Phil struggling with a trolley overloaded with cases, she thought her new life had started out pretty well.

'I'll get a taxi. You wait here with the bags.' Phil gave his instructions and jogged off towards a line of parked cars.

'What do you think of it? It's God's country, isn't it?' Phil asked as the cab pulled away from the curbside. Now that he was home his accent appeared to be broadening by the minute.

Carol looked out of the open car window and the warm breeze swept the hair away from her face. They were driving along the shores of Botany Bay and Carol had to admit that, even through her very tired eyes, it looked beautiful. The temperature was rising rapidly now and Carol undid the top two buttons of her blouse. It was an action that did not go unnoticed.

'We've had a beaut summer, and it looks set to

continue. You will be brown in no time.' Phil's eyes were smiling as he spoke and Carol could feel his joy at being home.

'What do you think of that?' Phil asked excitedly, pointing towards the front windscreen and their first glimpse of the white rollers that came in endless waves and tumbled onto the golden shore. 'Can you swim?' He asked.

'I can.' Carol's reply was guarded. 'But, you are not getting me in there.'

'You'll love it.' He gave her hand a reassuring squeeze and then, self-consciously pulled his own away.

The taxi rounded a sweeping bend and climbed a slight hill that overlooked the beach. It came to a halt outside a small wooden bungalow with a red, corrugated, iron roof.

'Here it is. Home sweet home.' Phil announced as he jumped from the cab and held the door open for Carol.

She got out slowly, not taking her eyes from the old property whose lemon painted wooden walls were losing the battle against the ravages of time and salt spray. While she stood studying her new accommodation Phil paid off the taxi and was struggling with the cases.

'Let me help you.' Carol laughed when she saw him trying to negotiate a gap in the crumbling wooden fence that had once boasted a garden gate. Before she could move he was through the narrow opening and tottering up the weathered cement path that led to a wooden verandah that ran the width of the house.

Phil's strength failed at the last minute and he stumbled up the two steps and onto the verandah. The bags fell from his grasp and tumbled noisily onto the wooden boards.

'Are you alright?' Carol called out and ran to where he sat, surrounded by the fallen cases.

'You bet. Never better.' He smiled back and got to his feet. 'Come on in.' He turned the key in the lock and stood aside to let Carol enter.

An old rug lay over bare boards and a faded lumpy sofa sat in the middle of the lounge room. There was no hall to separate the front door from the rest of the house and as the door opened Carol thought she had travelled forty years back in time. The only concession to the present was a bean bag that sat in one corner of the room. Carol walked further into the house and looked inquisitively through the doors leading off from the lounge.

'What do you think of it?' Phil asked, placing the bags on the floor next to the sofa. Carol did not know what to say. She had not seen a house quite like it. It was all so different from what she was used to and again a feeling of distance and separation came over her.

'It's great. Very nice.' She knew it was an inadequate reply but the many hours of travel and the simple bewilderment at being where she now stood addled her brain.

Phil saw the strain in her eyes.

'You look beat.' He said and picked up her bags. 'This is your room.' He disappeared through one of the doors. 'The bathroom is in there.' He re-emerged from the bedroom and pointed to another door. 'Take a shower and go to bed for a few hours and later this afternoon I'll take you for your first Aussie beer.'

Carol went into the room that was to be hers, at least for a few days. Like the rest of the house it was very sparsely furnished, a chest of drawers, a cupboard and a very old bed. She lay down and felt her body sink into the thick mattress. She delighted in the relaxation but knew there was the film of twelve thousand miles to wash from her body.

She unpacked hurriedly, found her toiletries and went into the bathroom. There was an old steel tub with a shower rose projecting from the wall. She closed and locked the door, undressed and stepped into the bath. She pulled the shower curtain across and turned on the water. It felt wonderful to have the jets of warm spray on her body, cleansing and reviving. She turned her face to the water and shook out her long brown hair. She shivered as life surged back and with the water playing on her skin began thinking of the man on the other side of the door. The more she thought about him the more she wanted him to come in. She could not help herself. She began to feel alive and eager to start her new life.

'You tart.' She whispered and laughed to herself.

While Carol was in the bathroom Phil had been busy preparing the spare room for his guest. He also put the kettle on and when she finally came out thrust a hot mug of coffee into her hand.

'What do you want to eat?' He asked while heading for the kitchen.

'I never want to see food again.' Carol called after him. She walked over to the well-worn sofa and flopped into it. The revival was over. The hours of discomfort and fatigue washed over her again. Phil returned from the kitchen with a sandwich that could have doubled for a house brick.

'You looked shagged.' He said with candid honesty. 'I've got your room ready.' He led the way into the bedroom. Carol's eyes focused on the bed and she could remember little more from that moment until she awoke six hours later.

Carol's eyes opened and she felt an instant panic come over her. 'Where was she?' She looked round the room without recognising anything. Her heart beat faster and she found it hard to catch her breath. She then remembered Phil and everything fell into place. She lay back on her pillow, let out a sigh of relief and looked up at the cracking paint on the ceiling.

There was a knock on the door. In a wild rush Carol reached for her brush and having run it through her hair a few times called out for him to come in. Phil entered carrying a cup of tea and a tin of assorted biscuits.

'I thought I'd better wake you or else you wouldn't be able to sleep tonight.' He said and handed her the tea. 'How did you sleep?'

'Like a baby.' Carol replied, sipping her tea and looking enticingly over the rim of the cup. Phil moved uneasily trying to keep his face from betraying his desires.

'Well, when you're ready I'll take you for a drive around. I'm just going to collect my car from my folks place. I won't be long.' He smiled and left the room. Carol heard the front door open and close with his passing.

By the time he returned Carol was dressed and ready to go exploring.

'What do you want to see first?' He asked.

'It's your city. You decide.'

'Okay, it'll be getting dark soon. Let's go into town and get a drink and a bite to eat.'

Carol was rested and the thought of food was now more appealing than it was a few hours ago.

For such a young man Phil had some pretty old possessions. At least that is what Carol thought having seen his house and now his car. Phil proudly told her that it was an FJ Holden.

'You don't see many of these around.' He said triumphantly.

'I bet.' Carol smiled and got in.

They followed the coast passed sandy beaches and rocky headlands until they reached the Old South Head Road. It was the long way round but Phil was eager to show off the prettiest parts of the city. Carol sat quietly, commenting, more interested in simply sitting and absorbing as much as she could of the scene around her. 'It's fantastic.' She thought as she looked out to sea and then back along the rugged coastline. The sight she saw next took her breath away. The road veered away from the sea and Sydney Harbour extended out in front of her. Flotillas of small boats dotted the blue waters. In the distance, the orange rays of the setting sun shone through the grey metal girders of the Harbour Bridge and were reflected in the tall, glass, towers of the city's skyline.

'Best city in the world.' Phil stated, not expecting a reply.

Carol looked out of the car window and tried to store everything in the inner eye of her memory.

'I'll take you through town and we'll have dinner in The Rocks. I know a great place, you'll love it.' Phil's voice was full of enthusiasm and Carol knew that he was enjoying his role as tour guide.

They drove along the harbour foreshore, passed pretty parks and through fashionable suburbs until they climbed the hill that led to the infamous area of Kings Cross.

'This place looks lively so early in the evening.' Carol innocently commented.

'Wait until later on. You won't be able to move for tourists and tarts.' Phil replied smilingly.

'Oh,' said Carol, nodding and staring even harder.

Phil drove through the red light area, passed the Botanical Gardens and onto Circular Quay, where late commuters jostled shoulder to shoulder to catch trains and ferries out of the city. As they drove passed the station Carol could see the ferry terminal lying behind and watched as a large green and white boat moved away from the quay and out into the harbour. Her thoughts were interrupted by Phil announcing their arrival.

'There it is. The Rocks.' He turned right and drove under the bridge. Carol was not impressed and Phil saw it in her face. 'Looks a bit rough, doesn't it?' He asked and continued. 'It's the oldest part of Sydney. This is where it all began and where there is now, the greatest pub in town.' Before she could comment the car stopped outside an old, run down, public house whose stone walls could have been hewn by the city's first colonial settlers. 'We'll have a drink here and eat afterwards'.

Phil led the way inside. The interior was as rundown as the outside. However, what the place lacked in decor it more than made up for in atmosphere. As they stepped up to the scarred and beer stained wooden bar the drinkers around them erupted as one voice to sing a medley of songs from the First World War. They were both led and accompanied by an ageing three piece band that comprised a piano, a one string base and the spoons. Each was played with skill and enthusiasm. While Phil was ordering Carol stood back and looked around. There were groups dressed in formal wear rubbing shoulders with workmen in sweat stained blue vests and shorts.

Phil placed a large, ice cold glass of beer in Carol's hand, stood back, raised his glass and, over the noise of the singing, proposed a toast.

'Welcome to Australia. I know you'll love it.'

'It's great to be here and I'm sure I will.' Carol laughed.

It was all but impossible to talk while the songs were belting out and so Carol had time to reflect. Just outside the pub door stood the Sydney Harbour Bridge. Beside her, singing along with the best of them, was an Australian who, in a short time, had come to mean a lot to her. She was riding high and it worried her a little.

After another beer and a lot more songs Phil suggested it was time to move on. The restaurant was only two hundred yards down the road. It was cut out of the rock at the base of one of the bridge pylons. The atmosphere inside was in keeping with the area and its history. Old prints of Port Jackson and convict art hung from the bare stone walls. The staff were dressed in colonial costume. The menu offered, 'Colonial dishes to feed a growing Nation.' The food was hearty and delicious; and, coupled with a bottle of red wine, soon had Carol relaxed and very pleased with the hand fate had dealt her.

They talked of their past lives and filled in gaps not covered in earlier conversations. Carol omitted to mention Peter Wells. They also spoke of the future and Carol was both surprised and disappointed to learn that Phil only had six days before he had to leave for the Army. 'It was not long,' she thought, but then realised that she too had to take the next step on her journey. She was committed to see Jane's uncle and reasoned that it was for the best. She did not want romantic ties altering her plans this early in her adventure.

'How are you feeling?' Phil asked, draining his glass.

'I think that last Irish coffee has finished me off.' Carol replied, wiping the last traces of fresh cream from her lips.

'You've had a long journey. It'll take a couple of days to adjust. We had better be going.' Phil paid the bill and they walked out into the warm night air. It was a beautiful evening with the harbour magically reflecting the city lights in its still waters.

'It really is fantastic.' Carol exclaimed to herself as much as to anyone else.

On the drive back to the house neither spoke more than a few words. It did not seem necessary. By taking back streets Phil got them home before Carol expected it and despite her tiredness she did not want to go inside.

'Is there anything else to see?' She asked.

Phil thought for a while and then put the car into first gear. He drove for a short distance and they came to a spot overlooking the beach. He pulled in and turned off the engine. They sat motionless, looking out to sea, each realising the situation they were now in but not sure what to do about it. It was an emotional standoff with both wanting to get closer to the other but neither wanting to compromise the relationship that had built up between them. Consequently they sat, admired the view and then returned to the house feeling self-conscious about their private thoughts.

Phil unlocked the front door and stood aside to let Carol pass. He switched on the lounge room light.

'Do you want a coffee?' He asked, thankful for something innocent to say.

Carol politely declined and they both made to go to their respective bedrooms, but something was holding them back. It was Phil who spoke first.

'I want you to know how great it is to have you stay.' He said, moving closer.

'It's wonderful to be here Phil. I owe you a lot.' Her words broke the spell. Phil did not want to appear to be foreclosing on a debt and Carol regretted the connotation of having to pay for his kindness. She lifted her face to his and kissed him on the cheek.

'Thanks for everything. You are a lovely man.'

She turned and walked into her bedroom, closing the door gently behind her.

The next five days were ones of joy and excitement. Phil was determined to show Carol all that Sydney had to offer. They visited the beaches, drove into the mountains, spent a lazy day on the harbour and dined in intimate restaurants. Phil even took Carol home to meet his parents.

She was the first English girl to have sat at their table and to Carol it appeared that the only knowledge Phil's father had of England was that they could not play Rugby League and their cricket team were a load of crocks. Mrs. Sewell maintained a shy silence, only speaking to answer questions or to offer more food from the serving dishes at the centre of the table.

'I thought I'd take Carol down to the south coast for a couple of days.' Phil announced boldly and Carol looked to his parents. She could not tell how they regarded the living arrangements that existed between her and their son. They appeared to be a very conservative couple and Carol did not think it wise to flaunt what to them may be an immoral liaison. Phil appeared oblivious to any such consideration.

'We could stay at Ted's cottage down at Hyams Beach. He won't be using it mid-week. I'll give him a call and see if I can go over and get the keys.' Phil sprang from the table and ran to the telephone that sat on the window sill in the hall. Carol was on her own.

'You will love Jervis Bay. It is such a beautiful spot.' Carol looked towards Mrs. Sewell as if to get confirmation of what she was hearing. The mother smiled and Carol knew she was accepted. They talked about the bay and Carol learned that the family used to go there a lot when Phil was a boy.

'Philip used to love the Navy ships that anchor in

the bay. He was mad on the Navy at one time. We even thought he would go to the Naval College. That is down there you know.' As she spoke Mrs. Sewell relived those passed days while Carol felt herself grow tense. 'He went off the idea of becoming a Naval Officer and now look at him, joining the Army as a soldier. I'm not a snob, but it does seem a waste.' The conversation was cut short as Phil re-entered the room.

'It's all set. We can pick up the keys on our way home and we will set off early tomorrow morning.'

Carol could see that he was excited about the idea, while for her, the past was closing in.

They left early next morning and were on the southern outskirts of Sydney as the rush hour traffic passed in congested streams in the opposite direction. The miles that separated her from the city liberated her soul. Her thoughts of the previous evening were senseless. She was as free as the open spaces that now greeted her eyes. She was happy and moved closer to the man who helped make her so. Phil took his eyes from the road, looked into Carol's face and smiled. Nothing was said, but a bond was strengthened.

The countryside became greener as they passed into the dairy lands of the Illawarra.

'This is more like England.' Carol commented, as they passed fields dotted with dairy cows.

'Don't go getting homesick on me.' Phil answered and smiled.

'No worries about that.' Carol answered in her best Australian accent.

After three hours of driving Phil announced that they were nearly there. It was news that was eagerly accepted by his passenger who was coming to the conclusion that once you have seen one gum tree, you have seen them all.

They turned off the Princes Highway and onto a road that snaked through tall trees that, in places, blotted out the sun. Carol became excited when she saw a sign warning of the danger of kangaroos crossing the road.

'Are we really going to see kangaroos?' She asked, expectantly.

'Sure we are.' Phil answered confidently and pointed out of the side window. 'There's one now.'

Carol followed the direction of his outstretched hand and saw the body of one unfortunate animal lying dead by the side of the road.

'That doesn't count.' She said. Sad and disappointed that the first kangaroo she should see in Australia was the victim of such an untimely death.

The uneven surface of the road made the last few miles a bone jarring ride; however, any discomfort was forgotten when the car topped the brow of the last, pot holed, hill. Jervis Bay stretched out before them, its clear blue waters bounded by a ribbon of the whitest sand Carol had ever seen.

'That looks a pretty spot.' Carol said, pointing to a clump of white wooden buildings with bright red roofs that were set on the edge of the blue water.

'It's the Naval College.' Phil answered. 'I wanted to go there once. Don't know why I didn't really. I must have been going through my rebellion against authority stage.' He steered the car off onto a side road that was no more than a dirt track that led down to a cluster of old wooden cottages. 'This is Hyams Beach. The cottage is just over there.' He drove a little further and stopped next to a small building that sat on the headland overlooking the bay.

'I can't get over how white the sand is. It's beautiful.' Carol exclaimed.

'Prettiest spot in the world.' Phil replied and Carol had to agree. Phil went to unlock the front door while Carol walked to the rear of the car and started to remove the luggage from the boot.

'Come and have a look at your new home.' Phil called from the house.

Carol collected two cases and carried them inside. The cottage had only two rooms. The kitchen and living area occupied most of the available space. A blue beaded curtain led the way to a small bedroom. Carol walked around, put her head into the bedroom and then it occurred to her.

'Where is the . . . ?'

'Round the back.' Phil anticipated the question and pointed through the window towards a small wooden shed.

'Real back to nature stuff ay?' Carol laughed and Phil changed the subject.

'Let's unload our things and go for a walk along the beach.'

Carol walked up to her knees in the warm, clear blue water. She looked out towards the entrance of the bay. It was dominated by a cliff that rose dramatically from the sea. The bay was calm with only the occasional set of ripples on its surface as soft breezes passed over the water.

'It's so peaceful here.' Carol sighed and put out her hand to Phil. 'Thank you for bringing me.'

They stopped walking and turned toward each other. Their bodies drew together and their lips met. They kissed long and passionately as the ebb and flow of the tide washed the waters about their feet. When, finally their lips parted, Carol's mouth broke into a mischievous smile and kissing him quickly on the lips she ran off into the soft white sand. Phil gave chase and brought her down with a flying tackle from behind. They rolled in the sand, their bodies entwined and kissed again.

'I know, let's eat out tonight.' Phil said, when they finally sat up and dusted the sand from their bodies. Carol looked about her.

'Where are we going to find a restaurant around here?'

Phil pointed along the beach.

'Right there.' He said triumphantly. 'We'll have a Barbie.'

'Great!' Exclaimed Carol and her eyes widened with excitement. Hand in hand they returned to the cottage, got the car keys from the table and drove to the nearby General Store to buy the food they would eat that night and for the next two days.

Done together even the mundane task of shopping became an exciting experience. As they came out of the store Carol looked up and down the street. This was the Australia she expected to see, right down to the men in their shorts and long socks. On their way back to the car Carol turned to Phil,

'The only thing missing are the kangaroos, and I don't mean the dead ones.'

'Well, I don't know about the roos, but what say we go back for a swim? This shopping is hot work.' Phil suggested.

They returned to the cottage to change and it was while Carol was standing naked in the box like bedroom she realised there was only one bed. Despite the warm feeling she held for Phil, her sense of betrayal was even greater. 'How dare he take her for granted.' Taking a bikini from her suitcase she put it on angrily while her mind raged with indignation. 'She had not encouraged him. It was his idea to come here and now she knew why. He was not going to get away with it. Just let him try it on.' Carol reached for her towel and marched out of the bedroom. She may have once wanted all that Phil was planning, but now, she was feeling used and angry. Her eyes were hard and her face set in a mask of menacing defiance.

She looked around the living room and saw the object of her wrath bending over a bed and tucking the trailing edge of a blue sheet under the mattress. She stood dumbfounded, unable to speak.

'Carol, what's wrong?'

'What's wrong?' She replied in a tone of confused agitation. 'Where did that come from?' She pointed at the bed.

'It's one of those divans that turn into a bed. I thought I would make it up now rather than wait until tonight when we'll be tired. Which one do you want?' He waited for a reply, not understanding Carol's hesitation; but, happy to stare at her taught body trimmed by the material of her swimsuit.

'I'll take the one in the bedroom, if that's alright with you?' The answer finally came in a matter of fact tone. She was not going to let him know what she had just been thinking and how childish she now felt.

'Let me finish that. You go and change.' She said.

The water felt beautiful against her body. She did not hesitate on entering but ran straight in. The waves washed onto the beach as the swell from the open sea came to its relentless and turbulent end. The white water felt cold on her stomach as the sea touched the bare skin above the waistline of her bikini. She gave a scream and dived into the next oncoming wave. She swam under the clear water for a short distance, surfaced and looked back to the beach. Phil was entering the water with a lot more hesitation and Carol looked long and hard at the muscular body that a short while before she had rejected with indignation. 'I must have been insane,' she thought and called to the slowly advancing figure.

'Come on in, it's great!'

'It's freezing!' Came the high pitched reply.

Carol swam toward the flinching brown figure and when she was only a few feet away, stopped, stood up with a hand full of water and threw it over his half submerged body.

'You ratbag! I'll get you for that!' He screamed and ducked his body under the water. 'Now you're in for it!'

He called and swam towards her. Carol tried to run away but her legs became like jelly as his thrashing body drew nearer. Very quickly he was next to her and she felt his arms go around her waist lifting her into the air. She screamed as she left the water, flew a few feet through the air and re-entered with a splash of salt spray. He came after her and gathered her to him again. Carol melted against his body and with arms about each other they kissed. The water flowed between their bodies, sealing their embrace. Carol could feel the emotion building within him and the pressure of his body excited her to a point where she no longer cared for the principles that earlier meant so much. Their lips parted and Carol was picked up and carried through the water, cradled like a small child. They kissed again. The feeling was getting stronger and they both knew where it was leading. Looking into each other's eyes the world seemed to stand still. Phil released his grip and Carol's feet touched the sand.

'We should set up for the barbecue.' He said, trying to control the emotion in his voice. 'Let's go and collect some stones and firewood.' He took Carol's hand and they returned to the beach.

They walked along the sand dunes that separated the beach from the bush behind. Together they collected the stones that Phil set in a circle to form a fireplace, and the wood that he used for fuel. By the time the fire was ready the shadows were lengthening in the evening sun. Carol and Phil returned to the cottage to change and collect what they needed to cook a meal out of doors.

When they got back to the beach the sun was

disappearing behind the tall, Blue Gum trees, and, out to sea a bright three quarter moon was rising above Point Perpendicular. The sky was empty except for the moon and a few of the brightest stars that sparkled against the deep blue mantle. The orange glow from the setting sun transformed the whiteness of the sand into a golden ribbon that stretched as far as the eye could see.

'It is even more beautiful when the sun goes down.' Carol said to herself as she walked down to the beach. Phil had gone on ahead and already a fire was burning in the stone fireplace. Carol came down and sat beside him. Two thick steaks were cooking on the burning embers. Phil took out a bottle of wine from the portable cooler. Pouring two glasses he handed one to Carol.

'Here's to you.' He raised his glass to touch hers. He wanted to say more but was unable to find the words. They both took a sip and Carol leaned over and tenderly kissed his cheek.

The bay was bathed in moonlight and the stars shone in the night sky. Heaven and earth blended in a beautiful blackness that engulfed the young couple now silhouetted by the flicker of the firelight.

The food was eaten, the wine drunk and the flames became glowing embers. Phil stoked the dying fire as he watched Carol looking pensively across the water. She felt his eyes upon her and also felt an attraction far stronger than she had felt before. Perhaps it was because she had not wanted to get involved that she had denied these feelings. Whatever the reason, it lost its meaning in the burning depths of the fire. Their bodies met and they drew together. Carol looked up into the glittering blackness and closed her eyes as the passion she had wanted to control took possession of all of her.

Carol opened her eyes and looked into the serene face of the man lying on the pillow next to her. She had fought for what felt an eternity to stay out of the situation in which she now found herself, and wondered why she resisted something that felt so natural. As she stared into Phil's sleeping face her mind re-traced the steps that had brought her there. So much had happened in such a short time, and, in two days they were to be torn apart.

'Why did life have to be so complicated?' She asked herself.

As if stirred by her troubled thoughts Phil opened his eyes.

'Hello.' He said and moved closer to give Carol an affectionate kiss on her pouting lips.

She replied and kissed him back.

It was an awkward time for both. The romance of the night had given way to the reality that comes with the sun. Each knew the feelings they held for the other, but, could not be certain that these were shared. Phil spoke again.

'It was a beautiful night. You're beautiful. Come here.' He reached out and drew her to him. The uncertainty passed. They embraced and the passion that was kindled with the fire returned and burned more brightly than the night before.

'Is this where you bring all your girls when you want to seduce them?' Carol asked as she went out of the door and into the sunlight.

'Only the Pommie ones.' Phil replied and patted her shapely bottom. They walked arm in arm to the car. 'I'll take you around and show you some of the other beaches and we can stop for lunch in a pub somewhere before heading home. I don't want to leave it too long before makin' tracks, it's a long drive and tomorrow's our last day.'

'I don't want tomorrow to come.' Carol said sadly and moved closer. 'I don't want this time to end… ever.'

Phil cursed himself for being so thoughtless. 'It doesn't have to.' He said and looked into Carol's eyes. He kissed her to break the spell.

They walked back to the cottage and packed their cases in silence. They had found something in this place and were taking it out into the world. The real world. They loaded the suitcases into the car.

'Look!' Phil cried pointing towards the entrance of the bay. 'There's some ships coming in.' Carol looked at the grey forms as they glided over the still surface of the water. 'Destroyers. I can't make out their numbers. I used to know the numbers of all the ships when I was a boy.'

Phil was so intent on trying to identify the ships he did not notice the change that had come over Carol. Her body grew taut and her eyes hardened as if to defend herself against an impending attack. The ships drew nearer and it was as if her past life was being carried before them like the waves at their bows.

'Let's go, Phil. You said we had to get going.' Carol went to the car and got inside. 'Why does it have to come back to me?' She asked herself, anguishing over the past and the life that would not let her go.

Chapter 8

The wind lifted the white spray and carried it in silver sheets across the heaving flight deck. The Officer of the Watch pulled the bridge window down so that he could feel the freshness of the North Atlantic morning. The bow rose and fell as Sovereign's grey mass punched through the sea.

The sun had risen an hour before and Peter had been there to record the bearings and elevations of the stars that were so quickly hidden by the brilliance of its rays. He had put a fix on the chart and was now standing at the back of the bridge looking out over the white capped sea.

'The Captain's compliments sir.' Peter looked around and acknowledged the Bosun Mate's salute. 'The Captain would like to see you in his sea cabin. Sir.'

'Very good.' Peter's manner did not betray his curiosity. He moved to the starboard side of the bridge and followed the passageway aft to the small cabin that was the Captain's home while the ship was at sea. He knocked twice.

'Enter.' The stern voice barked back.

Peter walked in to find the Captain dressed in a thick burgundy dressing gown with matching carpet slippers and clutching a pink signal sheet in his right hand.

'Good morning Peter. Please excuse the rig, but I thought you would like to know about this straight away.' He raised the signal in front of him. 'How would you like to go on this year's Far East Deployment?'

Peter did not know what to say. He did not want to leave the ship. He had organised her routine for the coming year and wanted to see the job through. However, he also knew that to go on a deployment East of Suez was a career opportunity not to be missed.

The Captain could sense Peter's dilemma and enjoyed seeing this usually inscrutable officer now showing signs of concern. He did not let him suffer too long before continuing.

'I don't just mean you. I am talking about Sovereign. The old Pegasus can't make it. Her boilers have finally given up the ghost and she has to go in for immediate refit. We are her replacement.'

Peter could not believe what he was being told. A Far Eastern Deployment meant that Sovereign would be flagship and he the Squadron Navigator. There would be a Rear-Admiral embarked affording him the chance to demonstrate his skills before a man who could accelerate his already rapid promotion. Once again he appeared to be in the right place at the right time. Peter fought to contain the excitement these thoughts generated. The Captain was talking again and Peter listened impassively, his face once more a mask of his emotions.

'We have been ordered back to Portsmouth where we will undergo a three week self-maintenance period. We sail on February 20th and embark the squadrons on the 22nd. When we get back to Portsmouth you will have to get together with the pilot of the Pegasus and get their itinerary. If you think the schedule needs altering let me know. Now, get us back to Pompey by 2000 tomorrow. On your way out will you tell the Bosun's Mate to get Commander (S) for me? Thank you, Peter.'

The meeting was over and the Navigator left his Captain padding around his cabin in his bedroom slippers. Peter knew that his own excitement was also shared by his commanding officer, and, for all the same reasons.

'Finished with main engines. Thank you Coxswain.' The Captain's voice was as crisp as the January breeze that cut across the harbour. He turned to his Navigator. 'You better get across to Pegasus Peter and don't let your jubilation be too obvious.' The Navigator saluted.

'Aye aye, sir.'

Both men smiled in their conspiracy, each aware of the opportunity fate had placed in their path.

Peter arrived at Sovereign's gangway just as the lines were being doubled up and secured. He saluted as he crossed the brow and walked briskly down the uneven steps to the stone wharf.

Pegasus was already in dry dock and one of her huge propellers was missing, leaving a naked stump extending from beneath her stern. Peter walked alongside the grey hulk. He had always marvelled at the majesty of the aircraft carrier at sea, but now, set in that giant hole in the ground, that mystique was stripped away.

Peter walked to the after gangway and continued up to the quarterdeck of the Royal Navy's oldest aircraft carrier. The gangway staff saluted smartly as the unknown officer boarded their ship. Peter returned the courtesy.

'Good evening. I am Lieutenant-Commander Wells. I have come to see your Navigating Officer.'

'Very good, sir.' Replied the Quartermaster. 'The Bosun's Mate will take you to see Commander Goodman.'

Peter followed the Ordinary Seaman and found himself noticing the change that comes over a ship when it goes into dockyard hands. It was a sad sight to see wooden duckboards running the length of main passageways; pieces of machinery in various stages of repair; and, to smell the stench of oil that only a ship fighting for its life can emit.

Peter was taken to the wardroom where the big bulk of the Navigator sat slumped in an armchair. A cup of coffee sat beside him and he appeared to be working on a crossword puzzle from the evening paper. Peter dismissed his guide, stepped over the coaming and entered the silence of the wardroom. He walked across to the big man who was the personification of the depression that now enveloped HMS Pegasus. There would be those who welcomed the change in plans, but most of the ship's company would have been looking forward to that all too infrequent trip to the Far East.

'Commander Goodman.' Peter stood at attention

and addressed the sporting pages of the Portsmouth Evening News. I am Lieutenant-Commander Wells, Navigating Officer of HMS Sovereign.'

The paper was lowered and a large black bearded face looked up at the intruder.

'I've been expecting you. You are here to take my trip, you lucky bastard.' The large frame rose from the seat and extended his right hand. Peter was relieved to see the stern face of the senior Commander break into a smile. 'Sit down. What d'ya say your name was?' Asked the Navigator in the lazy speech of the upper classes. Peter introduced himself again. 'D'you want a cup of coffee, Peter? You might as well, there's not a lot else to do around here.' Peter agreed and the big man motioned to the wardroom steward.

'I've got the ship's programme for the deployment here.' The Commander patted a thick folio on the table next to him. 'We'll go through it over coffee.' He turned his attention to the smartly turned out Leading Steward who was at that time pouring a cup of hot brown liquid into a white Admiralty cup. 'Make that two would you, Johnson?'

The next three weeks were ones of intense activity for Sovereign and her crew. Stores came aboard in a never ending stream. Stokers and dockyard workers toiled around the clock to ensure that her machinery, from the main engines in her bowels to the catapults on her flight deck, were fully operational. Sailors from the Seaman Departments of; Gunnery, Radar and Communications attended courses at their respective schools ashore.

Under simulated conditions they practised the skills that would be needed in the busy months ahead. Advanced parties from the Fleet Air Arm readied the carrier for the arrival of the squadrons. Their job would not really get underway until the aircraft and their supporting services embarked off the coast of Cornwall in the weeks to come.

The days alongside passed all too quickly for those men with hearts committed ashore. On the last Saturday before departure the Wardroom marked the ship's imminent sailing with a party. Coloured lights festooned the quarterdeck and brightly painted canvas awnings shielded the area from the cold winter wind. The wooden deck had been scrubbed to a white brilliance by a legion of Ordinary Seaman who recently joined the ship for their first taste of life afloat. It was not what they had expected.

The wardroom was decorated with bright signal flags placed, under the meticulous eye of the Chief Steward, to present a crescendo of colour that would dazzle even the most inebriated eye. The ship's cooks displayed their skill on long tables weighed down with mouthwatering creations from delicate canapés to sweet delicacies that added inches to the waistline by simply casting a longing glance in their direction.

The first guests started to arrive at 1900, while Peter was completing the tying of his bow tie. He donned his mess jacket, checked his appearance in the mirror and hurriedly left for the wardroom. He was not looking forward to the evening's activities. Gone were the days when the anticipation of meeting a pretty lady added a dimension of excitement and challenge to the event. As he descended the ladder that led to the wardroom deck Peter could hear the groundswell of music and voices. He entered the crowded anteroom and made his way to the bar. He looked about him and was relieved to see that he had beaten the 'brass'.

'Gin and Tonic, please.' Peter gave his order to the steward behind the bar as he made a vertical stroke on the bar chit. He looked around the wardroom once more. It was rapidly filling with officers and their ladies. 'Wives and sweethearts,' Peter thought of the naval toast for Saturday, 'may they never meet.' He raised his glass and drank. He knew that, for some, those words would certainly ring true in the months ahead.

'I guess we better enjoy the wardroom while we can, ay Peter?' Peter looked around and into the crusty old face of the Boatswain. He considered the statement he had heard a number of times before and wondered if the aircrews could really be that bad. He nodded to the Boatswain but was not going to commit himself to condemning a group of men he had yet to meet. As he pondered the question a silence descended on the wardroom. Peter saw all the heads turn towards the door. He looked over in that direction and could just see the balding head of the Captain and the greying hair of Rear-Admiral Harrison. Over the past weeks he had met the Admiral on a number of occasions and found him to be a man of humour and high expectations.

As quickly as it fell so the crescendo of party noises rose again. Peter moved away from the bar. He felt uncomfortably exposed. He was one of the few officers not escorting a lady and having made an appearance was already planning his escape. An escape it would be, a breaking out from a situation in which he felt himself a prisoner. He walked through the crowd acknowledging greetings and passing social pleasantries as he made for the door. He stepped out into the passageway and turned to walk back to his cabin. He had only gone a few yards when he stopped and reconsidered. 'What am I doing?' He thought. 'I am dressed up like a tailor's dummy, I might as well make the best of it, but, not here.' The decision made, he climbed the ladder that led to the quarterdeck. He stepped through the hatch and onto the white wooden deck. There was a winter chill in the air. Peter walked over to the makeshift bar that had been placed on the port side, away from the gangway. He ordered his second drink of the evening and moved across to the wooden guard rail that skirted the deck. Taking a sip of his gin and tonic he looked through the gaps between the awnings and studied the lines of an RFA tanker secured alongside the fuelling wharf on the Gosport side of the harbour.

'Hello, Peter Wells isn't it?'

Peter was startled to hear his name spoken and looked to see who was addressing him. He was taken completely off guard when he stared into the face of a pretty young woman.

'Hi, I'm Susanne Harrison.' She extended her very slim hand to him. 'My father has mentioned your name quite a bit recently. He doesn't usually bring his work home. You must have made an impression. I suppose I should not be telling you this. Anyway, I wanted to meet you and now I have. I saw you leave the party. I knew it was you from the description I got from Daddy. He said you were young for your job and you are aren't you?' Peter shuffled uneasily, shrugged his shoulders and remained silent. 'I left my drink downstairs. Do you think I could get another one over there?'

This was Peter's chance, at last he had a platform from which to launch himself into the conversation. He took her order, excused himself and went to get the drink. He returned, presented the glass and was about to say something when the talkative young woman started again.

'Are you looking forward to going to the Far East? Daddy is.' She went on to recount the story of her childhood in Singapore while Peter sipped his gin and nodded interestedly. At least he hoped he appeared interested; because, the longer she talked the more difficult it became for him to listen.

'What a shame,' he was thinking, while his head nodded as she spoke. 'Such a pretty girl.' His eyes darted over the firm lines of her compact figure. She was a small girl and Peter had to look down into her, rounded, cherub-like face. Her whole appearance was rounded from her high cheek bones to the fullness of her breasts and the curve of her back and bottom. Her hair was chestnut brown and cut in a page boy style that framed her face. Peter looked into her deep brown eyes and found himself regaining interest in whatever she had to say.

'I talk too much, don't I? Don't answer that because I know I do. It's only because you make me nervous.'

Peter was now well and truly lost for words. He

agonised over what to say and marvelled at this girl who said whatever came into her head.

'Say something.' He told himself and then blurted out, 'there is absolutely no cause to be nervous.' He then berated himself for sounding so fatherly. 'Why don't we go down and have a dance? It is rather cold up here.' He had taken the initiative and also knew that anything was better than trying to sustain a conversation with this young lady. As he followed her down the ladder he hoped that fast music was being played in the wardroom.

A number of eyes turned to watch them enter and notice was taken of who escorted the Admiral's daughter. Susanne took Peter across to her parents, who were talking to the Captain and his wife. Peter thought he saw a glint in his Captain's eye that suggested his Navigator was certainly playing his cards right.

'If only he knew,' thought Peter, recalling how he came to be in this situation. They chatted for a while and then Susanne took hold of Peter's hand.

'Peter promised me a dance.' She proclaimed, while pulling him towards the dance floor. Peter excused himself and tried to depart with dignity.

'He does not know what he is letting himself in for.' The Admiral remarked to his group who all laughed as one.

As if by arrangement, as soon as they reached the area set aside for dancing the tempo of the music changed. A slow tune was played and couples either moved closer together, thankful for the chance of intimacy, or left the dance floor in an embarrassed rush. Peter cursed his luck, but knowing there was no turning back, put his left arm around Susanne's waist and held her hand with his right. They stood a respectable distance apart and did not speak.

'What a relief,' Peter thought as he held her and lost himself in the music. It had been a while since he was in female company. As they moved together he felt himself unwind. The records changed and he relaxed his hold on Susanne's hand. He pulled her closer and placed both arms around her trim waist. Susanne responded and increased the pressure of her hand on Peter's back. It was he who resumed the conversation, asking all the standard 'get to know you' questions. He learned that she worked in Plymouth as a nursery school teacher, and, he guessed she must be about twenty two years old. She and her mother had come up to stay with her father prior to his departure. Peter stopped asking questions and lowered his head so as to be able to place his cheek against hers. They were now moving as one.

He felt a fluttering start in the pit of his stomach and travel in a gathering wave throughout his body. He hoped his partner did not detect this surge of sexual excitement. He could not believe that it was happening again.

The music changed tempo once more and the bodies on the dance floor parted.

'Would you like to get something to eat?' Peter asked, as they walked from the dance floor.

'I would like to get some fresh air first.' Susanne replied. They left the wardroom and returned to the quarterdeck. Peter collected their drinks and they walked as far away from the other couples as they could get. Peter wondered at the quiet change that had come over the Admiral's daughter. 'She is lovely, but a little strange,' he thought and then made a decision. 'What the hell it is only for one evening.' He recalled how exciting she was to hold.

'How would you like to have a look over the ship?' He then remembered to whom he was talking. 'I suppose you've seen it all before?'

'Never at night.' Susanne answered with a sparkle in her eyes.

They put their half-finished drinks on the guardrail and Peter led the way to the ladder that gave access to the flight deck. A light breeze cut keenly across the open expanse of deck. Peter put a protective arm around Susanne's shoulders and she came closer.

'Watch out for the wires.' Peter warned, pointing to the oily cables that ran parallel to each other across the rear section of the flight deck. These were the arrestor wires which, when caught by the trailing hook of a landing aircraft, brought it to a spectacular and rapid halt. Susanne looked down and narrowly missed tripping over the first of the messy cables. They walked diagonally across the deck to the island on the starboard side. The hatch was open and Peter motioned for Susanne to go inside. He followed and they stood in a dimly lit space at the foot of a steep ladder, bathed in red light.

'I'll go first,' said Peter and set off to climb the ladder. Accustomed to ship's steep ladders Susanne knew why she was to go second. She smiled at Peter's chivalry. Peter climbed the steps and called back for Susanne to be careful. He waited at the first deck and then led the way up the final flight.

'Where can I get a drink?' Gasped Susanne when Peter announced they had arrived. 'I should have brought my glass with me.' She said, only half-jokingly.

They were on the bridge and Peter signalled for her to come over to the big airline style chair that sat, raised up, on the port side.

'Come and sit here and get your breath back.' He said. Putting his hands around her waist he lifted her into the Captain's chair. She looked around at the many instruments that were arrayed in front of her and then lifted her eyes to look out of the bridge window. It was a clear night and the lights of the harbour and surrounding towns sparkled like the stars that hung over the white scarred silhouette of Portsdown Hill.

Seeing this pretty girl in his own territory caused Peter to go silent. He knew that in a few days' time it would be her father walking this bridge and here he was trying to seduce his daughter. It was a dangerous game. As if by telepathy the Admiral's daughter leaned down from her high perch and put her arms around Peter's neck. He looked into her burning brown eyes and kissed her parted lips with the passion of a man who had denied himself such feelings for far too long.

Their lips parted and Susanne slid from the chair and into Peter's arms. She kissed him affectionately on the neck and then as quickly as his passion was aroused so it subsided. Peter once more considered the implications of his actions. 'Damn it.' He thought. 'Not here, not now.' He gently kissed Susanne on the lips, squeezed her body to his and then released the pressure.

'We had better get back to the party.' He said and

took her hand. He led the way back down the ladders and took a different route back to the wardroom so as to avoid the, now, biting night air.

Susanne was disappointed by the hasty retreat, but knew the reason behind it. Being the boss's daughter had many disadvantages, but she was not going to give up that easily.

'Will I see you before you sail?' She asked as they neared the sound of the party. Peter quickly considered the question.

'There is only tomorrow and I have a few things to go over before we sail.' He paused. 'How about coming aboard for dinner?' It was not the answer she wanted but it was a compromise. It was not the answer Peter wanted to give but it was the only sensible one. The date was made. 'Speaking of food, why don't we go and see the creations the chefs have prepared for tonight?'

Neither had a big appetite so they just toured the tables, commenting on the marvellous selection of food and its imaginative presentation while sampling various dishes as they went. The food appeared to regenerate Susanne's tongue as she began firing questions at Peter about his past life. He went on the defensive and withdrew into himself. This getting to know you ritual forced him to think of events that caused him pain and to expose failures to a virtual stranger. He knew then that this was why he shied away from starting new relationships.

He tried to turn the tables and get Susanne to talk about herself, as she had so freely earlier in the evening. It did not work. The more he tried the faster came her questions in return, until the question he dreaded most was asked.

'Do you mind if I ask you a personal question? It doesn't matter, I'm going to ask it anyway. Why aren't you married?'

Peter felt a sickness in the pit of his stomach. The spark of anger was ignited within him and he felt belittled by his own lack of control. It was another failure and all failure stemmed from that incident he did not want to remember. His anger turned inward as he re-lived those months of separation and divorce. However, Peter could only take self-recrimination for so long and then a safety mechanism was activated in his mind. He directed his rage toward his ex-wife because she had not listened, had not understood.

'I was married.' Peter said the words abruptly, hoping to end the line of questioning.

Susanne was visibly startled. She was certain he had not married because of the Service. A silence fell between them and Peter thought that the end of the conversation and the relationship.

'Do you have any children?'

Peter could not believe it. Like a terrier with a bone she was not going to let it go. He steadied himself to answer.

'Yes, a boy, although I haven't seen him since he was a year old.' Peter could see the disbelief and dismay in the young woman's face and so continued. 'My wife married again and we thought it best that the boy only know one father.' Peter had won. Susanne asked no more questions.

'I am afraid I'm going to have to break you two up. It is time we were off, Susanne. Sorry to have to take you away.' The Admiral smiled like an indulgent father who was expecting a scene at his intrusion.

Peter returned the smile, relieved to be free of the questions, anxiety and self-recrimination. Susanne was not so quick to perk up and her father attributed that to disappointment at having to leave so soon.

The gangway staff snapped to attention as the senior officers and their ladies approached. No further words had passed between Peter and Susanne and the Navigator was thinking of ways to say farewell to his partner. He then remembered the dinner invitation. As the Admiral and his wife stepped onto the gangway Peter turned to Susanne. She halted and looked questioningly at him.

'Will I see you for dinner tomorrow? Around seven o'clock?' Peter asked.

'I will look forward to it.' Susanne replied demurely. Peter put out his right hand in an awkward attempt to shake hands and said goodnight. Susanne leaned forward and gave him a discreet peck on the cheek.

'Goodnight Peter.' Stepping onto the gangway she walked carefully down the uneven steps. Peter saluted and stood looking down at the black car that was to take the Admiral and his family home. Susanne glanced up as she got into the car and then she was gone. The car pulled away with Peter watching it until it turned and went out of sight behind an old red brick dockyard workshop.

Peter stepped back from the rail and walked across the wooden deck. Other couples were still enjoying the festivities, but, he had too much to think about to even consider joining in again. He climbed the ladder to the flight deck and retraced his earlier steps to the bridge. He sat down on the Captain's chair.

'Of all the people to tell his secrets to, the Admiral's daughter, what stories she could tell her father. Damn it.' Peter's mind was a cauldron of angered thoughts and the fire that fed them flared up again. 'I thought I had put all that behind me. Damn Damn Damn!' He struck the arm of the chair with a heavy blow from his right hand. The sound echoed around the steel structure of the bridge.

'Is anything wrong, sir?' Peter was startled by the voice of the Quartermaster.

'No, no, carry on.' Peter tried to inject some composure into his voice. 'That's put the lid on it,' he thought, 'just my luck to be here when the security rounds go through, now the whole ship will have a story to tell. The Navigator and the Admiral's daughter. The Navigator knocking seven bells out of the Captain's chair at midnight.' He could just imagine how these two incidents would be linked by the overactive imaginations in the ship's company.

He got out of the chair, walked round and down three steps to the Admiral's Bridge. 'The day after tomorrow how would he be able to face the man who would be pacing this space? What a disaster this evening turned out to be.' He remembered tomorrow's dinner engagement. 'All was not lost.' He thought.

The following day the weather deteriorated. Rain fell in torrents and huge water droplets ricocheted off the steel deck as the relentless flood met the unyielding metal plate. Peter spent the greater part of the day in the chart house. He studied the programme for the coming months, paying particular attention to the itinerary for the first five days. During this time a squadron of six ships would assemble. Sovereign would sail from Portsmouth in company with the anti-submarine frigates; Consort and Constant, and the Royal Fleet Auxiliary tanker, Provider. On the second day she would be joined by the guided missile destroyer Salisbury and the stores ship, Ocean Ranger. On days three and four the Fleet Air Arm squadrons would practise deck landings and then embark with their arms and services. Throughout this time Sovereign's own crew would have serious work to do moulding themselves into a unified team capable of reacting swiftly and skillfully as a maritime fighting unit. Operating in a multi ship environment demanded a high level of professionalism from the Commanding Officer to the most junior sailor.

Peter turned his attention to the departure plans. He removed the relevant charts from the folio and laid them out on the table. He rechecked; tracks, bearings, wheel-over points, the Harbour Pilot manual, and all sources of information that would help him take Sovereign to sea. As he worked, the rain continued to fall. By late afternoon his task was completed. He strolled around the bridge looking out at the sheeting rain. He hoped that by tomorrow morning the skies would have cleared. Holding onto this thought he walked over to the bridge ladder and descended to the passageway that led to the wardroom. He felt he had earned a cup of coffee and a chance to relax. Throughout the day he had not allowed his mind to wander from the duties of a Squadron Navigator. As he drank and unwound he thought about his dinner engagement. He was not certain that she would turn up, and he was not sure he wanted her to. He then considered the implications of not seeing the Admiral's daughter.

'Were the events of last night to have repercussions?' He finished his coffee and stared into the empty cup. Peter knew that if Susanne did not appear then there were consequences he would have to live with for at least the duration of the deployment. He replaced the cup in its saucer and with his hands on the arms of the chair lifted himself to his feet. He felt weighed down by his thoughts;

'I don't need this aggravation.' He said to himself and walked over to the Duty Steward to warn him there would be one extra for dinner.

The pipes sounded round the dockyard as each ship marked the ceremonial of sunset. 1900 had come and gone. Peter stood on the quarterdeck looking down on the wharf below. It was a cold, wet night. He moved back from the guardrail and paced the deck. He hated to be kept waiting. On this cold night and under the watchful eyes of the gangway staff Peter became impatient. After last night's episode on the bridge the crew could now talk about the night the Navigator got stood up. He walked back to the gangway, trying to disguise his annoyance. He looked at his watch. It was ten past eight. He had to know whether she was going to arrive.

Peter left the brow and returned to his cabin. He knew he had the Admiral's telephone number written on the deployment notes. He found it and went along to the wardroom. All eyes fell upon him as he entered alone. He walked over to the telephone, looked at the paper in his hand and dialed the number written on it.

While waiting for the call to be answered Peter looked round the wardroom. As his gaze fell on the faces of the assembled officers not one of them could hold his eye.

'2076.' The male voice on the other end of the line sounded sharp and angry. Peter wanted to put the receiver down but he was committed, trapped by the piece of black plastic he held in his hand. He had to answer,

'Hello, is Susanne Harrison there please?'

'Who is this?'

'Peter Wells.' Peter hesitated wanting to hang up. 'Susanne was to have dinner with me this evening.'

Peter knew he was talking to the Admiral, but could not bring himself to open a conversation. The Admiral appeared to be in a very bad mood.

'Susanne is here, but she will not be going out again. Not for a few days anyway.' Before Peter could ask what he meant the agitated voice continued; 'she had an accident on her way to see you, Peter. She rolled her car. It's written off and she nearly was too.'

'How is she?' Peter interjected.

'In shock. The doctor says that it's not serious and there is nothing broken. She's a lucky girl.' Peter did not know what to say next and was relieved when the Admiral spoke again. 'I will not be coming with you tomorrow,' he said gruffly. 'I will join with the squadrons. Fleet Operations know and so does Captain Harlow.'

Peter felt that he was being dismissed.

'Please tell Susanne I called and give her my regards. I hope she is up and about soon. Good night, sir.' With a silent sigh of relief Peter hung up the phone. He stood looking at the receiver and fought to gather his thoughts.

'I hate bloody telephones.' He cursed as he walked away from the bar on which the offending instrument was perched. With every step he analyzed what the Admiral had said. 'On her way to see you, Peter.' 'Did he really blame me? He couldn't. Hell, what a mess.' He concluded.

'Bad news, Peter?' The voice of the Officer of the Day, brought him out of his quandary.

'Yes. Susanne's had a car accident. She's okay, except for shock.' Just saying these words helped to clear his mind. He turned to the steward. 'My guest will not be coming for dinner. Will you tell the chef and let the gangway staff know.'

Peter did not want to be drawn into a conversation about the accident and so, having informed the staff, he left the wardroom. Following the passageways and climbing the many ladders he made his way to the safe haven of the chart house.

'He can't blame me for God's sake.' Peter said to himself, as he switched the desk lamp on and sat down in the old leather chair in the corner of the small cabin. 'Bloody hell.' He cursed as he recalled the telephone conversation and the events of the past two evenings. 'Stupid girl.' He exclaimed to the emptiness around him as he turned his anger on Susanne Harrison.

Peter sat rigid in the chair and stared out of the small scuttle into the dark, wet night, losing track of time as he wrestled with his thoughts and fears. Eventually, giving in to reason, he rose from the chair and left for his cabin.

'I should send her some flowers.' He felt better for having made a decision.

The sky was dark and threatening, but the torrential rain of the previous day had stopped. In its place a fierce wind cut across the surface of the harbour. It was 0930 and aboard HMS Sovereign Special Sea Dutymen had closed up.

'We're going to really need the tugs this morning, Peter.' The Captain remarked in what was the first exchange of words between them. Under normal circumstances this would not be unusual as the Captain had full confidence in his Navigator and knew that all the preparations for getting underway would be carried out as a matter of course. However, on this morning, Peter was feeling particularly sensitive and he felt the silence between himself and the Captain keenly.

'Rear-Admiral Harrison will not be sailing with us.' Harlow spoke again. 'I understand you know about the bad luck with his daughter. It was a foul night last night.'

'Excuse me, sir.' The voice of the communications rating broke into the conversation and ended it before Peter could find out whether the blame he felt the Admiral attributed to him was a belief now shared by his Captain. 'The tugs want to know whether they can button on, sir.' The sailor with the telephone handset relayed the message.

'Give me the phone.' Replied the Captain. He spoke into the handset and told the tug masters what he expected of them and then returned the set to the sailor.

'Tell the hands to fall in for leaving harbour.' The pipe was made and down on the flight deck blue clad figures appeared from the shelter of nooks and crannies and lined the edge of the long deck. The sympathies of those fortunate to be enclosed within the ship went out to the men who had to line the decks and stand exposed to the chill bite of the February wind.

1000 hours and the Royal Marine Band struck up with a crescendo of sound that carried on the wind across the crowded dockyard. To the music of 'Hearts of Oak' the great grey mass of the aircraft carrier came alive. The main engines turned the screws that dug into the murky water of the harbour, causing it to boil with white surging foam.

'Slow astern starboard, slow ahead port.' Harlow gave his orders crisply into the rubber encased microphone that connected him with the wheelhouse. 'Let go aft.' The order was relayed to the quarterdeck. Using the bow line and with the assistance of the tugs Sovereign's stern moved away from the wharf.

'Let go forward.' The final order that separated the ship from the shore and the crew from their loved ones was passed.

Down on the wharf arms were waving and faces looked up, eagerly trying to find their men among the line of blue uniforms. Eyes filled with tears and some had to seek comfort on the shoulder of those standing next to them.

Aboard Sovereign those with nothing to do but stand and watch also felt the emotion of farewell. Lumps came into throats, eyes became glazed, hearts weighed heavily for men whose life of home and family was being taken away, to be replaced by the transient existence of the sailor and the inadequate link of the written word.

Sovereign turned to face the harbour entrance and the sea beyond. Astern, the two escorting frigates were taking up station, standing like two menacing sentinels awaiting their mistress, their sleek hulls adding to the threatening scene of thunderous clouds and turbulent seas. The signal hoists at their yardarms flashed tongues of colour against the sombre background.

The tugs slipped and in line ahead, with Sovereign as the guide, the men of war sailed majestically out of harbour. In one hour RFA Provider would slip and proceed to rendezvous with the squadron in the towering seas of the English Channel.

As Sovereign entered the open sea Peter put a fix on the chart and handed over to the Forenoon Officer of the Watch. Throughout the ship the Special Sea Dutymen were falling out from their stations and their places taken by the first sea watch of the long deployment.

'Are you happy?' Peter asked as he concluded his handover.

'Yes. I've got her.' Replied the Officer of the Watch.

'Very good. I'll be in the chart house if you need me.' Peter moved over to the starboard side of the bridge and looked back at the receding landmarks of Portsmouth. He thought of Susanne and hoped the flowers had arrived.

The Officer of the Watch put his binoculars to his eyes. The white flashing light of a signal lamp stabbed out of the predawn sky.

'It's Salisbury, sir.' The yeoman completed writing down the message and handed it to the Officer of the Watch.

'Bosun's Mate, give my compliments to the Navigator and tell him we have visual contact with Salisbury and that the Captain is being informed.'

Both Captain and Navigator arrived on the bridge at the same time.

'Good morning, sir.' Peter said as the compact figure of the Captain climbed into the chair on the port side of the bridge. 'Morning Peter.' Harlow replied, taking the signal pad from the Yeoman and smiling as he read the message written upon it; 'Greetings Sovereign. May we join the party?' Harlow had known the commanding officer of Salisbury since their days together as cadets at Dartmouth.

'Yeoman, make to Salisbury it is good to have you with us. I hope you brought the dancing girls.'

The signalman's face remained impassive as he took down the message and transmitted it by flashing light across the dark seascape.

'Well Peter, what do we have planned for today?'

The Captain turned his attention to the day's programme and the Navigator outlined the series of Jackstay transfers and underway replenishment that would mould the squadron into a unified operational team. He handed the Captain the list of times and ships that would be taking part in each.

The morning sky was becoming brighter and the rays of the sun pointed like the spokes of a wheel through the broken cloud. Harlow looked across the ink black sea toward the now visible Salisbury.

'When she's in station, let me know. I am off to have my breakfast.' The Captain climbed down from his chair and left the bridge.

Peter remained, chatting to the Officer of the Watch and looking out at the force that was assembling. To starboard the bow of the frigate Constant sliced through the rolling swell and in the gathering light Peter could make out the figures of sailors on her upper deck. Astern, the lumbering form of the Provider rose and fell as she followed in the disturbed waters of the carrier's wake. Peter spoke to the Officer of the Watch.

'Tell your relief that we will commence the first RAS with Provider at 0930. Special Sea Dutymen to close up at 0900. I'll be in the chart house if you want me.'

The ships closed each other like two great leviathans. As they came abreast the huge force of suction set up between their two hulls threatened to unite them in a disastrous embrace. The sea between them was melting into a cauldron of white foam. A whistle sounded, followed by a single gunshot and a metal bolt hurtled across the turbulent chasm. The distance line was paid out; ten, twenty, thirty feet. The numbered squares passed between the two ships with each coloured square telling the margin that separated their pounding hulls. The line reached one hundred feet and went taut. The ships were in station. More whistles sounded. Both crews were ready.

On the bridge Peter checked the course repeater and the distance line. Down on the fuelling point the crews were hauling on the line that, yard by muscle punishing yard, brought the giant fuel hose closer.

'Keep away from the side!' The Petty Officer in charge of the fuelling point bellowed to the young sailors under his charge. 'Look at the line, two six. Heave!' He urged his men on. Most of the fuelling party had performed such underway replenishments before, but, for some, seeing such big ships in close company was an awe inspiring sight. The guardrails were down and just a sideways glance revealed the boiling cauldron waiting to claim a careless victim.

With every pull on the line the black hose came closer. It crossed the gunwale and the fuelling crew fought to take charge and marry the hose to the fuelling point in the carrier's decks.

'Steady!' Roared the Petty Officer. 'Keep the line straight.' Out of the corner of his eye he saw the last man in the line moving closer to the edge of the ship. 'Hey! Watch what you're doing. Move back...' Before he could finish the command the heavy fuelling hose lurched to the side and, momentarily out of control, rebounded against the young sailor.

'Man Overboard! Disengage!'

Even before the sailor had left the deck the Petty Officer was screaming the alarm. Everyone watched as the figure tumbled, as if in slow motion, towards the boiling sea. He hit the churning whiteness and was gone. His body did not even make a splash as it was engulfed by the wave crests that appeared to reach up as if to catch their helpless victim.

'Man Overboard. Starboard side.' The message came loud over the bridge intercom.

'Disengage!' Harlow called from his vantage point

on the wing of the bridge. He had not seen the man go over but now strained to see the body in the raging sea between the ships.

'All lines clear, sir.' The message came from inside the bridge but the Captain had already seen from his position high over the ship's side. The order was already on his lips.

'Revolutions 270. Port thirty.'

Sovereign shuddered under the sudden increase in power and healed over as her rudders bit into the sea. Crusader, as guard ship, was astern of the replenishing ships. She slowed her speed and posted extra lookouts. On board Salisbury a helicopter was scrambled. Another lifted off from Sovereign as she completed her turn and steadied on the course she was steering when the accident occurred. She too now reduced speed.

'Get all non-duty personnel up onto the flight deck.' Harlow barked. 'We'll need all the eyes we can muster for this job, Peter.' The Navigator nodded in silent acknowledgement.

Everyone in Sovereign, and in every other ship, knew that to find the sailor would be difficult. To find him alive would be a miracle. Eyes scanned the sea, praying they would be the ones to see the man in the water, willing it to be so. The Captain spoke to the Officer of the Watch.

'Get the man in charge of the fueling point and find out who it is we are looking for.'

A death like veil fell over the bridge as each man thought of the nameless sailor in the water.

'Captain, sir. It's Salisbury. She has a contact and is closing to investigate.' The Yeoman's voice broke the silence.

'Where is Salisbury?' Harlow asked.

'Port quarter, two thousand yards, sir.' Peter replied. Harlow moved to the bridge wing and raised his binoculars to his eyes. The Wessex helicopter from Salisbury flew low overhead, its blades chopping at the air. The grey hull of the destroyer lay still in the water.

'From Salisbury, sir. They have got the man.'

The communicator's message brought the Captain over to the telephone. All eyes turned to the small figure dressed in an off white submarine jumper that was tucked under an oversized uniform jacket. No one could make out what was being said, but, when he replaced the receiver everyone on the bridge knew that what they feared most had happened.

'Ordinary Seaman Matthews is dead I'm afraid.' The Captain's words cut through all who heard them. The dead sailor was only a boy. His death would cast a shadow over the squadron and every man in it. Harlow moved over to the ship's public address system, removed the microphone and flipped the switch to transmit.

'This is the Captain speaking...'

Peter stepped into Flyco. He looked out of the windows that commanded a panoramic view of the flight deck and the airspace around the carrier.

'If he can't put it down this time he has to go home. We'll have to get a replacement.' Commander Air's voice was tinged with resignation and disappointment.

Peter looked out and watched the jet fighter bank and circle in the clear blue sky astern of the carrier. He had come to the flying control position on orders from the

Captain. The 'old man' had been keeping a tally of the number of times the aircraft had touched down and then powered back into the sky. He was becoming impatient.

'Who's up there, Bob?' Peter chose his moment carefully. Bob Keller was a worried man. The confidence of the young pilot at the controls of the aircraft would by now be severely shaken. Commander Air knew that this last attempt could very well be just that.

'Lieutenant James.' Keller answered and continued, '...and God knows if he is ever coming down.'

'The skipper says he gets one more crack at it.' Peter delivered the message.

'You don't have to tell me Peter. I've already given the order. James doesn't know it, but if he doesn't get down this time I'm sending him back to the air station.'

Peter looked down on the flight deck and up into the sky above the rolling metal landing strip. His eyes scanned the horizon for the lone aircraft. A movement caught his eye and he concentrated his gaze. He saw it. A small dark shape hurtled towards twenty thousand tons of moving steel that must look like a table top to the young pilot at the controls.

The Flyco door opened and a middle aged pilot dressed in flying overalls entered. Peter looked at the stranger's shoulders and saw two and a half gold rings. He also noted the pilot wings sewn on his flying suit. Commander Air lowered his binoculars and looked over to the door as the officer entered.

'Hello Steve, thanks for coming up.' The two pilots shook hands. 'Steve Marks, this is Peter Wells.' The commander made the introductions and then returned his attention to the aircraft that was now closing rapidly. He spoke again without taking his eyes from the approaching aeroplane.

'What's wrong with him Steve?'

Peter then realised the significance of the officer's presence. He was the leader of 809 Squadron. Lieutenant James was one of his boys. The fighter pilot replied;

'I don't know. He worked well on the circuits and the touch and goes. He judged the wires well on the strip ashore. It must be first night nerves. He'll do it this time.'

Marks was a good squadron C.O. who looked after his men. He knew that it was he who had declared James ready for the 'real thing'. If that young pilot failed they both failed and both would pay the price. That price was a lot higher for the man in the cockpit. His life depended upon a cool professional approach to the problem that was now racing relentlessly toward him. If he tried too hard to win his place among the carrier's squadrons then his pride might rule his judgement and the sea would embrace his fall.

'His hook is down.' Commander Air's call directed everyone's attention to the steel blue shell that was closing fast above the aircraft carrier's stern. The aircraft appeared to be falling out of the sky in what was nothing less than a controlled crash. The scream of the engines sent shock waves through the flight deck crews as the fighter roared over the round down and hit the deck with the full force of its engines powering the aircraft into the unyielding surface.

'He's down and he's got the wire.' Cried Marks, who instantly breathed easier.

The twin engined fighter hit the deck, hurtled forward and then stopped abruptly as the hook that trailed beneath its fuselage caught the arrester wire. The nose of the aircraft bowed down as the forward momentum was taken away, and then rose again as the plane came to rest. The roar of the engines subsided. The hook was disengaged and the arrester wire clattered noisily along the deck until it came to rest in its position parallel to the other cables at the end of the flight deck.

Commander Keller gave the order to suspend flying operations and then turned to the leader of 809 Squadron.

'Tell Lieutenant James that I want to see him in my cabin as soon as he has finished debriefing.'

Marks raised his eyebrows as he passed Peter. Both knew the meaning of the commander's instructions. Lieutenant James had joined HMS Sovereign but may soon wish that he had not.

'Flying operations over for now, Peter. You can have the ship back to do whatever it is you 'Fishheads' do.'

'You are too kind, sir. I'll convey your message to the Captain.'

'You do and I'll have your balls for breakfast.' Peter turned to leave. 'By the way.' Keller's voice stopped him. 'We have one more arrival today, but I am sure you are prepared for that.' Peter went cold. The arrival of Rear-Admiral Harrison had been put to the back of his mind. Once again the questions and doubts flooded in and Peter walked back to the bridge deep in thought.

'Who was the pilot? The Captain asked when he saw Peter return to the bridge. There was no response.

'Pilot!' At the sound of his unofficial navigator's title Peter returned to the present.

'Yes Sir?'

'I said, who was that pilot?' At this point the Captain threw back his balding head and laughed. 'I knew these damn birdmen would complicate things around here.' He said and laughed again. Peter, who was still not sure what was going on, waited for the Captain's jollity to subside.

'Well Peter, who was that young flyer?' The reworded question was immediately understood by the Navigator who went on to tell his, still smiling commanding officer, about Lieutenant James and the interview Commander Air had in store for him. 'Bob will sort him out.' The Captain commented and then turned his attention to the other air matter of the day. 'Now, for this afternoon. I want you on the flight deck for the arrival of the Admiral. There will be a departmental briefing at 1700 and he wants you to brief him before that takes place.'

'Very good sir,' replied the Navigator, disguising the questions rising again to dominate his thoughts.

The shrill of the Bosun's call heralded the arrival on board of the Flag Officer Commanding the British Squadron. Captain Harlow stood in the lee of the bridge island and as the 'carry on' sounded, removed his cap and ran in a low crouch towards the helicopter. The blades of the Wessex thrashed at the air in a lazy arc causing a downdraft of air that buffeted the two senior officers as they shook hands. Both men then moved toward the protection of the island where the Captain introduced his Executive Officer and then Peter. The Navigator saluted, 'Good afternoon Peter.' The Admiral said and shook his hand.

'Good afternoon, sir. Welcome aboard.' Peter replied, looking into the older man's face to see if he could read any greater meaning in his expression. The Admiral turned to the Captain,

'Let's get on with the briefings then Jerry,' he said and marched off ahead of his entourage.

Inside the metal cocoon of the aircraft carrier's island the sound of footsteps on deck plates preceded the advance of the party. Peter followed the Admiral, staring intently into the back of the senior officer's head, trying to penetrate the thoughts he so keenly wanted to unlock. As they reached the grey door of the briefing room the Admiral stopped and signalled for those behind to go in ahead. As Peter drew abreast he put out his hand.

'One minute, Peter.' The Admiral said, and taking an envelope from his jacket pocket held it out to him. 'Susanne asked me to give this to you.'

'How is she?' Asked Peter, thinking quickly and looking unruffled

'A lot better. A little subdued, but that is no bad thing.' Harrison smiled. 'Now let's go inside and you can tell me what's in store for us.' He placed his hand on Peter's shoulder and directed him to go in ahead.

'What was in the letter? The Admiral appeared happy enough. Perhaps all his fears were groundless?' Peter tried to put these thoughts out of his mind as he concentrated on his briefing. He was relieved when the Admiral felt satisfied he had been brought up to date and dismissed him. Once alone in the passageway the usually calm Navigator could scarcely hide his impatience to tear the envelope from around the letter and read the words he believed held his career in the balance. As if reading something he shouldn't he stole a glance over his shoulder to confirm he was alone. He stared at the blue paper and the rounded handwriting and then scanned the two pages. He checked how the letter began, and, more importantly, how it ended... 'Love, Susanne.' Instantly he felt better and read the letter more thoroughly.

The more he read the more of a fool he felt himself to be. Susanne apologised for missing their dinner engagement, told of the accident and her recovery, said how much she had wanted to see him before he sailed and how she hoped they would see each other again on his return. Peter's face broke into a smile, 'how could he ever have believed that a young woman, even an Admiral's daughter, could affect his career. She was attractive enough, but, to see her again? He was not sure.' He re-read her final words and then, tearing the pages into four, walked out onto the upper deck and threw the pieces to the wind. He watched as they floated down to the white capped surface of the sea.

The effect of having five hundred extra men on board was reflected at dinner on the first night of the Air Squadrons' embarkation. Each of the long tables was packed with officers talking and eating. The noise level prompted the old Bosun, who had joined the Navy as a boy sailor at the start of the Second World War, to lament the invention of the aeroplane. There were many who shared his view.

As Peter entered the wardroom he was taken aback by the increase in numbers. He then noticed the composition of the tables and smiled to himself. Seated before him was a living example of tribal behaviour. The ship's officers did not sit with the aircrews and even the squadrons did not mix. Peter walked over to the senior officer's table and took a seat next to the tall, willowy figure of the Supply Commander.

'It must be the tourist season.' Peter quipped as he sat down.

'They must like the place, because they keep coming back every year.' The Supply Commander retorted dryly.

As he ate, Peter's eyes scanned the crowded room. He reflected on the youth of the aircrews and focused on a particularly boisterous table situated close to the door. Over the din he thought he heard a name he recognised.

'Oh come on Jamesey, don't be a cretin. You just could not get it down.'

'What do you know? I was just making sure that I didn't go over the side. They are not very good at picking you up around here.' The wardroom fell silent. The atmosphere became instantly electric, volatile, as if whatever happened next could destroy the world bounded by the pale blue walls of the wardroom. It was as if everyone had been waiting for something to happen and now it had. A movement at the next table caught Peter's eye. He watched as the Senior Engineer struggled to get out of his seat. He was held back by restraining hands. Among all of them it was this officer who felt the loss of Ordinary Seaman Matthews the most. The young sailor had been in his division, he was his responsibility.

From a foolish remark a gauntlet had been thrown down and now all waited to see if it would be picked up. The Engineer remained in his seat. Across the room a daunting figure rose to his feet. Peter had seen the big man earlier that afternoon defending his officer, now, he was standing over him like a threatening cloud. The Senior Pilot spoke in a deep, resounding voice.

'Lieutenant James. Come with me.'

The younger man looked up with a face drawn with uncertainty. He pushed his chair back and got to his feet. Lieutenant-Commander Marks walked from the wardroom and the Lieutenant followed, his eyes set straight ahead, not daring to look at the faces of his fellow officers. The tension was broken, voices once again filled the room. The threat had passed.

In the anteroom, after the meal, Peter was approached by an embarrassed and angry man. As the only ship's officer Steven Marks had so far met he addressed his apology to Peter.

'Please convey my regrets to all those hurt by what was said this evening. Lieutenant James will be making his own apology to the Executive Officer tomorrow morning and you can rest assured that the mouth will not flap out of line again. I will see to that.'

Peter smiled. 'Let's forget it. How about a cup of coffee and you can tell me what makes you want to crash land an aircraft onto a piece of metal, the size of a postage stamp, in the middle of a perpetually moving ocean.'

'Thanks.' The pilot said, almost in a whisper, and then perked up. 'You must have a lot of time on your hands.'

Chapter 9

Carol looked out at the brown landscape of the Australian bush. The ground was flat with hills rising, blue to the eye, on the far horizon. Clumps of white trunked ghost gums stood, like skeletal sentinels over the arid earth. The gentle motion of the train rocked her body and held her in a half dream state that caused her mind to wander over the past and her hopes for the future.

'Tea, coffee, sandwiches?' The voice of the steward roused Carol from her state of limbo. She stared at the boyish figure in his ill-fitting uniform and flowing blond hair. It was good to have something different on which to focus her attention. 'Can I offer you anything?' The youth came to the side of his trolley and pressed himself against the edge of Carol's seat. 'It's a long journey, not much to see, you must be getting bored.'

Carol raised her eyes above the poor cut of his light blue trousers and returned his gaze. He was very young she thought and wondered if he really was trying to pick her up. 'If that was his intention he was out of luck.' She smiled to herself.

'No thank you,' she cooed, 'I have everything I need for the moment.' Carol looked straight into the young man's face and playing him at his own game held his eyes until he could no longer return the attention. He moved behind his trolley and pushed it forward and away through the carriage. Carol wondered whether the loose fit of his trousers might now prove to be a godsend.

Outside a flash of colour caught her eye. A flock of pink and grey galahs flew low over the parched scrubland. She watched as the pink cloud swirled about the sky until they appeared to come to a decision and, as one, flew away from the speeding train and up into the highest branches of the gnarled sun bleached gum trees. 'This is Australia', Carol thought. 'This is as far from Number 11 Laidlaw Crescent as I can get.' Sydney had been a romantic interlude, a way station on her journey out of the past. Phil was lovely, but it had all been too easy, too fast. That is why she had not slept with him on their last night together. She had just gotten herself out of that sort of situation and was not going to fall straight back into the same trap. Phil had been very good about it. He said he understood, but she felt his disappointment. Putting her hand in her pocket she withdrew a silver key and stared at it recalling his final words.

'Take this, if things don't work out you will always have somewhere to stay. I love you very much, Carol.' He had held her hand as he gave her the key. She had felt the caress in his touch and the sensation remained with her. Carol had brought men down to size in the past, she had even prided herself on it. However, with Phil she had watched him get smaller even before the train had left him in the distance, standing alone on the grey platform. She felt sorry. He deserved better.

Carol had not wanted to impose herself on strangers, but Jane had been adamant that her uncle would love to have her stay. The old man appeared eager enough when she telephoned last night. From Jane's account her uncle was a colourful character and the next few weeks promised to be interesting. Staring out at the passing bush she let herself be taken by the gentle motion of the train. Her eyes grew heavy as she settled back in the seat, emptied her mind of thoughts and fell asleep.

'G'day Carol.' The greeting came from a small man dressed in khaki shorts and shirt. He waved a dusty brown slouch hat above his head. He walked with a swagger as he approached and held out his hand. 'It's lovely to see you my dear.' He said and clasped her hand in his own.

The old man's skin felt like leather and his lined face looked as if it was made with the same material, cured in the sun. His face beamed with pleasure.

'C'mon let's get you out of this sun. We don't want you to burn on the first day.'

Carol bent down to pick up her bags but was stopped by her host.

'Don't worry about those, Eddie will get them.' Carol looked round to see the porter. A young aboriginal boy approached sporting a broad grin that exposed brilliant white teeth that cut a bright line across his dark face. Jack took hold of Carol's arm and led her along the platform. She jumped as the train that had brought her, to what looked like the middle of nowhere, moved off, gradually gathering speed until it disappeared into the shimmering haze. They walked through a rusting metal gate and Jack pointed to a battered Land Rover parked in the dust. 'There's the car.' He said and Carol watched as Eddie threw the bags into the back and climbed in himself. There was no covering over the rear section of the vehicle and Carol felt sorry for the small boy being exposed to the harsh outback sun. Jack opened the passenger door and Carol climbed aboard. The door was slammed shut and the small man hurried around the front of the car and climbed into the driver's seat.

'Hold on m'dear.' With that warning he put the Land Rover into gear, wheeled in a circle of red dust and drove out onto the open road. 'I've been looking forward to your visit ever since Jane wrote and told me you were coming to Aus. I've had a room made up. You may find it a little primitive but it's clean and the mossies won't get you.'

The Land Rover sped down the ribbon of black tarmac. Carol looked ahead at the watery mirage on the road. Perspiration beaded on her brow and she could feel a rivulet of moisture run down between her breasts. She fiddled self-consciously with the front of the dress to try and prevent it clinging to her body. Jack glanced at his passenger and continued his unbroken conversation. It had been a long time since he had someone to talk to, especially someone who was female and attractive.

A dirt road appeared ahead on the left hand side and the car was turned violently to negotiate the corner. Carol fell against Jack and she fought to regain her upright position. Jack's hands stayed on the steering wheel, but he took his eyes off the road and smiled at Carol. She looked out of the rear window and saw the aboriginal boy scrambling about on the floor trying to stop himself and the bags being thrown from the car.

'We've got to get home pretty quick. I've got the vet coming round.' The old man explained, as he centred the wheel and the vehicle steadied. Carol just shook her head as she sat upright and gripped her seat with both hands. The dirt road ran between two low hills and as they passed between them Jack pointed ahead,

'There she is. That's my property.' He exclaimed.

Carol looked to see a low wooden structure with a rusting corrugated iron roof and bounded by a large verandah. Lines of fences formed two large paddocks and there was a long wooden stable near the house. It all looked rather run down and not like the farms at home at all.

'How much of it is yours?' Carol shouted over the noise of the decelerating engine.

'All of it.' Jack replied proudly, '...as far as the eye can see and beyond. Thirty eight square miles in all. This is not your English farm y'know?' Carol did not say that the thought had crossed her mind.

The car was going slower now and turned into the gate that had been opened by another aboriginal boy who had seen the car's trail of dust rising over the hill. Jack stopped the vehicle outside the house and quickly leapt out to help Carol from her seat.

'Welcome to Callala.' He made a sweeping gesture, removing the hat from his head and pointing it toward the house. He then turned to the boy, who was running back from the gate. 'Joseph, help Eddie with the bags.'

The sound of squeaking hinges and the slamming of a door caused Carol to look to the front of the house. A middle aged aboriginal woman walked out onto the verandah and down the four wooden steps to the driveway.

'Hello miss. Did you have a good journey?' She asked.

Jack walked between them.

'Ah Carol, this is Mary, my housekeeper. Whatever you want Mary will get for you. She's a beaut.'

Carol looked into the smiling face of the woman and suddenly felt a very long way from home. She then remembered she had been asked a question.

'Oh yes, thank you. Although I am a bit tired and very hot.'

'You come inside out of the sun.' Mary said and returned to the house. Carol looked round for Jack, saw that he was supervising the unloading of the bags, and then followed the housekeeper.

Once inside Carol was surprised how cool it was and immediately felt better. Mary disappeared into a side room and returned with a long, cold glass of orange juice. The hinges of the screen door squeaked, the door slammed and Jack entered the house.

'Okay, where's mine?' He called. Mary hurried away and returned with a frosted can of beer.

'Has the vet called yet?' Jack asked and there followed a conversation that excluded Carol, and which she welcomed. She had the chance to survey her new surroundings.

'It's not unlike Phil's place,' she thought, 'only bigger.' The lounge room contained an old leather suite that looked as if it had come to Australia at the same time as Jack. The decor was old, dark and refreshingly cool. Three rooms ran off from the lounge and Carol could see the brown landscape of the bush through the windows at the far end of the house.

His conversation over Jack returned his attention to his guest.

'Sorry to ignore you m'dear. Now Mary will show you to your room and you can settle in. I've got to go out for a while. I'll see you later.' Jack turned to his housekeeper.

'I'll be back at four. Take good care of our guest. He then smiled at Carol.

'See you later.' He turned and disappeared out of the front door.

Carol followed Mary down a long hallway and into a large square room. A double bed with a roughhewn headboard lay against one wall. An old wooden wardrobe and a chest of drawers, with a hastily erected mirror, stood against another two. Her bags were lying on the bed.

'The bathroom is at the end of the hall and here are some towels.' Mary placed two frayed cotton towels on the bed. 'If there is anything you want, just ask.'

Carol was left to unpack. As she transferred her clothes from the suitcase to the old chest of drawers she felt uneasy. She did not think she was prejudiced but in this house she felt an oddity. Jane's uncle appeared to have not only cut himself off from his family, but his own race as well. 'Perhaps it was only her increased sense of isolation that highlighted this difference in Jack's lifestyle. When in Rome.' She philosophically mused. Then a more immediate concern caused a momentary panic. She had nothing to wear. One pair of jeans was not going to be enough if she was going to have to live in them day and night.

'Bugger!' She swore and slammed the lid of the suitcase. She paced the room until, with resignation, she realised there was nothing she could do about it and that she might as well freshen up and get a few hours' sleep. The hours of travelling were catching up on her and she was dying to wash off the layer of dust that had settled on her during the madcap ride from the railway station.

'You decent?' Jack called through the door.

'Yes, come in.' Carol replied and covered herself with a sheet. As the old farmer entered Carol noticed a pair of trousers draped over his left arm and a pair of boots in his hand,

'Here, you'll need these if you are going to help with the mustering. You do ride, don't you?'

'Too right.' Carol replied in as broad an Australian accent as she could muster. Now he was talking her language.

'Beauty.' When you're dressed, come outside and I'll show you round the place.' He turned and closed the door behind him. Carol looked at the trousers.

'He certainly thought of everything,' she thought and smiled.

'How d'they feel?' Jack asked, as Carol came out of her room.

Carol felt self-conscious in the form fitting jeans. At home she would not have thought anything about the close fit of her clothes. But, here, surrounded by the rugged masculinity personified in the Australian bush, she felt exposed. She looked into the staring eyes of the old man but could not hold his gaze.

'Come on I'll show you round.' He called to her.

Carol went out of the back door still wondering how he had been able to find clothes to fit her. He offered no explanation and she was too embarrassed to ask. The screen door shut behind her and the bright afternoon sun hurt her eyes.

'You'll need a hat.' Jack said and took a mental note to get one. They walked past a few ramshackle sheds to a large fenced paddock and some stables.

'You said you could ride.' Jack commented.

'Oh yea. I love it.' Carol eagerly replied.

'Good. You can help with the muster tomorrow. I bet you've never ridden horses like these.' He pointed to five stocky beasts that stood silent in the shaded stalls. 'Cattle horses, all you have to do is stay on board. They'll do the rest.'

'Don't worry about me. I'll stay on.' This was something she knew about and the old stockman would soon learn that there was more to her than a well shaped pair of jeans. Jack pointed to the paddock,

'Tomorrow this will be full of cattle and my financial troubles will be over. Let's take the jeep and I'll show you some more of the place.'

They walked round the side of the stables to where an old Second World War Jeep was parked. They climbed in and Jack brought it roaring to life.

'Hang on. There's no roads out here.' Jack laughed as the car bucked over the uneven ground and sped down into the valley. Very soon the house could no longer be seen. The open land that bordered the property gave way to trees with bark bleached white by the sun, and scrubland fighting to survive without water.

'Look!' Yelled Jack, removing his hand from the steering wheel and pointing out to the right. 'Bloody roos. I hate the bastards.' He aimed the speeding vehicle in their direction.

'What are you doing?' Carol cried as the jeep closed in on the grazing animals.

'Look at them. They're eating me out of house and home, the ratbags! Give me that rifle.' He pointed to the weapon strapped behind the rear seat and, with one hand on the steering wheel, turned the car in a skidding arc and brought it to a stop in a choking cloud of red dust.

'Hurry!' He cried, 'I'll get the bastards!'

Carol sat rigid looking in disbelief first at her driver and then at the animals that had offended him.

'What is going on?' She thought.

'The rifle!' Jack turned and pushed Carol out of the way as he reached for the weapon. Suddenly Carol realised what was going to happen and she found her voice.

'What are you going to do? No you can't!' She put her hands up to wrestle the rifle from the hunter's shoulder.

'You don't understand.' He hissed through clenched teeth, and put down the gun. 'Bugger it.' He swore resignedly as the live targets turned and bounded off into the cover of the tall gums trees. Jack leant over the Jeep's steering wheel and turned his head to look at his passenger. 'When you have been here a little longer you will understand why I have to keep them down.'

'I never will.' Carol replied passionately. 'How could you kill such beautiful animals?'

Jack raised his eyes and hands to heaven, gave a sigh of exasperation and then pulled on the ignition button to bring the Jeep back to life. Still shaking his head he wheeled the vehicle around and away from the battleground.

'I'll show you the work we have for the next few days.' He said, trying to quickly change the subject.

The Jeep sped over the humps and bumps hurling Carol out of her seat on numerous occasions and nearly out of the car on one. The dust was heavy in the air and settled on the skin forming red rivulets where perspiration mixed with the dry grit. Jack aimed the vehicle at a low hill and, as they became airborne, appeared to turn it in mid air and steer it through a narrow gate. At this point Carol closed her eyes and only opened them on her driver's command.

'Look! There's the little beauties.' Jack was pointing to a large number of cattle grazing off the ungenerous vegetation. Carol could not help thinking how thin they looked. Not her idea of beef cattle at all. Her face must have given her thoughts away as Jack was quick to point out that the meager rainfall had taken its toll that year.

'Still, they'll fetch a passable price and I'll keep going for another year.' He stopped the car while he continued talking. 'We'll drive them back into the paddock you saw earlier. You said you could ride. Tomorrow we'll see, but, as I said, all you will have to do is hold on.'

Before Carol could rise to the bait Jack put his foot down on the accelerator pedal and drowned any protest in a crescendo of engine noise.

'We'll go back now.' He yelled. 'Mary will have some tucker ready and you can get an early night. Big day tomorrow.'

Carol seethed with anger as she held on during the wild ride. 'How dare he patronise her.' She thought. 'Tomorrow I'll show him.'

These thoughts tormented her all through dinner. Even while she answered questions about home her mind would not let go of the vow that tomorrow these Australians would be laughing on the other side of their faces. She even took these thoughts to bed and despite her tiredness they held sleep at bay for a few restless hours.

The sound of movement and laughter drew Carol away from the breakfast table and out into the yard. She smiled as she watched the antics of the aboriginal hands as they prepared the horses for the day's work. Then, the smile froze on her lips. She watched as one of the lads minced up to the smallest of the horses, mounted side saddle and then fell over backwards onto the ground. Carol turned on her heels and stormed noisily back into the house.

'How dare they.' She swore, burning with indignation. Back in her room she picked up the hat Jack had found for her and, slapping it against her thigh, marched through the house and went outside.

'Good. You're here Carol.' Jack's voice barely penetrated her temper. 'Zac's saddled up the small one.' He pointed to a compact little horse that looked very disinterested at what lay in store. Jack continued. 'He's a good little horse. Remember, just stay with him.'

'Thanks.' Carol curtly replied, 'I'll do my best.' Deftly she sprang into the saddle, turned to the stockmen and called; 'Right. Let's go to work.' Digging her heels into the horse's flanks she galloped out of the enclosure and into the open country.

Jack looked puzzled and shrugged his shoulders to the boys;

'You heard the lady. Let's go to work.'

The coolness of the fresh morning air calmed Carol's anger and she soon realised she did not know where to go. It dawned on her that it did not matter, because her horse did. Without directions from his rider the little horse galloped over a low ridge and down into a valley that opened out onto a flat plain. There, dotted about the brown landscape, were the cattle. Once again Carol was struck by how thin they looked.

'They'll take some fattening up,' she thought, 'and they won't do it on this.' Her eyes looked around at the dry grass and the dead bark of the trees. The main party soon caught up and she heard Jack's voice.

'Okay, let's round them up.'

The aboriginal riders tore away in all directions to get around the herd. Carol quickly became caught up in the excitement of the muster. She ran and wheeled her horse while waving her large brimmed hat, encouraging the reluctant livestock with wild whoops and yells.

By early afternoon the herd, apart from a few strays, was assembled and moving in an ambling pace towards the holding pens.

'How d'you like it?' Jack called across to Carol, who was riding on the other side of the herd. Her face reflected her pleasure.

'It's great!' She beamed back at him. In the excitement of the morning she had forgotten about her vow to show off her riding skills to these 'cowboys'. Instead, she had been caught up in the muster and simply enjoyed herself. For Jack and the boys, Carol's riding skills had not gone unnoticed.

The dust rose in a red cloud about the cattle and stained the wet skin of the riders. Carol heard Jack calling to one of the hands and looked over at him. On the far side of the herd and down in a hollow she saw two stray cattle grazing undisturbed as if they thought that by ignoring the passing of their friends they would be ignored.

'I'll get them!' Carol called and wheeled her horse about and cut round the herd. Once clear she dug her heels in and horse and rider ran as one towards the straying beasts. The rush of wind in her face and the thrill of feeling her horse's legs picking his way over the uneven ground heightened her excitement. One misplaced hoof would mean disaster.

'Come on!' She urged as the adrenalin in her body made her heart beat faster and her head spin with the thrill of danger.

As Carol approached, the two strays raised their heads. It did not take the two animals long to realise that what they saw approaching was the end of their freedom. At least that is how it appeared as the two, normally sluggish beasts, turned on their tails and ran for the sanctuary of nearby trees.

Carol turned her mount to head them off. Taking the reins in her right hand she removed her wide brimmed hat with her left and waving it up and down tried to divert the stampeding cattle from their headlong flight. Very quickly she was ahead of the chase and wheeled her horse to cut off their advance. The cattle slowed and turned. Carol shouted commands as she felt victory to be hers.

'Yah. Get round!' She leaned out of the saddle and almost touched the animals with her hat. The perspiration ran down her face and her body ached from the strain of the chase. Dust clouded her vision, but, still she rode like the wind. The cattle were now running in circles, churning up the ground beneath their hoofs. Carol and her horse were moving as one and never before had she felt such exhilaration on horseback.

The pace was slowing and Carol was ready to cut off any breakout by her quarry. Then, while she turned round and her back was presented, the cattle bolted again. Responding quickly she was soon up with them.

'Turn you bastards!' She screamed as frustration and anger poured out from her tortured body. Leaning out of the saddle she thrashed the air with her sweat stained hat. 'Argggh…' Carol's cries died in her throat as she felt herself slipping. Suddenly the world of speed turned into one of slow motion. She was falling. 'What's happening?' Her mind fought to function as the world began to spin. She was falling, falling…

'Go get the jeep Zac…and be quick.'

The words were mere whispers from another dimension as Carol felt hands loosening the belt around her waist. Her eyes opened slowly and the light of the outback sun caused such pain she thought her head was going to explode.

'Just lie there Carol. You'll be alright. Take it easy.' The words penetrated the haze of pain. She then felt the buttons of her trousers being undone. She tried to raise her hands to stop the trespass but they would not respond.

'Relax Carol. You've had a fall, but everything is okay.' The voice was gentle and the hands left her stomach. She felt better.

How long she lay on the hard ground she had no idea. She did not care. All she knew was that by keeping her eyes closed the pain in her head was kept at bay.

'Okay I'll lift her into the back. Zac, you support the head, and, be careful.'

Carol recognized Jack's voice but had not heard the car arrive. Perhaps she had blacked out again. Strong arms went about her body and lifted her off the ground. It was comforting to be held and consciousness drifted away again.

'Concussion. Nothing broken. Let her rest and keep her in bed for a day or so.'

The voice carried through the closed door as Carol lay on crisp white sheets and looked around her room. Her head pounded but the pain was now bearable. She could open her eyes without it feeling like her skull was going to split in two. How long she had been in bed and how she came to be there was a mystery to her. Looking up at the plastic lamp shade she forced herself to concentrate. Nothing came, only the sickening nausea of concussion. Voices on the other side of the door interrupted her thoughts.

'What about X-rays?' She recognised Jack's voice.

'I don't think it will be necessary, unless there are any complications. Keep an eye on her. I'll call again tomorrow.'

The voice receded and Carol could hear the two men walking up the passageway towards the lounge room. She put her hand up to her head, expecting it to be covered with bandages and was relieved to find there were none. Waves of tiredness drifted over her as the effort of just raising one hand seemed an exhausting exercise.

'Good morning. Miss.' Carol stirred when she heard the sound of china upon metal. Mary put the tray on the bedside table. 'How you feelin' today?' She asked as she helped her patient to sit up against the headboard.

'Not too bad. A little headache. How long have I slept?'

'You've had a good night's sleep. It's now eleven in the morning, but you've got to stay in bed. Doctor's orders.'

'May I come in?' Jack asked, putting his head round the door. Mary turned to leave.

'Now you eat your breakfast.' She said as she passed

the old man and left the bedroom. Jack walked over and sat on the edge of the bed.

'You're looking good.' He said and put his right hand on Carol's knee. As she felt the pressure of his touch it triggered a film in her mind. She remembered the hands loosening her clothes after the fall and it sent a chill through her whole body. Once again her expression betrayed her thoughts.

'Are you all right?' Jack asked.

Carol made excuses about still feeling fragile. He said he understood, gave her leg a squeeze and left her to her thoughts. She watched as he walked out of the room, and, pulling the bedclothes up underneath her chin, laid back on her pillows.

'What was wrong? Why did she feel threatened?' She looked at the tray of food by the bed, but had no appetite. Turning onto her side she drifted back into a tormented sleep.

It was another two days before Carol felt well enough to leave the house and venture out into the sunshine. She walked over to the stables to say hello to the horse that had unseated her. The young stockmen were pleased to see her up and about. They joked about her fall and this time she laughed with them. She was accepted and now felt at ease with these boys.

'Ah Carol, there you are.' Jack's voice startled her. 'Do you feel up to a bit of prospecting?' She looked puzzled and he continued. 'There is a river not too far from here and its bed is paved with gold.' He smiled and his leathery face cracked into a million fragments. At that moment Carol felt a fondness for him that she had not experienced before. 'He's not such a bad old stick.' She thought. And Jack continued. 'You'll have to do a bit of climbing, nothing too steep. Want to give it a go?' Without a moment's hesitation she accepted. 'Good on yer. I've got the pans in the jeep. I'll get Mary to make us some tucker.' The lines on his face stood out like the cracks on a dried up river bed.

Jack drove sedately as he guided the Jeep between the trees and rocks. Carol was grateful for his consideration. Her head no longer felt as fragile as an egg, but she did not want to put her recovery to the test.

They drove up into the tree line where the air was cooler and the vegetation a little greener. There were no tracks up there and how Jack knew where he was going was a mystery to his passenger. They had been driving for nearly an hour and a half when the car slowed down and turned off in the direction of a craggy peak.

'Nearly there now.' Jack announced. 'We'll park over there, by Watchtower Rocks.'

Carol looked up at the formation of stones that did look like a tall tower standing guard over all that lay below. Jack put the Jeep into low gear and it felt as if the old vehicle was willing itself to climb the last hundred yards of steep and rocky ground. Eventually they arrived at a clearing and the engine was switched off.

The 'Watchtower' rose above them almost blocking the mid-morning sun. Carol thought she was on top of the world. The view was breathtaking. The blistered land she had come to know stretched away in the distance while around her green leaves and coloured flowers blossomed in the cool mountain air. While she lost herself in the unspoiled beauty of her surroundings Jack unloaded the car and was soon ready for the next part of the journey.

'Follow me and watch your step.' He cautioned as he strode off up the ridge. Carol looked at the old stockman and marvelled at his fitness. 'Perhaps he's not as old as he looks,' she pondered. This line of thought was terminated by the necessity for concentration as she negotiated the narrow path that led to the base of the 'Watchtower.' Once there, she looked down on the valley below.

'Incredible!' She exclaimed. 'It's like being in another world.'

The steep sides of the hidden valley rose sharply and the bright glint of sunlight on the valley floor betrayed the water flowing there. Holding onto outstretched branches and sharp edged rocks Carol followed her guide downward.

'It really is like being on another planet,' she sighed, looking up at the overhanging mantle of eucalyptus leaves that shielded them from the world above. She gazed along the valley floor and the river which flowed like liquid crystal over golden pebbles.

'Do you want to eat or make your fortune first?' Jack asked as he unloaded his back pack onto the dry shingle of the river bank.

'What a daft question. I can eat anytime. Lead me to the gold.'

'You'll need this.' Carol was shown a metal pan and told to follow. They walked to the water's edge.

Squatting by the shallows Jack took the pan in both hands and immersed it just below the surface of the water. Gathering a small amount of silt he lifted it out and began moving the container in a circular motion. His brow furrowed. The lighter sediment and water rolled around the edge of the metal pan and was tipped away while the heavier deposits remained in the bottom. Jack examined the residue and then poured it back into the creek.

'Oh well, nothing here.' Carol looked shocked when he threw the dirt away. 'You've seen how it's done, now see if you have more luck.' He handed her the pan.

Carol took it, and following instructions, went through the same procedure. With only the silt remaining she felt sure there was gold in her hands. Jack looked through it.

'Nothing there m'girl. Have another go.'

'Nothing there.' Carol retorted. 'You said there was gold up here.'

'And so there is, but it has to be found.' He answered.

'You said the river bed was lined with it.' Carol pressed her point.

'Perhaps I did exaggerate.' The bushman conceded. 'Have another go anyway. I'll get the grub. This prospecting lark is hungry work.' He went away grinning while Carol refilled the container and gazed hopefully into the collection of stone and sand.

'Hey! Look at this!' She called excitedly and ran over to Jack. 'I've hit pay dirt. I'm rich, rich!' She cried with delight, hoping she had found something worthwhile in the sparkling fragments that lay in the bottom of the pan.

Jack took his time examining the find. He ran his finger through the silt. He swirled the contents around the bottom of the dish. He even tasted a little bit on the end of his finger. Finally he spoke.

'Well, you may be a Pom but you sure can pan the best piece of sandstone I've seen in a long time.'

'Sandstone! You bastard!' Carol cried and threw the contents of the pan over his feet. 'Anyway, when was the last time gold was found out here?' She asked. Jack cradled his chin with his hand and thought for a while.

'About '58. I think.'

'That's not too long' Carol's excitement grew again.

'1858.' Jack replied.

Carol looked round for something to throw. Jack retreated to the food sack.

'Don't do anything rash.' He said in mock horror. 'Kill me and you may never get out of here, and remember, good cooks are hard to find.'

He set about building a fire and Carol raised her hands in resignation. 'Anyway' she thought, 'he has brought me to one of the prettiest places I have ever seen.'

'Perhaps I'll get lucky.' She said philosophically and returned to the stream to try her luck once more.

The blue smoke from the fire rose lazily through the canopy of branches. The rocks from the creek provided a framework for a safe fireplace and the aroma of steaks cooking made Carol's stomach rumble in anticipation.

'This is the life,' she thought as she took a break from prospecting and looked along the river to where it disappeared round a far bend, funneled in its journey by green leaves from overhanging trees.

Jack presented her with a plate piled high with salad and a freshly cooked steak. He produced a bottle of red wine and two glasses.

'To gold.' He held out his glass as he proposed the toast. Carol laughed.

'To us.' She replied and touched her glass to his.

They ate in silence, words appearing unnatural in the quiet setting. Carol kept looking about her in an attempt to bring the beauty within herself so that she may never forget this place.

After the food was eaten and the wine bottle was empty Jack broke the silence.

'You had such a good technique panning for gold, how about trying it with the dishes?'

'You press your luck, and, don't think I couldn't find my way out of here if I had to.' Carol smiled as she spoke. 'Come on, give them here.' She took the metal plates and cutlery to the water's edge and waded in. 'It's bloody cold.' She called in her best outback accent.

After the work was done they sat by the bank throwing small stones into the mirror like surface of the creek.

'I'm afraid we can't stay too much longer.' Jack advised. 'It'll take some time to get up the valley and there's the drive home. We can't do that in the dark.' Reluctantly Carol had to agree.

They extinguished the fire, collected their things and, with Jack leading the way, walked back up the valley wall. Once at the top Carol looked down for a last glimpse of a magical spot she never wanted to forget.

'We'll have to come back here again.' She said softly.

'Why, haven't you got enough gold for one lifetime?'

'I'll give you gold!' Carol removed her hat and hit the stockman across the back of the head. Making a run for the jeep Jack pretended to try and start it before Carol could get on board. She ran after him, jumped onto the running board and scrambled into the passenger seat. Her head spun a little from the sudden exercise, but the sensation quickly passed and she thought no more about it.

Jack maneuvered the car down the mountainside and onto the plain below. They reached the house just as twilight was giving way to the night and the stars were shining boldly out of the clear black sky.

'It has been a wonderful day. Thanks for taking me.' Carol said as the car came to a stop outside the house.

'My pleasure m'dear, my pleasure. Now, go inside and wash up. Old Mary will have some dinner ready for us.' He replied.

'More food!' Carol exclaimed.

The following day Carol returned to the saddle and over the next week helped with the working of the property. In her free time she would go for long rides, either alone or with Jack. When he rode with her he would recount fascinating stories about the bush and its people, and she would wonder that he was born an Englishman.

With the passage of time she came to know him, although, she was no closer to understanding the way he lived than she was on the first day of their meeting. He had told her tales, both tall and true, about his life at 'Callala'. He made her laugh and he made her think. There were so many questions she wanted to ask. Questions born of things left unsaid by this exiled Englishman with the broad grin and empty eyes. He never spoke of England or his family and when Carol tried to guide the conversation along these lines the illusive bushman would change the subject.

What intrigued Carol more than the old man's abandonment of his family was his apparent withdrawal from his race. Over the past days he told stories but never mentioned friends. He spoke as if nothing existed beyond the sun bleached fences of his property.

One night over dinner these thoughts were interrupted by Mary bringing a coffee pot to the table. She looked at the middle aged aboriginal woman, overweight but with an attractive open face and dark eyes that shone like bottomless pools. Carol could contain her curiosity no longer and as the housekeeper left the room asked;

'Why have you cut yourself off so completely, Jack?'

The question was badly phrased and Carol hated herself as soon as the words left her lips. Jack's hand froze as he reached for the coffee pot. He turned his head and stared at her. Carol looked away.

'Sorry.' She apologised. 'None of my business. I am sorry.' Writhing with embarrassment she rose from the table. 'I hope you will excuse me, I think I'll have an early night.' The floor was not going to open up and swallow her and so the only thing to do was run. Pushing her chair away from the table she hurriedly rose to her feet. Excusing herself once more she walked passed the back of Jack's chair. He put out his hand and took hold of her arm.

'Don't be silly. Come on and finish your coffee, sit down.' He looked up into Carol's face and his eyes seemed to be asking her to stay. Carol stopped and returned to her seat. He topped up her cup and began to talk. 'You're right. I have cut myself off. I've broken away from everyone and everything that has bound me to the past. People expect too much and give too little, and that especially goes for families. This is my home now and they are my family.' He pointed after Mary and continued, 'They ask for no more than a roof over their heads, food on the table and a bit of money in their pockets.'

While she listened Carol recalled what Jane had said about her uncle and she was puzzled. 'If he had exiled himself from his family, where did Jane fit in? How did she manage to arrange this visit?' There was only one way to find out.

'What about Jane? You keep in contact with her.'

Jack's expression hardened and there was a short silence before he spoke.

'When I got Jane's letter it was the first time I had heard from her, or anyone in the family, for ten years.'

Carol was stunned. She sat back in her chair and stared into the stern, lined face

'Then why…?'

The old farmer cut her off and completed the question for her.

'Why are you here? Curiosity. The same reason Jane told you to come here and why she asked me to have you. You are expected to go back and tell them how 'old Jack' is getting on. Aren't families wonderful?' He ended sarcastically.

Carol was embarrassed and speechless. She chided herself for her curiosity.

'I am glad you did come to stay.' Jack said and extended his hand across the table top. Carol raised her eyes and took the thin, leathery hand in hers and gave it a squeeze.

'So am I.' She whispered. 'It has been fun, but now, I think I'll go to bed.'

She rose from the table, walked to the door but hesitated before leaving. Turning back to face the old man she said.

'I am not a spy.'

Jack's face broke into a broad, compassionate grin.

'Hell girl, I know that. See you later.'

Giving a smile and a self-conscious wave Carol left the room. As she undressed her mind went over the conversation she had just had and she seethed inside. 'How could Jane do it to her? The price of her accommodation was to be information; well, she would not pay it.' Carol felt sympathy for the exiled bushman. They were both escaping from relationships and here they were, in the middle of nowhere, away from the ties of families or friends.

Carol had not been asleep long when she stirred, roused by a presence, a feeling she was not alone. Her body went rigidly still and an icy chill travelled down her spine. Her eyes widened as she tried to stare into the darkness. It was not a dream, she was certain there was someone in the room with her. She dared not move. Panic took hold of her and she lay, too scared even to turn her head towards the sound of a floorboard creaking in the centre of the room. She felt helpless and frightened, waiting in the darkness and unable even to scream.

Something touched her leg. It was a hand, hot and clammy, exploring under the thin cotton sheet that covered her. A cry died in her throat and she gasped in horror as the hand slid between her thighs, forcing her paralysed legs apart.

'No. No!' She cried as her body reacted to its violation.

'Don't cry, don't cry. It's alright. It's me.' Jack's pleading voice made Carol once again go rigid. She could feel his breath on her face and smell the brandy carried upon it. She began to fight back, resisting the pressure of his body.

'Don't. No!' She gasped and struggled to remove the hand from her stomach. Swinging her legs to the edge of the bed she tried to roll free, but, Jack was too strong and, pinning her hands to the pillow, lowered his face to hers.

'Come on Carol.' He hissed through clenched teeth as he fought to maintain dominance. 'We're the same you and I. We understand each other.'

Carol cried aloud as she felt his moist lips touch the skin of her neck.

'Carol please.' Jack's voice was gruff with passion. He released the grip on her left hand so that he could feel the curve of her breast.

With one arm free Carol struck out and lifting her body from the bed, tipped her attacker onto the floor. His body struck the wooden boards with a resounding crash and his sprawling arms upset the bedside table, sending it spinning across the room. Carol rolled her feet onto the floor and stood up. Her eyes were now accustomed to the darkness and she could see Jack's small frame lying curled up on the floor. The room fell silent.

'Are you all right, miss' Carol was startled by the sound of Mary's voice and the knocking on the door. She looked down at the crumpled man on the floor and could hear a low moaning cry coming from him. She moved closer, hesitating with each step, while the housekeeper kept pounding on the door. 'Is everything okay?' She asked again.

'Yes.' Carol answered, at first uncertainly and then with more confidence. 'Yes. I'm fine. Thank you.' She was strangely thankful that Mary had not forced open the door and wondered at herself for not telling the truth. She then looked down at the old man who was openly crying now and hiding his face in his arms. Carol bent down and put out her hand to touch his back. He shrank away from her, rolling into a cringing ball. She moved over to the door and slid her hand over the wall, feeling for the light switch. The glare from the bulb seemed to exaggerate the tragedy. The body, that only moments before, was so strong and demanding now shrank away from the light and heaved with the sobs of a broken man. Carol knelt beside him.

'Why Jack? Why?' Her voice quivered with emotion.

'I'm sorry. I'm sorry.' Was all he said, over and over again. Carol felt her strength returning and with it came anger.

'Come on, get up!' She tugged at the arms that shielded the old man's head. Her fear was gone. It was she who was now in charge. 'Get up I said!' She nudged the crumpled body with her foot. Jack stirred and rose to his knees. Carol stood back and pulled her nightdress down in an effort to cover her nakedness. 'Come on Jack. Get up and get out!' She hissed.

The small frame of the farmer was hunched forward, his eyes stared at the floor.

'I've missed so much out here and you.' He sobbed as much to himself as to Carol. 'You reminded me of all I never had. You were my last chance.' He finally raised his eyes and managed to look at her. Carol's burned back in fury;

'And you thought you were going to get it this way?' She hesitated and then spoke with authority. 'I'm leaving today. Get Zac to take me into town as soon as it gets light.'

'Don't go, please don't go.' Jack pleaded.

'Fuck you! I want you to get out of this room and I don't want to see your face again. If Zac is not there at daybreak the whole world will get to know what a bastard you are. Now, get out!'

Jack backed toward the door, felt for the handle, turned it and hurried from the room.

'Shit.' Carol sighed and slumped on the bed. She looked at the closed door, jumped to her feet and went to put a chair against it. She could not return to bed and so collected her suitcase from on top of the wardrobe and began to pack. She glanced at the clock. A quarter past two, she had a long wait until dawn.

Her hands trembled as she packed. Once that was done she dressed in the clothes she had arrived in eleven days before. Moving across to the window she opened the curtains. The moon bathed the ground in a shining blue light that picked out the tall gum trees on the far edge of the yard. She lost herself in the quiet emptiness.

The darkness gave way to the golden rays of the morning sun. Carol raised her head from her hands. She had fallen asleep and now grimaced at the effort of straightening her cramped body. The light streamed through the window and formed a halo around the suitcases now standing in the middle of the room.

'That's it.' She said to herself. 'I'm out of here.'

She walked across the room, removed the chair she had put there as security and opened the door. Picking up the cases she left the room without looking back.

The hallway was still in darkness. She walked silently towards the front door. Her body was on guard, expecting Jack to appear from the shadows.

'I hope Zac is there,' she thought as she reached the lounge room. She went to the front door and opened it. The screen door squeaked on its hinges. Carol was careful not to let it slam shut. She looked out into the yard.

'Thank God.' She breathed the words out loud.

There was the Land Rover with Zac standing by it. He walked over and took the cases from Carol's hands.

'G'day miss.' He said politely.

'Morning Zac.' She replied and thought what a farce this all was. 'Did he know why she was leaving at this hour? He must be curious.' She thought. She looked around but there was no sign of Jack.

'The boss sends his regards and hopes you have a good journey.' Zac interrupted her thoughts.

The cases were thrown in the back and Zac walked round to the driver's door. Carol took a quick look around and entered the cabin. Zac started the engine and drove the car in a dusty arc away from the house. As they headed for the open road Carol wondered if her departure was being observed. She could not stop herself looking back. She glanced at the curtained windows but nothing stirred.

'The train to Sydney doesn't come through until one o'clock this afternoon. Do ya want to go to the hotel and wait there?' These were the first words spoken on the journey and were only said when the Land Rover passed the first wooden buildings of the small town.

'No thanks. Take me to the station.' Carol replied and they returned to silence until the station was reached. Zac stopped the car.

'D'yer want me to stay?' He asked, in total confusion.

'No. Just get my bags and you can go.' Carol grew impatient. It was important now to be free of 'Callala', to be alone and back on her own.

Carol did not wave as the Land Rover pulled away, she simply watched until it was out of sight. Turning back to the railway station, which was no more than a platform and a bench, she raised her arms and took a deep breath of fresh morning air.

While the taxi drove through the quiet Sydney streets Carol cradled the key in her hands. She was on her way to Phil's house and sadly reflected that she needed its refuge so soon. She thought of Phil and wished he would be there. It would be three more weeks before he completed basic training. Three more long weeks before she would see him again. The bravado of the morning had faded with the setting sun. Carol now wanted someone to comfort her. To reassure her.

'Which house do you want, lady?' The taxi driver asked as the car pulled into the sleeping street.

'Number Eight'. Carol checked the tag on the key ring.

The taxi stopped and the driver went to retrieve the cases from the boot.

Carol followed the driver through the wooden gate posts and up the path to the house. She paid the fare and tipped him for his courtesy. As the key turned in the lock she felt like a house breaker. The door opened and she switched on the light. Emptiness engulfed her. She did not belong there. Every room felt hostile. She had forsaken this house and now it was rejecting her. Carol fearfully wondered if Phil would do the same.

She picked up her cases and carried them into the bedroom. The bed was made and she guessed that Phil's mother must be keeping an eye on the house. She made a mental note to telephone her in the morning. She looked at her luggage.

'I can't be bothered,' she said to herself as she unlatched the first case. She was lonely and miserable, the unpacking could wait. Letting her clothes lay where they fell she undressed and went into the bathroom. The shower's warm jets failed to revive either her body or spirit. She dried, returned to the bedroom and curled up in the bedclothes. Drawing her legs up under her and embracing the pillow Carol longed for sleep to take away the emptiness that clawed away inside.

The next two weeks were the loneliest Carol could remember. She told Phil's parents she was living in the house and they invited her for dinner, but Carol never fixed a date. She tried to write to Phil but no matter how many times she sat down before the blank pages of a writing pad the words would not come. She was alone and unable to cry for help.

In the early mornings she walked along the beach, staring out into the foaming breakers. The salt mist clung to her skin and matted her hair. She would sit on the sand and let the grains run through her fingers. She watched the world come to life but did not feel part of it. The sight of couples jogging along the beach cut into her, but she could not look away. Hours went by and the sun was high in the sky before something inside told her to return to the house. Once behind its closed doors she would hide like a recluse.

Towards the end of the second week Carol decided she had had enough. She caught a bus into the city and made her way to the airline office. 'It was time to go home.'

Light rain started to fall as Carol got off the bus. She could see the office on the other side of the busy street and putting a newspaper above her head darted between the moving cars. Once outside she looked in at the posters advertising some of the world's most exotic resorts. She noticed a picture of Windsor Castle and read the words, 'Come to Britain.' A smile crossed her lips.

Many people were lined up at the counters and Carol stood watching them. She looked at the faces of the would-be travellers, so full of excitement and anticipation. She noticed an elderly man take out a cheque book and begin to write. How much of his life's savings was he spending she wondered. She had made that financial commitment as well as the more important commitment to herself. A new beginning. Another bite at the apple ... and she had failed.

As her hands went to open the double glass doors she hesitated. She had been let down in the past, but, she had never disappointed herself, she had never failed herself. For a moment she was fused to the door as these thoughts tumbled through her mind. She looked over at the photograph of Windsor Castle and, at that moment, knew she was not ready to go back. Turning on her heels she looked for a place where she could get something to drink and a bite to eat.

Seated by the window Carol drank a mug of black coffee and looked at the job section of the newspaper that only minutes before had shielded her from the rain. There were a number of vacancies for staff at the many wine bars that were springing up around the city. She took out her pen and circled one of the names she knew to be close to the house. That evening Carol was pulling corks and enjoying the company of young people who poked fun at her 'Pommie' accent.

The days ceased to drag and thoughts of home were confined to letters sent to her parents. A walk along the beach was no longer a lonely vigil, but a time for plans and dreams. Letters began arriving from Phil. He told of training exercises that kept him away in the bush and the life of a Private Soldier in an Infantry Regiment. Carol read and re-read everything he wrote. From guarded emotion his letters came to express a deep feeling. Carol was reminded of the last words he said to her on the dark platform at Central Station. At that time his love was flattering, even comforting to a girl so far from home. Now, with each letter her own involvement was becoming more serious. The bond grew stronger. Phil called it love, Carol was still unsure. She knew the artificial emotion created when the written word was the only communication. However, she did sign her own letters with, 'Love', and, she could not hide her excitement as the day of his home coming drew nearer.

The sound of a car engine drew Carol to the front window. Her heart leapt in her breast. She felt like crying. Running to the front door she flung it open and ran onto the verandah. Phil was paying the taxi driver. He turned, picked up his bags and faced the house. To Carol he appeared taller, stronger. The khaki of his uniform accentuated the tan of his body. The wide brim of his slouch hat shaded his face, but, his white teeth flashed in a smile of pure joy. Carol ran along the path and threw her arms around his neck. Tears ran down her face. It was so good to have him back, to have someone to hold and to be held. Phil gently pulled her away and looked into her tear filled eyes. Love welled within him. He took Carol's face in his hands and kissed her lips with a tenderness that made both their bodies quiver. The weeks of pent up emotion were about to explode within and from them. Their lips parted and they looked again at each other.

'Come on.' Phil broke the spell. 'Let's go inside.'

Carol picked up the lightest case and took his hand. For the first time in many weeks she felt safe.

'It is great to have you back.' She said.

Phil lowered his head and kissed her tenderly on the cheek. It was a reassuring gesture and Carol felt warm inside.

Once behind closed doors they let the cases fall to the floor and kissed again, long and hard. There was no need for words. They were now together and they needed each other.

'I must have a shower.' Phil whispered and traced Carol's profile with his finger.

'Good. So must I.' She whispered and grinned impishly up at him.

The water played on their bodies. Carol tingled as Phil's hands cupped her breasts and his lips caressed their fullness.

'Beautiful.' He sighed. 'You're so soft. You have no idea how I've longed to hold you. At times it was all I could think of, all that kept me going.' Their lips met and they kissed, their tongues meeting and exploring. Carol moved her legs and allowed Phil's hands to glide over her body. She looked down and took him in her hands. Bending her knees she lowered herself and with her lips tracing the contour of his body took him in her waiting mouth.

Phil stroked Carol's hair as he lay beside her.

'You're beautiful.' He said quietly and leaned over to give her a light kiss on the lips.

'You're not so bad yourself.' She replied and they smiled together. 'How long am I going to have you for?' She asked.

'Monday morning.' Phil became serious. 'I have to report to Holsworthy.'

'Two days.' Carol was horrified. 'Two days. That's all?'

'I thought I told you in my last letter.' Phil tried to defend himself.

'You most certainly did not. You know you didn't.' Carol felt cheated and betrayed.

Phil backed down and spoke quietly;

'Okay, you're right. I didn't know how to tell you.' He waited before saying more. 'I join the battalion at Holsworthy, just west of Sydney. I'll be there for six weeks before going up to the jungle training centre in Queensland. After that… Vietnam.'

The meaning of what had just been said did not immediately penetrate Carol's cloak of annoyed frustration. She then stopped suddenly and looked at him.

'Vietnam.' The name was barely audible. Phil nodded and tried to smile.

'How long for?' Carol asked.

'A year.' He tried to sound matter of fact but the emotion gave an edge to his voice. This was what he joined for. He had been proud to enlist rather than wait for his conscription papers. Now there was only one regret as he looked into the moist eyes of the girl he loved. 'Come here.' He reached over and drew Carol to him. 'I'm going to be around for the next six weeks and they will not all be work. Let's make the most of it.' He gently kissed her and held her close. 'It's your weekend, what do you want to do with it?'

Carol snuggled into his muscled body and replied urgently.

'Make love to me.'

Chapter 10

The Indian Ocean reflected the pale blueness of the cloudless sky and the gentle swell failed to disturb the glass like surface. The horizon looked a hundred miles away in the noon day sun.

'Stand by, stand by... mark!' The voice of the Navigator's Yeoman was crisp and loud as he counted down the seconds from his chronometer. At midday Peter had to take the last sun sight before landfall was made on the west coast of Australia. It had been a long trek across the Indian Ocean and most of it in weather so bad that the use of the heavens for navigation was out of the question. 'It's good to see the sun, sir.' Commented the Yeoman as Peter noted the angle on the sextant arm into his orange notebook.

Peter quietly agreed but within himself he was rejoicing in the relief of obtaining this crucial fix of the ship's position. The morning stars had given him a location and the mid-morning sun had confirmed it. This last sight would prove beyond doubt that after all those days in the wilderness he was on course for his landfall at Geraldton, Western Australia.

The fix was transferred to the chart and Peter ran the track on to calculate the time when land would be sighted. He then went to the bridge to inform the Captain and the Officer of the Watch.

Captain Harlow was perched high in his chair, his head bent in deep concentration as he read the latest signals to his ship. In the past weeks he had not spent many hours away from that chair and the strain of command was etching a few more lines into his stern face. Peter waited by the chair until his presence broke into the Captain's consciousness.

'Yes Peter, what is it?'

'Landfall, sir. Geraldton 1930, the Abrolhos Islands will appear an hour before at 1830.'

'Very good. Would you let the Admiral know? He's been asking.'

'Hello, Peter.' Admiral Harrison was on the bridge wing overlooking the flight deck. 'It's good to have some tropical weather for a change.'

Peter readily agreed. The first leg of their deployment had been one continuous storm passage down the west coast of Africa. Even the six days since leaving Cape Town had been marred by torrential rain and high seas.

'I expect to make landfall at 1830, sir.' Peter reported.

'That's good news.' Harrison replied with a smile. 'I don't mind telling you that I will be glad to be getting ashore for a few days. Three days in Cape Town was not long enough. Before all the political ruckus we used to spend weeks down there. Lovely place, cracking girls.'

Peter smiled, knowing the Admiral's fondness for the ladies. He also knew that he protected his own like a hawk. This made Peter uneasy in his company. Peter had received five letters and a postcard from Susanne, but had barely been able to compose two pages in return.

'Are you going to the civic reception in Perth, Peter?' The Admiral asked.

'Yes sir. I am.' Peter answered guardedly.

'We didn't see very much of you in Cape Town.'

'No sir. The bad weather necessitated changes in the programme and I wanted to go over the coming exercise schedule without the interruptions one gets at sea.'

'Good for you, but you don't know what you missed.' The Admiral's face broke into a broad and knowing smile.

'Will that be all, sir?'

'Yes, thank you. 1830.' The Admiral repeated the time of landfall and looked at his watch.

Peter returned to the chart house happy to be free, but, aware that his reputation as a Navigator rested on sighting land at the time he predicted. Not only his ship, but the whole group, would know if he was wrong. It was now thirteen hundred and time for lunch.

Peter looked at the clock on the chart house bulkhead. It read '1815'. He felt the adrenaline surge around his body. Six days at sea and he had to hit the target right on the nose. His pride as a navigator depended upon it and his ego demanded it. He left for the bridge.

Behind the formation of grey ships the sun was setting. On board Sovereign the bridge lighting was set to dim. The Captain sat in his usual perch, looking directly ahead as if expecting to see land before the radar detected it on its orange screen.

'Good evening Peter.' The Officer of the Watch greeted the Navigator. Both men looked at the radar screen and then at each other. Everyone on the aircraft carrier's bridge, and on the bridges of the other ships, felt the tension of the situation. Peter felt a momentary panic attack. 'What if he was wrong?'

The second hand clicked mechanically round the black face of the bridge clock. The crackling voice on the intercom cut through the silence. The Officer of the Watch picked up the rubber microphone and depressed the trigger to answer,

'Bridge.'

'Contact bearing 080, twenty miles, bearing remains steady.'

'Very good.'

As soon as he heard the word contact Peter moved over to the radar screen on the front of the bridge. He concentrated on making his movements as controlled as possible. Inside, his whole nervous system went into overdrive.

Peter looked at the screen and delighted at the first golden flicker that appeared on the edge of the circular dish. He noted the range displayed at the top of the screen. A great weight lifted from his shoulders when an outline, that could only be land, gradually took shape in front of his eyes.

'We have land, sir.' Peter reported to the Captain. Harlow's reply was matter of fact.

'Very good.'

Peter inwardly thanked him for his restraint. Any other reaction could have been construed as a lack of faith on the Captain's part.

Noting the range and bearing Peter went to the chart and looked for prominent landmarks that would show up on a radar screen. He returned to the radar and noted three more contacts which he transferred to the chart. He now breathed more easily.

'Got it.' He sighed under his breath and the relief flowed through his body. He put the fix on the chart and ran the track on for the next fifteen minutes.

'Well, where are we Peter?' The Captain could contain himself no longer.

'The Abrolhos Islands, sir.' Pointing to the chart Peter indicated their position and pointed out the relevant landmarks. 'I suggest we stay on this course for another fifteen minutes and then come starboard to 180 degrees.'

The Captain looked at the chart and pointing to the mainland let his finger rest on the group of islands.

'Not bad, not bad at all.' He said.

The breakwaters at the entrance to Fremantle Harbour reached out like welcoming arms into the blue waters of the Indian Ocean. In line astern Sovereign led the formation between the stony sea walls. White clad sailors lined the decks and looked down at the crowds who had gathered on the shore to welcome them.

'It looks like we're in for a good time.' A voice on the aircraft carrier's flight deck broke the regimental silence. The Chief Petty Officer in charge was quick to respond.

'The next man who makes a sound will not get to sample anything except permanent gangway duty.'

He need have said nothing as the Royal Marine Band struck up and drowned any further conversation.

The harbour wharves were crowded with the green-grey hulls of the Australian warships. Captain Harlow had the con and Peter was able to take in the scene. He knew the Australian ships that were to take part in the coming exercise and now identified them as Sovereign glided past on her way to her berth at the far end of the basin.

On the starboard bow lay the Australian Flagship, an aircraft carrier only a little older than Sovereign. The Bosun's call sounded and the ship's companies on both vessels came to attention.

Once the Woomera was clear astern the Captain maneuvered his ship alongside the wharf. It was a delicate operation, made even more so by the knowledge that the Australians would be watching. It was now the Captain's turn to demonstrate his skills, and this time, to an international audience.

The bulk of the carrier shuddered as the engines were put astern. Forward motion was slowed and the bow edged into the dockside. Peter watched as the bow line was passed between ship and shore. He turned to check that the stern tug was pushing Sovereign into the wharf. 'Nicely done,' he thought when he heard the Captain's order to, 'finish with main engines.'

Harlow came in from the starboard bridge wing and snapped an order to the Officer of the Watch.

'Fall out Special Sea Dutymen and be ready for the

Admiral who will be going ashore as soon as the brow is secured.' He did not wait for an acknowledgement but walked briskly through the bridge and into his sea cabin.

Peter moved to the table and gathered his charts and instruments. As he walked to the chart house he nearly fell over the Captain who was bustling out of his sea cabin with his steward in hot pursuit. Peter smiled, realising that the skipper was wasting no time in moving back into his more spacious day cabin while in harbour.

'Are you coming to the reception tonight?' Peter was surprised by the Captain's question.

'Yes sir.'

'Good. See you there.' The Captain continued on his way leaving Peter to wonder why everyone was so interested in his social life.

The wardroom was bustling with activity. The weeks at sea with only a short break ashore at Cape Town were about to be redressed. There were a number of functions arranged and it appeared that all those who were not on duty had a place to go. Peter walked over to the bar and ordered a gin and tonic.

'Heart starters, ay?' These words from the Senior Engineer made Peter look up from his glass.

'Yes.' He replied. 'Trying to get into the swing of things.'

'These younger ones don't need any encouragement.' The older officer observed. 'Look at them. Do you think we should let them loose on these quiet people?'

Peter looked round the crowded and smoke filled room. He smiled and nodded his head.

'A hole and hair and the rest is just gash.'

No one knew whether the wardroom fell silent because of the comment or whether it was quiet when the statement was made. Whatever the sequence there was now an unnatural stillness over all. Peter looked about him and his eye settled on a group of young pilots and one face stood out from the crowd.

'Lieutenant James. It had to be.' He thought and shook his head in resignation. The Engineer's eyes followed Peter's stare.

'I hope they are not coming with us.' He said with great feeling. Peter did not reply. He did not have too, it was understood.

The Executive Officer entered the wardroom and his commanding voice broke the embarrassed spell.

'Would all officers attending the civic reception please proceed ashore as the transport is waiting.'

Peter drained his glass and was relieved to see that Lieutenant James had not made a move. 'It may not be such a bad night after all.' He conceded.

The spacious reception hall was filled with uniforms, dinner jackets and ladies dressed in evening gowns. The official party greeted the guests as they entered. Peter stole a glance at the attractive young woman standing behind the Mayor. 'Was he dreaming or did he see a flicker of interest in her eyes?' He then recalled an Australian Naval Officer standing by her side and reasoned that she must be with him. He tried to dismiss her from his mind. A waiter proffered a silver tray on which were standing a dozen long stemmed glasses brimming with champagne. Peter took a glass and looked around the room. It resembled a giant school assembly hall with portraits of the Queen and Duke of Edinburgh dominating one wall. Maroon curtains covered the other three walls and folding chairs were lined up along two of them. A large buffet was being arranged underneath the Royal portraits.

'Quite a turn out'.

Peter looked to see Steven Marks standing beside him, and, agreed.

'Everything is bigger in Australia.' The aviator continued as a tanned young woman with an ample cleavage walked by.

'Right again.' Peter said, and smiled.

'I spent two years down here just after I got my second ring. It's a great place.' Marks gave a brief account of his time on exchange service with the Royal Australian Navy.

'Have you got any friends here tonight?' Peter asked, moving his glass around in a sweeping arc as he spoke.

'Oh yes. You probably saw them as you came in. Follow me.' The pilot threaded his way through the crowded room so quickly that Peter soon lost sight of him. Standing on tiptoe he craned his neck to relocate his guide.

'Peter.' He felt foolish when he turned round and looked into a pair of sparkling blue eyes, but it was not the owner of those eyes who had spoken. 'Peter, this is Jennifer Hale.' Steven Marks made the introductions; 'and this is Jim Hale, a Senior Pilot aboard the Woomera.'

'It is her.' Peter recalled the face of the girl he saw on entering the reception. He remained silent.

'I was telling Peter that he should try and get a posting to Oz. He would love it.'

'I'm sure he would.' Jennifer answered seductively. Further conversation was interrupted by a speech of welcome and an invitation to enjoy the hospitality of the city. Taking a sidelong glance at Jennifer Hale, Peter wished that he could. He was intrigued to see that she was looking at him. Peter considered the implication of that look and decided he was not going to get involved. The speech concluded with an invitation to the guests to enjoy the buffet that boasted some fine West Australian seafood.

'What a good idea. I'm starving. Come on everyone, before the locusts get at it.' Jennifer said, taking hold of Peter's hand and pulling him after her. Peter looked at Steven Marks and then at Jim Hale but they were both lost in conversation and oblivious to all except the flying qualities of a Grumman Tracker anti-submarine aircraft. 'Do you like lobster?' Jennifer asked as they neared the table.

Peter said that he did and, although feeling awkward at being the center of this pretty lady's attention, also felt the thrill of it.

'You wait here and I'll get you a selection.' Jennifer instructed and walked off to the buffet.

'Jennie taking good care of you, Peter?' Jim asked as he walked up from behind.

'Yes thanks.' Peter tried to sound detached.

'That's good.' The Australian replied and returned his attention to Marks. 'Come on. Let's you and me get stuck in.' Jennifer returned with two plates piled high with salad and seafood.

'After this you will have to come back to my place.' She said and Peter nearly choked on a lobster tail.

'Are you alright?' She asked with real concern.

'Yes.' Peter coughed, fighting to regain his composure. 'It went down the wrong way.'

'Don't die on us Peter. We have a war to fight in a few days.' Marks joked referring to the forthcoming exercise. 'Jim commands a Tracker squadron in Woomera.'

Peter looked at the Australian pilot and thought that here was a way to get out of the situation he felt himself to be headed. He turned his attention to Jim Hale.

'I have never seen one of those aircraft. In fact, I have never flown from an aircraft carrier.' He looked at Steven Marks. 'These 'airey fairies' won't let me near an aeroplane.'

'What!' Jim cried in simulated horror. 'You don't know what you're missing.' He then paused, 'I'll tell you what, at the end of the exercise you come over and I'll take you up. What do you say?'

Peter considered the offer. He would have no trouble in hitching a ride on one of the helicopters across to the Woomera and the Captain should not object.

'You're on.' He answered enthusiastically.

'Great. I'll send you a signal when I've set it up.'

'You must be mad.' Jennifer interjected. 'He can't drive a car let alone a plane; and, talking of driving, have you invited these guys back for drinks after this show packs up?' She looked at Jim and he was quick to reply.

'I was getting round to it, what do you say gentlemen, a few cold ones to commemorate the landing of the Royal Navy on Australian shores?'

'Don't mind if I do.' Steve Marks replied eagerly.

Peter stole a glance at Jennifer. 'It was dangerous, but what the hell.' He thought.

'I'd love to.' He answered.

'Love to what? You dirty bugger.' Steve joked.

Peter felt embarrassed and prayed he had not been so obvious. He said nothing and hoped the moment would pass quickly.

The four continued to talk, eat and drink until Jennifer suggested it was time to leave. The reception was coming to an end and the wine waiter had not circulated through the crowd for at least fifteen minutes. They placed their wine glasses on the nearest table and walked to the door. Jennifer went to collect her wrap and Peter turned to Jim;

'How do you manage to live on the West Coast when the Navy is concentrated on the east?' The answer only served to confuse Peter more.

'It's not my place. Jennie owns it. I only use it when I find myself over here.'

He was even more perplexed when Jennifer returned with a spring in her step and took his arm;

'You drive Jim. I feel like living dangerously.' She gave Peter's arm a squeeze and guided him through the door.

The house was situated on the coast overlooking a long sandy beach and the white capped waters of the Indian Ocean. Jim poured the drinks while Peter took in the view.

'You have a beautiful place here.' He said admiringly.

'I'll show you around.' Jennifer was quick to offer and turned to Steven Marks. 'How about you Steve, want a stickybeak?' The pilot smiled wryly,

'No thanks, I'll stay here and keep an eye on the barman.' Jim passed Peter his drink and told him to take it with him. Peter accepted the glass but found it hard to look his host in the eye.

Jennifer led the way through the split level living area and onto the bedrooms. Peter did not linger. He moved her quickly along by asking to see the garden.

'Certainly.' She replied with a smile on her full, red, lips.

'Oh God.' Peter said to himself as he instantly realised the implications of his request.

A stone patio stretched the width of the house and extended out into the spacious back garden. On one corner sat a barbecue like a small red alter and Peter walked over to it.

'Every home should have one.' He commented, running his hand over the rough surface.

'Oh yes. I love eating out.' Peter cleared his throat, took a long draught of his gin and suggested they return to see how the others were getting on.

'You are always running away Peter.' Jennifer took his hand. 'You should learn to slow down.' Peter felt the inviting pressure of her fingers.

'Damn it Jennifer! What are you trying to do?' He could play the game no longer and his voice held the tone of frustrated exasperation. Jennifer looked surprised.

'What do you mean?' She answered innocently but her lips pouted and her eyes sparkled with invitation. Peter blinked and held his eyes closed while he took a deep breath.

'What do I mean? This is what I mean.' He said in exasperation, holding up their entwined hands.

Jennifer looked puzzled;

'You aren't married are you?' She asked. Peter could not hide his amazement.

'No! I'm not married.' He over emphasised the 'I'. Jennifer started to laugh and continued until tears were running down her face.

'Oh Peter, you are priceless. I don't know whether you have been at sea too long or not long enough.' She stopped to wipe the tears of laughter from her cheeks, and then asked; 'who is my husband?' Embarrassment led to annoyance as Peter tried to regain some ground.

'Jim of course. I'm not blind.'

Silence separated them. Jennifer read the signs and knew she had gone as far as she dared with this man. When she spoke again her voice was soft and understanding.

'Jim is my brother.' She paused and smiled, 'older brother, of course.'

Peter felt foolish but relieved. Slowly, a smile came to his lips.

'Please forgive me. I didn't mean to.' Thinking of what would be inferred Peter decided that he had said enough.

Jennifer kissed his cheek;

'You Navy men are so naive. Come on, let's go see my 'husband'. She squeezed Peter's hand and promised she would not say anything.

As they re-entered the lounge room Jim was the first to comment;

'And where have you two been? Check their clothes Steve and see if they have sand in their pockets.'

'Lovely house, Jim.' Peter said in an attempt to counter any further questions.

'Thanks. Our father gave it to us, but Jennie is the one who lives here full time.' He waited a moment before adding, 'Although it beats me how she manages to pay the bills. She's never in a job long enough to pick up the pay cheque.'

Jennifer poked her tongue out at him and retorted,

'I know I have a big brother who will always help me out.' They both smiled and the subject was dropped.

'How about a barbecue tomorrow night?' Jennifer asked enthusiastically. 'Peter said he liked outdoor cooking, what about you Steve?'

The senior pilot had to decline due to a previous appointment with the Royal Australian Air Force at their base north of Perth.

'That's a shame,' Jennifer replied and turned to her brother, 'we can still have one, can't we Jim?'

'Whatever you want.' He agreed and looked at Peter. 'What do you say?' The Navigator readily agreed.

They had another drink before Jim drove the men back to the ship. As they passed through the deserted streets of Fremantle Peter could not get Jennifer out of his mind. He was already impatient for the next eighteen hours to pass so that he may see her again. Jim stopped the car at the foot of the officer's gangway. They shook hands and bid each other good night.

'I'll collect you at 1900.' Jim confirmed, as Peter left the car. Ascending the gangway Peter felt his pulse racing in anticipation and a smile crossed his lips as he returned the Quartermaster's salute.

Peter looked into his wardrobe and thought about Jennifer's comment from the night before. He concluded, 'conservative yes, naive no.' The comment had been on his mind all day. He analysed his life and agreed that it was cloistered. He considered his relationships and recognised they had not been very successful, but, he did not attribute that to being naive.

'Lieutenant-Commander Wells, please report to the quarterdeck.' The metallic voice of the ship's public address system saved him from further soul searching. He looked at his watch and thought that Jim was early.

His heart skipped a beat as he stepped through the hatch and out onto the quarterdeck. Jennifer Hale was standing and talking to the gangway staff, her slim figure accentuated by a cotton dress, held against the curve of her body by the gentle sea breeze. She looked over as Peter approached and her face showed her obvious pleasure at seeing him again.

As he took her hand Peter thought how lovely she looked. He then realised she was alone.

'Where's Jim?' He asked, but did not really care.

Jennifer explained that her brother had to remain aboard the Woomera and would not be joining them. Peter expressed his disappointment and hoped it sounded sincere.

On the drive to the house Peter did his best to keep the conversation away from himself and was relieved when Jennifer proved to be a willing talker. He was interested to learn that she received an allowance from a doting father and thought back to the conversation on the previous night. Jim had teased her about her numerous jobs and Peter wondered what her brother really thought of his younger sister.

The car travelled along the ocean's edge and Peter looked out at the twilight sky.

'Penny for them.' Jennifer said, not liking Peter's momentary detachment. He looked at her and smiled.

'Nothing really. I was just admiring the sunset.'

'Beautiful isn't it.' She agreed. 'It looks even better with a drink in your hand. Let's see if we can get there before it gets dark.'

The car sped forward forcing Peter back in his seat as Jennifer put her foot to the floor.

'Jim does that.' She commented.

'Does what?' Peter replied.

'Goes silent when I put my foot down. He doesn't trust me, how about you?' Peter wished she would not look at him while she was driving and answered nervously.

'Aren't there laws against this sort of thing?'

Jennifer laughed.

'Coward!' She scoffed. 'Don't worry we are nearly there, hold on.' She drifted the big six cylinder car around a curving right hand bend and then, decelerating rapidly, turned sharply into a white concrete driveway. 'Big stop!' She cried and applied the brakes firmly. Her passenger pitched forward and then fell back in his seat. 'Come on, the sun has almost gone.' She dashed out of the car, slamming the door behind her. Peter sat for a while shaking his head.

'Fast lady,' he said to himself and got out of the car. By the time he reached the front door Jennifer had prepared two drinks.

'Gin and tonic, ice and lemon,' she held out a glass and he accepted it with gratitude. It had been quite a drive. They moved to the large bay windows and watched the dying moments of the day.

Jennifer stood close to him and he looked down into her eyes. She responded by giving him a quick kiss on the cheek that took him by surprise, and, almost before it had time to register she was on her way out of the room.

'I'll make the salad and you can cook the steaks.' She called back over her shoulder.

Peter followed his hostess. Jennifer switched on the patio lights and refilled Peter's glass,

'It's thirsty work.' She said.

As the meat sizzled on the hot plate Jennifer came out from the kitchen and, holding onto Peter's arm, nuzzled next to him.

'Smells good.' She sighed.

Peter felt the thrill of her touch and the frustration when she rushed away to get the rest of the food.

'How do you like it?' Peter asked when she returned to the patio. Jennifer's eyes twinkled in response,

'Anyway you want.' She replied and held his eyes with hers.

Peter felt uneasy. He was not in command and he did not mind, nor did he want to control the desire that was like a fire within him.

'Must not forget the wine.' Jennifer said and ran back into the house. She returned with two chilled bottles and two long stemmed glasses. 'Hope you like white wine,' she said and handed him the corkscrew.

Peter opened the first bottle and filled their glasses, 'Cheers,' he smiled and touched his glass to hers.

'To us.' Jennifer responded and brought her full lips to the glass. Peter could not take his eyes away and stared as she drank the wine. She looked over the rim and held his gaze. He was the first to look away.

'Right, let's eat.' He said and took the steaks from the fire.

'Delicious.' Jennifer placed her empty plate on the tray beside the barbecue. 'You are an excellent chef.'

'Thank you.' Peter bowed his head and continued. 'It is such a beautiful way to have a meal. Look at those stars.' They looked up into the night sky.

'Let's go for a walk.' Jennifer suggested.

Peter hesitated as once again the initiative was taken from him, and, he could have kicked himself for his reply.

'What about the washing up?'

'Oh Peter!' Jennifer scoffed and rose from the patio chair. 'That can wait.' She said and then added, 'But if it will make you happy we can take them into the house. I have a lady who comes in every day, she will clean them.'

Peter was not surprised and smiled. He carried the tray into the kitchen.

'Just leave it there,' Jennifer directed. 'I'll get rid of my shoes.' Peter remained anchored in the kitchen until he heard her calling. 'Come on Peter.' She was standing barefoot by the open front door.

Arm in arm they descended the steps that led down to the driveway. Jennifer snuggled close as they crossed the road and walked onto the grass verge that bordered the beach.

'You had better take your shoes off before we go any further.' Jennifer softly advised. Barefoot and holding onto each other they walked down to the sandy beach.

The sound of the sea was like muffled thunder. The white foam glistened as the waves hit, swept up the sand and retreated, to be replaced in a relentless cycle of movement and sound. Jennifer ran off into the darkness.

'Race you to the water,' she called the challenge as she ran. Peter followed, struggling to keep his footing in the soft sand and cursing himself for not doing more exercise during the long weeks at sea. He peered into the darkness as he ran and at the water's edge quickly retreated out of the way of an incoming wave.

'Don't be a woos, come on in.' Peter stopped and looked in the direction of the sound. Jennifer waved to him. 'Come on, it's really warm.'

Peter was out of his depth even before he got to the water. He was in a quandary; he had just eaten, he didn't think it felt that warm, he had his clothes on. While looking into the rolling sea his own world stood still. He could not believe his own senses anymore. Jennifer came towards him, her naked body streaked with foam and glistening with sea water. Peter stood rooted in the sand, his hands, still holding his shoes, hung down by his sides. She came closer. The sea washed around his ankles as Jennifer put her arms around his neck.

'I see I will have to take you in hand.' She said and

drew Peter's lips to hers. The contour and wetness of her body triggered the passion within him. His arms enveloped her and they lost themselves in a kiss. As their lips parted Jennifer took her hands from around Peter's neck. Slowly, and, meaningfully she undid the buttons of his shirt, loosened the buckle of his belt and slipped her hands into his trousers. As she caressed him Peter thought he would explode. He kept telling himself that this could not be happening and just when it looked as if the night would be over before it began, the touch was withdrawn. She took her hands, placed them on Peter's chest and eased the shirt from his back.

'You don't need this,' she purred and threw the shirt onto the sand. Her attention then returned to the trousers and with sensual ease ran her hands down Peter's thighs. Feeling that he should regain some of the initiative Peter removed the rest of his clothing and threw them back up the beach.

'That's better.' Jennifer sighed and pressed her body to his. She looked up into Peter's face and they kissed again. 'Come on.' Once more the young woman took the lead as she held Peter's hand and led him into the rolling waves.

'Blimey that's cold!' He exclaimed as a wave slapped against his flat stomach. Jennifer laughed and scolded him for his cowardice.

They swam into the calmer water behind the breakers. The lights from the houses sparkled along the shore and the beams from the headlights of passing cars stabbed into the darkness.

Jennifer swam close and at times held onto Peter,

entwining her legs about him. Every touch was exciting. The rolling of the swell and buffeting from waves pushed the swimmers closer to the beach. As his feet touched the bottom Peter held out his arms. Jennifer came to him and held on. The need within them required no words and instinctively they made their way to the shore. Ignoring their clothes they walked to the back of the beach where low sand dunes offered some seclusion from the road beyond. In an embrace they lowered themselves onto the sand and, without words, made love.

'This sand gets everywhere.' Jennifer laughed as she spoke.

'You are not wrong.' Peter agreed and laughed with her.

They kissed gently and Peter stroked a few grains of sand from Jennifer's stomach. He looked at her nakedness and once more the feeling of disbelief clouded in on him. It was Jennifer who supplied the reality.

'Come on, we better go.' She rolled over and got to her knees. Peter jumped to his feet and helped her to stand. 'Where did we leave our clothes?' She giggled.

'They are probably out in the Indian Ocean by now.' Replied Peter, who was only half joking. He set out to look for them.

Walking back along the beach Peter felt self-conscious once more. It was with relief that he found his clothes and hurriedly put them on. Jennifer slipped the dress over her head and the thin cotton material travelled downward, hiding the delights of her body like a curtain dropping over a stage. She held her underwear in her hand and Peter became aroused again as they returned to the glare of the street lamps. They crossed the road and walked up the driveway to the house.

Jennifer entered first and threw her bra and panties onto the sofa.

'I better get you back.' She declared. Peter was stunned and looked hard at the disheveled and exciting figure of the woman to whom he had just made love. Jennifer continued, 'I have a very early flight tomorrow. I am going to the east coast for a few days.'

Peter did not understand, but, the spell had been broken and all he could answer was,

'Okay.'

Back in his cabin Peter tried to piece the evening together. It was as if he had spent the last few hours in a fantasy land. He looked at his watch, 'two hours ago we were on the beach,' he thought and shook his head. 'I just don't believe it.'

Jennifer had hurried him out of the house and on the drive back to the ship displayed no sign of the passion that only minutes before had consumed her. She only talked about her trip to Sydney and how she hoped they would see each other again.

Peter paced the small area of his cabin, stroking his brow.

'See each other again.' He said to himself and laughed.

For the remaining days in harbour the Squadron Navigator once again retreated from the social scene. Steven Marks returned from duty ashore and was disappointed when Peter would not talk about Jennifer

Hale. The pilot refused to believe there was nothing to tell. Eventually, to save embarrassment, Peter said that he hoped to see her again in Sydney. It was a lie, but kept Steve happy and put an end to his questions. The more Peter thought about that night the greater became his resentment. He had been manipulated, it would not happen again.

On the day of sailing there was a lot to be done. A letter arrived from Susanne Harrison. Peter read it quickly and threw it into the top drawer of his desk. He wanted to be free and was very happy to be going to sea.

The Navigator stood on the bridge and watched the Port of Fremantle pass astern. Sovereign led the British squadron out into the Indian Ocean. The Australian ships had departed two hours earlier and in three more hours the two navies would commence the first in a series of 'mini wars' that would keep them at sea for the next two weeks and take them from the coast of Western Australia to the eastern edge of the Great Australian Bight.

'Signal, Sir.' The Yeoman handed the pink slip of paper to the Navigator. Peter read it through tired eyes. The past days had been among the toughest he could remember. To sleep for more than four hours at a time and to live without alarms, darkened cabins and hastily eaten meals was like a dream to him. As he read the message his face broke into a smile.

'Damn me, he has remembered.' Peter's spirit lightened as he contemplated the adventure. He was going to fly off an aircraft carrier. All he had to do was get permission from the 'Old Man.'

'No! If you want to kill yourself why don't you do it in one of our own aircraft?' The Captain's tone was final. Peter's disappointment was acute and it must have registered on his face as Harlow offered an explanation. 'You are too valuable to risk on a joy ride, Peter. You are the Squadron Navigator and we have a lot of miles to steam before we see Pompey again.' The Captain's tone mellowed. 'Getting home is only the beginning for you. I cannot allow you to risk your future.'

Peter stood while the Captain spoke. He listened, but could not accept the arguments. He had to answer.

'Sir, the main exercises are over. My work is up to date. I will only be away from the ship for eight hours, and if anything should happen,' Peter hesitated, 'it is my life.'

The craggy face of the Commanding Officer looked long and hard at his Navigator. After a reflective silence he spoke,

'Peter, I told you when we started this deployment that our careers were bound together and the success of one would automatically benefit the other. That situation has not changed. I do not intend to be remembered as the Captain who lost his Navigator off the coast of South Australia.'

Peter listened and recalled that earlier conversation. He remembered being proud to be taken so much into his Captain's confidence. Now, he resented being a tool to fashion another man's career. He had to fight on.

'I appreciate what you are saying sir.' Peter hoped to placate the Captain before going on, 'but, there has not been a flying accident on this deployment and I do not recall any Fleet Air Arm casualties, either with us or the Australians, for some time. I believe that you are over stating the dangers, sir.'

Harlow looked at his Navigator. He could see the determination in his eyes and the rift forming between them. He brought his hand to his chin and tugged reflectively. Eventually, the silence was broken.

'All right. You can go, but, if you kill yourself you will have to answer to me, sooner or later.'

Peter acted quickly so as to deny the Captain any opportunity to reconsider. He thanked him, saluted and hurried to the main signal office to acknowledge his invitation.

At 0800 the following day Peter was strapped into the right hand seat of a Wessex anti-submarine helicopter and flying over the open ocean that separated the aircraft carriers of the two navies. White caps topped the waves and a rolling swell ran over the sea. Peter looked out of the open door and felt exhilarated by the speed and the close proximity of the water below.

The characteristic greenish paint of the Australian carrier stood out against the darkness of the sea, and, the metallic greyness of its flight deck appeared to rise to meet the approaching helicopter. Peter watched the large ship roll and held his breath as the helicopter's wheels hit the moving deck. He held on, expecting the aircraft to bounce, and was relieved when he heard the pitch of the engine change and realised the machine was going to stay where it had been placed. The Pilot indicated for Peter to undo his harness.

Jumping down onto Woomera's flight deck Peter was greeted by his host for the day. They shook hands.

'Glad you could make it Peter.' Jim Hale's smile reflected his sincerity. He directed Peter to the bridge island on the starboard side of the flight deck. They moved through the hatch and into the relative tranquility of the superstructure.

'Is there anyone you want to see before we go along to the briefing room?' Jim asked, thinking Peter would want to meet his opposite number in the Australian ship.

'I came here to fly. I can talk ships when I get back. Where are we going today?'

The Australian pilot directed his guest to follow him. They descended a ladder and walked along a narrow passageway until they came to a door with the sign, 'Flight Crew Briefing Room.'

'In here Peter.'

'Good morning gentlemen,' Jim greeted the men in the crowded room and took his position on a rostrum in front of the assembled aircrew. Peter nodded when he was introduced and hoped that he did not look as out of place as he felt. Jim went on to outline the programme for the day's flying.

Three Trackers were to do a fly past over one of the larger towns in the bush country to the south of Adelaide. It was to be the highlight of their annual carnival and Jim pointed out that, for some of the inhabitants, it would be their first contact with the Navy. He gave details of the operation and concluded

'Let's give them something to remember.'

The airmen stood up as their commander left the

room. Back on the flight deck Jim introduced Peter to his crew, and then led the way to the Grumman Tracker that was waiting on the flight deck. The size of the machine surprised its newest crew member and Peter said so.

'It would not look so large if we had a bigger carrier.' Jim explained. 'When we land there is only three feet clearance between the wing tip and the island. Not much margin for error.' Peter wished he had kept his thoughts to himself. He climbed two steps and entered the tubular body of the anti-submarine aeroplane. To his right was the pilot's position with its array of dials and instruments that gave the Navigator a fleeting sense of admiration for those who chose to fly.

'Just move to the centre of the aircraft, Peter.' Jim's instructions moved him along until he was standing between two electrical displays and the crew seats. 'You take the port one.' Jim indicated and Peter moved out of the aisle and sat down. 'I'll leave Barry to settle you in and I'll talk to you later.' Jim moved forward to take his place in the left hand seat.

Barry Noyes was the Observer responsible for the underwater sensors and weapons. He helped Peter into his safety harness and then explained some of the gadgets that were in front of him. As he listened Peter knew that only half of what was being said was registering in his brain. The thought of the imminent take off was driving all other considerations from his mind. By his left shoulder there was a small, oval, window and Peter looked through it to see the blades of the port engine rotating into life.

'Now for the second best sensation in the world.' The Observer said smilingly.

The aircraft moved slowly forward until coming to a jerking halt on the catapult runway. The twin engines screamed as the pilot opened the throttles to give them enough power to keep them flying once the catapult had done its job.

'Stand by for take off.' Jim gave the warning and Peter sat back in his seat. He glanced out of the small window beside him, but, with the first hint of movement looked straight ahead and braced himself.

The steam catapult hurled the Tracker from the carrier's deck like a stone from a slingshot, and all those inside, were pushed back in their seats, their faces contorted and grotesque.

For a few seconds the aircraft flew out of the pilot's control. As it passed over the end of the flight deck it dipped towards the sea and Peter let go an involuntary gasp as he felt the aircraft fall away. Free of the catapult's thrust the pilot regained control and the turboprops clawed at the air, gaining height with every rotation of the blades. Peter felt relief and then exhilaration surge through his body. The Grumman Tracker banked to the left and climbed while Peter looked down at the sea as the world dropped away.

'What did you think of that?' Jim's voice crackled in his headphones and Peter could not disguise his excitement.

'Fantastic!' He exclaimed. 'Bloody marvelous!' Jim laughed and spoke again.

'Tony will fly it from here, so things should be even more exciting.' He joked at his Co-Pilot's expense.

The aircraft continued its spiraling climb until

the designated altitude was reached. Peter, his nose pressed against the window, caught sight of Woomera and thought how immense these ships appeared when standing on their bridge and how insignificant it now looked against the backdrop of the never ending ocean. It then occurred to him that in a few hours he would be landing on that minute image in the sea.

Peter felt something touch his arm and looked round to see the Observer pointing through the starboard window. Peter craned his head to see the other two Trackers forming up alongside. On the carrier's deck they had looked so ungainly, now airborne, they assumed a natural grace. Peter watched and felt a child's excitement at what he was experiencing.

The starboard wing suddenly dipped and his stomach felt hollow. The change in altitude had come without warning. Peter looked to his right and watched the sea below pass before the window. Barry Noyes sat back in his seat to give his passenger a better view.

'What do you say Peter, is this the life or isn't it?' Jim's voice echoed in Peter's headset and echoed his own thoughts. The aircraft regained level flight and Jim spoke again. 'Come on up and have a look around.'

Peter was helped out of his harness and walked forward. Jim looked round and smiled. His face mirrored the pride he felt in his aircraft and his job. The co-pilot had the controls and Jim explained the panel of instruments. Peter appreciated the technical side of flying, but, it was the thrill of being airborne that made it an adventure. He stayed talking to Jim until the rugged South Australian coastline passed beneath them. Jim advised his guest to return to his seat and strap in.

The brown, scorched scrubland stretched out as far as the eye could see. Herds of cattle appeared as if they had been sprinkled over the landscape. The pilot's voice sounded over the intercom,

'Okay hang on, we're going to take a closer look down on the deck.'

Instantly the nose of the aircraft dropped. Peter could feel the gravitational forces pressing his body back in his seat. The engine noise increased and his pulse began to race once more.

The aircraft levelled off and Peter strained at his harness to look up the aisle and out of the cockpit windows. The ground appeared so close that it could be touched. Sheep in the field ahead exploded in a white cascade of frenzied movement, running in all directions to escape the alien above their heads. Peter sat mesmerised as the ground passed beneath him. Jim's voice brought him back to reality,

'We are going back up.'

The nose rose sharply and the aircraft banked to port. Peter looked out of his window and saw the other two aircraft hedge hopping across the flat land. They too then rose and followed their leader.

The formation flew on for another half an hour before the 'target' town was seen on the horizon. The co-pilot took the Tracker up to a higher altitude and Peter watched as the other aircraft took station alongside. Jim's voice filled Peter's headphones again.

'Hold onto your hats, we are going down.'

Once again Peter was hurtling towards the earth and moving his body to get a better view. Galvanised tin roofs glistened in the sunlight. Peter's imagination reverted to childhood games of war. The town became an enemy stronghold under attack with waving crowds its defending forces. As the aircraft passed low over the buildings Peter looked down, almost expecting to see burning devastation and the tell-tale trails of pursuing missiles. The Tracker's nose lifted and the formation banked to starboard for a second pass over the town.

In line ahead the group streaked above the rooftops and cheering people gathered in the main street. Peter pushed his face to the window in order to see as much of the show as possible, and then, without warning, the aircraft moved violently from side to side. Peter sat back in his seat and shot a glance to the Observer.

'What was that?' He asked, his eyes wide and the colour momentarily gone from his cheeks.

'Just saying goodbye.' Replied the grinning young officer waving his arms to portray the waving motion of the aeroplane.

A sigh escaped from Peter's throat, he relaxed and threw his head back. They were soon climbing again.

'How's that?' Jim's voice echoed around the aircraft. 'Let's go home.'

The Tracker banked and began a slow turn towards the coast. Jim spoke into Peter's headphones.

'Enjoying yourself?'

The enthusiasm in Peter's voice was unmistakable and the Australian smiled as he recalled the reserved officer he had met two weeks earlier.

For Peter the flight back to the Woomera was a time for reflection. The formation maintained a level flight and there was none of the high jinx of the outbound journey. Rarely, in all his years at sea, had Peter felt such exhilaration. There was a challenge in navigation, but not the immediate thrill and bravado he had experienced that day.

The flat, sun bleached land, gave way to the jagged cliffs of the Great Australian Bight. The sea now lay below, dark and menacing. White streaks of foam ran along its surface and Peter knew that the return to the carrier would not be as easy as the departure.

The minutes passed and then he heard the co-pilot's voice in his headphones,

'There she is. I have her visual.'

Peter's heart jumped in his chest. Looking down the aisle and out through the forward windows he saw the small, green form of the Australian aircraft carrier cutting through the choppy sea. The adrenalin was flowing again. Peter expected the ship to look small, but not that small. To land on the tiny floating platform now below them seemed impossible. He sat in that awkward position unable to take his eyes from the carrier. He remembered being told that there was only three feet of clearance between the Tracker's wing tip and the carrier's island superstructure. He cursed his memory for choosing that time to recall the information. He then also remembered that it was the co-pilot who was to do the landing. Peter sat back in his seat.

The Observer was watching his passenger's face and knew the doubts that were playing on Peter's mind.

'Doesn't look like Heathrow Airport does it sir?' Peter turned and smilingly shook his head. The Observer spoke again. 'You know the drill sir. We line up on the orange lights down on the deck and just follow them in. The Lieutenant has done it many times.' Jim's voice cut in and curtailed any further reassurances.

'Right Peter, Tony will take us down last. We will stand off to port while the other two land on. This will give you a chance to see what it looks like to put one of these beauties down from our end.'

'Thanks for the sideshow, but I am not sure that I want to look.' Peter replied with his tongue in his cheek and his heart in his mouth.

'Well don't. I never do.' Jim retorted. Both men laughed and some of the tension was relieved.

Peter leaned out once more to look ahead. The destroyer that was acting as guard ship passed underneath. Off the stern of Woomera the Search and Rescue helicopter hovered only feet above the jumping waves. To Peter, both were grim reminders of the danger inherent in carrier operations.

Woomera loomed large as the Tracker passed above it and made a sweeping turn to port. On her deck the crews were assembling in readiness to meet the first of the arrivals. Peter watched the roll of the ship and noted the arrestor wires that would halt each aircraft's headlong race to the sea. A figure appeared on the wing of the carrier's bridge and for a moment Peter wished he was down there, back in his own environment and not suspended a thousand feet above with only one way down. The sea became empty once more as the carrier slipped astern. The aircraft continued its slow turn.

'Take a look out of your window Peter.' Peter could see the carrier once more and above its stern, as if drawn by a giant magnet, the first Tracker was making its approach. Everything appeared to be happening in slow motion as the two drew closer and closer together until the aircraft was flying only a few feet above the flight deck. In the blinking of an eye the aircraft landed and the union was complete. Just as quickly its forward motion was halted by the extended length of the arrestor cable. Peter watched as the wire was released and slithered back along the deck to regain its position parallel to the others ready for the next arrival.

At the time when the second aircraft was thundering onto Woomera's deck Jim's co-pilot was making his approach. Peter strained at his harness to watch the landing through the pilot's windows. As they descended emptiness clawed at his stomach. The flight deck loomed ahead, its metal blackness a threatening and unyielding barrier. Peter sat back in his seat, his heart pounding in his chest.

A single, hollow, thumping sound marked the aircraft's arrival on board. The Tracker continued its forward momentum although, to Peter, the engines sounded quieter. The aircraft ran on and Peter thought of the carrier's metal island and the clearance margin with the wing tip. He then realised that it was not the starboard wing that was taking his attention. It was the port. The aircraft was falling away. The port wing was dropping. He looked to his window and saw the foam from the carrier's bow dancing up at him. 'God! We are going in!' The thought instilled fear but not resignation. Pulling his upper body out of his seat he looked forward in time to see Jim's hand reach out for the throttles and return power to the dying engines. Agonisingly the aircraft clawed its way back from the brink. Peter sat back once more and fought to regain his breath. Beside him the Observer sat staring out at the sea that had nearly claimed them.

'Right, now listen here.' It was Jim's voice quiet and deliberate. 'Tony thought he had the wire and we all now know that he didn't. He is taking her round again and we will be having coffee in the briefing room in about ten minutes. Sorry for the delay.'

Peter knew why the Lieutenant had to be given a second chance. He only wished he did not have to be around for the training session.

The aircraft completed its circuit and descended for the second attempt. Once again Peter was staring out ahead, only this time, he was trying to land the plane himself, using concentrated will power. The deck rose to meet the incoming aircraft and Peter assumed the brace position long before impact. Looking straight ahead he tried to think of something besides the imminent encounter of metal upon metal.

The edge of the deck appeared out of the corner of his eye and he tensed, waiting for the moment when the wheels would touch and the trailing hook would grasp the life saving wire. The world stood still, suspended above a narrow platform on a rolling sea.

A body jarring jolt announced their arrival. They

swung from side to side as the aircraft fought for stability after its full power landing. The engines roared and Peter sat waiting for the headlong rush to come to an equally violent halt. He sat rigid, his body forced backwards by the high speed of the advance.

'Come on, come on.' He repeated to himself under his inhaled breath.

It could not have been more than a few seconds from the time the undercarriage struck the deck to when the arrestor wire was engaged, but, it felt like an eternity. The aircraft stopped suddenly pitching all those inside forward in their harnesses. Peter stared out of the window and fleetingly wondered how Tony had missed the wire the first time. Such thoughts were soon replaced by the relief at being back on board. The bridge island passed by the starboard window as the Tracker taxied along the deck and turned into its parking spot. Once again Peter was pitched forward as the brakes were applied. The engine noise died away and Jim spoke into the headphones.

'Well we're home. How did you like it Peter?'

Peter's reply was already on his lips.

'Whatever they are paying you, it is not enough.'

'That's what we've been saying all along.' Jim responded and continued. 'Come on let's stretch our legs.'

Peter unbuckled his harness and moved to the exit door. He ducked his head as he went through and stepped down onto the flight deck. The fresh salt air felt good and to move cramped limbs was wonderful. Peter bent down and touched his toes. It was then he noticed a crowd gathering around the aircraft's nose wheel. Standing up sharply his gaze focused on a stream of liquid running down from the undercarriage and onto the flight deck. The Observer walked passed and Peter put out his arm to stop him.

'What is that?' He asked, pointing to the now glistening pool on the deck.

'Hydraulic fluid, sir.' The Observer answered soberly. 'If we hadn't got down that time, we wouldn't have got down at all. On the deck that is.' He raised his eyebrows. Peter thanked him for his explanation.

'Perfect end to a perfect day.' He said to himself and smiled.

'What's so funny?' Peter looked to see Jim coming out of the island hatch. Peter pointed to the nose wheel.

'Do you have any more surprises?'

'All in a day's work for a steely eyed Navy pilot.' He joked, and went on to explain the problem that could have cost them a lot more than the aircraft.

'I think I'll stick to navigation.' Peter replied, and nodded his head.

Sydney Heads rose from the sea like craggy sentinels. An orange ribbon of morning haze hung low over the coast line. Sovereign wheeled over, rolling in the long swell, while astern the frigates followed in the carrier's wake. Two days earlier Salisbury, in company with RFA Provider, was detached from the squadron to proceed to Melbourne for an eight day courtesy visit. It was a time to relax after an exacting period at sea. However, on the flagship's bridge the Navigating Officer was not looking forward to a week of idleness.

South Head passed astern and Peter gave the helm order that brought the lumbering bulk of the aircraft carrier around onto a new course and into the protection of one of the world's most beautiful harbours.

A passenger ferry, painted green and white passed close alongside, its decks crowded with people eager to get a close look at the visiting warships. Directly ahead, a speed boat cut under the carrier's bows.

'Bloody fool!' Harlow growled, his face bearing the strain of the days and nights at sea.

As Sovereign rounded Bradley's Head the Sydney Harbour Bridge came into view, dominating the western end of the waterway.

'Magnificent.' The Captain muttered and turned to Peter. 'It seems an age since we discussed coming here, ay pilot? To think, if the old Pegasus had not burst a boiler we would now be shivering somewhere off the coast of Norway.'

'Do you think we should send them a postcard sir?' Peter suggested with a broad smile on his face and the Captain laughed heartily at the idea.

The exclusive houses, apartments and yacht moorings of Sydney's fashionable harbour suburbs glided passed on the port side as Sovereign neared the naval base at Garden Island. The Captain took the ship and Peter stood back to monitor the commands and ensure they were carried out quickly and correctly.

From the Naval Headquarters, situated on a hill overlooking the dockyard, the shrill sound of a Bosun's call was heard. The ship's company was brought to attention and the courtesy returned. The tending naval tugs secured alongside and, in consort with the carrier's main engines, brought the great ship to rest by the wharf.

As in Perth, the Admiral was the first to leave the ship and Peter wondered how he managed to get from his bridge to the brow in such quick time. He watched as a pale blue car whisked the senior officer away. He then turned to leave the bridge.

While walking to the wardroom Peter considered his itinerary for the week long stay in Sydney.

'First, a good night's sleep, starting tonight.' He said to himself. He would avoid the ship's cocktail party at all cost. A quiet meal ashore and an early night was the extent of his plans; but first, a cup of coffee and then off to Fleet Headquarters for a meeting with the Operations Officer.

The black coffee and comfortable winged chair provided the first hint of relaxation Peter had felt for three long weeks. He sat back and stared at his surroundings without his mind taking anything in. It was only on hearing his name for a second time that he realised the steward was standing beside him.

'Excuse me sir. The Admiral would like to see you in his cabin.'

'What now?' Peter answered incredulously. He had just watched him go ashore. The sailor nodded his head.

'Yes sir, right away.'

'Very well. Thank you.' Peter drained his coffee cup and placed it back on its saucer. 'No rest for the wicked,' he thought as he hauled his body out of the arm chair.

Taking his cap from the peg outside the wardroom

he walked briskly to the Admiral's cabin. With his cap under his left arm he knocked twice on the imposing teak door.

'Come in.' The command was short and sharp.

Peter turned the brass door knob and entered the rarefied atmosphere of the Flotilla Commander's inner sanctum. Rear-Admiral Harrison was standing behind a large pedestal desk, his hands resting on the back of a green leather chair. He moved around to the front of the desk and greeted Peter with an outstretched hand.

'Hello Peter, glad they found you.'

They shook hands and Peter looked into the Admiral's eyes. As soon as he walked into the cabin he sensed something was not quite right. Now, he could see in the older man's expression an uncertainty that was out of character. Peter shifted his weight from one foot to the other and glanced about the large cabin. He saw her sitting in the chair, partially hidden by the alcove that led to the Admiral's sleeping quarters; but, his mind tried to deny what his eyes were telling him.

'Hello Peter.'

'Susanne is down here staying with friends.' The Admiral interjected into the awkward situation. He could not know what was going through his Navigator's mind and Peter did not want him to.

'It's lovely to see you again Susanne, and looking so well.' Peter found his voice.

'You are looking good too, Peter.' She replied with a smile on her full red lips.

'I know you two have a lot to talk about, but, it is going to have to wait.' The father broke in again. 'You have an appointment with Fleet Headquarters Peter and I have to get Susanne to the hairdressers. You will have tonight to catch up on old times.'

'Oh Daddy!' Complained Susanne.

'Don't you 'Oh Daddy' me young lady.' The Admiral countered. 'I told you we would not be here long. Peter is a busy man.'

'I know.' She answered and shot a meaningful glance at the Navigator. He immediately felt guilty about the letters he had not written and Susanne had drawn first blood.

'Be here at 1900 Peter, I am having drinks for the Department Heads before the cocktail party gets underway.' The invitation was delivered as a directive and Peter felt the trap close around him.

'Yes sir, I look forward to it.' He lied and looked at Susanne. 'I will see you tonight then?'

She nodded and stood up. Walking across the room she took Peter's hand.

'It is good to see you again.' She said, and Peter could feel the tenderness in her touch. He squeezed her hand and replied.

'You too.'

The Admiral broke up the reunion.

'You don't want to be late, Peter.'

'No sir.' He answered and looked at Susanne. 'See you tonight.' He walked to the door, opened it and left without looking back. Once in the passageway he headed for the upper deck. 'What next?' He asked himself.

Out in the air the sun made him blink his eyes until they grew accustomed to its bright light.

'She didn't look bad.' He thought, recalling the trim figure sitting crossed legged in the arm chair. He had to admit that he was still interested.

'So much for an early night.' He said to himself.

Peter could hear the sound of raised voices as he turned the corner that led to the Admiral's cabin. He found himself contemplating the property of alcohol that caused those drinking it to assume that all others about them were going deaf.

He was late, but, not hurrying. The afternoon had provided a useful period for reflection and planning. He had come to the conclusion that nothing had changed. Susanne had to be handled gently. She could still help him, and she could certainly hurt him. He was determined it should not be the latter.

The Royal Marine sentry opened the door and Peter entered the smoke filled cabin. He looked at the scuttles. They were open but the still night air was not helping the ventilation.

'Ah, Peter. Good to see you. Gin and tonic, isn't it?' Rear-Admiral Harrison greeted him warmly and signaled to the steward. He gave the sailor the order and returned his attention to the Navigator. 'A profitable visit to Operations, I hope?'

Peter recounted his visit to the Naval Headquarters until his drink arrived. The interruption afforded him the opportunity to look away and scan the crowd. He noticed the Captain having an animated conversation with a very fashionable lady bedecked with opulent jewels and an ample bosom. 'They look too at ease to have just met.'

Peter thought and his eyes moved on. There were other civilians intermingled with the senior ship's officers, but, no sign of Susanne. 'Where could she be?' He wondered. He had arrived late to ensure that she would have been there before him. The Admiral was speaking again and Peter gave up the search. They were joined by the Supply Officer and shortly after the Executive Officer swelled their group. Peter sipped his drink and feigned interest in their conversation while he reviewed his own plans for the evening.

The meeting between himself and Susanne had taken on the guise of a contest. In the Admiral's cabin that afternoon she had taken the opening point and now, by her lateness, she had won another. Peter was now desperately looking for points. The highly polished teak door then swung open and in she came. It was a superb entrance. The room fell silent as all heads turned to look at the late arrival.

'Stunning.' Peter stared over the Admiral's shoulder and admired the vision that stood before them. The white evening dress took the form of her slender body and accentuated the brown silkiness of her skin. Her hair was pinned back, highlighting her high cheekbones and the fullness of her lips. The whole party remained transfixed, until the Admiral broke the silence.

'You are here at last my dear.' He scoffed and took her hand. She walked further into the room, her eyes glancing about her until they found their target.

'What is he standing back there for?' She asked herself. Almost without realising it Peter had moved himself back into the crowd. She looked into his eyes and noticed the hesitation. 'She had not had a chance to really get to know him; but, was this really the dynamic man that her father talked about so often?' She wondered. 'Come over here!' Her eyes tried to convey the command and just as she thought he was making a move her hand was taken by the Captain and the moment was lost.

Peter felt rooted to the spot. He was quite relieved to see the 'old man' move in, but, at the same time felt cheated.

After sharing a few pleasantries with the Captain, Susanne circulated around the room with Peter following her progress, unable to take his eyes from her. 'Damn it!' He thought, 'I must see her.' Maneuvering himself out of the group he positioned himself so that Susanne would pass him when next she moved. His change of station did not go unnoticed. Susanne skillfully ended the conversation she was having with the Engineer Officer and a civilian guest and turned to face the man she had come to see.

'Good evening, Peter. I did not realise Daddy had invited so many guests.'

Peter returned the greeting and, looking around, agreed that there were indeed a lot of people present. Even more ineptly he told her what had been on his mind ever since she entered the room.

'You look lovely this evening.' The words exploded from his lips.

'Only this evening?' She teased, enjoying watching him wrestle with his discomfort, but also sensitive to his pride. 'Thank you, Peter. Actually I feel pretty jaded after that long air journey.'

Well, you hide it well. May I get you another drink?'

Peter felt happier now the conversation was underway. Susanne looked down at her empty glass.

'I don't think I will have another one here. We still have a cocktail party to go to.' Like Peter, she was happy they were talking and did not want to have him disappear now. 'Are you enjoying Australia?' She asked. Peter felt uncomfortable but answered without delay,

'What I have seen of it.' His mind's eye flashed back to the night on the beach in Perth. He still found it hard to believe it had happened. Susanne continued with the sign of a little edginess in her tone.

'You did not say much in your letters. I wondered what you did for relaxation.'

Peter recalled this forthright manner on their first meeting. It was not a part of her character he appreciated. He replied impassively,

'Not much to tell really. Actually we have not had a lot of shore time since leaving home. It has been a busy trip.'

'So my father has said. My mother doesn't believe him either. You men always stick together.' Before Peter could reply to the subtle accusation the Admiral broke into the conversation.

'Sorry to interrupt, but, we must be getting along to the cocktail party. Peter, you will escort Susanne won't you? There's a good man…'

So ordering, he left them slightly embarrassed at being so blatantly thrown together.

Peter had come to know Susanne's father and discreetly looked about him to see why the Admiral had been so keen to delegate the escorting of his daughter.

The reason was not hard to find, and it was going to upset Sovereign's Captain who had been outranked as the Admiral took his lady's arm and escorted her, her jewels and her bosom out of the cabin.

'Shall we go?' Peter asked and made a flourish with his right hand in the direction of the open door.

On their way to the party Peter asked Susanne about her trip and, as he remembered, she was only too willing to talk. As they neared the ladder that led to the wardroom, he had to interrupt for fear she might ignore the hole in the deck and take all the steps in one stride.

'Thank you. I did see it.' She pointedly replied.

'Things are not going too well,' he thought. Susanne was on edge and he did not know what to do about it.

The sound from the wardroom indicated that a number of guests had already arrived.

'We'll have to stop meeting like this.' Peter quipped as they entered the scene of their first encounter.

Susanne smiled but did not reply. Peter raised his eyebrows and was relieved to catch the eye of a passing steward. He turned his attention to ordering the drinks and when he looked back found Susanne in conversation with Commander Air.

'Peter, I have been invited to meet some of the aircrew boys, will you come along?' Susanne asked. The Commander was quick to interject.

'We can't have a 'fishhead' crossing the picket line, ay Peter? Besides, being around too many general list officers makes them nervous. They've only just got used to me.'

'You go ahead,' Peter answered, 'I'll wait for the drinks.' He winked at the pilot. 'Don't leave her alone with them, you know how they get when exposed to too much female company.'

'Sounds fun.' Susanne giggled. 'Lead on.' She gave Peter's hand a squeeze and walked off into the crowd. The drinks arrived and Peter sat down at a small table.

'Good evening, Peter.'

The female voice startled him, but he recognised it instantly. He looked up and into the sensual face of Jennifer Hale. The vision had an immediate effect on his body and mind. The blood began to pound in his veins and his heart beat faster.

'Jennifer, what are you doing here? I thought you were only staying in Sydney for a few days.' He stood up and made a move to shake her hand but she moved to one side and kissed him gently on the cheek.

'What sort of greeting is that?' She pouted.

'It was such a surprise.' He explained weakly.

'I thought Jim told you that I was staying on over here. I was hoping you would look me up.'

'Yes of course.' Peter lied not wanting to get into long explanations and excuses even though the Australian pilot had said nothing about his sister's movements. By this time Peter knew he was in trouble and was looking around for avenues of escape.

'Where is Jim?' He asked, hoping that her brother would be the one to get him out of the dangerous predicament into which he was heading.

'He's around here somewhere.' She answered disinterestedly and then asked. 'Now what have you been up to since I last saw you?' Her eyes appeared to sparkle and the corners of her mouth turned up in a mischievous grin. 'Have you got the sand out of your shoes yet?' Peter could not stop himself from smiling.

'It really does get everywhere, doesn't it?' He joked, suddenly finding himself enjoying this encounter.

'What does?'

'Oh no!' Peter closed his eyes. What he feared most had happened and by the tone of the question he knew the situation was already critical. He turned to Susanne and stepped back to allow her into the conversation. It came as a further shock to see that she was accompanied by Lieutenant James. The young pilot spoke up.

'Good evening, sir. I return Miss Harrison to you, much admired but otherwise intact.' He smiled at Susanne and she too looked as if she had enjoyed herself.

'Cheeky bugger.' Peter swore to himself, but also realised he had been given breathing space on Susanne's question. He thanked the Lieutenant and returned his attention to the two ladies. 'It is either a feast or a famine' he thought as he made the introductions and hoped the previous subject would be dropped.

'We were just talking about sand.' Jennifer breezily spoke up. Peter went cold. He stole a glance at Susanne. She looked puzzled and he prayed she would not delve any further.

'Any sand in particular?'

'That's done it.' He told himself as he watched the battle lines being drawn. For the first time he really noticed the difference in accents and this seemed to heighten the tension. It was becoming an international issue and he felt dangerously exposed. Jennifer fuelled the flames.

'If Peter has not told you I am sure there must be a reason. Perhaps we should change the subject.'

Peter prayed for the deck to open and swallow him, but, knowing that such a merciful release would not be forthcoming he had to say something. Realising that it was Jennifer who was the danger he addressed his opening words to her.

'Actually, Susanne and I have not had a lot of time for talking.' He went on to explain the circumstances of their meeting earlier in the day, but avoided any mention of their previous relationship. In his mind there was nothing further to explain. The Australian girl turned to Susanne,

'You must get him to tell you about it when you have more time.' She smiled and looked at Peter. 'I must go. Give me a call if there is anything I can do for you.' Leaning forward she kissed him on the cheek. 'Bye.' She purred and waved with her finger tips.

Peter breathed a little easier as she walked away, at least now he had only one to deal with.

'Who was that?' The question came like the thrust of a knife and before he had time to answer Susanne was again on the attack. 'You could have spoken up for me a lot stronger than you did. You made me sound like a casual acquaintance. How dare she!' In her indignation she did not know who had annoyed her the most and who to attack. Her eyes flamed with rage.

Peter was confused and uncertain. He too did not know whether it was he or Jennifer who was the major source of Susanne's anger and he did not have to wait long to find out.

'I can see now why you were too busy to answer my letters. Oh Peter, you must think me such a fool.' The last words were said with a sadness tinged with a newly realised determination. 'As you seem to get on so well on your own I will leave you to it!' She stormed off leaving Peter open mouthed and without a chance to offer either a defence or protest.

'Well I'll be damned.' He said to himself and looked around to see if anyone had witnessed the scene.

'She has a mind of her own and a temper like her mother's.'

'Oh no!' Peter thought as he heard the voice and saw his world crumble before his eyes. His stomach tightened as he turned to face the Admiral.

'Let her go and cool off. She's tired. I don't think she's recovered from her long journey yet.' The father's voice was sympathetic.

'Yes sir.' Was all Peter could find to say as he wondered what the next move was going to be. The Admiral spoke again.

'I don't know what it was that you two were discussing, but it looked pretty lively.'

'He is now fishing,' thought Peter and resolved to disclose as little as possible.

'A silly misunderstanding, sir.' He answered and the Admiral appeared to accept the reply.

'She is just a girl really. She thinks she knows it all, but, we who have been around the block know otherwise, ay Peter? Don't let it spoil your evening. It will all be different in the morning.' Peter had to bite his tongue to stop himself saying, 'Yes sir,' once again. Instead he nodded his head in acknowledgement. That appeared to be enough as the Admiral smilingly took his leave and returned to his group. Peter also had to smile as he watched the fulsome lady take his arm and welcome him back with eyes that sparkled like the emeralds about her neck.

Peter drained his glass. He had a lot to think about and this was not the place. Moving through the mass of bodies he was stopped by the strong arm of Steven Marks.

'Going already?' Peter had hoped to make a clean escape.

'Yes, I have done my duty.'

The pilot appeared agitated and replied quickly.

'Jennifer Hale is here. She is looking for you.'

Peter looked away not wanting to have this conversation. Looking back he said soberly,

'I know. She found me.'

'Well?' Marks kept digging.

'Well what?' Peter answered with irritation in his voice. 'There is no 'well' there never has been.' He hoped that a show of annoyance would curb any further questions. As he spoke, something over Marks' shoulder caught his eye. He was staring so hard that even the pilot turned to look.

'You don't have to worry about her anymore.' Marks commented when he realised who Peter was looking at. 'She is having a good time.' Peter was speechless with disbelief and injured pride. 'How could she?' He thought, 'not James!' Susanne was laughing and clearly enjoying the young man's company. At that moment Peter wanted her, and seethed with irritation. 'How dare she make a fool of him. It was he she had come all this way to see. He knew it was.'

'Are you okay, Peter?' Marks became concerned by the stern silence and the look of anger on Peter's face; but fortunately, misinterpreted the Navigator's concern. 'James is really not that bad. A little headstrong and a bit flash, but, not stupid. At least not when it comes to Admiral's daughters.'

Peter was not really listening but realised he had to pull himself together. 'What the hell,' he reasoned, 'if that is what she wants.' He looked back at Marks.

'Well, you keep an eye on him. I've got to go.' Without giving Marks a chance to reply Peter moved on and out of the wardroom.

Once free he walked briskly to his cabin, changed into civilian clothes and made his way to the gangway. The Quartermaster put away his magazine and stood to attention when he saw Peter approaching. He saluted as the Navigator walked across the brow. The cool night air felt good after the stuffiness of the wardroom. Peter walked down the wooden steps and onto the dockside. He did not know where he was going and it did not seem to matter. As he walked images of the evening flashed before his eyes. He tried to analyze but ended up dismissing them as being of no consequence. It was an indifference he could not sustain.

At the main gate he showed his identity card to the dockyard policeman and walked through.

'Taxi mate?' The casual questioning voice brought

Peter out of himself. He looked down at the red and blue cab parked alongside the curb, opened the rear passenger door and was about to get in when the driver spoke again. 'What's wrong with the front seat?' Peter had forgotten the unwritten law of the Australian taxi driver.

'Oh, right.' He replied, closing one door and opening another.

'Yous must be a Pom.' The driver stated without fear of contradiction. 'Yous blokes always go for the back seat. Makes a fella think you don't want to sit next to him. Sort of like yous are better than us.' Peter was wondering if he really deserved this tirade when the driver laughed and added, 'of course we all know yous can't beat the Aussies.' He looked at his passenger. 'Don't worry about it mate, where d'ya wana go?'

Peter was caught out yet again. He had been so preoccupied with the evening's events and so taken aback by the driver's opening remarks that thoughts of a destination had not occurred to him. He looked at the driver and raised his hands in resignation.

'You tell me.' He said and continued. 'Where is a good place to go for a quiet drink?'

'Sheila's?' Was the driver's immediate reply.

'No. Just a quiet drink.' Peter answered firmly. He had had enough of 'sheilas'.

'To each his own.' The driver was not going to be outdone and having made his point relented and said; 'Okay, I know a bonza place.'

The key turned in the ignition and the car raced away from the curb, performed a sweeping left hand turn and headed up the hill towards Kings Cross. As they passed the flashing neon lights of Sydney's red light district the driver spoke again,

'If you change your mind, here's the place.'

Peter did not doubt it as he looked at hundreds of neon signs depicting scantily clad women and watched energetic barkers practically dragging passing males inside for a closer look.

At the centre of the Cross the taxi turned left and headed down the New South Head Road towards the wealthy suburbs on the harbour's southern shore. Peter looked out at the glistening reflection of the harbour lights in the gentle rolling blackness of the water, while the driver kept up a constant commentary as to where they were and what they would see next. Peter was thankful he was not expected to add anything to the conversation.

The cab drove for another few minutes before turning off the main road and into a small car park.

'Here yer go sport.' The driver cheerily announced. 'Yer might even strike lucky in there.' Were his parting words as he put the car in gear and headed back into the traffic.

Peter watched the taxi drive away and then turned to see where he had been dropped. It looked to be a small restaurant and bar, very dimly lit with small table lamps flickering through shuttered windows. He walked inside feeling ill at ease.

'May I help you?' A young waitress appeared from nowhere.

'Where is the bar, please?'

'This way sir.'

Walking behind the girl he could not help admiring her trim figure corseted in a black pencil line skirt. 'Perhaps he hadn't had enough of sheilas', he thought. They passed by the restaurant and out onto an enclosed verandah that overlooked the water. Peter was shown to a table and his order taken. He sat quietly looking around him until the gin and tonic arrived. He took a long drink and sat back in the wooden captain's chair.

'What a day.' He said aloud and noticed heads around him turn to watch the man who was talking to himself. After the second drink he was feeling better and more able to relax and appreciate his surroundings.

'It is a beautiful harbour.' He said, but, this time to himself. He looked out at the moored boats and distant shoreline. A ferry sailed passed, its decks ablaze with golden lights.

'Six more days', Peter mused and suddenly felt very lonely. The third drink arrived and he paid the bill. He had had enough and was not enjoying drinking alone. He asked the waitress to order him a taxi and sat back to finish his drink.

At that moment the peace of the evening was shattered by the sound of laughter and raised voices. Peter looked round but could not see who had just entered the restaurant. He smiled thinking it good to hear someone enjoying themselves.

The waitress returned to say that his taxi had arrived. He rose from the table and walked towards the exit. Passing the restaurant he looked to see who was making all the noise.

A raucous group sat around a large table with one

man sitting unsteadily in a chair facing six frothing glasses of beer.

'Rather him than me,' Peter thought and then, as he stared, felt himself go cold. He stood rooted to the spot and stared at the shaded profile of a young woman sitting beside the slouching guest of honour.

'It can't be.' He said so loud that the waitress asked if he was talking to her. He mumbled an apology and she returned a quizzical look before going back to her work. Peter remained transfixed, his heart pounding in his chest.

'Excuse me,' it was the waitress again, 'your taxi is outside.' Peter took hold of his tangled emotions and thanked her. At that moment he was torn between confronting the apparition and leaving before he too was seen. He chose the latter. He turned and left the restaurant. The night air felt cold and he began to shiver. The taxi's door was open and Peter got in the front passenger seat.

'Where to, mate?'

'Garden Island.' It was all Peter could do to answer. The car drove away with Peter in a trance, desperately trying to recapture the image in his mind's eye. It had been dark and only a profile, but, it was her. He was sure of it. 'Why didn't he go and make sure?' He berated his own uncertainty.

The driver sensed his passenger's mood and left him to his thoughts until the cab pulled to a halt outside the dockyard gates.

'That'll be three dollars and thirty cents, mate.'

Peter looked round in surprise at where they were. The journey had passed without him noticing the miles or the landmarks. He paid the fare and bid the driver good night.

Walking through the silent dockyard he studied the ships that were secured alongside, but, no matter how hard he tried to concentrate on their lines the question kept returning.

'Was it her?' He said aloud and repeated the question.

The stone walled buildings echoed his footsteps and at that moment he could have been the only person on earth. 'This is where I belong,' he thought; but, visions of the past played in his mind and robbed him of his certainty. He thought of Angela, and his son and then Carol. He thought of her most of all.

'It couldn't have been. The light playing tricks. That's all.' He told himself.

Rounding the last of the dockyard buildings the imposing form of Sovereign loomed out of the night. Orange light from the row of tall wharf lamps cast an eerie glow over the sleeping giant.

Peter walked up the gangway and gripped the rails firmly in his hands.

'Let's get back to sea.' He said to himself. He looked up at the bridge, to the only place where he truly felt secure.

Chapter 11

Carol stirred, awakened by a sense of loneliness. She reached over and felt the rumpled sheet. Like a frightened child she sat up, panic biting at her. She looked at the clock on the bedside table. It was only 4am. 'Where was he?' She heard the sound of water running in the bathroom. 'What's going on?' She tried to clear her head; then, as Phil came out of the bathroom it all fell into place. He looked strong and imposing in the starched khaki uniform. His boots shone like onyx. Framed by the door he appeared taller.

'I didn't mean to wake you.' He said softly as he walked to the side of the bed and sat down.

'I forgot you had to leave so soon.' She replied, nuzzling into his chest and putting her arms around his belted waist. He bent down and tenderly kissed the top of her head.

'It has been a lovely weekend.' He murmured into her tousled hair. Carol tightened her grip and hugged his hard body to her.

'I don't want you to go.' She said, her voice muffled

by his shirt. Carol dreaded the return to the loneliness of the past weeks. She felt secure and happy in his company, although she knew, from the moment their lovemaking finished on his first night home, she would lose him again. Behind the joy of the past two days was the knowledge that no matter how close they became, on Monday morning he would be gone.

Phil's attempts to ease her anxiety served only to aggravate the situation. He promised to telephone whenever he could.

'Anyway.' He said. 'I will be home on the weekend after next.' Carol reacted sharply, giving vent to her disappointment.

'It's okay for you. You will be running around the bush playing soldiers. What am I going to do?'

Carol regretted the outburst. Phil was shortly to be gone and this was not how she wanted to be remembered. 'Oh Phil I'm sorry.' Tears came to her eyes. 'I get so lonely when you are not here.' Her body trembled as she fought to stem the flow.

'I know, I know.' He tried to comfort her, not really knowing at all and thankful when Carol gradually calmed down. He wiped the tears from her cheeks.

'I must look awful.' She said, and forced herself to smile. Phil gently brushed his lips against her ear.

'You are beautiful and I love you.' He whispered.

At the sound of these words Carol went tense and, almost against her will, her guard went up. She could not reply, the words would not come. She just did not know. Instead, she turned to her lover and laying back on the bed drew him to her. They kissed longingly, desire flooding back into their bodies. It was Phil who pulled away first.

'I really must be going.'

'I know.' Carol whispered back and kissed him playfully. 'You have sexy lips.'

They both smiled and this was the signal for them to part. Phil walked over to his suitcase and fastened the catches. The metallic clicks as they came together sounded very final in the quiet of the morning.

'Have you had breakfast?' Carol felt she had to say something to break the threatening silence.

'I've had coffee.' He replied, lifting the case onto the floor.

'I thought an army marched on its stomach.' Carol retorted and Phil returned to cradle her face in his hands.

'If I had time for breakfast, I would have had time for you.' He kissed her and added, 'I should have put the alarm on earlier.' Carol was quick to reply

'No, we should have gone on all night.' They laughed and kissed again. This time it was Carol who broke away.

'I thought you said you had to go.'

'You're right.' Phil said resignedly.

Carol got out of bed, picked up her dressing gown from the floor, where it had fallen the night before, and walked through into the lounge room. Phil followed, carrying his suitcase in one hand and large brimmed slouch hat in the other. Carol opened the front door. It was still dark outside and the morning air caused her to draw the night gown more tightly about her body. Phil passed by, pushing the wire screen door open with the edge of his case.

'I'll be right back.' He said as he walked across the verandah and down the wooden steps to the path. He placed the case in the boot of the car and ran back to the house. He took Carol's hands in his own and looked into her eyes.

'It is good to know that I have you to come home to.' He said and kissed her tenderly on the lips. The embrace grew more intense as their bodies drew together and they held each other, not wanting to part. 'Carol, I do love you.' He said as he hugged her to his chest. She tightened her embrace but did not answer. A shiver ran down her spine. 'You better go inside or you'll catch a chill.' Phil said as he felt Carol's body shake in his arms. They parted and Carol wrapped her dressing gown around her once again. 'I'll ring tonight.' Phil said as he walked off the verandah, and then added, 'make sure you're in, or I'll get suspicious.'

Carol smiled and blew him a kiss.

'Just make sure you call, or I'll be furious.' She replied.

Phil opened the car door and slid his long frame behind the steering wheel. The engine spluttered to life in the still morning air. Carol heard the gears engage and watched the wheels begin to move. Phil waved once more, put his foot on the accelerator pedal and pulled away from the curb without taking his eyes from Carol. She blew him another kiss and smiled as she thought it lucky there were no other cars on the road. She watched until the rust streaked rear of the old car reached the end of the road and turned out of sight around the corner.

'Alone again.' She said to the empty street and the sleeping houses. 'What am I doing here?' The question rattled around in her mind as she walked back into the brightly lit lounge room. Looking around at the worn out sofa, the age stained wall paper with its curling corners and gaping seams, she began to laugh.

'It's mine, all mine.' She laughed, raising her arms above her head and opening out her hands as if accepting a tribute of all that surrounded her.

Gradually she lowered her arms and came to realise that here indeed was a home of her own. She went to the kitchen and switched on the kettle. As it boiled she looked about her. The white painted ceiling was yellowing and the walls showed numerous signs of overactive chip pans. The cupboard doors closed with varying degrees of success and those that refused hung at drunken angles from their hinges.

The kettle steamed its signal of completion and coated the adjacent walls with rivulets of condensation. At first Carol was unaware the water was boiling away. While her eyes were inspecting the house her thoughts were wrestling with her conscience. 'While Phil was away this house was hers.' As hard as she tried to bury it beneath feelings of warmth and gratitude, this knowledge kept percolating to the surface of her consciousness. 'She was free at last.'

'Shit, the kettle!' She cried, reaching to remove the plug from its socket and almost scalding her arm in the process. By this time the walls were running with water and the corner of the kitchen, where the kettle stood, looked like a railway yard in the grand old age of steam.

'Thank God for that.' Carol said as she peered into the scalding bowels of the kettle and saw there was enough water remaining for one cup of coffee.

A street light twinkled through the kitchen window and the darkness was giving way to the golden redness of another day. A gusting wind had risen with the dawn and dared anyone to venture out on this autumn morning. Carol picked up her cup and walked to the bedroom. She snuggled down into the sheets, sipped her coffee and considered where she would go from here.

The weeks of Phil's training did not pass as swiftly as Carol had imagined. He came home on three weekends during the six weeks and telephoned regularly. The life of a soldier agreed with him. On each homecoming Carol saw him grow in confidence and felt him gain in strength. She found herself living for these weekends, longing for the companionship. The days in between blended into an indistinguishable morass of routine and boredom. On more than one occasion she told herself that she might just have well stayed in Portsmouth,

'At least it was spring at home.' She would argue to herself.

Towards the end of the six weeks Carol had an idea that kept her occupied for those last and longest days of all. The thought of spending those days with only the turning of a calendar to mark their passing could not be endured without something to look forward to.

'You've got something to look forward to darlin'.' Pat, the manager of the wine bar where she worked, took pleasure in teasing her about her love life. He got a bit close to the mark sometimes, but, Carol enjoyed the banter. She felt accepted and was happy in her new life.

'I have dreamed of that so many times I thought I would go blind.' Phil sighed, rolling onto his pillow, a feeling of relief and contentment washing over his body. He turned and cupping Carol's breasts in his hands kissed the soft flesh, brushing his lips from one to the other. 'You are gorgeous.' He whispered and transferred his lips to her waiting mouth. Carol caressed his face with her finger tips.

'You're not so bad yourself,' she smiled tenderly and then added, 'but, we do have a party to go to.'

'Spoil sport.' He answered.

On arriving home earlier that afternoon Phil had been told of the evening planned for him. The evening that Carol had been planning for the last two weeks. He was not convinced that it was a good idea. He had his own plans for his first night but Carol was so excited that he could not disappoint her. He consoled himself with the thought that it would only be for a few hours and right now they still had an hour before they should start getting ready. Circling his arms about Carol's body he drew her to him and kissed her open lips. Her legs entwined with his and he felt her draw him to her. Locked in the embrace he tingled as her hand moved down his body and guided him into her. He gasped with ecstasy and Carol increased the pressure in her thighs.

'I'm going to rape you.' She declared softly, her voice heavy with desire.

'Make way for the hero!' The call echoed through the quiet restaurant as the door was flung open. There was the sound of a mock bugle call and the group stood to attention while Phil entered in front of them. Inside the restaurant all heads turned towards the sound.

'Keep the noise down guys.' Phil pleaded, embarrassed at being the centre of attention.

A waitress approached and ushered them to a secluded corner in the dark restaurant.

'Can't see a bloody thing.' A voice called out of the gloom.

'Cut it out Pat, you'll get us thrown out.' Scolded Carol. 'This is Phil's evening.'

'I think ol' Phil is more interested in the night, ay mate?'

'What's the use?' Carol conceded and sat down.

Drinks were ordered and when they arrived Carol stood up again to propose a toast. Before she could say what was in her heart Pat spoke up.

'You Poms are really hooked on ceremony.' Carol was quick to reply with a newly acquired local expression.

'Up your nose with panty hose, Pat.'

'That's a bloody good toast. I'll drink to that.' He raised his glass and downed the schooner of beer in one draught. The rest of the party dissolved in fits of laughter. Pat turned to the waitress. 'Six beers here, love!' He pointed wildly in the direction of Phil.

'What are you doing Pat?' Carol had stopped laughing and was now a little concerned.

'I'm buying a beer for my mate. One each from all of us. You can make six more toasts.' The group once again started to laugh. Phil slumped in his seat as the six schooners of lager were placed on the table in front of him.

'I give up.' Carol sighed and then reached into her purse to remove a small, neatly wrapped parcel. She kissed Phil on the cheek and asked him to hold out his hand.

'What's this?' He asked, staring at the package that lay in his palm.

'Just something to take with you .. to remember me by.' Her voice betrayed a sadness that suddenly engulfed her. Phil gave her a kiss while the rest of the table cheered and the moment passed.

'Good on ya mate.' They raised their glasses and all drank to the soldier.

'Rather you than me.' Pat declared and Phil was quick to respond.

'Don't be so sure Pat, old pal. They may raise the conscription age and your birthday will come out of the ballot. I'll see you up there.'

'Thanks, you're a real mate, but, I'll wait and see you when you get back if you don't mind.'

The table fell suddenly silent as each thought of the war that was being fought by Australian soldiers and claiming Australian lives. Carol broke the sombre spell.

'Come on Phil, open your present.' She ordered, digging him in the ribs.

His hands went to the parcel and Carol looked around. She felt someone over her shoulder and it made her uncomfortable. Phil noticed her unease.

'What's wrong, babe?' He asked.

'Nothing.' Carol shook her head. 'Someone just walked on my grave that's all.' She immediately regretted her choice of words as the table fell silent once again.

Phil made a big show of unwrapping his present and the buzz of conversation returned to the table. Carol cautiously turned and looked over her right shoulder. A shadowed figure stood in the doorway. She stared, trying to focus on the darkened face, knowing it wasn't a stranger. Behind the figure a door opened and for an instant light fell upon him.

'Peter!' Carol rose out of her seat but the figure was gone. She ran to where he had been standing and looked around. The door to the restaurant kitchen opened again and she blinked her eyes in the bright light. As it closed she was plunged into an even greater darkness. She moved towards the front door, pulled it open and ran outside. She wrapped her arms about her and let the heavy door slam shut. At the roadside the red tail lights of a taxi were moving away. As it turned into the traffic Carol strained to see the figure in the passenger seat, but he was obscured by the driver and the car was soon out of sight.

'Carol what's wrong?' Phil was standing in the doorway, his face lined with concern. 'What are you doing out here?' Carol stood staring at the spot where the taxi had been and then turned to him.

'I thought I saw a ghost.' She cried and huddled into his chest. He cradled her in his arms and led her back inside. As they neared the table, conversation stopped. The silence emphasised the discomfort everyone was feeling. Once again it was left to Phil to restore the facade of normality.

'Carol thought she saw someone she knew, but, it wasn't. Now, what about this present? I hope one of you ratbags hasn't opened it while I was away.'

They all smiled with relief and gratitude. Carol gave his hand a squeeze. Phil then set about unwrapping the present.

'Don't forget the card.' One of the girls in the party exclaimed as Phil ripped the paper from the small container. He stopped and searched through the crumpled debris. He found the card and held it up.

'What does it say?' The same voice enquired. Phil read the words to himself, looked at Carol and kissed her.

'Come on. Let's have a look!' The voice became more insistent.

'It's private.' Phil answered quietly and put the card into the inside pocket of his jacket. The table erupted in a crescendo of jeers and calls of, 'spoil sport,' while Phil continued opening the present.

The last pieces of wrapping paper were removed exposing a small black velvet box. Phil lifted the lid,

'It's beautiful.' His voice was tender with emotion. 'Thank you Carol, you're beautiful.' He placed his arm around her shoulder and drew her to him. They kissed amid renewed cheers from around the table.

'Let us see it then.' Pat's loud voice drowned out the rest. Phil took the gold fountain pen from the case and held it up. Once again everyone at the table erupted in cheers and whistles.

Carol heard none of them. Her world had been turned upside down and her mind was full of images.

His face, voice, body, touch. She knew it was him. There was no doubt in her mind; but, what was he doing there? Why had he just stood there and why did he disappear? These questions would give her no rest and the evening that was meant for Phil passed without him again entering her thoughts.

On the drive home Phil fought to control his anxiety. He had watched the change come over Carol and had spent the evening trying to stop the others noticing. Jealousy was stirring within him and he knew that if he did not discover the identity of the shadowed figure then anger would be his next emotion. Already his stomach was tightening at the thought of Carol with another man.

'Who did you see, Carol?' The question shot from his lips like the bullet from a gun. He had wanted to be more subtle, to mask his feelings, but, he was under threat and it was worse not knowing who was stepping so menacingly into his life.

Carol was startled by the urgency of the question but too tired to give an explanation. All she wanted was to be left alone with her thoughts; to shelter within herself and not come out until she was certain she could not be hurt. She answered distractedly.

'Not now Phil, please.'

They continued their journey in silence until he could contain himself no longer.

'I want to know who you saw. I have a right to know.'

Carol's emotions exploded, detonated by his claim upon her.

'You have no such right! You don't own me. Nobody

owns me. Why don't you just leave me alone?' Carol sat back in her seat and glared straight ahead.

Phil gripped the steering wheel with his knuckles whitening under the pressure of the torment that raged within. He felt powerless, unable to influence what was happening around him.

'Don't shut me out.' He said, almost in a whisper. The tears started to run down Carol's face.

'Oh Phil. I don't want to.' She sobbed.

Phil said nothing, but, willed her to open up and say more.

Carol looked in her purse and took out a small, white, lace handkerchief. After drying her eyes she looked at the material now stained black with streaks of mascara.

'I must look a mess.' She said, trying to smile and regain her composure. Phil remained silent, but turned to smile at her. They were almost home and his hopes of getting an explanation were fading with every passing street lamp. He could not open the wounds again, it would have to be Carol's decision and she had receded once more into silence.

He parked the car and switched off the engine. The world was now silent. They sat for a short while and then Phil moved to open the door. He stopped as Carol's hand rested on his thigh. Looking into her eyes he saw an uncertainty he had never noticed before. She spoke as if it was her confession.

'The man I think I saw was the main reason for my coming to Australia.'

Phil's eyes widened and he caught his breath.

Questions welled in his throat, but, Carol continued, forcing him to almost choke on each unuttered syllable.

'We lived together for a short time, and I loved him.' She stared into Phil's face and saw a man who wanted to know but no longer wanted to listen. His eyes flickered with uncertainty and fear. 'I don't know what he is doing here. It probably wasn't him anyway. It couldn't have been.' She spoke the words but did not know who she was trying to convince. Phil listened and plucked up courage to speak.

'You said he was the reason for you coming to Australia, why?'

Carol kept her eyes upon him.

'Yes that's right. He was. When we finished I wanted to get away as far as possible and start again.'

Relief flowed through Phil's body. Carol had come to Australia to start a new life and that life included him.

'Carol, I love you.' He sighed and in the confined space of the car's front seat, placed his arms about her and hugged her to his chest. His strong arms made Carol feel secure and comforted, but, the images continued to play behind her eyes.

'Let's go inside.' She whispered and softly kissed his lips. Their bodies parted.

'I do love you.' Phil said so seriously that Carol felt herself tremble. She cradled his head in her hands and kissed him again.

'Come on.' She said, 'Let's go to bed.'

Next day, there was still tension generated by unanswered questions; however, fearing a return to the tears and recriminations of the previous evening Phil asked no more questions. 'Besides.' He reasoned, recalling the warmth and openness of her body. 'Last night she was mine.'

As if to reinforce his claim Phil suggested they have lunch with his parents. It was not Carol's idea of an exciting outing, but, was happy to go along with anything that kept him from thinking too deeply about what had happened. She now felt guilty about the words she spoke and the feelings she held inside. Whatever she did, Peter Wells was now within her. Looking in the mirror he stared back at her. She had lain in Phil's embrace and it was Peter who caressed her.

Once the dinner plates had been put away Carol went into the lounge room. The morning papers were draped over the coffee table. She picked one up and disinterestedly thumbed the pages.

'Coffee or tea?' The voice boomed from the kitchen.

'Coffee please.' Carol replied and went back to her browsing. Turning the pages she came to the society section and her heart stopped. The black, capital letters, of the headline leapt from the white background;

'FLEET RECEPTION ABOARD BRITISH CARRIER'

Carol sat mesmerized by the meaning locked in the words.

'It was him.' She whispered and scanned the pages of photographs. She then saw the name Sovereign, and the memory of a short and bitter conversation she had with Jane came into her mind.

In an attempt to reunite the couple her friend had told her of Peter's posting to the aircraft carrier. It was information Jane had received via her Royal Marine husband. She had hoped to use it to bring the couple back together. Carol soon quashed that idea and had told her friend to mind her own business. Carol smiled as she realised her friend was going to get her wish.

Carol went back to the beginning and examined each photograph in turn. Her disappointment grew when she did not see a picture of Peter. She then read each caption searching for his name. Feeling cheated she read the small article that explained about the visiting ships and hope was rekindled when she read that the Sovereign would be open for public inspection on Sunday 7th April.

'That's tomorrow!' She exclaimed.

'What about tomorrow, dear?' Mrs. Sewell was carrying a tray on which sat cups, saucers and a sugar bowl.

'Oh.' Carol replied shyly, embarrassed by her own enthusiasm. 'There are some British ships open to visitors tomorrow, I thought Philip might like to go along.' She always used his complete name when talking to his mother. Mrs. Sewell's answer came as a surprise.

'Not tomorrow dear, Philip has football training.' Carol could not believe what was being said.

'Football training?' She answered incredulously, 'what football training?'

The mother knew she had said the wrong thing and a pregnant silence followed. Carol glared in the direction of the kitchen, waiting for Phil to appear. Mrs. Sewell retreated and went to warn her son.

Phil entered the room and sheepishly grinned at Carol.

'Get in here.' She commanded through gritted teeth. Phil obeyed and walked towards her with his hands raised in resignation. He went to speak and was silenced by Carol's threatening tone. 'What is this about football training, and why tomorrow?'

Phil could understand her annoyance at him having made plans to go to football; but, could not figure the significance that tomorrow appeared to hold. He could not think of any prior arrangements they had made, and was not going to ask questions. A quick explanation followed by a lot of apologising looked to be the answer. He went on to tell of the inter service rugby competition that was to be held on the coming Wednesday and how he had been chosen to play for his battalion. He then apologised for not telling her earlier and explained that he was waiting for the right moment. The firm set of Carol's mouth told him that there may never have been a right moment.

'What about tomorrow? What am I supposed to do?' Carol's annoyance gave an edge to her voice.

Phil had not thought about it. He shrugged his shoulders and moved his mouth causing his lips to disappear. Carol then answered her own question.

'I'll tell you what I am going to do. I am going to look over this British ship.' She tapped the newspaper article for emphasis. 'I am going to surround myself with British men who know how to look after their women.'

By this time Philip's parents had entered the room and, out of the corner of her eye, Carol saw Mrs. Sewell raise her eyebrows to her husband

'Silly cow.' Carol thought and returned her attention to Phil, who was just getting ready to defend himself.

'They will be there on Wednesday.' He said weakly, but, it was enough to momentarily confuse Carol and upset her train of thought.

'Who will be there on Wednesday?' She asked.

'The RN'ers. It is a competition between our three services and the Poms. It should be a good day.' Phil's father turned away.

'He should not be sounding so enthusiastic,' he thought and was surprised when Carol remained silent. It remained quiet for some time before Carol spoke again. This time her tone was calm and conciliatory.

'All right, you go to your training and I will go to the ship. We can meet back at the house later in the afternoon.'

'I can collect you at the dockyard.' Phil suggested, eager to maintain her good humour.

'That won't be necessary. I'll be okay.' Carol nonchalantly replied.

The crowd jostled outside the dockyard gates. Carol had arrived early and was now having to fight to keep her place at the head of the queue. She was rolled one way and then another like a piece of flotsam in a human sea, and she hated it. Throughout her discomfort she thought of the times Peter had taken her aboard his ship. How grand she had felt, walking passed the tourists at Portsmouth Dockyard on the arm of a handsome naval officer.

'Where had it all gone?' She sighed.

'Five minutes to go.' An eager young voice in the crowd called out and the assembled masses began to push forward like a mindless army storming a fortress wall. Carol stood her ground but felt herself being carried by the tide.

A few more minutes passed and a dockyard policeman appeared by the gate. He looked at his watch and then out into the crowd. The human wave surged forward again. The policeman looked at his watch once more and then withdrew a key from his breast pocket. Moving deceptively fast he inserted, turned and withdrew the key before the crowd could advance and trample him underfoot. The double gates swung open and Carol was carried forward with her feet barely touching the ground.

Carol hurried along to escape the stampeding herd, but was soon overtaken by a swarm of young boys. They were running headlong in the direction of a large, grey mast that towered above the dockyard buildings. Carol realised that if she did not quicken her pace she would be at the back of the line when the tide arrived at the ship's gangway. Her pace and her heartbeat accelerated. Very soon she would know if Peter Wells was the shadow that haunted her. Over the past twenty four hours she had almost convinced herself that it was not Peter she had seen in the shadows.

'Even if Jane was right, he was probably no longer on the ship,' was the argument Carol used to convince herself that the past was really, just that. However, it had not been persuasive enough to keep her from today's pilgrimage.

Rounding the end of the last building her breath was

taken by the sheer size of the aircraft carrier. 'If he is on there I will never find him,' she thought. She slackened her pace until the jostling she received from the other visitors prompted her to get back in the race.

At the foot of the long wooden gangway she stopped and looked up at the metal structure towering above her. Her foot stepped onto the bridge that would take her back into the life she thought she had left behind. Feelings of excitement and uncertainty caused her heart to beat faster, and beneath her light woolen jumper her breasts rose and fell in seductive harmony.

That morning Carol had dressed carefully. She needed the jumper because of the fresh autumn breeze, but, she also knew that it complemented her with a subtle sexuality. Her jeans were tight and tucked into grey boots which accentuated the firmness of her thighs and the length of her shapely legs. As she picked her way over the raised planks of the gangway she did have second thoughts about the height of the heel on her boots.

On board the ship a junior sailor greeted each visitor with a smile and a 'Welcome Aboard' brochure. His eyes widened and his smile broadened when Carol put out her hand.

'Thank You.' She said and smiled, knowing her outfit was working and so dispelling any further doubts about the heels being too high. Whatever the obstacle she would overcome it. It was a strange feeling being back on board a naval ship. Carol felt it was almost like being home.

'Excuse me, miss.' The apologetic voice intruded into Carol's reminiscences. 'If you would follow the arrows, please.' Carol looked along the deck and noticed the red cardboard arrows suspended from rope guidelines. She then noticed the reason for the sailor's concern. The crowd was backed up behind her. She excused herself and moved on a few paces. A polished wooden board caught her eye and on it was written a list of officer's names.

'This is it! Now I will find out!' She said to herself, and, moving out the way of the advancing visitors she studied the list more closely. Her eyes did not have to look far before she saw it; LCDR P. WELLS – NAVIGATING OFFICER – ABOARD. She held her breath as she stared at the gold letters. He is here. He is on board.' The thought made her head swim and she looked up and down the deck, expecting him to appear at any moment. She had not dared believe that it really was Peter at the restaurant and now the proof was before her, printed in gold on a mahogany board.

She thought of having him called to the gangway, but remembered how he had slipped away that night. 'Besides,' she decided, 'it was too obvious.' She re-joined the crowd and was swept along by their momentum.

The inspection route took the visitors through the hangar, up onto the flight deck, where Sovereign's aircraft were safely displayed behind rope barriers, and into the bridge island. It was here that Carol felt very close to Peter Wells.

'This is the chart table.' The voice of the guide made Carol jump and she turned, expecting to see Peter standing beside it. The sailor continued; 'The chart house is along this passageway.' He pointed to the port side of the bridge. 'I am afraid it is not open to visitors today.'

Carol's whole body went as cold as ice.

'He must be there.' She whispered to herself. As the crowd moved away, she crept along the passageway. Craning her neck as she tried to see inside the little room.

Lieutenant-Commander Wells... telephone... wardroom.'

The stentorian sound of the ship's public address system caused Carol's heart to jump into her throat. She looked around guiltily to see if anyone had seen her, and, then realised that at any moment he would come out and they would meet face to face. Her whole world was reduced to the space she now occupied and time stood still.

'Where is he?' Carol became concerned when the door to the chart house remained firmly shut. She waited, but eventually, giving away to her impatience ran and looked into the small room.

The door was locked and he was not inside. The world that had enclosed her now fell apart. At first she did not know what to think, and then, her thoughts turned in on herself. 'What had she done to deserve this? Why did she have to chase after this man?' Her inquisition was interrupted by the bemused voice of the guide.

'Excuse me miss, you aren't allowed along there, sorry.' Carol took command of her emotions, apologised and rejoined the group. 'Well, where is he then?' She thought. She felt humiliated and angry, but the need to see him would not go away.

Each step now tormented her. The tour was almost over and every stride took her closer to the gangway. Once more she considered introducing herself to one of the crew and asking for Peter to be piped.

'Mind your head on the hatch.' The sailor warned as the leading member of the group lowered himself down the ladder that led back to the gangway.

Carol had decided to ask the Quartermaster to contact Peter; however, the closer she came to the Leading Seaman the weaker became her resolve. By the time she was beside him the idea seemed ridiculous.

Leaving the ship, all the plans she had made crowded in on her. She felt cheated and miserable.

'What do I do now?' She asked herself, as the tears began to appear in the corner of her eyes. She stepped onto the concrete wharf and walked away from the ship. She was thankful that Phil would not be at the dockyard gates to meet her. At that moment all she wanted was to be alone.

'Still at rugby.' She said aloud as the taxi pulled up outside the house.

'What's that?' The driver asked, and Carol felt foolish at being found talking to herself.

'Oh nothing,' she replied, 'how much do you want?' The driver gave her a salacious grin and told her the fare.

Carol was still in a quandary as she walked up the path and onto the verandah. She could not clear her mind of the nagging questions about her future. The front door swung open as the key turned in the lock. Throwing her handbag onto the sofa she looked around the shabby room and slammed the door behind her.

'Damn and blast!' She cried in exasperation. 'Where do I go from here?'

It was then that her eyes settled on the black plastic

form of the telephone, sitting on the gnarled wood of the sideboard. Slowly, she walked over to it. 'I could still ring him,' she thought, 'it might be easier than meeting him face to face.'

Purposefully she reached for the directory and flicked the white pages until she found the number of the naval dockyard. Taking the receiver in her left hand she began dialing the number... it was ringing!

The insistent tone sounded in her ear and the longer it remained unanswered, the greater became her doubts.

'What am I doing?' She sighed but could not let go of the receiver. Eventually a stern voice answered,

'Naval dockyard. Which ship?'

Carol was surprised by the immediacy of the question and blurted out the name.

'Sovereign.' Once again the ringing sounded in the handset.

'I can't do it.' She told herself, but was still unable to put the telephone down. Her hands became moist with the tension of waiting.

'HMS Sovereign... Quartermaster. Can I help you?'

The sudden sound of a cockney voice shocked her and Carol took the handset away from her ear and stared at it in disbelief. She could still hear the voice repeating the ship's name and Carol slammed the receiver down. The room fell into a stunned silence punctuated only by Carol's panted breath. Breaking away from the telephone she collapsed onto the old settee.

'It's over,' she sobbed, 'finished, dead!' She beat the chair's weathered arm with her fist. 'I came here to start a new life. I don't have to go back. Blast him!' The tears rolled down her cheeks. 'Blast him.' This time the words trailed away into silence.

'Lieutenant-Commander Wells... telephone... wardroom.' Peter heard the pipe as he was leaving his cabin. He hurried along the cream painted passageway of the senior officers' accommodation, his mind thinking of a route to the wardroom that would avoid the crowded upper deck. He loathed open days when his ordered world was invaded by hordes of people who came to pry and point.

On entering the anteroom the Leading Steward handed him the telephone.

'Hello. Lieutenant-Commander Wells speaking.'

The silken voice of Jennifer Hale purred down the line.

'Hello Peter. I've been waiting for you to call.'

Peter changed the receiver to his other hand and shuffled his feet nervously. He explained he had been busy and hoped it sounded convincing.

Jennifer dismissed his excuses and went on to invite him to a party she was having that evening. This was the call Peter had dreaded. He had no desire to get involved again with this woman and although he was half expecting the call he had not prepared an excuse. He was against the wall and thinking fast. A lie was the only solution. He apologised and said he had a prior engagement for that evening.

'Anyone I know?' Jennifer inquired sarcastically. Peter retained his composure and said he did not think so, but refrained from saying more. Sensing Jennifer was experiencing a rare moment of uncertainty he apologised again, thanked her for the invitation and before she could recover the initiative, hung up. Peter caught the wardroom bar steward's eye.

'Gin and Tonic, please.' The steward smartly filled the order.

'You sound like you need it.' The voice of Steven Marks brought Peter back to the present.

'You're not wrong,' he smiled in reply and asked, 'will you join me?'

'Why not. The sun is over the yardarm.'

'Since when has that stopped the Fleet Air Arm?' Peter joked.

'True, true.' Marks conceded

The men took their drinks and went to sit in the chairs away from the bar.

'So what's new?' Marks asked and before Peter could reply, continued, 'are you going to Jennifer's party tonight?' Peter shook his head and told him about the telephone call. The pilot could not understand the decision and said so. 'I thought you two had something going?'

'Just shows how wrong you can be.' Peter replied.

'I guess so.' Marks smiled, took a sip of his Brandy and then asked; 'What about the rugby on Wednesday, are you going to that?'

Peter had been interested in the sport since his days in the first fifteen at Dartmouth, although now, he considered himself strictly a spectator. He had heard of the forthcoming game and had already decided to go along to cheer on the ship's team. Steve was obviously pleased and Peter wondered why this pilot should concern himself with his social welfare. The question had to be asked and the reply was equally frank.

'Because you work too hard and you can be a miserable sod at times.' Peter laughed and raised his glass.

'Cheers. Cruel but fair.'

The next two days bore out what Steven Marks had said. Peter lost himself in his work. He had to plan the next phase of the deployment which would take them to Singapore where the navies of four countries would battle it out in a ten day exercise in the South China Sea. It was important work, but, even Peter knew it need not have occupied so much of his time. He was also well aware of why he had to keep so busy. The vision he saw on Friday night had shaken him and he did not want time to question how he had planned and lived his life.

It was a cold wind that blew off the harbour and across the rugby field at Rushcutters Bay. There were already a lot of vehicles in the car park when Peter arrived with Steven Marks and two other officers from Sovereign.

'That wind is going to cause trouble.' Peter commented to the agreement of the other three.

They left the car and walked towards the playing field. Groups of spectators stood huddled around the pitch.

'There are the Pongos.' Marks pointed to a dark green bus just entering the grounds and then added, 'they will be the ones to beat. They have not been at sea for the past two months.' The others looked at the bus and nodded their heads soberly.

'Who did we draw in the first round?' Alex Simpson, one of the ship's Direction Officers, asked. Peter looked down the list of the day's fixtures.

'We're in luck. We don't meet the Army until the second round. They might get tired by then.'

'Fat chance!' Marks retorted and pointed to the bus that was disgorging a stream of extremely big and fit looking young men. 'Look at those chaps.'

Alex Simpson was more confident,

'They are only soldiers, and Australians at that.'

'Don't let them hear you say that. They look mean enough already.'

The men laughed and continued their stroll, talking of the matches ahead and admiring the setting. The playing field was tucked away on the harbour foreshore and set amidst a leafy park.

'Where are our boys' Alex asked, as it looked as if all the other teams had arrived and were already warming up.

'There they are!' Steve Marks pointed to a light blue bus just entering the gates of the park. 'Better late than never.'

From the time his eyes opened that morning Phil had not stopped talking about the rugby competition. He had spoken of little else since the training session on Sunday. This suited Carol who was left with her thoughts and did not have to explain her occasional periods of silence. There were times when she thought the future held nothing and the past only tormented her. She was thankful for Phil; but, knew that it was too convenient.

The demarcation between love and security was too blurred. Nothing was clear anymore. At times her desolation was so complete she felt physically ill and her head would pound until it felt like it would burst with the pressure of her tormented thoughts.

The only decision she reached was to live from day to day and let the future take care of itself. The only certainty was that the memory of Peter Wells would not leave her. She now mourned his loss like that of a loved one taken too soon. The irony was she thought, 'the body was still there to haunt her.' Even now, sitting alongside Phil as the car negotiated the dirt road that led down to the park, Carol nurtured a secret hope that Peter Wells would be there waiting for her. She hoped, but dared not believe it.

Peter had never mentioned rugby during their time together and she often wondered how he looked so fit when he appeared so disinterested in sport. At the time she was glad, knowing that sport would have distracted him from her and she already had enough competition with the Navy. 'I lost him anyway,' she sadly concluded.

'Looks like I'm late.' Phil said, pointing to the bus parked under the trees. He made no mention of why they were behind schedule. Carol looked stunning and his friends would be choked with envy. He parked the car, kissed Carol and ran out onto the field to warm up with his team.

'I'll see you before the game starts.' He shouted back, the words barely audible as the wind caught them and carried them along with the swirling leaves. Carol remained in the car until she heard the shrill sound of the referee's whistle. Reluctantly she stepped out into the chilling breeze. Without warning a gust of wind took the beret which she had meticulously put in place, and, with it the hair style she had spent hours getting right. Bending down she retrieved the hat and contemplated returning to the car to use the mirror to readjust her appearance. She dismissed the idea as vanity and continued on her windswept way to the white lines that marked the boundary of the rugby field. Heads turned as she approached. Phil ran over to her.

'Wish me luck.' He said as if he was about to embark on a mission of life and death.

Carol gave him a kiss on the cheek and felt the eyes of his team mates upon her. He smiled and ran back to rejoin them. 'He has got a nice bum.' She thought.

The referee's whistle sounded and the oval ball was kicked high into the air. Carol's eyes followed the trajectory until it was caught and hidden from view by half a dozen heaving bodies. She did not understand the rules, but, appreciated the potent combination of strength and stamina that the game demanded.

A mountain of bodies was forming in the middle of the field and Carol was concerned that Phil was at the bottom of it. She scanned the players who were still on their feet and with relief saw him standing on the far side of the field. Then, as if by illusion the ball was flying once more. It fell into Phil's hands and he was running with power and purpose towards a human barrier of white and blue jerseys. Carol marveled at his speed but had to shield her eyes as two burly Australian sailors halted his advance and buried him under a mass of vengeful flesh.

When she looked again the world froze in front of her eyes. It was like stopping a moving picture in order to concentrate all attention on one frame.

'Peter!' She exclaimed so loud that those about her looked and smiled, thinking her concern was for someone caught in the melee out on the field. She stared across the green pitch and knew she was holding his gaze. Their eyes cut across the distance with invisible lines of force and a silent voice. He began to move. He was walking alongside the playing field in the direction of the car park. Carol snapped out of her trance like state. He was getting away. Her whole being cried out for someone, or something, to tell her what to do. Instead, she stood rooted to the spot, in a state of indecisive torment.

His pace quickened and all Carol could do was watch, her eyes never blinking for fear of losing sight of him. At the end of the field he turned and strode behind the goal posts and continued to the corner flag. They were only separated by thirty yards when she lost him behind a crowd of burly spectators. She caught her breath and stood on tiptoe to try and catch sight of him again.

'Hello Carol.' Peter Wells stood behind her.

She remained motionless for a second before her reflexes prompted a response.

'Hi.' She replied weekly, as disbelief clouded her mind. They shook hands formally, neither knowing what to say next.

'You are looking well.' It was Peter who spoke first. Carol thanked him and stood admiring his tanned face. His dark hair was lightened by the sun and she was surprised to see it longer than he used to wear it.

'What are you doing here?' He asked, conscious of the embarrassment caused by their prolonged silence.

Carol told of her brief stay in Australia, omitting to say why she had come, or where or with whom she was staying. She also did not mention having seen him five nights previously.

'We are playing games again,' she thought and then it was her turn to ask the questions. She learned more about his posting to Sovereign and the progress of the deployment so far. As Peter described the ship's visit to Perth he could not help thinking about his night time swim in the sea, but, managed to disguise his thoughts behind superficial descriptions. The conversation became instantly more meaningful when he said,

'I thought I saw you on Friday night, at a restaurant in Elizabeth Bay. I was not sure so did not stay to find out. You know how it is.' Inside he cringed at his own words. Even now he was not sure why he had not gone up to her on that night. 'Why he had not done it then, and yet now, as soon as he saw her, he could not stay away?' Reasons eluded him. Carol answered apprehensively,

'I was at The Swiss Cottage on Friday night, with a group of friends.'

'It was you, then.' The answer came out in a whisper.

The nature of the day's rugby competition called for short games in a knockout format and the first half of Phil's match had just ended. Carol looked over at the playing field and was thankful that he was not coming off. She watched him standing with the rest of the team sucking thirstily on half an orange. She did notice that he was looking across at her.

'What are you doing here today?' Peter asked.

Smiling coyly Carol looked towards the playing field.

'I have a friend playing for the Army side.' She answered.

'Oh.' Peter said in an unguarded moment. He then realised that she would not be there alone. The shrill sound of the referee's whistle interrupted the conversation.

The players, some running, others tiredly jogging, made their way to their allotted positions on the field for the second half of the game. Peter followed Carol's eyes and although not knowing who, knew that out there was someone who occupied a place in her life. After the short silence conversation and questions came easier. Once again Peter was the first to speak.

'Would your friend mind you talking to me?' He pointed to the pack of players as he spoke. Carol's mouth curled in a half smile.

'Oh, I don't know,' she replied slowly. 'If he thought you were a stranger trying to pick me up he would probably laugh it off. If he knew that you were the man from my past,' she paused. 'I don't think he would be too impressed.'

They smiled in their conspiracy, and the question opened the way for a deeper conversation and a revelation from Carol about her personal affairs.

Peter was not surprised. Having stood with her for only a short time he felt the attraction, the magnetism she had always generated. He knew she could have any man she wanted.

While they talked the bond, that was once so strong, was being renewed. Their bodies, drawn together by an unforgotten passion, communicated to each other in movement, stance and touch.

Time passed without either noticing the minutes and they were both surprised when the game ended and the players started walking from the field. Carol felt a momentary panic at being found out and yet she did not want Peter to go. He noticed her agitation and knew the reason for it.

'I think it's time I left. My friends will be wondering what has happened to me.' He took Carol's hand and held it in his. 'It has been lovely seeing you again. Let's not lose touch, call me. We sail on Monday.'

It was a hurried farewell. Peter could see a serious young man walking toward them and did not want to wait around for introductions that would require explanations.

'Bye.' Carol called after him as he walked away.

'Who was that?' Phil's voice preceded him by about ten yards. Carol tried to look composed and lied.

'Just someone trying to pick me up. You should not leave me alone with all these men around.'

'Well I'll be around for the next half hour and then our next match is against the Poms. Whose side will you be on?' Carol felt her face redden. 'Don't answer that. I couldn't take the disappointment if you said the wrong thing.' He smiled and leaned forward to kiss her.

'A narrow escape,' she thought as their lips met, knowing she did not have an answer.

For the rest of the day Carol darted glances at Peter

across the grass pitch. She felt thrilled when she caught his eye, but cheated when he did not come over and talk to her again. For fleeting moments she despised him for his caution. It came as an even harder blow when she realised he had left the grounds. Her eyes searched every inch of the field, the car park and the approaches to the recreation ground.

'How had she missed him? Why hadn't he attracted her attention before he left?' The day ended as it had begun, with Phil preoccupied with rugby and Carol's thoughts dominated by Peter Wells.

The next day, Phil was suffering the after effects of three games of rugby and Carol felt like a recluse, happy to be left alone with her thoughts.

On waking that morning her immediate impulse was to telephone Peter. Throughout breakfast her conversation was desultory, prompting Philip to comment that she did not seem to be on the same planet. She made the excuse that he would be leaving soon and she was beginning to miss him already. He came to hold and comfort her and she had to bite her lower lip to hold back the tears of shame. Her thoughts gave her no peace.

'Why should she be doing this for a man who showed so little interest in her? Why couldn't she be happy with what she had?' She did not know the answers to these and other questions. She did know that she would make the telephone call.

Later that morning, on the pretext of having to go to the local shops, Carol took the car and drove to the telephone box by the beach. Phil had offered to accompany her and it had taken some fast talking to convince him she could get the shopping alone and that he should take it easy after the exertions of yesterday.

As the front door closed behind her the feeling that she was embarking on an act of treachery enveloped her. It was as if she was being driven to betray Phil and rebel against the comfortable routine their relationship had become.

Carol stood in the red wooden call box and the ringing tone of the telephone sounded in her ear. The call was answered and this time she asked for the wardroom of HMS Sovereign with bravado. The duty steward answered and she had another wait while he piped for the Navigating Officer. The minutes passed in impatient agitation and then she heard the heart fluttering sound of Peter's voice. Her own trembling as she spoke.

'Hello Peter, it's Carol Adison.' The formality of her introduction sounded ridiculous to her as it echoed in the line.

'Carol, I've been waiting and hoping you would call.' The tone of Peter's voice conveyed his pleasure more than his words. He went on to apologise for not signalling his farewell on leaving the football match. 'I thought I better keep a low profile.' He explained. Carol countered by saying that apologies were not necessary, but the memory of her annoyance registered in the back of her mind.

They spoke of their happiness in meeting, the coincidence involved and the possibility of seeing each other again. On the last point Carol became serious, as her conscience troubled her for the second time that day.

'Will I be able to see you before we sail?' Peter asked.

There was a moment's silence before she answered. Her voice heavy with guilt and resignation.

'Phil leaves for a course on Saturday afternoon.' She could not believe she was doing this, but carried on. 'I will call you around four.' That was just what Peter wanted to hear.

'I look forward to seeing you again. We have a lot to catch up on.' He answered happily.

The longer the call went on the faster Carol's courage drained away, until she had to say that she must go. Reluctantly they said their goodbyes and Carol held onto the receiver until she heard the line go dead.

'I've done it.' She sighed and pushed on the heavy door of the telephone box until it gave way and opened. Once in the open she furtively looked around and hurried to the car. On the drive back to the house she almost forgot to buy the groceries that were her alibi. When she did finally arrive home Phil commented on how long it had taken and Carol was forced to lie again.

'The shop was packed.'

'Chatting up the fella behind the counter more like.' Phil replied and Carol's heart stopped beating.

The remaining two days before Phil left to rejoin his unit were a living hell for Carol. She admitted to herself that she had been a bitch in the past; but, never had she strung a man along so flagrantly before. Even as they made love on that last morning she was conscious of playing a part, determined he should not become suspicious at any cost.

Saturday afternoon they drove to Central Railway Station to collect Phil's rail pass and for him to start the first leg of his long journey to the Jungle Training Centre in Queensland. Both were quiet as they left the house behind them and drove into the busy city streets. It was Phil who broke the silence.

'It is only for three weeks and then I'll be home again. After that there is three weeks back at Holsworthy and then two weeks leave before I have to go up top. We will have lots of time together.' He thought the words would help ease the pain of this parting and was surprised when he saw tears come into Carol's eyes. 'Don't cry. It's only for a short time and when I come back, well,' he waited before adding, 'who knows what might happen.' He looked meaningfully into her eyes and she knew exactly what was being said, and, at that point she nearly broke down.

'Oh Phil' She cried sadly and then caught her words.

'I love you Carol and that is what will keep me going until I see you again.' He placed his hand on her thigh and squeezed softly. He then leant over and gently kissed her cheek. She could not look at him and sat staring at the road ahead with unseeing eyes.

They parked the car and walked hand in hand to the RTO Office. Some of the men from Phil's unit were already there and they welcomed him like school boys meeting after term break. He introduced Carol to some while others just smiled or leered from a distance. Looking at his watch he suggested they collect the bags and make their way to the platform.

Nearing the gate a sea of green surrounded them and Carol moved closer so as not to be trampled under black, spit polished, boots or jostled by swaying khaki duffle bags. Phil felt Carol move against him and guided her to a quiet corner, away from the tide of travellers. He put down his bags and removed his wide brimmed hat, placing it on the top of the upright duffle bag. Taking Carol in his arms he drew her to him. Their faces came together and their lips met. They kissed long and passionately until an alarm sounded in Carol's head and she pulled away. For a brief moment they stood looking at each other and then Phil kissed her again;

'I do love you and don't you ever forget it.' He said and smiled as he carefully replaced his hat, fitting the brown leather strap under his chin. I better get on the train.'

Carol walked with him to the departure gate and stayed there while he found his warrant and showed it to the ticket collector. Before passing through the black, wrought iron entrance he turned and quickly kissed Carol for the last time.

'Bye.' He whispered and taking a firmer grip on his bags, walked away. He looked back and Carol waved as the tears tumbled down her cheeks.

She stayed, looking through the rusting ironwork of the platform barricade until the train rumbled into life and moved laboriously along the platform. Phil hung out of an open window, craning his neck for a last glimpse of her. He waved as the diesel engine gained momentum and carried him away. Carol watched as the last carriage snaked around the track and disappeared behind a soot encrusted siding. Slowly turning away she rubbed the last tear from her eye and began the walk back to the car.

On the drive to the house she felt miserable as

thoughts and recriminations fell in on her like the suffocating snow of an avalanche.

'What was she doing to him? It was his car? His house? He thought she was his girl!' She then thought of the telephone call she had arranged to make to Peter.

'I really am a bitch.' She said aloud, knowing she was going to make that call.

The front door swung open and as Carol entered the old living room she felt as empty as the house. Her eyes fell on the telephone and as if drawn by a force outside herself she slowly moved towards it. Her hand rested on the receiver.

'Pick it up.' A voice was commanding her. Her hand remained poised but did not move. Abruptly she turned away.

'I can't. Not so soon.' She whispered and walked into the kitchen.

A mug of coffee made her feel better. She looked at the clock on the wall. Four o'clock. It was now time. Telling herself this is what she wanted she walked back into the lounge and made directly for the telephone. She dialled the number.

'Good afternoon. Wardroom. HMS Sovereign.'

She was through and there was no backing out. She asked for Lieutenant-Commander Wells and waited, her eyes glancing around the now familiar room.

'Oh come on!' She urged as the empty minutes ticked by. Peter's voice was then heard and all her doubts disappeared. They talked as old friends now at ease with each other. An unspoken commitment to reunite had been made and for Carol the guilt that had weighed so heavy upon her was replaced by the desire to be with this man she thought she had left behind.

'When can I see you?' Peter could contain the question no longer, and for an instant Carol felt uncomfortable. Visions of Phil's farewell were projected vividly in her mind. She physically blinked her eyes to shrug them off and answered.

'I will be outside the dockyard gates at eight. I will see you there.'

'The gates?' Peter replied in amazement.

'Well, you can't come here.' Carol replied and the line went silent.

'You are right of course.' Peter acknowledged and then had an idea. 'Why don't you come aboard? We can have a few drinks and then go on for dinner somewhere.' Carol's reply came without hesitation,

'No. Thank you. I would prefer to meet on neutral ground if you know what I mean?'

Peter said that he did and they went on to make their plans for the evening. Carol replaced the receiver and she was smiling.

Chapter 12

Peter turned away from the telephone, a broad grin displaying his pleasure. He glanced at the clock on the bulkhead, 'only four hours to wait,' he thought. Collecting his papers he left the wardroom. There was a lot to be done.

'Excuse me, sir.'

Peter stopped and looked around to see who was addressing him. The Captain's steward spoke again.

'The Captain's compliments sir. He would like to see you in his cabin.' A frown crossed Peter's brow.

'Very good.' He replied sternly and followed the Leading Steward to the Captain's cabin.

The sailor knocked on the door and a gruff voice called for them to enter. The steward stood aside to allow Peter to enter first. Captain Harlow's face broke into a more congenial mould when he saw his Navigator.

'Peter, glad they found you. Come and sit down.'

Peter became guarded. 'How long is this going to take and what does he want?' He thought anxiously.

The Captain offered him a cup of coffee but Peter

declined not wanting the meeting to take any longer than necessary. As if reading his thoughts Harlow continued.

'The Admiral is having a barbecue tomorrow to mark our last day in Sydney and he would like you to attend.'

Peter was taken by surprise and there followed a moments silence that the Captain took as a refusal.

'Do you have other plans?' He asked.

'No.' Peter both thought and replied quickly. 'No, not at all. I would like to come. May I bring a friend?'

'I don't see why not. You've not been wasting your time in Sydney, ay Peter?' The Captain smilingly replied and went on to outline the plans for the afternoon. 'The do is being held in the grounds of the Fleet Headquarters. It gets underway at 1400. I look forward to seeing you and your companion then.'

This signalled the end of the meeting and Peter rose from his chair and bid the Captain good afternoon. He closed the door behind him and considered the consequences of what had just been agreed. 'Susanne was bound to be there,' he thought, and that worried him.

Preparing for the evening Peter now had even more to think about and by the time half past seven came around he had decided nothing except to take events one at a time. It even occurred to him that Carol may not want to see him again after tonight. A lot had happened since they were together in England.

He walked briskly along the wharf and was at the main dockyard gate by five to eight. He showed his identity card and passed through. Looking around he noticed Harry's Café de Wheels was already doing a healthy trade from sailors starting their night on the town. There was no sign of Carol.

The minutes passed and his eyes scrutinised every car that came into view. He walked out into the middle of the road where the vehicles not allowed into the dockyard turned around. This afforded him a better view of the two approach roads from Kings Cross and Woolloomooloo. There was still no sign of her.

He looked at his watch and started to worry. It was twenty minutes past eight. The thought that this had happened before crossed his mind as he recalled Susanne Harrison's non-appearance due to a car accident two months before. He returned to the pavement and leaned against the blue wooden wall that formed the pedestrian entrance into the dockyard. More minutes passed and a feeling of self-consciousness came over him as he felt the inquisitive stares of the dockyard policemen on duty.

'Where was she?' He asked himself through gritted teeth and began pacing once again. As he moved away he missed seeing the taxi that just pulled up short of the gates.

'Hello Peter.' Carol called gently.

He turned with surprise, caught off guard.

'You look like you've seen a ghost.' She teased. He apologised and walked over to her. They kissed automatically as old friends do.

'I had trouble finding a taxi.' She explained, knowing there was a car at the house she could have used. Peter dismissed the apology as unnecessary.

'It's just good to see you.' He said and took her hand.

'Let's take your cab.' They waved to the taxi that had not yet driven away. Bundling into the back seat Peter gave the driver the destination

'I really can't believe it.' Peter said as the car darted between the fast moving traffic.

'Believe what?' Carol asked.

'That we are together, in a taxi, in Sydney. It really is incredible.'

'It's fate.' Carol replied and squeezed his hand.

The taxi came to a halt at the foot of a towering, circular building on top of which sat a revolving restaurant that afforded a panoramic view of the city and beyond. Peter helped Carol from the car and then turned to pay the fare. Arm in arm they walked into the building and caught the lift to the top floor. Peter had booked a table and they were taken to the bar while it was prepared. Carol looked down on the sparkling lights of the city.

'It really is Fantasy Land.' She said in a low, amazed voice. Peter nodded and followed her gaze out into the glittering night. He turned to face her.

'It is lovely to see you again.' His tone was husky with emotion and his stare so piercing Carol had to avert her eyes.

In the intimately lit restaurant the months dropped away. Carol told of her adventures in the outback and her life in Sydney. She talked about Phil, how they had met and how much she owed him. Peter listened but said little.

The food was excellent, the wine relaxing and the mood seductive. There was one question Peter had to ask and he hoped he already knew the answer. The sound of soft music surrounded them and they got up to dance. They moved as one, their bodies in harmony, each movement a caress.

'Why did you come to Australia?'

Peter prayed he had judged the moment correctly. Carol's eyes hardened for an instant and then she smiled. Her lips parted to reveal pearl white teeth that contrasted beautifully with the soft tanned skin of her face.

'You know why.' She answered and rested her head on his shoulder. 'I loved you Peter. I think I still do.'

Their lips met and nothing existed outside their embrace. Their bodies stayed together not caring that the tempo of the music had changed.

'Would you like coffee?' Peter asked and then suggested they have something in it. He ordered two Irish Coffees and then returned his attention to Carol. He became serious for a moment. 'I don't want to drag up the past,' he began awkwardly, not sure of the words he should use to express his feelings. 'We had a very good relationship until, for reasons we both know, it went wrong. I can't guarantee it will succeed a second time but I would like to give it a try. I don't want to lose you again.'

The arrival of the coffee delayed Carol's answer and caused Peter to think he had revealed his feelings too soon. He was both surprised and relieved when she leaned across the table and kissed his open lips.

'I don't think you have to worry about that.' She sighed.

Peter paid the bill and extended his hand across

the table: 'Where do we go from here?' He asked and caressed her hands.

'Well, we can't go to your place and we certainly can't go to mine.' Carol replied with a grin on her lips. Peter smiled and answered;

'Well, we will just have to find a place of our own.'

The receptionist presented the key and after a professional glance refrained from asking if there were any bags to be taken by the bellman.

They stepped out of the lift on the third floor and walked slowly to their room. A cloud of guilt descended on Carol as a vision of Phil walking away along the platform caused her to shiver and falter in her step. Peter looked at her.

'Is anything wrong?' He asked with concern and placed his arm around her shoulder.

Carol shook her head, but Peter knew what the problem was for he too felt out of place. The surroundings and the inevitability of what was going to happen made it all feel disturbingly mechanical. He looked again at Carol.

'Are we doing the right thing?' He asked and Carol now smiled back at him.

'I don't think we have any choice.' Peter kissed her gently on the lips.

'I think you're right.'

The room was large with a double bed dominating the other pieces of furniture and standing as a symbol of why they were there. Once again self-consciousness separated them. Peter walked around opening all the cupboards, looking into the bathroom and when he returned Carol was sitting on the end of the bed.

'You are very pretty.' He said from across the room and held out his arms to her. Carol came to him and their lips met, fusing their bodies into one. Their hands moved in caresses, at first uncertain and soon demanding. As Peter manipulated the clip on the back of Carol's dress she touched his lips with hers and whispered in a voice heavy with desire,

'Let's take a shower.'

With bodies still wet from the warm jets of water they wrapped themselves in a large bath towel. Carol's breasts pressed against Peter's chest and his hands floated down her back and onto the roundness of her bottom. Gentle pressure forced her to him and she felt the urgency of his desire against the soft flesh of her stomach. Moving her hands down his body she held and gently guided him into her.

'Carol, I do love you,' he sighed as she stroked and fondled him with the light touch of a temptress.

Before it was too late Peter placed his arms about her, bent down and picked her up. As he carried her to the large bed his tongue explored the pink hardness of her erect nipples and the softness of her rounded breasts. He placed her on the crisp white sheet and ravaged her with his eyes as she lay naked and open before him. Her eyes burned back and her lips parted invitingly. Peter cradled her head in his hands and drove himself into her.

Lying back in each other's arms they felt relaxed and warm. Carol cuddled into the roughened contours of Peter's neck.

'I love you,' she whispered, 'and I don't want this to ever end.'

Peter turned on his side and stroked her cheek. He kissed her tenderly so she would have to believe what he was about to say.

'We have wasted too much time already. I want you back now and forever.' A glistening tear formed in the corner of Carol's eyes.

'Oh Peter,' she sighed and two pearl like droplets of water slowly glided down her cheeks. Peter's lips lightly followed their tracks until their mouths met and they kissed.

The morning sunlight filtered through the net curtains and played on the faces of the two lovers. Peter opened his eyes gradually and squinted as the morning rays shone in on him. He moved his head to look at Carol and smiled at the peaceful expression on her sleeping face.

'What are you smiling at?' Her tired voice startled him.

'I thought you were asleep,' he answered defensively.

'If you are going to take advantage of me I want to be awake.' Carol teased and rolled on top of his taut body. 'I love your chest.' She cooed, running her fingers through the tight, black curls of hair that covered the front of his body.

'Is that all?' He replied and thrust his thighs against her.

'Oh no.' She answered and straddled her legs around him. They made love slowly with the morning sun bathing them in its golden light.

'I must look a mess.' Carol said as she tried to arrange her dress and smooth out the wrinkles that had gathered from its spending the night on the floor.

'What about me?' Peter laughed, rubbing the black stubble that covered his chin.

They smiled in the fullness of their love and not caring about the consequences.

'So, what are we going to do today?' Carol asked excitedly and raised her eyebrows as if she knew the answer even before she asked the question.

'Not that. At least not straight away. You are insatiable and I love you.' Peter replied, taking hold of her trim waist. He then asked, 'How about a barbecue?'

Carol was stunned for a second.

'Where did you get that idea?' She answered and thought for a moment. 'Yes. All right. Where shall we have it?'

Peter moved uneasily and hesitated before answering.

'Well, I have an invitation to attend our Admiral's get together at Fleet Headquarters this afternoon. Would you like to go to that?'

Disappointment was Carol's first reaction. She wanted Peter to herself and thought he would want the same. Turning away she looked out of the window. Peter noticed her change of mood and quickly back peddled.

'We don't have to go. It's just an idea.' He knew this to be a lie and prayed Carol would agree. She did not answer for a long time.

'Okay. It should be fun. Like old times ay?' Relief washed over Peter like a wave over a rock.

'Good. We'll do that.' He said and continued. 'I think we should keep this room for another night.'

'It sounds better all the time.' Carol giggled. The thought that Peter might like to spend the last night before sailing on board his ship had crossed her mind.

Peter returned her smile and went on;

'We better go back to your house and get you some more clothes and something for this afternoon.'

Carol became serious once more.

'I think I had better do that myself.' No further explanation was necessary.

'You're right. I'll go back to the ship and get what I need. We will meet back here later in the morning. Now that's settled, what about breakfast?' Peter asked.

'I thought you already had it.' Carol replied, smiled, and raised her eyebrows.

Driving back to the house in the back of the taxi Carol had time to think about what had happened and to think about Peter. She knew he had not changed, but, she was not going to let that stand in the way this time. 'Anyway,' she reasoned, 'it will make up for the time when I had to fight my way into that bloody dockyard.'

Peter was grateful not to see anyone he knew when he returned aboard; although, he did feel a little conspicuous as he passed the gangway staff with fifteen hours of growth on his chin. He thought he detected a wry smile on the face of the gangway sentry but, decided that he was being over sensitive.

Back at the hotel he sat by the open window looking out onto the road and watching for the taxi that would bring Carol back to him. The breeze was cool on his face, the roads deserted and Peter felt alone with his thoughts. The minutes passed and he was surprised to find that he enjoyed the solitude. It was one of those rare moments when everything seemed to come together in a revelation that mystics spent a lifetime to discover. He had been given a second chance and he was going to take it.

An old white car, streaked with rust, stopped at a parking meter opposite the hotel. This activity on the deserted road attracted Peter's attention. He stared at the lone vehicle and was astounded when Carol got out of the driver's door.

Leaning out of the window he waved and called her name. She looked up, smiled and waved back. The warmth that flowed through his body proved to him that here was the girl he wanted to marry.

He watched as she crossed the road and entered the hotel. Excitedly he ran to the door and grasped the handle. He waited for the knock on the door and on opening it took her in his arms. The sweet fragrance of her body aroused him and in a voice deepened by desire said, 'I love you Carol,' and hugged her tightly to his aroused body. She looked up at him with laughter in her eyes,

'I love you too, but, I don't think we have time to do anything about it right now.' Peter laughed and they kissed playfully.

'You are gorgeous.' He sighed and reluctantly let her go.

'So are you.' She replied, affectionately touching the end of his nose. 'Let's go see the Admiral'

The morning breeze had abated by the time the first

guests arrived on the lawns that surrounded the Naval Headquarters. The old Holden drove up to the main gate and stopped alongside the wooden checkpoint.

'Lieutenant-Commander Wells and a guest.' Peter called into the office. The policeman checked his list, saluted and instructed them to proceed.

'You pack some punch these days.' Carol said cheekily.

'You better believe it.' He answered, only half in jest. They drove up the long hill that led to the Headquarter's building and stopped in the car park at the foot of a stone staircase. The engine was switched off and Peter turned to his guest.

'The more things change the more they stay the same, ay?' Carol nodded and leaned across to give him a kiss.

'Once more into the breach.' She responded with another quotation. They climbed the steps and on nearing the top heard the sound of voices raised in enjoyment.

'Sounds pretty lively.' Carol commented. Peter was relieved that they were not the first to arrive.

As they negotiated the last uneven step a red and white striped awning came into view, dominating the skyline. The tantalising aroma of meat cooking on a barbecue hung heavily in the air.

'Peter, glad you could make it.' Rear-Admiral Harrison came forward to welcome the latest arrivals.

Peter introduced his guest and the Admiral's eyes widened in appreciation.

'Come on.' The Admiral beckoned, 'let me take you to meet the other guests.'

They followed the straight figure of the Admiral into the main body of the assembled party. He turned and addressed the new arrivals.

'You will know most of the people here, Peter, so I will leave you to do the introductions.'

Peter nodded and cast an eye around the guests. Steven Marks was there, as were all of Sovereign's Department Heads. Where the ladies came from he did not know, except for one.

'Hello Peter, I haven't seen you for a while.' The barbed tone belonged to Susanne Harrison. She was standing alongside a young pilot and Peter went on guard. He returned the greeting and introduced Carol. While he spoke he could feel the two women eyeing one another in the intense manner that only they can, and, get away with. The ladies shook hands.

'Will you be staying in Australia long?' Susanne asked in a tone that was both polite and probing.

Carol had to consider her answer carefully. 'It was a good question,' she thought. She glanced at Peter and, after a moment's pause, replied.

'I will have to wait and see. I have only been here a short time and already so much has happened.'

Peter placed his arm around Carol's waist and gave her a supportive squeeze. He smiled and addressed the pilot.

'What is everyone drinking, Mr. James?' Peter knew the young man's Christian name but wanted to make the distinction between himself and the Lieutenant. He hoped that by doing so Susanne may also be more easily curbed. The pilot took their orders and went off to have them filled.

Susanne once more opened the questioning and engaged Peter in conversation. While they spoke Carol became intrigued to know where this pretty girl fitted into Peter's life. She concluded that if it was not for this mystery the afternoon would have been a typically boring naval event. She was almost disappointed when Peter managed to break away from his inquisitor to show her off to the Captain and the other officers.

It was not until she saw the respect he commanded that Carol fully appreciated the heights to which Peter had risen. Never before had she fully understood the forces that drove him. Now, her eyes were opened and she felt ashamed of her selfishness. She discreetly held his hand for reassurance and to signal her newly realised understanding. He received and held it firmly.

With the lengthening shadows cast by the afternoon sun came the cool easterly breeze from the ocean. Guests were making their farewells and Peter thought it time to make theirs. There were not many hours left and he did not want to squander precious minutes when the prospect of empty months lay ahead.

The Admiral eyed Carol as he bid her goodbye and said he hoped they would meet again.

'I thought Peter had been wasting his time down here.' He joked and Peter knew that Susanne need no longer concern him.

The car drove down the hill and around the red brick buildings of the dockyard. Peter looked back at Sovereign's towering masts and thought of tomorrow's ten o'clock departure.

'Let's go back to the hotel.' He said.

They made love with the fierce intensity of people who know they are on borrowed time and want to lose themselves in the certainty of the present. When it was over they lay quietly in each other's arms.

It was not until the alarm rang at 0530 that Peter's mind was finally made up. He looked into Carol's half-awake eyes and drew her to him. The softness of her body felt indescribably alluring and in a voice breaking with emotion he whispered,

'I love you. I don't think I ever stopped loving you. I just denied it. I don't want to lose you again.' He stopped and swallowed. 'Carol, will you marry me?'

Carol's eyes filled with tears, her heart pounded and she could scarcely believe what was being said. She fought to clear her head and then abandoned herself to the joy that consumed her.

'Oh yes, yes...' Her words were muffled as their lips met.

They dressed and had breakfast in the room. Everything now felt so natural. They made plans for the three months ahead when Sovereign would return to Portsmouth. Carol decided to return to England within the week in order to start looking for a house and to set the wedding arrangements in motion. She told herself she no longer had reason to remain in Australia.

Peter had to be aboard by 0730 and the farewell was hard for both. Never before had he regretted a departure. Going to sea had always held the prospect of a new challenge. It was always an adventure. Now he yearned for the woman he would be leaving behind.

Carol parked the car outside the dockyard gates and Peter glanced at his watch. 0720. They put their arms about each other and kissed in the impossible hope that time would stand still.

'Oh Peter, I will miss you.' Carol cried, her face wet with tears. He could not answer so kissed her gently and tenderly while easing their bodies apart.

'I have to go.' He said, and looked around at the other members of the ship's company saying their farewells to girls met during the short stay. Stepping out onto the curbside he opened the rear door and removed the small case that contained his civilian clothes. A passing sailor saluted and Peter returned it smartly. That was the signal for him to assume his role as Squadron Navigator, HMS Sovereign. He walked to the front door and kissed Carol through the open window. She made a move to get out but he stopped her.

'I have to go. I will see you on the 11th July. I think it's a Monday.' He forced himself to smile and then added, 'Wear a mattress on your back.' Carol laughed through her tears and they kissed.

'Write a lot,' she pleaded, 'I do love you.' They kissed for the last time and Peter gently broke away.

'I love you too.' He answered and began the long walk back to the Navy.

Carol left the car and followed until the policeman on the gate indicated she could go no further. Peter looked back and waved.

'He looks magnificent,' she thought, his white cap cover reflecting the morning sunlight and his two and a half gold stripes appearing to glitter on the sleeves of his jacket...

'.. And he's all mine.' She said out loud.

Carol watched Sovereign's departure from Mrs. Macquarie's Chair, a lookout situated a short distance across the water from the dockyard. Her eyes scanned the aircraft carrier's bridge to catch a glimpse of Peter, but, could not be sure it was him she saw among the uniformed officers on the high platform.

The lumbering grey mass with white water churning under its stern moved inexorably out into the channel. Carol's tears once again began to fall as the distance between her and the ship grew greater. Sovereign turned and pointed her bow towards Bradley's Head and the open sea beyond.

Carol remained on the headland staring at the empty harbour. The occasional pleasure boat sped past, but, for Carol it was like staring into a void. Peter was gone and she would not see him for three long months.

During the next week Carol called at the airline office and booked her flight home. She gave her notice at the wine bar and wrote a letter to Phil.

This last task was left until the night before her departure. She knew that to stay and tell him face to face was the right thing to do, but, it was impossible. She could not face him knowing how badly he would take the news. Her first priority was to get home. She would feel that Peter was closer in familiar surroundings. There were also arrangements to be made. Such arguments could not disguise the fact that she was a coward, taking the coward's way out. She told herself that it was an image she would learn to live with.

At the wine bar Pat was upset by her decision but promised to explain, as much as he understood, of Carol's point of view to the young soldier. She left him her address and asked that he let her know how Phil was getting on.

As for the letter, she wrote that a complete break was the only solution and thanked him for his concern, kindness and love. It was totally inadequate, took the best part of the night to write and only ended when no more words could be found to justify her actions.

Nine weeks after stepping off the aircraft at Sydney's Kingsford Smith Airport, Carol Addison was in the departure lounge waiting to board the flight that would take her home. Pat came to see her off and when she asked him why he kissed her affectionately on the cheek and answered,

'Perhaps I love you. You have that effect on men you know.'

Chapter 13

Soon after Carol arrived in England a letter came from Pat. In the envelope was a newspaper clipping that told of the deaths of five soldiers and the wounding of seventeen others in the Phuoc Tuy Province of South Vietnam. It was among the highest casualty rates suffered by Australia in the war. The soldiers were from Phil's battalion but no names were given. There did not have to be. Phil had never written and now, he never would. A presence she had always felt was gone. Pat had not enclosed a letter and Carol concluded that he was either too sad, or too disgusted to write. She never heard from him again.

The wedding was a very private affair with Peter wanting as few reminders of his previous marriage as possible. Their life together began happily with both Peter's career and their marriage progressing successfully. However, the pressures that interrupted their first relationship came to disrupt the second.

On promotion to Commander, Peter was appointed

Executive Officer of the Navigation School at Southwick. In naval circles both events were regarded as triumphs for a young officer. Carol and he moved to an idyllic cottage in Meonstoke. A village set in the rolling hills of Hampshire, and one where the parish register boasted the names of other high ranking service officers, professional people and 'Gentlemen' farmers.

Since the days at Southwick Peter continued to prosper. In 1979 he achieved his Captaincy and the following year, command of one of Her Majesty's Destroyers. To his officers and men he was 'the oracle', the man most likely to succeed. Like all men they liked to be around success, and, in their eyes their Captain was supreme. No one in the ship, and only a few people elsewhere, knew that Peter Wells was not infallible.

Carol learned to live with her husband's obsession with success, just as she learned to live without his love. She also learned to live within herself. After so many broken dreams life became a sad disappointment, and life had not finished with Carol Wells.

In two weeks' time Peter Wells junior was coming to see the father he had never known. A young man who, to Carol, was a symbol of the children she never had and the selfishness of a husband who refused to even consider a family. It was a meeting she thought would never happen. Peter never spoke of his first marriage or his son. As the day drew nearer all her confused mind could think of was, 'why would he want to come on a Monday ?'

PART TWO

1981–

Chapter 14

'Hi Nick, I didn't see your name on the roster.' The three thin gold stripes on his jacket sleeves told that the man speaking was a Senior Steward, the second in charge of the thirteen man cabin crew aboard the Boeing 747.

The young man to whom he spoke positioned his black leather bag under one of the chairs in the small briefing room. Still trying to catch his breath he turned to answer; 'I was called out on an hour and a half standby, what a mad scramble. Who is the Flight Purser?'

The Senior Steward took out a crew list from his briefcase and read the name off the top;

'Don West, he's not bad.' He said and then added warily, 'except, he does have a thing about hats.'

'Oh No.' Nick put his hand over his mouth and pulled it down over his chin. 'I knew I would forget something in the panic.'

The Senior Steward suggested he go to the baggage room as they often had a collection of used hats left by forgetful crew members. Nick thanked him and hurried away hoping that one would be there.

When he returned, empty handed, the briefing room was full and the Flight Purser was seated behind the desk at the head of the room. His eyes narrowed as the last crew member entered and he disapprovingly looked at the gold wristwatch on his arm. Nick apologised and explained about his hat. The Flight Purser's reply was succinct;

'See the Captain when you get on board. Now let's get on with the briefing. Stephen Cartwright is your staff number correct and where do you want to work?'

There followed the routine check of staff numbers and the lottery to find which jobs on the aircraft each crew member wanted to perform. The choices went according to seniority and by the time the last job was reached so was the most junior crew member.

'Peter Wells, 25379, looks like you get the rear economy bar.' The Purser's voice still held its menacing edge.

'That's Nick not Peter. I don't use my first name.' The force of the statement caused the older man to look up from his paperwork and the others in the room to avert their eyes. The moment's silence was broken by a grudging acknowledgment and a continuation of the briefing procedure. The crew was told the passenger load, including the number of elderly or infirm as well as the number of babies and infants. The briefing was concluded with the Flight Purser asking if there were any qualified nurses on the crew and when no hands went up went on to ask the statutory safety questions;

'Nick Wells, where are the therapeutic masks stowed?' The answer was smartly and correctly given.

'Good.' The Purser acknowledged and concluded, 'let's have a good trip. See you all on the bus.'

The crew bundled out of the room with hands full of cabin bags and coat covers.

'Hello Nick.' The soft voice caused him to look behind and walk straight into a metal coat stand that stood by the doorway. He recovered noisily.

'I didn't know I affected you that much.' The pretty girl said, with a smile that accentuated her full, sensual mouth. She continued, her eyes wide with interest. 'I didn't see your name on the roster.'

'I was called out,' he answered.

'Good,' she said and smiled.

Nick stepped aside and let her pass through the door and out into the corridor.

'Pulled already?' The Senior Steward asked, flashing a glance towards the long legged stewardess walking through the swing doors to the waiting bus. Nick looked puzzled.

'I can't remember.' He replied and followed the girl onto the crew bus.

The bus stopped at the security checkpoint while the guard cast an eye over the identity cards of all on board. It then drove passed rows of parked aircraft until finally coming to a halt beside a semi-dormant white monster that would transport the crew and four hundred passengers to the blue waters and golden beaches of the Caribbean.

The blades of the four jet turbine engines turned lazily as petrol tankers and catering trucks ensured that both man and machine had enough to sustain them for the ten hour flight to Barbados via Antigua.

The crew bade farewell to the driver as they negotiated the steps and narrow doorway of the bus.

'Cheers, have a good flight.' He said to each in turn and then drove round to deliver his cargo of suitcases to the aircraft hold designated for crew baggage.

Meanwhile the crew, subdued by the thought of an aeroplane full of people and a long duty day, ascended the steps to the aircraft.

The interior of the cabin was a scene of organised chaos. Men and women with vacuum cleaners attacked the blue, well worn, carpet that had seen the soles of thousands of travelling feet; while others replaced the white headrest covers on each of the seats.

Silently and looking more like condemned souls than people just off to the beaches of the Caribbean the crew filed on board.

'Morning.' Came a greeting from inside the forward galley, where three men were loading enough meals for those passengers who would be sitting in the forward half of the aircraft. 'Give us a few minutes and we'll be out of your way.'

Nick said farewell to the Senior Steward who was heading forward into the First Class cabin.

'Oh yes, you're down the back aren't you?' The older man said with a smile that reflected his relief at not having to work in the crowded economy cabin.

Nick put his case behind his crew seat and proceeded to change out of his uniform jacket and into the maroon blazer that was the dress for cabin service. Once squared away he walked into the aft galley. One of the stewardesses was bent over and changing into her cabin shoes. Nick could not resist the temptation. He crept up, placed his hands on the girl's cello shaped hips and drew her to him.

'Stay like that,' he sighed, 'I think I'm in love.'

'Get off, you sex maniac. You stewards are all the same.' The broad beamed girl said as she straightened and stood up; but, not before pushing her bottom into his groin.

'You haven't changed since last week have you Nick?' A voice from behind called out.

'Oh hi Rog. I couldn't resist it, she's lovely.' He let go of the stewardess and turned to speak to the blonde haired steward who although only in his early twenties had a receding hairline that gave him a more mature look. Nick continued; 'Did you have a good stand-off?'

'Too short as usual.' The steward answered.

'I know what you mean.' Nick replied.

As they talked they set about preparing the galley and the after cabins for the onslaught of four hundred passengers.

'Who's looking after mothers and babies down the back here?' Nick asked.

'I am.' Nick swung around. 'Together again, Nick?' Her blue eyes appeared to widen as she spoke. 'It has been a long time.' Nick was baffled once again by this pretty girl who had spoken to him in the briefing room. As she walked into the galley he did not know what to say in reply.

'Stay away from him.' The other stewardess jokingly warned. 'His brains are in his trousers.' She turned to leave the galley and said; 'I'm going to check the toilets.'

'I'll be down there shortly!' Nick called after her, trying to take the focus off his present predicament.

'I'll get the safety equipment ready.' Roger said and left Nick alone with the pretty girl from the past.

'You don't remember, do you?' She asked with a quizzical smile on her lips.

Nick shook his head and admitted that he did not. Her answer surprised him.

'That's good. I thought you were ignoring me. I will have to jog your memory.'

She raised the hem on her skirt to reveal uniform grey stockings supported by a non-uniform red suspender belt. 'It is funny that we should be going to Barbados again.' She said, and shot Nick a knowing smile.

That was the key that unlocked the past. 'How could I forget?' He thought. His mind spun with a vision of a sandy beach, a full moon, rum punch and this girl lying astride him, naked, taking him into her. What he could not remember, and this worried him, was her name. Nick smiled and tried to brazen it out.

'I remember, I remember.' He said nodding his head and feigning recognition. He then did remember about his hat. They did not have one in the baggage room and the Flight Purser had told him to see the Captain. It was an escape from his embarrassment. He turned to the girl and taking her hand said;

'We'll talk later. Right now I have to see the Captain.' He hurried from the galley and headed forward.

'Have you seen the Captain yet?' The questioning voice of the Flight Purser barked as Nick's head appeared through the first class curtain. Nick replied that he was just on his way and climbed the spiral staircase to the upper deck of the 747. The stewardess who was looking after the upper deck cabin was just walking onto the flight deck laden down with cups of tea and sandwiches. She had the morning newspapers tucked under her right arm. Nick spoke, as he went in ahead of her.

'The Nigels have started already have they?' He joked in a whisper so as not to be overheard by the three men on the flight deck. 'I hope you have the Times crossword in there.' He said pointing to the newspapers. 'We won't be allowed to take off without that.' Nick winked at the stewardess and entered the flight deck.

The confined space was crammed with instruments, dials, panels and the three bulky figures of the technical crew. The Captain sat in the left hand seat, the back of his grey head bent over the controls. Nick waited until he saw him sit back;

'Hello Captain, my name is Nick Wells.'

The grey head turned revealing a round, red faced man who instantly reminded Nick of Santa Claus.

'Oh hello. Tea no sugar, just a dash of milk. Thank you.' Nick stepped back.

'Typical.' He thought and spoke again;

'No, Captain, the tea is on the way. I have been sent to tell you that I have not got a hat for this trip.'

'Why not?' Came the stern reply.

Nick could not believe that the loss of one hat could be such an important issue. He explained about being called out and forgetting it in the rush. The Captain listened and then ended the encounter by asking where the tea had gotten to. Nick's eyebrows raised to furrow his brow and he noticed a wry smile on the First Officer's lips. He had been listening to the conversation and his expression seemed to say, 'I have to sit up here with him for the next ten hours.' Nick nodded his acknowledgement and retreated from the flight deck. He spoke to the stewardess again as he left;

'Rather you than me, doll.' He hurried down the spiral staircase to the main deck.

Nick passed through the first class galley and walked down the other side of the aircraft's cabin in order to avoid another grilling about his hat from the Flight Purser. By the time he arrived back at the rear galley the Senior Steward in charge of the Economy cabin was there. He was a youngish man in his early thirties who sported a black moustache, neatly trimmed to a military style. His dark eyes stared and held Nick's.

'Hi Frank.' Nick said and reached out his hand.

'Hello chuck.' The Senior replied in a broad Lancashire accent. They shook hands. They had flown together before and each knew of the others likes and dislikes, on and off the aircraft. The thought crossed Nick's mind that a lot of the gay male cabin crew were sporting moustaches these days.

Preparations complete, the passengers began filtering on board. The voice of the Flight Purser crackled over the public address system announcing their arrival.

'Stand-by to repel boarders.'

Nick dreaded the opening stages of the flight when passengers tried to wedge bags that would fill a ship's hold into the limited stowages of the aircraft cabin.

Others wanted a 'smoking' seat but were allocated a seat in the non-smoking cabin, and, vice versa.

'Maybe I have been doing the job too long.' Nick said to himself as he set the smile on his lips and plunged into the fray.

'What is the problem?' He asked, having watched the flow of passengers come to a halt in a congested ball of humanity. An elderly couple were looking at their boarding cards and then turning their gaze to the seats around them, their faces registering their confusion. A vexed voice of a woman held up in the crowd rang out across the cabin.

'Excuse me, get out of my way, you are holding up the line.' She shrilled, trying to force her way through.

Nick asked her to wait for a second while he checked the boarding cards of the elderly couple and directed them to their seats. He then turned his attention to the terrier-like woman who was still straining at the leash.

'Now Madam, where are you sitting?' Her reply was short and to the point.

'Don't worry. I can find it.' He stepped out of the way rather than risk being trodden under foot, or battered to insensibility by her duty free bottle of Scotch and large bar of Toblerone.

Gradually, like the calming of the sea after a storm, the inside of the aircraft settled as everyone took their seats. Only a few remaining passengers straggled on board. The public address clicked into operation and the voice of the 'A' Girl in First Class welcomed the passengers aboard.

'That's sexy.' Nick thought, but could not remember

what the girl making the announcements looked like. He was not given time to ponder as the voice instructed the crew to stand by for the safety demonstration. Nick hurried to the equipment stowage but could not find the oxygen mask. He crossed the galley and looked in the stowage on the other side. That too was empty.

'Is this what you are looking for?' The girl from his past handed him the yellow plastic mask. 'Put it over your mouth and nose and breathe normally.' She said provocatively, using the words from the safety briefing. Nick smiled distractedly not knowing whether to be pleased or worried by all this attention. 'If only he could remember her name'. He thought.

Once the safety demonstration was over and each cabin was reported to be secured for take-off, the crew were directed to take their seats. They were on their way.

Ten minutes after the aircraft's wheels had left the tarmac the bar trolleys were wheeled out into the cabin. Forty minutes later they were followed by the hot meal carts. It was a synchronised system designed to feed and water four hundred people in the shortest possible time. However, there is always the special needs of the individual and the Senior Steward was the first to spot it.

'Nick, can you answer that call bell?' As a reflex Nick looked towards the blue light that was illuminated above the crew jump seat. Looking up and down the cabin he noticed a white light above one of the passenger seats at the rear of the aircraft. He went to see what was wrong.

He recognised the elderly couple who had been among the first passengers to board the aircraft.

'Is there anything wrong?' He asked and then his

eyes fell on the untouched meal tray in front of the old man. It was the woman who spoke:

'I am afraid my husband cannot eat this.' She said, pointing to the fillet steak on his tray. Nick looked at the man and instantly knew why.

'Of course Madam I will get something else.' The lady spoke again as if forced to give an explanation;

'We were so worried about missing the flight he forgot to put them in. His spare set is in our suitcase.' Nick knew all about being in a rush for the flight, but, could not suppress a smile. He reassured them and walked back to the galley to get a meal that did not require chewing.

It was another hour and a half before the meal was over and the trays collected in. The Senior Steward was preparing to screen the in-flight movie. Four hours had passed since the beginning of the flight and Nick still did not know the name of the mystery stewardess. He had expected to hear it during the bar or meal service but now knew that he had to ask somebody. He turned to the Senior Steward and asked;

'Have you got a crew list Frank?'

The Senior Steward searched in the pockets of his jacket.

'Yes somewhere here, why?' He replied.

'I want to know the name of the girl on the other bar, the one working with Roger?' Nick asked.

'It will drop off, you know.' The Senior answered and continued, 'I would not touch it if it was garnished with lemon on the side.'

'I know that Frank, but, could I have the name anyway?' The Senior looked down at his list.'

'Lynda Swan.'

'Of course.' Nick said to himself and repeated the name.

'What a waste.' Frank said and smiled at Nick.

'Thanks for the vote of confidence, but, I think I'll wait until they make it compulsory.' Frank's smile broadened and he replied;

'That won't be too long.'

'You could be right.' Nick acknowledged, only too aware of the number of gay stewards on the fleet. Armed with the name and spurred on by his memories Nick went in search of Lynda Swan.

'Lynda!' He called over the heads of the passengers lining up to buy their duty free alcohol, cigarettes and perfumes. She looked up with expectation in her eyes.

'See, I really do remember.' He said. She laughed revealing beautiful white teeth and eyes full of intent.

'I wondered when you would.' She replied and then noticed that all of the passengers standing close by were listening with interest.

The Flight Purser dimmed the cabin lighting and switched on the movie projector in each zone. The window blinds had been drawn and a calm settled over the darkened cabin.

'Now, hopefully, we can have a little peace and get a bite to eat.' Lynda spoke in a tired voice as she replaced the locks on her duty free bar. 'Are you eating Nick?' She asked.

Nick looked down at the pretty girl kneeling before him in front of the duty free trolley.

'Yes, okay.' He replied, trying to sound non-committal.

Lynda stood up and opened one of the many ovens that were crammed into the confined space of the aft galley.

'I put the meals on while the duty free bar was out in the cabin. They should be cooked. It's the usual, mixed grill, chicken or fish. What would you like?'

Nick opted for the fish. They placed the hot foils of food onto the plastic trays and left the galley. Nick and Lynda moved quickly through the galley curtain so as not to shed too much light into the main cabin. Keeping their eyes fixed on a point at the rear of the aircraft they walked quickly to the crew rest area.

'There's no one here.' Lynda said as she pulled back the curtain that shielded the four seats from the inquisitive stares of the passengers. They sat side by side and started eating. It felt awkward to finally be alone, where words did not sound so casual. It was Nick who spoke first.

'It's the Manager's Rum Punch Party tonight. Will you go along?'

'Will you?' The reply came instantly.

'All the rum you can drink in an hour, I never miss it if I get to Barbados on a Tuesday.' He answered with enthusiasm.

'Well, just save some for me.' She replied, placing the bread roll between lips moistened by the juice from the chicken.

Nick tried to steer the conversation onto the past to try and learn more about their last meeting, but, Lynda was more interested in the future and what adventures Barbados may hold. Nick stopped asking questions and concentrated on the food in front of him. When the meal was over Lynda was the first to make a move to leave.

'I had better get back.' She said, and, before Nick could answer she leant over and kissed him on the cheek. 'Until tonight.' She whispered.

The aircraft's wheels touched down on the shimmering tarmac at Barbados International Airport. Soon after the two forward doors on the left hand side of the aircraft swung open freeing the occupants trapped inside. The brilliance of the sunlight caused all not wearing sun glasses to squint as they exited the aircraft. While Nick said farewell to the passengers in his section his mind raced ahead to the evening and what it might hold.

'Do you want to stop at the shop?' The voice of the Senior Steward in charge of the First Class cabin brought the cramped mini bus to silence. The crew were halfway to the hotel and a decision had to be made before the last general store on the route was reached.

'How long have we got here?' A voice asked, from the back of the bus.

In the front passenger seat the Flight Purser turned around and looked back at his crew. His face had lost its menacing expression as if mellowed by the tropical evening air.

'We have tomorrow off, a shuttle to St Lucia the next day and home the following night.' He answered.

'Well, what do you think?' The Senior Steward repeated his question.

'Yes, we could do with a few crates.' Nick spoke for the rest of the crew.

The lights of the General Store came into sight through the ragged palm trees that bordered the pot holed road. The small bus stopped outside the wooden building that was built on a foundation of loose stones. The owner beamed a welcoming smile as he watched the airline crew enter his shop. He knew that his weekly takings were about to get a whole lot better.

'Okay, so that is three cases of beer and three bottles of rum.' Nick repeated the order for the confirmation of the crew. Two other stewards got out with him to help carry the stock. They returned a few minutes later.

'That should ensure a pleasant stay.' A voice called out from the back of the bus.

It was still quite a distance to the hotel and the crew had a chance to sample the beer before the lights of Bridgetown heralded that the hotel was not far away. Very soon the bus was driving down a dimly lit approach road that lead to the main entrance of the hotel. Porters were waiting to load the crew bags onto trolleys for transportation to the rooms. They saw the crates of beer and realised they needed more trolleys.

The crew checked in at the reception desk and milled around the lobby swapping room numbers and identifying their suitcases for the porters. Nick dropped the Bell Captain a tip for the carriage of the beer and the big man appeared satisfied. Nick then turned to the crew.

'A quick shower, change and up to the fort for the party. We don't have long. It only lasts an hour and gets underway at seven o'clock.' Almost as one the crew looked at the clock on the wall behind the reception desk. They had ten minutes.

'What room are you in, Nick?' He looked round to see Lynda with her pen poised ready to write down the number onto her crew list. The excitement of anticipation stirred within him. He checked his key.

'519.' He answered, and then asked, 'What about you?'

'531. See you at the fort.' She smiled and raised her eyebrows.

The air was balmy, still and heavy with the fragrance of the tropical blooms that grew in abundance in the hotel grounds. The Manager's Rum Punch Party was held on the battlements of a colonial fort, once used to protect the port of Bridgetown, but now part of the 5 star hotel. The lights of the city sparkled on the black sea while the stars above glittered in their dark mantle overhead. Nick could hear voices as he climbed the worn stone steps to the grassed area on top of the battlements. He looked over to see two tables bowing under the weight of glasses full of rum punch. The amber liquid with its decorative red cherry appeared to glow in the light from the ornamental torches that were positioned around the battlements. Nick collected a glass and walked away from the tables casting his eyes about the assembling crowd. He recognised the flight deck crew and then saw Roger coming up the steps followed closely by the girls.

'You are late, and one behind.' Nick said, holding

up an empty glass. The newcomers went along for their drinks and Nick went along for his second. They moved to the edge of the reception area where the battlements rose from the water's edge. Below the slow moving waves that lapped against the fortress wall lay canons, encrusted with two hundred years of sea life. They were exposed as the tide moved over them.

'This is the life.' Roger said, looking at the scene around him and the drink in his hand. The others nodded their agreement.

Nick sensed someone moving behind him and turned his head to see who it was. Lynda's blue eyes glowed brighter than the flames from the torches, whose light they reflected.

'Would you get me another?' She asked softly and handed him her empty glass.

'Sure.' He replied and then turned to the others. 'Anyone else for a refill?'

Loaded down with glasses he juggled his way to the bar and returned with a tray topped with brimming glasses of punch.

'Here, I brought you two.' Nick placed one in Lynda's hand and the other on the stone wall. 'It will save a trip.' He added. They both took a sip of the spicy cocktail and began to talk, ignoring those around them. Lynda had the advantage of knowing more about Nick than he of her, and he wanted to redress the balance. As they talked he also knew that whatever happened the last time they met, he wanted it to happen again.

As one glass was emptied so another took its place. As images entered Nick's mind so they became desires.

He knew the party would soon be over and it was his turn to make the move.

'After this is finished, would you like to get something to eat?' He asked.

'Sounds good.' Lynda answered eagerly. It had been a long time since she had eaten the meal on the aeroplane.

'We'll go along to The Swordfish shall we?' Nick suggested knowing that the little restaurant on the beach was popular with crews, but, also aware that it was close and its service fast.

The setting was made for romance. The waves from the Caribbean rolled onto the beach only feet away from the dining tables; but, Nick knew that with the number of times Lynda had been to Barbados he was not going to impress her with this restaurant. He often lamented the fact that the majority of girls with whom he flew had been, seen, and done more than he had around the world. They were hard girls to impress. However, tonight he hoped that the meal was just a formality, which was why it came as a shock to hear another man call out Lynda's name. Nick looked toward the intruder. He was an older man of stocky build with a thick shock of black hair that was greying at the temples. In the flickering light of the flaming torches the lines of his face appeared deeply etched. However, Nick had to admit that this man was a threat. The couple kissed and Lynda kept hold of the older man's hands as they talked.

Separated from the main group and no longer talking to Lynda, Nick felt vulnerable and self-conscious. He edged closer hoping to force an introduction and drive a wedge between them. He could not help thinking that Lynda was playing games and a slight feeling of resentment welled within him. It was a resentment tempered by desire and tinged with frustration. After a few minutes that felt like an eternity Lynda turned her attention to him once again.

'Nick Wells, this is Bob Farringdon, he is the Engineer off the other crew.'

The men shook hands and Nick asked the standard questions about the Engineer's trip, all the time wanting to know only one thing, how well did Bob Farringdon know Lynda Swan?'

'It's finished here, are you going to eat?' The Flight Engineer asked.

Nick felt his stomach go into a tight knot. Lynda explained that they were just off to The Swordfish and the Engineer asked if he could join them. Nick fought to appear unconcerned.

As they strolled through the hotel grounds and out onto the road that led to the restaurant the three chatted about their current trips and reminisced over passed ones. Nick kept alert so that he may find out more about this man who threatened his plans. They left the roadway and walked across an uneven patch of ground before coming to a pathway that led alongside the sand. The sea barely made a sound as it glided onto the beach. The lights of a cruise liner rounded the headland and moved silently across the bay towards the harbour entrance.

The three walked past a small green hedge that bordered the restaurant grounds and entered through a small open gate. The restaurant was a curious structure without windows or walls. The tables were set under a wooden roof into which slid the sides of the building, leaving an unobstructed view along the beach and out to sea. Most tables were occupied.

'There's one.' Lynda called and pointed to a small table just being vacated, close by the water's edge. They walked over and sat down. Nick seethed inside as the Engineer held Lynda's chair while she took her place.

'Creep.' He said to himself, picking up a menu to hide his embarrassment at not performing the courtesy himself.

The waiter soon arrived and their orders were quickly taken.

'What are you doing tomorrow?' Bob asked. Nick noticed that the question was addressed to both of them. He and Lynda looked innocently at each other and shrugged their shoulders. Bob continued; 'our crew are going out on The Captain Kidd, why don't you come along?'

The Captain Kidd was a sailing cruiser built to look like a pirate ship and designed to be just as lethal. For a set price they provided a five hour cruise along the coast, stopping for water sports and lunch while never stopping the flow of alcohol and live steel band music. It was a devastating combination.

'Sounds great.' Lynda was enthusiastic. Nick agreed. Bob explained that a bus would collect them from the hotel at nine o'clock.

The food arrived and they continued their conversation between mouthfuls of flying fish and sips of Pina Colada. Lynda had wanted a change from the rum punch and the two men went along with her decision.

'I didn't know how hungry I was.' Nick said, making short work of the meal.

While he had been eating the others talked freely. Once again Nick felt the evening drifting away from him. Coffee arrived and he drank it slowly while looking out at the small boats that bobbed at their moorings only a few feet from the beach. As his mind tracked from one transient thought to another he felt self-conscious and awkward. It was Lynda who brought him back.

'Are you ready to go Nick?' She asked, pushing her empty coffee cup towards the centre of the table. He took a second to understand the question and then said that he was. They stood up and once again Bob was quick to help Lynda with her chair. Nick clenched his fists in an attempt to relieve the tension in his body. As they walked back along the path he tried to unravel the confusion in his mind. Lynda had virtually ignored him throughout the meal and then had asked if he was ready to leave. It didn't make sense. There were times when he hated her for playing him along; but, he knew he wanted her more now than he had ever imagined in their earlier word games. His thoughts moved on to ways of getting what he wanted.

To this end Bob Farringdon played right into his hands and Nick gloated over the first mistake his rival had made that evening. The Engineer, either underestimating Lynda's tiredness after the busy flight from London or overplaying his own hand, asked if she wanted to call in at the hotel bar for a nightcap. Nick had waited, willing Lynda to answer no and unable to disguise his relief when she did so. That left the next move up to him. He had been virtually ignored for the past two hours and now had to devise a way to get this girl he had been sure was his so many hours before. He was not helped by the fact that all three had rooms on the same floor of the hotel and it was his room they came to first. If he had not thought fate was against him before, he was now convinced that it was. Turning to Bob he extended his hand and wished him good night. He then turned to Lynda and kissed her cheek. He wanted to whisper that he would be in touch but the moment was lost. Dejected he put his key in the lock and opened the door.

The room felt empty and the chill of the air conditioning was given a keener edge by knowing that he had failed. He felt for the light switch and the brilliance of the fluorescent bulb caused him to screw his eyes into a squint. Once accustomed to the brightness he looked around the white stone walls of the room. An abstract painting of bold yellow and green lines hung drunkenly over the bed. It was the first time Nick had noticed the work of art and he hated it. He hated the room, the silence, the disappointment. He swore in the emptiness and kicked the side of the double bed. It slid sideways on the smooth tiled floor and bumped the table standing alongside. The white plastic telephone rattled under the attack. Drawn by the sound Nick's eyes fell upon it. Crossing to the chest of drawers, where he had deposited the contents of his uniform pockets, he found the crew list he was given at Reception. He looked down the names until he came to the one he sought. The room number was scribbled beside it. In three strides he was standing in front of the telephone, the mouthpiece poised to his lips.

The purring sound in his ear told him that the machine was at his command. The index finger of his right hand extended towards the symbol that would connect him with the operator. He turned the dial until his finger was stopped by the plastic guard on its face and then he let it spin back to its starting position. The line went dead and then came alive once again as its signal was transmitted to the operator seated at the hotel switchboard.

'Hello, Operator, can I help you?' On the sound of the voice Nick placed the receiver back in its cradle.

'No.' He said to the now silent machine. He added the telephone to his hate list. It was impersonal, artificial. It made him feel furtive, begging. The moment was lost. There would be another. He turned his back on the object of his scorn and thought again. 'He could go and knock on her door.' He quickly dismissed that idea. His mind then set about analysing the events of the day, and all he could think was how the 'bloody' Engineer had ruined everything. He then felt his resolve return.

'To hell with it.' He said out loud. 'Faint heart never won fair lady.' His mind made up he walked back to the telephone and this time the call went through. Waiting for Lynda to answer he could feel the palms of his hands get moist. He shifted the receiver from his right to his left hand and brushed his free palm against the material of his trousers.

'Hello.' The questioning voice, sensual and feminine, startled him and for a moment his mind went blank.

'Hello.' The voice said again. 'She had not hung up. That was a good sign.' Nick thought and then managed to find his voice.

'Hi, Lynda. It's Nick. I hope I didn't disturb you.' It sounded so pathetic but, what else could he say? A debate raged in his brain, analysing and arguing every word he said.

'Oh no, not at all.' The answer came. 'I was just going to have a shower.'

Nick pictured the scene, the towel wrapped around her slim body, pulled tightly across her full and upright breasts; or perhaps no towel at all. The muscles contracted in his stomach and he stirred in anticipation. Awkwardly he moved his position. He had made the opening move and now had to sustain the momentum.

'I thought you may like a bedtime drink. I have got some brandy. How about a brandy coffee?' The proposition had been made. He now waited and part of him dreaded the reply. 'What if she said no?' He then remembered the Engineer. 'What if he was with her?' It felt like an eternity as he waited for the answer.

'I would love one.' Came the reply. 'How about you come round in five minutes. It will give me time to have a shower and slip into something.' The answer sent shivers to every extremity of Nick's body.

'Five minutes. I'll be there. Bye.' Replacing the receiver he could not believe his luck. 'I'm in.' His whole body screamed it out. He checked his watch. 'Five minutes.' He said and smiled, intoxicated by the prospect of what lay ahead.

Quickly he looked up and down the corridor and then knocked twice on the door. To his surprise the door slowly swung open. He entered the room pushing the door still wider. The room was empty and silent. 'Where was she?' He closed the door and moved further into the room. Looking around he noted that all the rooms in the hotel looked the same, the white stone walls, even the same gaudy painting. Only the occupant's belongings set it apart. The black suitcase standing in the corner, the high heeled uniform shoes standing next to it. The hint of perfume in the air. A sense of movement drew Nick's attention toward the bathroom and then Lynda appeared. His heart felt as if it had stopped beating and then, as he stared, it started to pound so loud he thought he could hear it. Lynda stood silhouetted against the bright light of the bathroom. A short, red, happy coat, decorated with gold embroidered Chinese dragons enfolded her. It ran down the line of her body, fell across the rise of her breasts and ended midway down her taut thighs. The two sides were held together by a red cotton belt that promised to untie at the easiest provocation. Nick tried to dislodge it by the power of hypnotic persuasion.

'You are lovely.' The words were barely audible as they slipped from his lips.

Lynda approached slowly, sensually.

'I didn't think you were going to call.' She replied, holding out her arms to him. He moved towards her. 'It has been a long time.' Lynda sighed, 'let us not waste anymore.' Her hands moved to the buckle on his belt and her fingers moved to unfasten it. Nick cradled her head with his hands and stroked her honey blonde hair. His lips travelled lightly across her face. Her hands caressed him. His body arched and his mouth sought the lips that were parted for him.

'Oh Lynda,' he sighed, his voice heavy with passion, his body consumed with desire.

He lay on the white cotton pillow supporting the yellow haired head on his chest. The golden rays of daylight shone through the cracks between the curtains. The morning chorus of birds heralded a new day. 'It had been a great night,' he thought and smiled as the events were re-played in his mind's eye. 'She certainly was inventive.' His smile broadened. He tried to look at his watch that lay on the bedside table. It did not feel that early and he remembered the plans for the day. Craning his neck he raised his head from the pillow.

'Can't you lay still?' Lynda's voice startled him. She looked up into his eyes and pressed her body against his. 'Your chest makes a lovely pillow.' She purred. Nick felt himself becoming aroused again. 'What is this I feel?' Lynda whispered, seductively moving so as to guide his awakened body into her. Nick felt driven by her sexuality and moved his hips easily, gently rocking their bodies beneath the bed clothes.

'We have a big day ahead.' Nick said with a smile.

'You're telling me.' Lynda replied, contracting and holding on until she felt him explode inside of her.

They laughed and kissed, making love was easy on that bright Caribbean morning.

'Come on we have got to get up.' Nick quickly kissed Lynda on the cheek and moved away.

'Again!' She demanded and they laughed together.

'We could stay here all day if you had not agreed to join that Engineer on that boat.' Nick taunted her.

'Me.' Lynda was quick to answer. 'I didn't hear you say no.'

'I never say no.' He said and patted the firm rise of

Lynda's bottom under the sheets. He looked at his watch and leapt from the bed. 'Hell, they will be calling for us at nine.' He exclaimed.

'What time is it now?' Lynda asked.

'Twenty to. I better get back to my room.' He stumbled into his trousers and did up the buttons on his shirt as he slipped into his shoes. Once dressed he gave Lynda a quick kiss on her lips. 'I'll be back in fifteen minutes.'

'That's the trouble with men,' Lynda complained in mock annoyance, 'once they have had you they can't wait to get away.' As Nick reached the door he opened it and turned to her,

'I will be back.'

'You better be.' She warned and threw a pillow at him.

Nick caught it and winked at her. He then slid through the open doorway and into the world outside. Looking up and down the corridor he was relieved to see that no one was about. He quickly walked to his room. His feet felt as if they barely touched the ground.

The sea shimmered in front of him and his eyes smarted from the salt water that leaked into the bottom of the mask. His chest felt tight and the air trapped in his lungs fought to escape its sinewy bonds. The wreck was visible but looked closer than it was in the crystal clear blueness of the sea. Brightly painted fish of all shapes and sizes flashed before the glass that protected his eyes. Taking greater control of his breathing Nick kicked his legs and pulled at the water with his arms in a last ditch effort to reach the barnacle encrusted hull of the wartime freighter that lay on the sandy seabed outside Bridgetown Harbour. It was no use. He swore at his lack of fitness and the previous night's rum punches as he turned back towards the surface. Expelling the air from his lungs in short bursts of bubbles that ascended passed his eyes like so many escaping prisoners he rose gently.

The black hull of the Captain Kidd was off to the right and he could see flailing arms and legs of other swimmers in and under the water. His eyes caught sight of a trim figure, barely concealed behind the crimson swimsuit. He swam towards the gently kicking legs and languidly moving arms that swirled the water along the contours of Lynda's body. With every stroke that brought him nearer he felt his desire growing. He struggled to control his breathing as the excitement of being so close to the body that had given him so much pleasure threatened to betray him to the sea.

Drawing near he reached out his arms, grabbing her around the waist, his fingers exploring inside the fine material of her costume. Then something he had not expected happened. Her body went taught and her legs kicked frantically as she tried to get away. Her thrashing arms churned up the water and hit Nick's face, expelling what air he had left in his lungs. He quickly surfaced to hear Lynda crying in panic and beating the water, wildly fighting to stay afloat.

'Are you alright?' The booming voice of a crewman on board The Captain Kidd rebounded across the water. All heads on the sailing ship were turned towards the threshing water. Alarmed now, Nick repeated the sailor's question.

'Lynda are you alright?'

Other swimmers were making their way back to the ship, some in alarm, some just curious at what all the commotion was about.

Lynda quietened when she heard Nick's voice and her eyes focused on his puzzled face. Then they hardened and bore into him.

'You bloody idiot!' She hissed, repeating it over and over as her body calmed down.

Nick waved to the ship and signalled that everything was under control. He then looked to Lynda.

'I'm sorry Lynda. I didn't mean to frighten you.' She swore at him again and swam towards the ship. Nick watched her go, powerfully, yet gracefully moving through the water. He watched as she pulled herself up the metal rungs of the ladder that was secured to the ship's side. He saw the crewman talking to her, a quick conversation and then she strode into the cabin at the stern of the ship and out of sight.

The excitement was over and the revellers returned to leaping from the ship's sides with wild, whooping yells. Nick decided that he better get back on board and try and put things right.

As he walked, dripping water onto the wooden deck, he stopped at the bar and collected a glass of rum punch. Holding it carefully and taking sips along the way he searched the decks and even stood guard outside the ladies washroom in case she had sought refuge in there. Eventually, he returned to the upper deck and walked forward.

'Lynda!' He called, as much in relief as in surprise.

She was sitting on the ship's rail talking to a sun tanned couple that Nick guessed must have been in their early forties. From their accent he guessed they were American.

'Lynda, I have been looking all over the boat.'

She shot him a disinterested glance and answered curtly.

'Well, you've found me.'

He self-consciously looked at the couple and then back at Lynda. He lowered his voice;

'I am sorry. I was stupid.' The apology hurt his pride, especially delivered before an audience. She was unforgiving.

'You're telling me. How could you do that? Just leave me alone.' So saying she excused herself from the group and walked briskly back towards the bar.

'She is a very angry young lady.' The comment came from the American woman and it took a moment for the words to register in Nick's consciousness.

'Yes, she is.' He answered distractedly, looking at the retreating figure.

The woman spoke again;

'Let's not let her spoil our fun.' She turned to the man sitting beside her and Nick revised his earlier estimation. He was much older; but, Nick was impressed by his athletic body. There was no excess flesh to be seen. The woman spoke again. 'Joe is just going to refill our glasses. Would you like one?' She removed the plastic glass from Nick's hand and gave it to her husband. At least Nick assumed he was her husband, there had been no introductions. The muscled body of the older man followed in Lynda's footsteps. They were alone and Nick could feel the electricity travelling between them. There was no other way to describe the atmosphere in which they now found themselves. It was as if they both knew that the other was there for the taking. Nick spoke first.

'What part of the States are you from?'

The lines appeared in white creases at the corner of her eyes as her tanned face broke into a broad smile. Nick felt uneasy.

'What's funny?' He asked awkwardly.

'I'm not from the States. I'm Canadian,' she paused and then smiled, 'you Australians never could tell the difference.' It was Nick's turn to smile.

'Touché.' He replied, and laughing together they held each other's eyes.

'Hi, I'm Tania.' The woman presented her hand and Nick took it eagerly.

'I'm Nick.' He said and looked into her brown eyes, unable to turn away.

The barriers tumbled down. Tania was eager to talk and for Nick just looking at her was enough, although he did contribute to the conversation when asked. While he spoke his eyes took in her whole body. He hoped his attentions would not be noticed, but, looking once again into her eyes he knew that they had.

'Joe, this is Nick. He's an Air Steward.' Tania addressed her husband who had returned with his hands full of drinks. The big man distributed the glasses and then shook hands with Nick.

'Pleased to meet you. I just saw your young lady at the bar. She's really knocking back the sauce.'

Nick shrugged his shoulders. Lynda was beyond his control, he had apologised what more could he do? Besides, he now had another interest.

The small ship was underway again and the sea breeze was refreshing after the still heat. Nick noticed that even with the new motion of the vessel Joe's muscled frame did not waver as if rooted to the deck like a giant mast.

'Where are you staying, Nick?' The big man's voice boomed in Nick's ear as the Canadian over compensated for the noise of the ship's engine.

'Over there.' He replied, pointing to the hotel perched on the headland. 'You can almost see my room.'

'That's a coincidence. We are staying there too.' Tania said and smiled directly at him.

Nick looked puzzled as he spoke.

'I didn't see you on the bus from the hotel.'

Tania was still smiling;

'You were preoccupied with a young lady at the time.' Nick glanced along the deck. While talking to Tania he had forgotten that Lynda was still on board. He sipped his drink and then saw her talking to the Engineer and a well endowed girl he recognised from the other crew.

'How long are you going to be in Barbados, Nick?' Joe's resonant voice brought Nick back to the conversation.

'Three days.' Nick answered. 'A shuttle tomorrow and home the following night.'

'They keep you pretty busy.' This time it was Tania who spoke, engaging him as much with her eyes as with her voice. Nick nodded and replied,

'Except for today, and I have my own plans for that.'

Tania was interested. Joe's eyes had just found the barely concealed breasts of the girl Nick had seen earlier.

'What might those plans be?' Tania asked provocatively. Nick felt that tingle of excitement that comes when the sexual game is being played and the stakes are getting higher. It's just like fishing he had always thought. The initial nibbles at the bait, curiosity on one side, anticipation on the other. Each one becoming bolder, swept in the inevitability of the flow until the excitement of the catch produces a frenzy in both. He didn't like fishing, but it made for a good analogy. Nick outlined his plans.

'Well, here we are for a start, and, a very good one it is too. Tonight I plan to carry on the momentum at the Winston Club.' He could see Tania growing more interested.

'Where is that?' She asked and Nick explained.

'A couple of minutes taxi ride from the hotel. It's great. The food is excellent and after dinner, drinks are half price and there is a disco on the beach. There's nothing like bopping and drinking a Rum Punch with the sand between your toes.'

'That sounds great. Will you take Joe and me? Show us the ropes.' The request was a thinly veiled invitation and Nick knew it. He thought quickly. He was not sure how he now stood with Lynda and he did not want to spend the evening alone. He arranged to meet them in the hotel lobby at eight o'clock. He even considered inviting them to the crew room for a pre-dinner drink, but decided that would definitely be asking for trouble.

'Will you dance Nick?' He no longer had time to

think about the evening as Tania took his hand. The steel band had started to play and he excused himself to Joe, who looked resignedly into his half empty plastic glass.

They danced to the reggae and calypso music and Nick drew applause from the crowd by limboing between Tania's legs while she poured her rum punch over his upturned chest. As he stood up Tania licked the rum from the matted body hair. Excited but a little embarrassed, Nick glanced over to Joe and was relieved to see that the big man was not looking.

'You are the best thing that has happened on this holiday.' Tania said as she held his hands and swayed her body before him. Nick smiled warily realising that he may be getting out of his depth. He was thankful when Tania asked if he would get her a drink. Obediently he moved towards the bar.

'You seem to be enjoying yourself.' Lynda's voice was edgy. Nick smiled.

'They are Canadians, on holiday. I am just being neighbourly.' This time Lynda laughed out loud.

'Oh Nick, you are incorrigible.' She leaned across and kissed him on the lips. 'Don't forget who you came with and don't get too neighbourly.' She continued to smile and stepped aside to let him order his drinks.

Nick looked blankly at the bartender who had to ask twice what he wanted to drink. Nick ordered three rum punches and then said to himself;

'I don't believe it, and I'll never understand them.' He thanked the barman, smiled at Lynda and walked back to deliver the drinks.

The ship's mainsail flapped in the light breeze as the skipper came into wind. The anchor was dropped and the Captain Kidd rolled on the gentle swell off the fashionable beach of Sandy Lane. As soon as headway was lost, speed boats surrounded the ship, tempting the passengers into water ski trips around the bay. Those who could do it and those who, because of the rum, thought they could, tumbled into the rocking boats. Nick stood leaning with his hands on the rail, looking down into one of the small craft.

'Why don't you have a go?' Nick turned and looked into Tania's mischievous face. He could not believe that she was into middle age. Where were the wrinkles, the sagging breasts? Even her backside was taught.

'Oh no, not me.' He answered. 'That is one thing I have never mastered.'

'You can swim though.' So saying Tania stood up on the rail and dived cleanly into the translucent blue water. She soon surfaced looking up at him, traces of water glistening on her face and shoulders. 'Come on,' she called, 'Jump!'

Nick did not acknowledge the call, he simply rolled sideways and fell like a bale of cotton over the side and hit the water with a geyser like splash. Tania laughed so much she nearly swallowed the greater part of the Caribbean.

'You are a fool.' She spluttered through the tears that were rolling down her cheeks and mingling with the salt water spray. They swam along and under the ship. There were no brightly coloured fish as there had been at the wreck, but, the sea bed was still sandy and with a deep breath Nick could just reach it.

'I do not want any of the funny business you played on that poor girl.' Tania warned smilingly.

Nick assured her that he was a reformed man. They laughed and swam to the anchor cable. As they held onto the metal links with their legs kicking gently beneath them Nick saw Lynda climbing down the ship's ladder and enter the water with a plastic card between her teeth. Another girl, who he did not recognise, followed close behind. Charged with curiosity he called out to ask what they were doing, and was, not surprised when Lynda took the card out of her mouth and replied;

'They have the most gorgeous clothes in the hotel boutique here and we are going to have a look.' Nick smiled and thought how no man could afford to marry a stewardess.

It was quite some time later when he saw the girls return. This time Lynda had a plastic bag clenched firmly between her teeth. All of the other people who saw were laughing and pointing at the heavily laden swimmer breast stroking her way towards the ship. Once aboard she held up her prize and everyone applauded loudly. Lynda made a curtsey and walked over to Nick who was now up on deck and clapping along with the rest.

'Look what I bought.' She said proudly and held up the wet bag. With a flourish she brought out a chic cocktail dress that was perfectly dry. 'Isn't it lovely?' She said, holding it in front of her.

'It certainly is.' It was Tania who spoke first.

'Thank you.' Lynda said shyly, and Nick was struck by how pretty she looked at that moment. Her face flushed with achievement and exertion. He spoke up and told her of their plans for the evening. Lynda agreed that it was a good idea. For a moment Nick was not so sure. Through a rum induced haze he briefly saw the complications that lay ahead, but, that moment passed when the boat's dinner bell rang.

After the bajan chicken and rice meal was eaten and the leftovers were cleared away the Captain Kidd weighed anchor and headed for home. The old wooden hull pounded into the waves that had risen with the afternoon breeze. Everyone either sat down or held on. Everyone except Nick. He swayed about the deck like a drunken sailor asking in an unsteady voice why no one would dance with him.

'Come on Nick. Sit down and stop playing the fool.' Lynda chided, trying to guide him back to the bench seats that skirted the deck. Nick allowed himself to be led, giggling and smiling benignly to all those around him.

'You are a fool.' Tania said to him, smiling and amused by his antics. Joe's face was impassive. 'The old stick in the mud.' She said to herself.

When the boat tied up alongside the wharf and the gangway was secured Nick, holding onto Lynda's hand, negotiated the narrow piece of wood with measured steps. The rum had done its work and the crowded minibus sped along the uneven roads to the noise of voices raised in song. Tania leaned across to Lynda;

'These guys here,' she said, pointing to the driver, 'must think we're mad. All reserved in the morning and out of our trees in the afternoon.'

'They must be used to it.' She replied with a giggle. 'It happens every time.'

317

On arrival at the hotel they stumbled from the bus and walked unevenly into the lobby.

'We will see you here at eight then,' said Tania, half asking and half telling the others.

'Okay.' Lynda answered. 'We'll see you then.'

The older woman looked to Nick for his confirmation, but, his eyes barely focused on the stone floor beneath his feet.

'Will he be all right?' She asked with concern. Lynda shook her head and answered;

'He better be.' She took Nick's arm. 'Come on you idiot.' She said and led him away.

'Did you see the state he was in?' Joe's voice was hard with disdain. 'How could anyone get in that state so quickly?'

'Oh Joe. Don't be so pious. Those rum punches were pretty lethal, and he is only young.' Tania came to Nick's defence.

'Trust you to be on his side. You hardly left him alone all day. You looked stupid. Why don't you at least try and act your age?' Jealousy was in his voice and Tania knew when to be diplomatic.

Her husband had not always been so staid. At college he had been the wild one of the group they used to go round with. There was nothing he wouldn't try. He knew no fear and Tania had found that irresistible. He had always been athletic and his physical strength had saved his body from annihilation on numerous occasions. From whatever adventure he had always returned smiling. They had married at the end of their college years when he was at his liveliest and most reckless. It was meant to be their greatest adventure.

Joe moved into the world of business with his characteristic bravado. He speculated wildly, buying one business after another with each failing through lack of knowledge and insight. Joe refused to be an employee, refused to be number two. As each attempt failed he attributed it to bad luck, poor support, even personality clashes with suppliers or colleagues. Eventually the failure spilled over into their marriage. Tania could no longer, and would no longer, ignore the moody silences, bouts of drinking and occasional flashes of violence. She had left him once, but returned believing that she could make a difference, and he would change. He did cut down on the alcohol and she even got him to accept a job working for someone else. He now made enough money to afford a holiday in the Caribbean each year, however, there was a cost. The spark had long gone out of their marriage and that inner drive that had first attracted Tania could now only be seen in the obsessive way Joe kept his body in trim. Physical fitness had become a religion to Joe Aspinal. It was the one occupation in which he was totally in control of his mind and body to the exclusion of all others.

'How was the Captain Kidd?' Anne, the girl who had been working the upper deck cabin asked Lynda as they went to refill their glasses. Lynda reached for the half empty bottle of white wine and topped up both drinks. She smiled as she recounted the day's events.

'So that is why he's not here.' Anne said. 'I knew there had to be a good reason.'

'He will be along.' Lynda assured her. 'I gave him a knock as I came to the room party.' She recalled Nick's drawn face, pained expression and disbelief that he had promised to have dinner with Tania and Joe. He promised Lynda that he would be along right away. She heard the toilet flush as she walked away. Lynda could not help feeling sorry for him.

The two single beds had been pushed against the wall and the balcony doors were wide open, all in an attempt to get as many people as possible into one small room. Two crews were combined in the evening's get together and people who had not seen each other in years were talking animatedly over glasses of beer, rum, wine or anything else they had brought along. It was the noise that told Nick he was nearing the room. As he entered the cigarette smoke burned his already smarting eyes.

'Ah, the sailor has finally made it.' Roger bellowed over the heads of the people standing by the door. 'Come here Nick my boy and have the hair of the dog.' Almost involuntarily Nick put out his shaking hand.

'Thanks.' He replied quietly and took a sip at the glass.

To his surprise, with each mouthful, he did feel better and said to his friend that this was the start of the slippery slope that led to alcoholics anonymous.

'I'll introduce you to the selection board.' Roger replied. The two stewards edged their way passed the crowd and out onto the balcony.

'You made it then?' The tone was thinly veiled with sarcasm and the Engineer was not smiling. Nick quickly noted that he was drinking with the two oldest men in the room. One he recognised as the Captain from their own flight, the other, he assumed to be the skipper off the other crew. Nick replied with a grin.

'Yes thanks. It was a good day wasn't it?' He was determined to show no signs of the queasiness he felt inside. A feeling he was pleased to note that was easing with every swallow of the rum he had in his glass. The Engineer smiled but did not answer, turning quickly instead to resume his conversation with the pilots.

'Who rattled his cage?' Roger asked, having monitored the conversation. Nick's grin turned into a genuine smile of satisfaction;

'He sees me as the reason he is not having his evil way with Lynda.'

'Well, he is still trying.' Roger lifted his glass to point towards the group. Lynda had joined them and was holding the three men spellbound. Nick thought of the saying about bees round a honey pot, or was it something about big black dogs he concluded, ungenerously.

Nick drained his glass and, taking those in similar condition from the people around him, edged his way across the room to the dressing table that was doubling as a makeshift bar. On the return journey he was waylaid by a steward from the other crew, a character he had not seen for over a year. They talked, condensing the months into seconds and their adventures into verbal comic strips. Walking back to his own group Nick smiled to himself thinking that in not many jobs did time stand still and so many different people float in and out of one's life as if they had never been away. 'The Flying Foreign Legion,' he thought about the expression and how well it suited airline crews.

'About time too! We are dying of thirst and you are doing a Royal walkabout.' Roger took his glass and said no more.

'You made it then.' Lynda had joined the group and spoke to Nick, after Roger had finished with him. Nick raised his hands in mock exasperation.

'Why does everyone keep saying that? Was there ever any doubt?' The group dissolved in hoots of laughter and when it subsided Lynda turned to Nick.

'We have to leave. Remember we are meeting Tania and Joe in the lobby at eight.' Nick glanced at his watch.

'Time for a quick one.'

Lynda stood firm.

'No there is not.' Taking hold of Nick's hand she led him through the crowd.

'I have this effect on women, when they want me, they have to have me.' He called back to the group who were grinning after them.

'Oh, come on Nick.' There was a hint of frustration in Lynda's voice and so he turned and followed her out of the room.

The Canadians were waiting in the lobby when Lynda and Nick came out of the lift.

'You are here Nick.' Tania said with laughter in her voice. Once again Nick threw up his hands.

'Give me a break.' He replied and Lynda spoke up.

'Everyone has been saying that and I for one think he deserves all the stick he gets.'

'You are a cruel woman.' Nick retorted and then breezily added. 'Well here we are, let's go for a drink.'

'Oh Nick!' The women exclaimed in unison.

Taking one on each arm Nick swept out of the lobby with Joe following quietly behind.

Over dinner they discussed those parts of their lives they did not mind exposing to the world. Nick could not miss the glossing over that the latter part of the Canadians marriage received. He was not surprised. A blind man could see the signs of a marriage being held together in a string bag. He could also not fail to recognise the huntress in the woman sitting opposite him across the table. She was the stereotype of the young man's dream. 'There again,' he thought, 'there is Joe.' He shot the big man a sideways glance. 'He is awesome.' He concluded and returned his attention to the conversation going on around the table.

'Shall we take the drinks outside?' Tania's voice was eager. 'I can hear music.' She added impatiently.

'Sounds good to me.' Lynda seconded the suggestion. 'But first,' she looked across to Tania and then to the men, 'will you gentlemen excuse us?'

'Why do they always have to go in pairs?' Nick asked the older man who just shrugged his shoulders and said nothing. It was an awkward silence until the ladies returned.

'What are you sitting there for?' Lynda called across the restaurant. Joe looked visibly uneasy as Nick got up from the table to join her. The music was loud and the dance floor was already crowded.

'This is a popular place.' Lynda sounded surprised and continued. 'Why have I not heard about it before?' Nick was quick to answer.

'You have never been on the town with me before.' Lynda looked puzzled and then asked.

'Why didn't you bring me here on our last visit?' Nick drew closer to her and lowered his voice.

'I don't think we went out much on our last visit.' Lynda's smile told him that she understood.

'Well, I am here now.' She bounced back, 'let's dance.' Taking Nick's hand she rushed toward the wooden dance floor.

'Come on Joe, let's dance.' Tania tried unsuccessfully to coax her husband away from the bar. Resentfully she stood watching the other couples enjoying themselves moving to the sensual beat of the reggae music. The excitement born of anticipation faded within her. At that moment she hated her husband. She looked out onto the sandy dance floor searching for Nick. Her eyes fell on him as he danced close to Lynda, and they did not leave him. She made her move.

'These songs are so long, how about letting me give you a break, Lynda?'

Without waiting for an answer Tania took Nick's hands and placed them around her waist. Lynda stood back, outraged and amazed both at the same time. It was a combination that left her powerless to protest. She walked back to the bar and noticed that Joe also looked very unhappy.

Tania kept hold of Nick as if afraid he would run away. When she spoke her voice quivered with desire. Nick knew that it was only a matter of time and the prospect both thrilled and frightened him. The music stopped and he made a move to leave the floor. The restraining arm about his waist held him firm.

'Wait.' The command was as firm as the grasp. Nick

looked down into her burning eyes and waited for what was to come next. To his relief the music started again. Tania's voice was commanding. 'We leave tomorrow. I must see you.' For a moment Nick was stunned. The urgency in Tania's voice worried him. 'Tomorrow morning at six o'clock. Joe goes for a run. He will be away for an hour. I'll see you then.'

Nick felt events passing out of his control.

'Tania.' Nick spoke not really knowing what it was he wanted to say. 'Why didn't you tell me before that you were leaving?'

'Would it have made a difference?' She quickly countered and he was left not able to answer. The seconds dragged as everything except his racing mind appeared to stand still. Eventually he was able to speak.

'But I have Lynda.'

Tania moved his hands so they rested around her neck. She spoke in a low, almost threatening voice;

'And you can have me.' They danced in an embrace, saying nothing, an awkward silence between them, until Tania spoke again. 'Tomorrow morning at six, keep your door open. I'll be there.' She kissed Nick gently on the cheek. 'Now let's go back and see what the others are up to.'

No sooner had they rejoined the group when Joe announced that it was time for them to leave. It was not a request and Nick felt himself redden as if the big man had overheard their plans. 'He knows.' Nick told himself and tried to look as relaxed and innocent as possible.

Tania insisted that he and Lynda stay and enjoy themselves, thanked them for a lovely evening and gave

Nick's arm an extra squeeze when she leant forward to kiss him goodnight. He watched as she walked away and felt his will go with her.

'Come on, let's dance.' Lynda took his hand and hurried back to the dance floor. 'It's early and we have all night.'

Reaching out his hand Nick felt the articles on the bedside table. He cursed himself for not leaving his watch on his wrist. His fingers traced the form of every object until they recognised the smooth surface of the watch glass. The muscles in his outstretched arm ached as he lay on his back, Lynda's head cradled on his shoulder, and his other arm running beneath her pillow. Gingerly he transferred the watch across the gap between the table and the bed. He barely breathed in the darkness, his eyes straining to see the luminous dial.

'What's the matter?' The drowsy voice startled him and Nick dropped the watch that landed with a metallic clatter on the stone floor. His heart pounded with shock and guilt. Since leaving the restaurant he had told himself that he would not open his door to Tania. Now, he knew that he would. He thought quickly.

'I can't sleep. I am going back to my room.' Lynda held out her hands to stop him;

'Don't go now.' She pleaded. 'Why do you have to go now?'

That night their lovemaking had been wanton. In the taxi from the restaurant their hands had explored, feeling, fondling, and exciting their bodies with the promise of ecstasy. Once in the privacy of the room their hands tore the clothing from each other's bodies. It was a lustful urgency and there was little trace of tenderness in their lovemaking.

'I have got to get a couple of hours sleep.' Nick tried to conceal the impatient edge to his voice and continued, 'and, if I stay here I am not going to get any sleep at all.' Leaning over he lightly kissed Lynda's lips and cupped her left breast and with a smile asked, 'Am I?'

'I guess not.' Lynda answered while edging her body beneath him. Nick smiled, kissed her again and pulled the sheet away. As he placed his feet on the cool floor he felt a force pulling him from the bed.

Dressing in the dark he retrieved his watch and saw that it was ten past five. He shivered with anticipation. He was leaving the known for the unknown, an adventure, an ego trip. It was all of these things. He looked down at Lynda and thought what she would do if she knew where he was going. The danger added further spice to the act. He checked his watch again. There was only forty five minutes to wait.

'I'll give you a bell later on.' He said, leaning across the bed. She nodded, they kissed briefly and he left the room, silently opening and closing the door behind him.

The morning sun filtered through the palm trees and the sky that was a deep red on the horizon rose to a brilliant blue overhead. Nick looked around to see if his exit had been observed by any passersby. He was glad that it was early and hurried to his own room.

'What are you doing up so early?' Nick froze in his tracks. His heart thumping in his chest. 'Not being a naughty boy are you?'

'Bugger.' Nick thought, damning his luck. He then thought quickly. The best form of defence is attack.

'Where have you been at this hour?' He countered and forced himself to smile confidently.

'You know me dear. So many men and so little time.' Frank laughed at his own joke and for a minute appeared lost in his thoughts.

'To each his own.' Nick joked and walked on wishing the Senior Steward a good morning. He glanced at his watch, only forty minutes to go. He quickened his pace but could not control his pulse. He reached the door of his room and tried to get the key to fit in the lock. Eventually it entered but would not turn in the latch. Withdrawing it he lost his grip and the piece of metal fell to the ground. Nick swore, bent down to retrieve the key and tried again. This time the door swung open and he was in his room. He switched on the light. After the glare of the morning sun the room was as dark as a cave. The curtains were very effective and Nick decided to leave them closed.

'What a mess,' he sighed, looking at the contents of his suitcase strewn about the room. 'I have got to get this cleared up and take a shower.' Having given himself orders he set about obeying them. He checked his watch again.

Towelling himself dry he walked out of the bathroom and over to the open suitcase. He looked into it and wondered what he should wear. It was then that a ray of doubt filtered into his mind like the arrows of morning sunlight that entered the room through a small tear in the curtain. Nervously he looked again at his watch as it lay on the dressing table. It was five minutes to six. It was nearly time.

'What the hell am I doing?' He asked himself, knowing that whatever it was he could not stop it. He shut the case. Wrapping the towel around him he went to the door. Excitement, fear, insecurity, and lust, all these emotions seethed inside him as he quietly opened the door and left it on the latch. He walked back to the dressing table and again looked at his watch. A shaft of light shot through the open doorway silhouetting the waiting body in its brilliance.

'Aren't you going to invite me in?' The voice was husky with emotion and that sense of menace that stirred Nick deep within himself. Not waiting for an answer Tania walked inside and gently pushed the door until the metallic click of the lock sealed them in their dimly lit world. Advancing slowly she let the purple robe drop from her shoulders revealing an evenly tanned body, rounded with age and not as taught as it had once been yet charged with the promise of mature sexuality. Nick stood transfixed like a rabbit in front of a bright light, a victim of his desires, waiting to be sacrificed.

'You aren't shy, are you Nick?'

Nick felt ill at ease standing before her covered only by a yellow hotel towel. It was not there long. Tania moved forward, removed it with one deft movement and caressed him shamelessly. He moaned at her touch, but could not move or return her attentions.

'Come here.' She guided him to the white sheeted bed and laid him down. 'You don't have to do anything.' She whispered.

'Oh no!' Tania exclaimed. The passion that had clouded her eyes was now replaced by fear. 'It's five past seven.' She rolled from the bed, her nakedness no longer a symbol of her dominance. She was afraid and the flight of the spirit had taken with it the power of the body. For the first time Nick noticed the lines and folds of the flesh. It was now left to him to take charge.

'Quick, get dressed.' He said and handed her the purple robe. 'Call me if he is not back yet.'

Nick ran to the door, opened it and Tania hurried passed and out into the morning sun. They did not kiss. Nick closed the door and returned to sit on the bed and wait for the telephone to ring. Once again he looked at his watch. The minutes passed and each felt like an hour. The call did not come. His stomach began to tighten. He looked at the watch again and then stood up and began pacing the room. His feet stuck to the cool tile floor.

Nick passed the next hour listening, in the curtained darkness, for the approach of urgent footsteps. His mind cried out to know what had happened while simultaneously fearing the consequences. Eventually he gave up the vigil and took another shower. Dressed in shorts and a tee shirt he felt more confident. He pulled back the curtains and let the light stream into the room.

'Eight fifteen.' He said to himself and began pacing once more. It was nine o'clock when the telephone finally rang. Nick jumped with surprise and looked at the white plastic form of the telephone. It rang again but he could not bring himself to pick up the receiver. The insistence of the bell echoed within him.

'You have got to answer it.' He told himself and moved slowly with his hand outstretched towards the machine. Like a coiled spring that has just been released his hand shot downward and took hold of the receiver.

'Hello.' His voice was unsure and guarded.

'Good morning. It is your early morning wake up call.' Lynda's breezy voice travelled down the cable and flooded Nick in a wave of relief. He could not answer immediately. 'Nick, are you awake?' She asked. He answered that he was and she continued, 'how about breakfast?' He was not hungry but it was a good excuse to get away from the hotel.

'I'll call for you in ten minutes.' He replied and hung up the telephone.

The room fell silent and Nick stared at the phone expecting it to ring again. He backed away from it and went into the bathroom.

Before leaving the room Nick looked over towards the telephone that appeared to dominate the bedside table on which it sat. It remained silent and he went outside. 'What a night.' He thought and took a deep breath.

They walked along the beach to a little restaurant situated high on the point overlooking the turquoise sea. They chatted while eating pineapple slices followed by an English breakfast that somehow felt out of place in their tropical surroundings. Nick sipped his coffee and reflected that he had made love to the girl sitting before him and yet knew nothing about her. He was then thankful that she knew very little about him. A flash of doubt crossed his mind and he wondered if anyone had seen Tania leaving his room. He then thought of Joe and what was going on in that room right now. 'Why hadn't she rung?' He asked himself.

Lynda had been watching Nick carefully and saw the worried frown appear on his forehead.

'What's wrong Nick?' She asked tenderly.

'Oh.' He looked into her concerned eyes and answered, 'Nothing, nothing at all, I was just thinking of what I have to do after this trip.' He thought fast and then thought again as he realised that he did have something serious to think about.

'What is that?' Lynda carried the conversation forward.

'I am going to see my father and my step-mother.' He replied.

'Why are you so serious?' Lynda continued.

Nick went quiet again and then answered slowly;

'I cannot remember my father and I have never met my step-mother.' It was now Lynda's turn to fall silent. She did not know what to say in reply. 'Oh, it's all right.' Nick realised her discomfort and continued. 'I was brought up by my mother and have a step-father and two step-brothers. So you see, I have more family than most.' He smiled self-consciously. Lynda remained silent. Nick went on to tell the story of his childhood that his mother had told to him. It was strange but he felt relieved to be telling someone else. The prospect of seeing his father was a daunting one, especially after what his mother had told him. He even suspected that she still loved him, so intently did she speak about him.

'You have never seen your father?' Lynda was incredulous and asked why? Nick was silent, thinking, and she regretted her curiosity. 'I'm sorry Nick. I didn't mean to pry.'

He looked up from the table and his eyes held hers. His lips broke into a broad smile and a dimple appeared on his left cheek. She loved that dimple, and, at that moment, she loved him.

'Let's have another cup of coffee and I'll tell you all.' He jokingly replied.

Over the dark, hot drink he explained that his parents had decided to break completely so that each could start again. Nick's father supported them financially. Very soon after the divorce his mother found and married his step-father.

'I was not told about my real father until I was twelve.' Nick explained.

'But that's not fair.' Lynda protested. Nick continued,

'Why not? I didn't spend my childhood torn between two fathers.' He then went silent for a few seconds. 'You know, I sometimes wish Mum hadn't told me about my real father at all. You have no idea how unsettling it can be to find that you have two fathers.' Nick drank his coffee, staring over the cup's rim towards the sea. Lynda stayed silent until curiosity got the better of her.

'Have you got any photographs?'

'Only ones taken when I was born, and we were both a lot younger then.' He smiled, but, Lynda could sense a feeling of unease. Nick continued. 'Well, all will soon be revealed.' He drained his cup and the conversation was over. He changed the subject to the day ahead and how they were to spend it.

'When is pick up?' Lynda asked.

'Five o'clock, and back here by midnight.'

'That gives us most of the day,' she said and added, 'and most of the night.'

The last words brought his thoughts back to the present and the telephone call he did not receive.

'Now what's wrong Nick?' Lynda was concerned and a little upset that he had not responded more enthusiastically to the prospect of another night together. The question made him jump.

'Oh nothing.' He gave no explanation. 'Come on, let's go to the beach.'

They waded in the shallow water along the shore. The sea was crystal clear and the shells and pebbles on the shallow seabed shone from the sand as the sun's rays played on the surface. Lynda wanted Nick to take her hand but he made no move to do so. Instead he bent down collecting flat stones and skimming them across the equally flat surface of the water. With every step he was thinking about Tania and what he should do. He also tried not to think about the consequences if Joe had found out.

The sun was climbing high in the mid-morning sky and its heat promised a hot day. As they neared the hotel Nick said to Lynda that he had to go to his room and would see her on the beach in ten minutes. Without giving an explanation he strode off through the palm trees towards the accommodation block.

There was no message under his door. He thought of passing Tania's room and quickly dismissed the idea as potentially suicidal. Still with no news he returned to the beach. Shielding his eyes from the sun's glare he scanned the sand. He recognised three people from the other crew and then saw his own crew's encampment. Trailing a sun bed behind him he made his way towards them. As he drew nearer he considered the tribal instinct that caused crews to congregate in enclosed groups to the exclusion of all others.

'Hi Nick.' The chorus of greeting rose from the sun beds scattered about on the fine, golden, sand.

'Where is Lynda?' Nick looked round knowing who asked the question and also knowing that all those camped there knew the meaning behind it.

'I don't know. I thought she was with you, Frank.' The group burst into a chorus of laughter. Nick turned his bed to face the sun and as he settled down thought of how quickly the involvement of he and Lynda would go round the airline routes. Jumbo Drums they called the grape vine that carried gossip worldwide in a matter of hours. There could be no secrets. Quickly these thoughts passed into oblivion as Nick fell into a deep sleep.

He awoke to feel the sun burning his back and to find himself alone on his section of the beach. 'Where have they gone?' His thoughts cried out as alarm swept over him. He fumbled under the sun bed for his clothes and the watch that was in one of the pockets. It was nearly midday. A surge of relief caused him to expel all the air from his lungs and it met the world with a loud hissing sound as it passed through his clenched teeth. He had not missed call time and he knew where the crew would be. Glancing over to the beach bar he saw them perched on its high wicker stools. Hurriedly he pulled on his tee shirt and walked over to join them.

'Hey, here's sleeping beauty.'

'What's wearing you out Nick? Anyone we know?' The comments came thick and fast as he drew under the thatched roof of the bar. His eyes darted along the row of chairs but his attention was arrested by a quiet voice off to his left. He turned to see Roger walking up to him.

'A guy called Joe is looking for you.' The words made Nick's blood run cold. Up until then he had always thought that those words were only an expression, but, right at that moment their meaning was only too clear. His thoughts ran through the possible reasons for the summons and came up each time with only one answer.

'Did you hear me, Nick?' Roger asked and repeated the message. Nick came back to the present. Calmly he asked where he could find the Canadian. Roger pointed towards the pool.

'He's over there.' Nick thanked him and turned to leave.

'Where are you going?' Lynda's voice halted his advance and stole his resolve. He was on the defensive again. His voice faltered when he spoke and he struggled to master his emotions. Fear, guilt, pride, Nick could not tell what made up his character at that time. A few hours ago he had been in an enviable position and he remembered those minutes with a lustful affection.

'Joe wants me.' He answered.

'So do I.' Lynda's reply was quick and smiling.

'Not in the same way I hope.' Nick found his ground and continued, 'where have you been all morning?'

'Looking at you flat out and dead to the world.' Nick grinned guiltily and Linda went on. 'You can't stand the pace.' Nick continued to smile but said nothing. 'Well, better not keep you. Are you sure it is not Tania who wants to see you?' She added pointedly. He kissed her gently on the lips and said he would be right back. 'Make sure that you are.' She called after him.

As he walked around the tables and chairs that skirted the pool area the fear returned. 'What would he find only a few more paces away?' He resigned himself to the fact that the big man had found out. That is why Tania had not phoned.

'I must be a lemming.' Nick said to himself as he climbed the four steps to the pool terrace. He looked about him and caught sight of the couple seated under an umbrella at the far end of the pool. Water splashed over him as two children jumped into the warm blueness of the tiled pool.

Joe rose to his feet as Nick neared the table. He looked bigger than ever and he was not smiling. Nick steeled himself for the worst.

'Well here goes.' He whispered to himself and straightened his body. Another few paces and he was facing Joe, the body builder. The men looked into each other's eyes while Tania remained seated. For those brief seconds no one moved. Nick did not know what to say so said nothing. 'Joe had summoned him,' he thought, 'let him make the first move.'

The Canadian's big right hand shot out from the side of his taught body. Nick stepped back so fast it was almost an involuntary action. His pulse pounded in his veins and he thought he felt the blow fall. His eyes then focused on the man's outstretched hand. Nick's face broke into a relieved smile not believing his good fortune. He took the big hand in his own.

'We are leaving in an hour and wanted to say goodbye.' Nick looked at Tania and saw that she was smiling. He could not concentrate for a second and just held onto the big man's hand. Eventually the words came and he wished them well. Tania was now standing and came over to the two men. Nick turned to face her trying to find the answer in her eyes.

'Good-bye Nick, it was nice meeting you.' She bent forward and kissed his left cheek.

'It was nice meeting you. Did she really say that?' Nick searched her face for answers but there was no indication that they had been anything more than holiday acquaintances. 'Was it an act?' Uncertainty shrouded Nick's mind like a fog. He was thankful that it appeared Joe knew nothing of that morning, but, he now felt both angry and embarrassed at being dismissed so lightly. 'Was it really that easy for her?' He questioned, looking again for the answer in Tania's tanned face. Joe interrupted his thoughts.

'Well, we better be going. We may see you next year aye?' Joe took his wife's arm.

'You never know.' Nick answered, glancing, at the man and then at his wife.

'Bye Nick,' was his only acknowledgement.

He stood and watched them walk away, his thoughts a mixture of relief and disbelief. He stood staring until they were out of sight. He shook his head, let out a big sigh and then turned and went back to the crew.

Lynda looked up from the table on which sat the tropical fruit salad she was eating.

'Back so soon.' She said, replacing her fork on the green plastic tablecloth. She noticed that he looked disturbed but said nothing. Nick pulled out one of the chairs and sat down.

'I think I'll have a rum punch.' He put his hand in his pocket and took out a small card that the receptionist had given him with his room key when he checked in. He signed the back of the drink voucher and handed it to a passing waiter.

'I can't refuse a free drink, it would be against the airline code.' He joked but was not smiling.

Silence fell between them and Lynda continued with her lunch. She glanced at Nick who was staring out across the beach and wondered why the departure of the Canadians should affect him so deeply. She knew that Tania had played up to him and had dismissed it as an older woman's fantasy. Looking into Nick's face she now was not so sure that that is all it was. Over breakfast she had loved getting to know him and felt close to him with an affection that went beyond sexual attraction. Now, he was distant and all because an older woman made eyes at him. She was not going to let him dwell on her for too long.

'What are you doing after lunch?' She asked and his reply was immediate.

'I thought I would have another one of these.' He pointed to the glass the waiter had just left at the table.

'Well, I have other ideas.' Lynda replied, placing her hand on the top of Nick's thigh and applying pressure with her fingers. She stared into his eyes and concentrated on burning the image of the older woman from his mind.

Nick rolled the glass around in his hands, took a drink, smiled and then replied.

'Sounds good to me.'

'Then, leave that, we have better things to do.'

'You do mean business don't you?'

'You better believe it.'

Nick was the first to rise from the table.

'Let's go.' He said and reached out for her.

'I thought you were never going to ask.' She said.

'Oh no. You asked for it and now you are going to get it.'

'Promises, promises.'

Nick put his arm about her trim waist and laughed. They had found each other again.

The persistent ringing of the telephone eventually broke through the barrier of sleep. Lazily, Lynda opened her eyes and looked dreamily at the telephone. Her mind was empty of thought except for the warm memory of their lovemaking. Nick had devoured her. He made love as though he wanted to possess her body and soul. She ached from his demands but held a feeling of total contentment and calm. Even the shrill tone of the telephone barely penetrated her waking mind.

Then, like a flash of light, the realisation came. Her hand shot out to the plastic receiver and she lifted it from its cradle. The echoing voice on the other end of the line was saying that it was 'call time' and 'pick up' would be in one hour. Lynda replaced the handset and looked about the room. Her clothes were strewn over every piece of furniture, she felt her hair and knew it was a mess. She looked at the still figure lying beside her. They had not meant to let this happen. A couple of hours in bed and then Nick was supposed to return to his own room so that she could get ready. An afternoon delight that was all it was meant to be. Gently she placed her hands on Nick's chest. The thick covering of black hair felt warm and sponge like between her fingers.

'Nick.' She whispered into his ear and kissed his temple. She repeated his name, only louder the second time. 'Nick wake up. It's call time.' As if programmed, the last words registered and brought an immediate response.

'Call time!' He sat bolt upright, his eyes staring in disbelief. So deep was his sleep that for the first few minutes he did not know where he was. All he knew was that it was 'call time.'

Lynda smiled back at him. She was out of bed now and walking towards the bathroom.

'It was great.' He said, now feeling the warmth generated by the memory of the past few hours.

'Yes, it was.' Lynda agreed and blew him a kiss as she closed the bathroom door behind her.

'I hate to love you and leave you but I've got a plane to catch.' Scrambling about the floor he gathered up his clothes and put them on. 'I see that doesn't bother you too much.' He called through the bathroom door. The shower had just been turned on. The door opened. Lynda had a towel wrapped about her, tantalisingly exposing the tops of her breasts and the shadow between her thighs.

'I would invite you in but I too have a plane to catch.' She teased. 'Give me a kiss and let me get ready.'

'Bloody hell, I'm glad to be back here.' Nick almost whispered the words as he entered the air conditioned lobby of the hotel. It had only been a fifty minute flight to and from St Lucia but what should have been three hours on the ground while the aircraft was re-fuelled, re-catered and cleaned turned into a six hour creeping delay due to engine trouble. It was a very long night.

'Oh Mr. Wells!' Nick had collected his room key and was walking away from the reception desk when the sound of his name being called halted his step. He turned back to the desk and saw that the receptionist was holding a small white envelope. 'Mr. Wells, this was left for you. The girl on duty forgot to give it to you when you left the hotel last night. I am sorry.' Nick barely heard the apology as he took the envelope from her hand. He wanted to tear it open right there and then, but a warning voice inside of him called for caution. He turned around and caught Lynda quickly looking away.

'Had she seen the whole thing? Did it matter if she had?' Nick thought on and knew that it did. He slipped the envelope into the back pocket of his trousers and walked over to identify his bag and give his room number to the bell captain.

'Nick.' Lynda's voice was soft and inviting, 'what are you going to do now? Do you want to come to my room or shall I come to you?'

'I'm knackered Lynda. How about we both get some sleep and meet for lunch. We could go to the place along the beach.' Nick was not sure that he was doing the right thing, but he wanted to read that letter. Lynda agreed but he could hear the disappointment in her voice.

They walked together to the south wing of the hotel and stopped outside a set of elevators. Lynda had to go up to the next floor.

'See you for lunch. I'll call you at midday.' Nick concentrated on sounding natural.

'Enjoy your reading.' Lynda said quietly as the elevator doors slid shut.

Nick put the key into the lock and entered the room. He placed his cabin bag in the wardrobe and sat down on the end of the bed. Before opening the letter he smelled it and was disappointed at finding it unscented. His thumb tore along the envelope's spine revealing one sheet of paper folded neatly inside. He withdrew and threw the thick paper of the envelope into the wastebasket. With a deft movement of thumb and forefinger the flowing handwriting was exposed. His eyes first scanned the lines and then concentrated on the message.

My Beautiful Nick,

Thank you for the most wonderful holiday I have had in years. Sorry for not phoning you. Joe came in soon after I got back to the room. He is out again now exercising on the beach. The only exercise I am interested in is with you my darling, Nick. Take care of that beautiful body and thanks again.

Much Love,

Tania

Having read it once, Nick read it over and over again. Rising from the bed he walked over to the chest of drawers and let the letter fall onto the wooden surface.

'Is that it?' He said aloud and picked the paper up again. 'Is that all?' He screwed the letter into the palm of his hand and then threw it to join the envelope in the bottom of the bin. It made a resounding thud against the metal as it landed.

A knock at the door diverted his attention and he went to open it. The porter walked passed him and deposited the suitcase onto the baggage stand by the chest of drawers.

'Have a good day man.' The young porter said breezily as he left the room and closed the door behind him.

Nick lifted the gold watch to his face. Ten to twelve, he had slept for only four hours and his mind and body told him that it was not enough. Laying there he argued the case for getting up. Their late arrival back at the hotel meant they would get only thirteen hours off before being called for the service home. If he got up now perhaps he could get another couple of hours sleep before pick up. On the other hand, if he went back to sleep he would not need those other few hours. He then thought of Lynda. He said that he would call her. That was not going to be easy. Perhaps he should stay in bed.

'No, what the hell.' He answered his own doubts and threw the covers off the bed. He quickly showered, put on a pair of shorts and a tee shirt and went over to the telephone. He dialled and waited for Lynda to answer. The prospect no longer daunted him, he no longer knew what he felt.

'Hello.' The drowsy voice answered.

'Hello Lynda. It's Nick.'
'What time is it?'
'Five past twelve.' He felt sorry for having woken her.
'What do you want?' The voice was still doped with sleep.
'We said that we would meet for lunch.' Nick began to feel agitated. He had not wanted to make this call.
'Oh no Nick. It's too early. I can't see you now. I've got to have some more sleep. I'll call you.' There was a short pause. 'Bye.' The line went silent.
'Women.' Nick sighed aloud. He picked up his wallet from the dressing table and left the room.

The first smooth glass of coconut flavoured nectar flowed over Nick's tongue, refreshing and reassuring him as it went. The second Pena Colada was taken slower and with greater appreciation.
'I thought I would find you here.'
Nick had not seen Lynda walk up to the bar and was surprised by her voice. She came behind and sat on the stool next to him.
'Have you been here long?'
Without saying anything he held up two fingers.
'You are knocking them back.' She commented, a little concerned.
'I'll be alright. One more and I will stroll down the beach for a bite to eat and may even get a couple of hour's kip before we are called.' There was silence before Nick spoke again. 'May I get you a drink?' Lynda looked at the cream liquid in the glass.
'I'll have what you're having.'

Nick turned to the barman and ordered two more drinks. There was another silence.

'Nick, about the phone call.' Lynda's tone was awkward and she paused between her spoken thoughts. 'I really was tired. I could not possibly have seen you then.'

Nick finished the last frothy remains of the Pena Colada and set the empty glass on the bar.

'That's okay,' he replied, 'I understand. I was too.'

'No you don't!' Lynda raised her voice and then checked her emotions. 'No you don't understand.' The two fresh drinks arrived. The bartender sat them down on the table and then retreated. Once alone Lynda continued, her voice now edged with emotion. 'I thought we were close you and I. It was special.' Her words trailed away as her thoughts took over. It was Nick's turn to talk and the alcohol made it all too easy.

'You say it was special, well it was; but, now, it's getting too heavy. All because an older woman wants a holiday thrill and writes a letter you become paranoid. I don't need it, Lynda.' His eyes stared into hers and then cut away at the end of the speech. There was another pause before Lynda spoke again.

'I don't know what went on between you and Tania, and if anything did go on I don't know when it could have, and, I am not sure that I want to know.' She stopped for a second and then asked. 'Is any of this making sense?' She lifted the brimming glass to her lips, as much for something to do as for the refreshment. Nick did the same and then replied.

'Lynda, nothing went on between Tania and me, except in her mind; but, there is more to it than that.'

He waited to see if she believed him before continuing. 'I am not ready to settle down to a steady relationship. If you thought that I was then I am sorry. I really am.' He stopped and shook his head. 'How did we ever get to a point like this?' Before Lynda could answer he went on. 'You know what I am like. Why do you bother with me?'

Silence once more fell between them. They sat perched on the high stools and sipped the sweet liquid lost in their own thoughts. Lynda spoke first and smiled into Nick's eyes.

'Do you want to start all over again?'

'I would prefer to start about half way through.' Nick smiled in reply.

'You are right.' She said. 'I do know what you're like. Maybe that's why I bother with you. Now, let's go and eat.' They laughed and put their arms about each other as they walked to the poolside café.

'I must go now. They will be calling us soon.' Lynda kissed Nick's cheek and rolled her feet onto the floor. Standing naked before him Nick admired her trim waist and the pert roundness of her breasts. Pushing himself up onto one arm he made his way to the edge of the bed. Placing his hands on her thighs he gently kissed her tanned stomach and traced the contour of her body with his lips.

Lynda's hands held his head against her stomach, holding his lips, burning into her softest flesh.

'Oh Nick.' She sighed, wanting to feel him inside her again, wanting to take him and to give herself to him. She repeated his name, unable to express the need within her. Her grip tightened around him and then she let him go. He looked up at her with an open, boyish face. Bending down she kissed his lips. 'Now, I must go.' She said, quickly covering her body with a white cotton beach dress. Nick followed her to the door, wrapping a towel about his waist as he went.

'No strings.' Lynda said softly and placed her lips gently onto his. Nick smiled and gave her hand a reassuring squeeze. They kissed again. Lynda opened the door and was gone.

The crew bus passed through the access tunnel and out along the airport's perimeter road. The crew reporting building was in sight when the Flight Purser rose to his feet.

'Thanks for your hard work everybody. Have an enjoyable stand-off and a safe journey home.' The crew thanked him in return.

'I hope you enjoy meeting your father.' Lynda spoke softly. Nick's meeting was their secret.

'Thanks.' He smiled. 'Thanks for a lovely trip.' He wanted to say more. He wanted to take her in his arms, but, this was London and the trip was over. It was like entering another world, the more ordered world of home, where past experiences became fantasies that would not survive the reality that was this real world. People who had been forced by circumstances to work and live in close proximity now said their goodbyes and scattered like leaves in the wind.

The bus came to a stop outside the crew reporting building they had left five days before. The crew collected their cabin bags and filed off the coach. Nick saw the driver lift his suitcase from the rear of the coach and place it on the curbside. He moved forward to collect it. As he did so he turned to Lynda.

'I will let you know how I get on.'

Lynda kissed his cheek.

'Good luck.' She whispered.

Chapter 15

The floral patterned covers that protected the arms of the winged sofa had faded with the years and there were one or two places where the cotton was wearing thin. However, sitting in the high backed chair felt very comforting. It was the kind of security that comes from being surrounded by memories and things familiar. Carol's mother entered the room carrying a tray laden with cups, cakes and a pot of tea.

Hastily Carol got up and cleared the coffee table of her father's old newspapers and stamp catalogues. She smiled as she placed them by the fireplace knowing that his tardiness infuriated her mother.

'Now my girl,' her mother set the tray down carefully, 'what is all this about?' Carol stared at her father's stamp books. 'You didn't come here to talk about stamps, or if you did, I'll get your father.'

Carol looked up and accepted the cup of tea that was handed to her. Her mind hedged around the question and the reason for her visit. Patiently her mother waited, sipping her tea. Only the clink of cups on saucers broke the silence until Carol spoke up.

'Peter's son is coming tomorrow.' The words exploded from her lips. Mrs. Adison placed her cup and saucer onto the table and then answered with amazement in her voice.

'Peter's son?'

Carol had not spoken of Peter's son for many years and her mother had all but forgotten that her daughter was a step-mother.

'Peter's son?' Her mother said again.

'Yes.' Carol answered.

'When did you say he is coming?' Mrs. Adison struggled to take in the news.

'Tomorrow.' Carol repeated and before the words were out her mother spoke again.

'How long is he staying for?' The mother's voice now sounded alarmed.

'Only for three days.' Carol was calming down as if to counteract her mother's agitation.

'How long have you known about this?'

'Three weeks.' Carol tried to sound casual.

'Three weeks!' Exclaimed her mother. 'Why did you wait until now to tell me?'

Carol felt herself becoming annoyed as she played with the handle of her cup and stared into the pale brownness of the tea. 'Too much milk,' she thought. Patiently, Mrs. Adison waited for an answer. Quietly and awkwardly it came.

'I have always put the knowledge of Peter's son out of my mind. It's been as if he didn't exist.' She stopped for a moment, lost in her thoughts. 'I wanted to believe that not thinking about him meant that he was not real, somehow.' Mrs. Adison put down her cup and moved next to her daughter. She put her arm about Carol's shoulders.

'What about Peter? How does he feel about the visit?' Carol stiffened and spoke with controlled deliberation.

'At first he was unsure. Can you imagine Peter unsure? Well he was. Then after a few days he declared that it was about time he saw his son again. It was his idea to let him stay for so long. The boy only asked to come for the day.' Her voice began to rise as she re-lived the conversation. 'He didn't even ask how I felt about it.' Mrs. Adison let a few minutes pass before she spoke again.

'How do you feel?'

Carol remained silent for a while longer.

'Oh, I don't know. Peter has a right to see his son. After all, he has gone almost twenty years without seeing him and all because she said it would be better that way.' Carol pronounced the word 'she' with disdain although, over the years, Carol had silently thanked her for that decision. 'I suppose I am interested to see what a son of Peter's looks like; but, why does he have to stay for three days?'

'Peter will be there tomorrow, of course.' Carol's mother made the statement sound more like a question.

'Yes, he'll be there, although he does have an appointment with Admiral Donnelly at two o'clock. The boy arrives at four.' Mrs. Adison looked concerned but not surprised.

'He has known about this visit for weeks, couldn't he have arranged a better time?' Mothers shared their daughters' anxieties over their husbands and Carol knew she had an ally.

'Oh he could have,' she paused for effect, 'but you know Peter.' The women shared expressions of resignation and annoyance. 'He did promise me that he would be home in good time.'

Mrs. Adison sat upright in her chair,

'Well my girl,' her mother always used this expression and Carol hated it. 'Your step-son is arriving tomorrow and you cannot think that fact away. You have to face it and make the best of it.' The advice was typical of her mother and Carol knew she was foolish to expect anything else, but was that really all she could say? Carol felt cheated and alone once more.

'Good afternoon sir.' Captain Peter Wells R.N, had his gold peaked cap tucked under his left arm and extended his right hand to the man responsible for his professional well-being. The Admiral rose from his leather chair and walked around the large table to greet one of his Captains. Clasping Peter's hand firmly in his own, he welcomed him warmly.

'Peter, please sit down, we have things to discuss.' The Admiral re-gained his chair and withdrew a thick manila folder from the top drawer of the desk. With great deliberation he laid it on the leather topped table and untied the draw strings that held the two flaps of the folder together. The contents of the file lay exposed in front of them both.

Admiral Donnelly, himself a young man for the rank he held, admired Peter's record. He looked up from the sheaths of paper and addressed the Captain,

'Well, Peter, you have been busy over the past few

years.' He paused for effect and not for a reply. 'Two years at Grenville as Exec, 76-78; command of Adventurer, 78-79; promoted to Captain and a job on the staff of the Commander in Chief Naval Home Command, 79-81; command of Belligerant and the Fourth Destroyer Squadron.' There was another silence. 'Not much shore time in there.'

This time Peter answered,

'No sir.' He felt that was all that was required at this stage.

'We can change that Peter.' The Admiral's tone did not betray his intentions.

'I prefer to be at sea, sir.' Peter spoke deliberately but with deference.

'I am sure you do, I am sure you do; but, I have plans for you Peter and these plans involve a year or two ashore.' Peter stared hard into the Admiral's face trying to read the meaning behind the words. The older man was giving nothing away. He studied Peter's file and only looked up to pass a comment or ask a question. It was as if he enjoyed toying with this officer. Peter sat rigid in the hard backed chair. There was so much he wanted to ask. Eventually Donnelly looked up. 'Now Peter, what about a cup of tea, or coffee perhaps?'

The question took him completely off guard and for a moment he hesitated,

'Coffee will be fine sir.' As he answered his mind was berating this man who held his life so much in his hands. 'Tea or coffee indeed! What does he think he's playing at?' Peter tried hard not to betray his feelings, but could not check his thoughts. 'Damn Gunnery Officers, they all think they are God's gift.' Everyone in the Navy knew the Admiral's background. A strict disciplinarian who had fashioned himself into the epitome of the pomp and ceremony that was the embodiment of the gunnery establishment at Whale Island in Portsmouth. On the island spit and polish was the way of life and discipline was its raison d'etre. This made the Gunnery Officer a unique member of the naval family. In a service that looks with a fond cynicism at anything too regimented the Gunnery Officer was a peculiar breed. In the form of Rear-Admiral David Andrew Donnelly it was a manifestation not to be taken lightly. Peter eyed the crisp creases of his jacket, the golden brilliance of the braid on his sleeves, the neatness of his grooming where not one hair dared move out of place, and, the square set of the jaw that told the world that here was a man with whom one did not trifle.

Moments passed and then the Admiral's Steward appeared through a side door carrying a sterling silver tray upon which were sat a matching coffee set with fine bone china cups and saucers. Peter took his cup and then sat back to await the Admiral's next remarks. There was a clink of porcelain as Donnelly put his saucer back on the tray with a flourish.

'Now Peter, back to the job in hand.' It was as if he had waited until Peter was drinking the hot liquid before speaking. Peter gave a muffled cough and set the cup and saucer back on the desk. Donnelly continued. 'There will soon be an opening at the School of Maritime Operations.' Peter knew it as the former Navigation school of which he had been Executive Officer in 1976.

He remained silent while the Admiral went on. 'The school needs a Commanding Officer, a Director of Studies if you will, and, I think you are the man for the job.' Peter sat speechless, all his faculties assimilating what he had just been told and trying to formulate the best response. He did not give one.

'I don't know sir.' Peter flushed with the bareness of his reply and the Admiral was quick to pounce on it.

'That is not like you Peter.' He waited for a few seconds. 'Now come on, give it some thought.'

The adrenalin was flowing more freely now and with it came confidence.

'I am not a teacher sir, certainly not a headmaster. I'm a sailor. I need to be at sea. I enjoy the command I have.'

The older man's eyes hardened and then, like the passing of a cloud, his face broke into a warm smile.

'Damn you Peter, but you can be a stubborn ass… let me put it another way.' He leant forward placing both elbows on the desk and cradling his prominent jaw on top of his clasped hands. 'You are an excellent navigator and an extremely competent tactical commander, but, you need more if you are going to the top in this Navy.' The Admiral was a master at the art of pregnant pauses. 'You will need a strategic understanding of maritime and other defence matters. The posting I am offering you will not only give you this, it will make you a part of it.' The smile had vanished once again and the dark eyes flashed, as if to reinforce the message the voice was conveying. Peter sat transfixed by the intensity of what he was hearing. 'As C.O. of the School you will be involved with senior officers from the other services and the Ministry of Defence in matters of strategic importance to this country, and...' He added, almost as an afterthought, 'You will be involved in training men to handle themselves and their material in this uncertain world of ours.' Peter ran his right forefinger along his bottom lip and held Donnelly's eyes with his own. The Admiral spoke on. 'You held the Execs job at Grenville for two years, so you have had experience in training.' He smiled knowing that he had countered one of Peter's arguments and continued, 'and here is something you may not have thought about.' For the finale the Admiral sat back in the leather chair. 'The second 'Through Deck Cruiser' will be commissioned in two years' time and she will need a Captain. Who better than the C.O. of the School of Maritime Operations? Even the timing is right.' Donnelly placed both hands on the arms of his chair signalling that he had rested his case, but, he had not finished talking. 'More coffee?'

Peter shook his head. 'No thank you sir.'

'Well, what do you say now?' The Admiral asked.

Peter knew that he had to accept, there was no doubt in his mind about that. However, he did not have to make it look as if he had been sold on the Admiral's arguments alone. Indeed, Donnelly had underestimated Peter, who had kept his eye on the aircraft carrier from the day its keel was laid. Although, he did have to admit that 'the old man' had got the timing right. He also knew that the next step after the command of such a ship was a Flag Rank. Through Deck Cruiser, Aircraft Carrier, whatever the government wanted to call it in order to get it accepted by the Treasury, to Peter it meant the second row of 'scrambled egg' on the peak of his cap and a thick band of gold on his sleeve.

It was now Peter's turn to maintain the pressure. He did it through silence, and he played it well. The Admiral had folded his arms and Peter could see by the furrow of his brow that he was impatient for an answer

'If I am offered the posting sir, I will be delighted to accept.' A smile crossed the Admiral's lips.

'Good man. Rest assured you will be offered the job, but, do not say anything about this interview.'

Peter nodded his agreement. There were now a few things he wanted to know.

'When is all this going to happen sir?'

Donnelly shifted his weight and made the leather of the chair squeak against the material of his trousers.

'You will hear in the summer, no later than August.'

'Not long.' Peter thought, and, felt a tinge of regret at having to give up his ship and the squadron. He enjoyed command at sea. In no other branch of the service was power so absolute.

The Hampshire countryside looked lush and green after the heavy rains of the previous night. On the hillsides bright clumps of daffodils swayed in the fresh spring breeze. As he drove, the thoughts of Peter Nicholas Wells were clouded by his mother's protests to the reunion with the father he could not remember. He recalled her questions and the one he had so often asked himself. 'Why now? Why after all these years of knowing he existed and doing nothing about it? Why had the need not arisen before?' He could hear her objections echoing in his ears. 'It will only upset you both. We agreed when we separated that it would be best for all of us if you did not see your father, and I do not see why that should change now.'

Nick had explained that it was because the man was his father, his real father that he had to meet him. His step-father was a kind and considerate man who treated him with the same affection as his two step-brothers, but for Nick there had always been something missing. He now hoped to find that link in a country house in Hampshire.

'I don't know why he wants to see you after all these years.' His mother had said, with uncharacteristic anger. This meeting had stirred emotions in her that Nick had seen before. He knew she still had a photograph taken on their wedding day that she kept hidden in a drawer in her bedroom. Nick had found it one day, many years ago, on one of his inquisitive expeditions that used to infuriate his mother. He had often been scolded for raking through cupboards and drawers and asked what he hoped to find. For Nick it was always a great adventure that often turned up treasures such as old coins, badges and his father's photograph.

As he turned off the main road and onto a lane that was signposted to Meonstoke, Nick recalled the moment he discovered the picture. He was twelve years old. He had taken it downstairs and asked his mother who the man was standing next to her in the uniform. He would never forget the pain that showed in her face at that moment. Tears welled up in her eyes and rolled in diamond like droplets down her cheeks. Nick smiled to himself, remembering that he had begun crying with her but not knowing why, only that his mother was unhappy and he had caused it. She had held his hand and taken him back upstairs to her bedroom where she returned the picture to its hiding place. She had then sat Nick on the bed and explained the father he had never known. At that age it had not meant a lot. He had his mother and a father who had been with him for as long as he could remember. He had two brothers and life was uncomplicated. Only as the years passed did the questioning begin. His mother, having told him the story, refused to mention it again. She had even forbidden him to tell his step-father that he had found the photograph. All she would say was that his father had abandoned him so that he could pursue his career and Nick could know a true family life. It had all been done for the best and Nick should count his blessings for having a step-father who loves him. From time to time Nick would sneak into the bedroom, remove the photograph and stare into it, hoping for an answer to his unspoken questions. Now he was less than three miles from the man who had eventually acknowledged his letter and invited him to stay.

Carol glanced at the kitchen clock as she hurriedly passed through on her way upstairs to the guest room. Her eyes fell on the dishes standing on the draining board.

'Bugger!' She cursed aloud. 'I thought I put those away. Look at the time. The boy is almost here. Oh, they'll have to wait.' Her mind made up she continued out of the kitchen and up the wooden staircase to the guest room. She opened the door slowly, half expecting to find her guest already inside. A breeze from the open window gently moved the net curtains. Carol walked into the centre of the room and looked about her. She thought that this was one of the rooms she rarely visited. She did not like entertaining and house guests were hard work to a woman who did not like housework or cooking. This had annoyed Peter on the occasions when he felt it important to entertain his superior officers. Carol would always find an excuse why she could not have anyone to come to the house and they would go out to a restaurant or club.

'It looks tidy.' She thought and was thankful for Mrs. Cotes, who came twice a week to do the washing and clean the house. Carol walked to the dressing table and looked at her reflection in the mirror.

'My god I look a mess!' She exclaimed, examining the faded and worn material of her jeans and the old white shirt that had once belonged to Peter. It was a little baggy but she was proud that, as she turned, the swell of her breasts could be seen pressing against the white cotton.

From outside the open window the sound of a car's engine travelled on the breeze. Carol ran to look out. The house lay at the end of the lane and the road stopped only a few yards passed their gate. She looked at her watch, ten to four. 'Peter should have been home an hour ago. He was cutting it fine.' She thought. Concentrating her vision she knew that she would be able to see the top of the car through the hedge that ran along the side of the house. Carol undid the window latch and swung the white painted wooden frame all the way open. The noise of the engine was now very near, but, still Carol could not see the car.

'Oh no!' She exclaimed. 'It can't be.' She could not believe what she saw as a white MGB wheeled noisily across the gravel driveway and came to a halt beneath the bedroom window. Carol watched as if spying on something she should not see. The car door opened and a young man got out, straightened himself and looked around. Carol moved away from the window but kept her visitor in sight. 'He is tall,' she thought. 'Taller than his father, but not as thick set.' She had always admired Peter's broad chest and the strength of his shoulders. Once again she came close to the window to try and catch a glimpse of the face of her visitor. It was too late, he had moved under the porch roof. The doorbell chimed twice.

'Where is Peter?' She whispered with anguish in her voice. She felt her confidence disappear into the silence that followed the chimes. Slowly she walked to the bottom of the staircase and stopped. Through the glass insert in the front door she could see his outline. The bell rang again.

Outside Nick moved away from the door and looked up at the house.

'Where is everybody?' He said to himself, worried by the silence and fearing that he had got either the day or the address wrong. Reaching into his jacket pocket he removed the now crumpled letter from his father. His eyes scanned the page. Confirming that he was at the right house he returned to the front door. His hand went up to the white button once more. Before he had time to place his finger upon it the door swung open. He hurriedly stepped back and nearly lost his balance as his right foot went over the porch step and onto the uneven driveway.

'Hello, you must be Peter.' Carol shook hands with her visitor in a forthright attempt to take command of the meeting from the start. The young man took the small hand and held it. He stood mesmerised by what he saw. He did not know what he had expected but it certainly was not a pretty young woman in tight faded denim jeans and loosely fastened shirt. Carol caught his gaze and self-consciously fiddled with a wayward button.

'It's Nick actually.' He answered.

'Pardon me.' Carol answered, forgetting what she had said.

'I'm Nick, not Peter. I use my middle name'. Their hands parted with Carol feeling very foolish. Peter had told her this, but at that moment her mind was all over the place.

'Of course, sorry.' They both smiled awkwardly and the moment passed.

'Where's my father? I thought he would be here to meet me.' The question rekindled the anger and embarrassment Carol felt over his absence, but she disguised her feelings well.

'He will be home shortly. He telephoned to say he may be a little late.' She hated making excuses. They both smiled once again. 'Let's get your bags and I'll show you your room.' Carol was thankful for the activity.

She held the front door open and Nick sidled through

with his suitcase. He was careful not to brush the paintwork. He already noticed that although the house was not particularly tidy, the paintwork was immaculate.

'Upstairs,' Carol instructed, 'follow me.' They were soon on the landing and Carol hurried ahead to open the door to the bedroom. Nick brushed passed her as he entered.

'I expect you could do with a drink after that long drive?' Carol asked as Nick placed his suitcase on the bed.

'That would be great. A cup of tea would go down well.' The reply surprised Carol who was expecting a young man to want something stronger.

'Of course.' She hesitated. 'Leave your bag and while the kettle is boiling I'll show you around the place.' Nick followed the trim figure of his step-mother out of the room.

In the courtyard that led from the rear of the house to the stables and fields beyond Nick tried to form the first impressions of his father's home. It was an imposing building, full of timbered character and well maintained, however, there was something unruly about the place. A certain scruffiness that undermined the image of the immaculate 'chocolate box' country house set among rolling pastures. Carol led the way to the stables.

'Here is my pride and joy.' She said with a voice full of warmth and a horse extended its chestnut brown head over the wooden door to greet her. Affectionately she petted the horse's neck. 'Do you ride?' She turned her attention to Nick.

'No, not really,' he hesitated. 'I have tried it a couple

of times but they have always thrown me off.' He pointed to the brown head as if it was the symbol of those who had unseated him. Carol laughed.

'I'll teach you. I can borrow another horse and we will go over the fields.' He smiled his acceptance and thought how this was not what he expected at all. They continued their walk around the courtyard and then returned to the house.

Over the rim of her tea cup Carol studied the face of her guest. She could see the square jaw line that was one of the features which first attracted her to his father, but, in Nick's face there was something different that set him apart from Peter. Carol struggled to find the answer and eventually it came. The eyes. There was a softness about the eyes that Carol no longer found in her husband. She had almost convinced herself that it was the rigours of the Navy and its responsibilities that had robbed Peter of this mark of tenderness for which she had so often looked. Here it was, in his son. 'It must be from his mother.' She concluded and this knowledge hurt her. 'It was childish.' She scolded herself, but could not hide the jealousy and frustration of being the second wife. Carol's eyes became more fixed on her visitor and she realised that seated before her was the living proof that Peter had been married before. Here was his only child. His son. His heir, and in the features Carol could not recognise was his mother. The woman Peter once loved and perhaps still did. The uncertainty was always there.

The tone of his voice intrigued her. It was uncanny to hear a London accent coming from a face so alike Peter's. His voice was soft, the dialect not harsh, but it was not the clipped and cultivated voice of his father. It was while she listened, her mind half concentrating, half analysing, that the sound of a car's wheels on the gravel driveway invaded her consciousness.

'It's Peter.' Realisation of his presence came as a shock and a feeling of guilt passed over her like a cloud travelling across the sun. She quickly stood up.

'That will be Peter. I wonder where he's been.' There was an edge to the question.

While they had been talking Nick was admiring the lady his father had married. Throughout this initial encounter the thought that she was not what he had expected entered, passed and re-entered his mind over and over again. He was already looking forward to the horse riding despite his previously embarrassing experiences. There had been times during their conversation when he felt uneasy under the stare of those deep brown eyes. The inky blackness of her dilated pupils had given a soft inviting aura to her face. It had made him move in his seat, play with his watch, clasp and unclasp his hands. Now the sound of car tyres on gravel gave him something else to think about.

As he followed Carol into the hall he let her get a few paces ahead. The car door closed, a few moments later the metallic sound of a key being inserted in a lock seemed to shatter the silence. It was then that Nick realised just how quiet the house had become.

The door swung open and there bordered by the dark oak frame was his father. Nick stood motionless, uncertain and overwhelmed. Captain Peter Wells RN stood before him, resplendent in the navy blue uniform with four gold rings and eight golden buttons gleaming in the sun's afternoon rays.

Carol kissed Peter and stood aside. Nick stayed still as his father moved toward him.

'Nick I am glad you have made it. It is very good to see you.' Father and son shook hands and Peter continued; 'Sorry I'm late but I had a very fruitful meeting with the Admiral.' Peter shot a glance at Carol and quickly returned his attention to his son. 'I hope you haven't been waiting long.' Nick blushed and was lost for words. Now that they were together what could he say to this man? What they shared in common now seemed to hold them apart. Peter continued and taking Nick's arm guided him into the lounge room. 'Has Carol shown you over the place?'

'Yes, thank you.' Nick replied quietly.

'Good. It is not all that grand but it does for us.' Peter moved across the room to a dark wooden cabinet and pulled down the ornately carved facade to reveal a line of spirit bottles.

'How about a drink?' Nick was still being swept along on the tide.

'A beer would be good.' He answered.

'Beer or Lager?' Peter asked, forcing Nick to think again. Even the most simple question took on a mind stretching quality. He recovered quickly.

'Lager, please.'

Peter looked to Carol, who had waited by the door, not venturing into the room.

'Would you get a lager out of the fridge?' He asked.

Carol turned and walked to the kitchen. She returned

with a frothing pewter tankard glistening with beads of condensation. Nick glanced at the inscription on the tankard's side; 'To Lieutenant Peter Wells from the wardroom HMS Hunter 1962.' Peter's eyes flashed between the tankard and his wife. Carol, who was still standing, looked composed and asked for a Cinzano and Lemonade.

'I think I'll have a gin and tonic.' The statement was made as much to himself as to the others. Peter prepared both drinks. 'I bet you're a dab hand at this?' He looked at Nick. 'I should let you do it.'

Nick smiled thinly and replied.

'Oh no, I'm quite happy having someone do it for me.'

'I bet you are.' Peter answered and raised his glass. 'To Nick. It is good to see you.'

Peter handed Carol her drink and they lifted their glasses in a toast.

'To Nick.' Carol repeated softly. The object of all this attention sat uncomfortably on the sofa.

'Well, I will leave you two together and go and see how the dinner is getting on.' Carol could feel the uneasiness in the room and was grateful to have an excuse to leave. Peter moved from the drinks cabinet and sat in a brown leather chair in front of the leaded window that looked out onto the driveway. Nick felt he should be saying something, but, the words would not come. He took another long draught of his lager.

'How is your mother?'

Nick's brow furrowed and he swallowed hard. The question caught him unawares and his answer was consequently terse.

'She's fine.' Once again there was silence.

'Do you have any brothers and sisters?' Peter continued.

'Two brothers.'

Nick went on to tell a short review of his family. He found that the more he spoke the easier the words came. It never occurred to him that his real father would know so little about him or his family. It was while he was recounting his background that Carol returned to say that the meal was ready. Nick drained the tankard and placed it back on the cabinet.

'You will have to tell me more.' Peter concluded the conversation. 'Now let's go and eat.'

Peter led the way out of the room and as he came abreast of the staircase stopped and turned to Nick.

'Tell Carol I won't be a minute. I just want to wash up and change. We don't usually eat this early. I expect she thinks that all you young fellows do is eat.' He smiled and climbed the stairs taking two at a time. Nick continued into the dining room. It was a small room, sparsely furnished and unimaginatively decorated. Nick sensed that it was a room not often used. The table was a solid piece of furniture, oval in shape and dark in colour. Around it sat six chairs that did not match in colour or style.

'Where is Peter?' Carol asked, her hands full of plates. Nick explained that he had gone upstairs. 'Well, if he doesn't get here soon we'll start without him. I'm not going to let it get cold.' She was openly annoyed. 'You sit here, Nick.' He moved to a place on the far side of the table. Carol left the room and quickly returned with a joint of beef on a silver carving tray. Placing it on the table in front of Nick she handed him the carving set. 'You must be good at this. I'll go and get Peter.' So saying she hurried from the room leaving her guest staring at the very well done joint of meat that sat blackened before him.

'If only she knew.' He said to himself as he tried to decide which end of the charcoal encrusted beast to attack first. On hearing footsteps in the hall he made a start.

Peter had changed into grey flannel trousers, a white shirt and a white round neck pullover. A naval cravat was neatly secured around his neck. The dark blue material contrasting with the whiteness of the other clothes.

'She has got you at it fast enough.' He commented on seeing Nick struggling with the joint.

'Either this knife is blunt or this meat is very tough.' Nick thought as he cut chunks of stringy beef off the dark joint.

Carol soon joined them and placed a bottle of red burgundy on the sideboard.

'Will you do the honours, Peter?' She asked as she took her seat next to Nick.

Peter took the bottle and pulled the cork. He filled their glasses. The action triggered a question.

'How long have you worked for the airline, Nick?'

The joint had finally been dissected and uneven chunks of beef lay piled on the serving tray. Nick gingerly placed the carving set on the tray and looked at his father.

'Just over a year.'

'Do you like it?'

Nick considered the question carefully before he answered.

'It's a good lifestyle, but the work gets to me sometimes.'

Peter picked up his glass and proposed a toast.

'To Nick. I hope this is the first of many visits.'

'Yes, you must come and see us whenever you like.' Carol added, smiling as she looked at her step-son.

Shyly he thanked them and took a drink of wine. The subtle beauty of Carol's expression stirred something within him and he found it hard not to stare. It was Peter's questions that kept Nick from betraying his interest.

'How did you do at school?'

Nick answered, as he neatly arranged the vegetables on his plate.

'Two 'A' levels in History and English Literature.' His voice indicated no sense of achievement. There was a pause while they each began their meal.

'Why didn't you go to university?' Peter could not conceal his disapproval.

Nick noted his tone but was not about to be intimidated.

'I wanted to see the world. See life itself rather than get it second hand from books.'

During this exchange Carol's eyes followed the men. She could not help feeling pleased with Nick's answer. Peter was so predictable.

'I suppose you can always go back to your studies. How old are you now? Twenty one, twenty two?' Peter did not wait for an answer. 'You could even join the Navy.'

This suggestion took Nick completely by surprise. He took a vigorous drink of wine. He said nothing and waited for whatever was to come next.

'You have the qualifications. You are fit and you have the right connections.'

Nick forced himself to eat and hoped he looked unconcerned. The conversation was turning into an interview and he did not like it. He took another drink before he answered.

'No. I don't think so. I'm not cut out for that sort of thing.' Peter was quick to respond.

'You don't even know what it's like. Why don't you let me arrange a meeting at Dartmouth for you? You could have a look round.' His voice was fired with enthusiasm. Nick held firm.

'No. Really. I'm not the military type.'

Carol could see the battle of wills and the shared character that marked them as father and son. She could see that Peter was pressing too hard.

'The Navy can't be every man's sort of life, Peter. Think of the competition.' She was trying to be flippant but also to make her point. It did not work. Peter retaliated with the authoritarian edge to his voice that she had come to hear more and more over the past years.

'The boy can't go on drifting forever, and I don't see that being an Airline Steward is a profitable career for a young man with intelligence.'

The table fell silent. Not even the nervous clink of cutlery against china was heard. The men stared at each other while Carol lowered her eyes to the table. The seconds were suspended in time and thought.

'I can understand why you say that.' Nick rallied to his own defence. His voice was calm and he did appreciate the point his father was making. Indeed, the thought had occurred to him on a number of occasions; however, he could not accept his father's attitude. 'We cannot all go into careers that we know will last all our lives,' he paused, 'I don't know what I will do for the rest of my life, but right now I am earning a good wage and seeing the world at the same time, and nobody tells me what to do.' He knew that this last statement was unfair but he had been in the airline long enough to realise that accountability was negligible. He held his father's stare until Peter smiled and looked at Carol.

'You are probably right.' He conceded, knowing he had gone too far. 'If you ever change your mind you know where to come.'

'Right.' Nick declared happily. 'I could not miss having a Captain speaking for me.' Nick had hesitated. He wanted to say something different. He wanted to say, 'with a Captain for a father,' but the words would not follow the thought. His emotions became a confused mixture of guilt and uncertainty. In his mind's eye was projected a vision of his step-father. 'Surely my loyalties must lie there?' He thought.

He looked across the table at the man he had never seen except through the eyes of a baby and as he did so he felt the bond between them. A unity that defied his conscience. He felt calm. A decision had been reached deep within himself. Although, he did not know if he would ever be able to give voice to his feelings and address the man before him as father.

Unaware of the troubled thoughts in his son's mind Peter went on to reveal his own good news.

'You would not only have a Captain on your side, you would have a Rear-Admiral. Or at least you would if you waited four more years.' With a flourish he finished his wine and refilled the glass. 'I think I told you that I was late because I had to see the Admiral.' He described the meeting in detail while Carol listened abstractly. She had heard it all before. Peter was now so engrossed with his news that he failed to see the disinterest in his wife's eyes.

Nick listened and asked the relevant questions. He knew that Peter was speaking on his favourite topic and dutifully gave his attention, while knowing Carol was not giving hers.

The meal was completed, although no plate was returned empty. Carol was quick to remove the evidence.

'I will bring the coffee through to the lounge.' She said. Nick's offer to clear away the dirty plates having been declined, his eyes now followed Carol out of the room. He was embarrassed when Peter's voice interrupted his thoughts.

'Nick. Would you like a port?' Peter pushed his chair back and rose from the table. He led the way back to the lounge.

'I can't remember whether you said you wanted it or not.' He said and handed Nick a glass of the ruby liquid. They sat in silence until Carol arrived with the coffee.

The rest of the evening was passed quietly with Nick recounting anecdotes of his experiences in the airline. Carol was fascinated by the different cities he had seen and the things he had done.

'It sounds like a very exciting life.' She exclaimed and caught Peter's reproachful stare.

Nick smiled.

'It has its high points,' he then paused, 'it is also one of the most exhausting occupations you can imagine and right now it has caught up with me.' He drank the last drop of coffee and set the cup on the tray,

'I hope you will excuse me if I crash out. The old time changes take their toll.' Carol smiled with gentle eyes.

'You will find towels on the end of your bed.' Nick nodded and thanked her.

'How about a run tomorrow morning?' Peter asked and surprised Nick by the question. It took him a little time to collect his thoughts.

'I'm afraid I didn't bring my gear. I didn't think I would need it.' His tone was both apologetic and surprised.

'Never mind.' Peter replied, 'next time you come down bring your shoes, there's some lovely countryside round here. Good running.'

'I'll remember that.' Nick replied and then turned to Carol. 'Thank you for the dinner. A home cooked meal was just what I needed.'

Carol smiled back at him and answered.

'Good night, Nick. Sleep well.'

'Good night.' He echoed and looked toward Peter seated in the leather arm chair. 'Good night.' He felt as if he wanted to add something else but knew that he could not. The word would not come to his lips, although it played in his head. The two men looked at each other as if they both heard it. Nick turned and left the room.

He was tired and yet sleep would not come. He was in his father's house. He had sat at the same table. It was as if he had found himself and, at the same time, lost another part of him that was familiar. He thought of his stepfather, the man who had nurtured and guided him into manhood. He had two sons of his own and yet treated Nick as equal to either of these. It was not his fault that Nick had always felt an outsider. Nick loved his mother and yet resented her for trying to hide the truth about his father from him. He had seen the photograph and the tears on his mother's face. He knew that she too was not sure that the life she had was the life she wanted. Now, he had met his father, talked, drank and eaten with him. He was still unsure of his emotions. In making this journey he had not known what to expect, although he did have expectations. Having met the man he was now filled with doubts. He had wanted to call him Father, Dad, but, the words would not come. There was a barrier through which he could not penetrate, a distance that alienated feelings and frustrated emotions that for so long had been waiting to be fulfilled. The sound of approaching voices drew his thoughts outside of himself and into the corridor on the other side of the bedroom door. He listened, eavesdropping on the conversation, controlling his breathing so even that did not muffle the sound. Carol sounded annoyed and as she passed his bedroom door Nick caught the tail end of the conversation.

'You invited him down, you arrived home late and now you say you have to work tomorrow. Tomorrow is Saturday for God's sake. Why can't it wait?' Peter's voice was louder, his tone more menacing.

'In a very short time I will have to hand over my ship and I know she is not ready. I need every day between now and the hand over date, whenever that may be, to get my ship ready. It is my reputation that is at stake here.' Carol was quick to interject.

'And it is your son who is in that room.'

There was silence. Nick heard a door close. He lay looking out of the window. The curtain moved gently in the night air.

Without looking at his watch Nick knew that it was late. The sun's piercing rays flooded the small room with brilliant golden light. Nick squinted into the lengthening day and maneuvered the upper part of his body off of the bed. There was no sound from outside his room and then it occurred to him to check the time.

'Eleven o'clock, it couldn't be.' His mind insisted as his eyes stared into the yellow face of the watch. In resignation he relaxed and flopped back onto the bed, covering his face with his folded arms.

He lay there, staring out at the strange yet homely room and wondered what the day would bring and pondered at what had passed. It had not been an easy reunion and the barriers were still there, but, he could not hide away in bed all day and he had to admit that he was looking forward to seeing Carol. Having made the resolve for action he sprang from the bed, wrapped a towel around his waist and walked out of the room and along the landing to the bathroom.

'Good morning.'

The bright and airy voice caused Nick to jump with

surprise. Automatically his hands went to the towel to check that it was secure. He looked at his hostess and admired the sexuality of the woman ten years his senior.

'You must have needed sleep.' Carol toyed with him, forcing him to stand before her bare chested and on edge.

'I am sorry. I didn't mean to sleep so long.' Carol dismissed his apology as unnecessary.

'I'll make us some coffee and then we can go for a pub lunch.' Her face radiated warmth and in her eyes was a hint of pleasure. 'You see, you really have timed it very well.'

She brushed past him in the narrow passageway. The touch of her floating hair on his naked shoulder aroused a feeling within him that he did not want to admit. He pulled the towel tightly about his waist.

The pine table sat in the centre of the kitchen. Its surface bore witness to its years. As Nick entered Carol set a steaming mug of coffee on the gnarled wooden surface.

'Would you like anything for breakfast?' She asked. Nick declined, remembering what she had said about going out and not wanting to hold her up any longer.

Carol was dressed in jeans that gave a sensual outline to her figure. A pale blue sweatshirt draped her breasts, hiding and yet not concealing their fullness. Nick admired her covetously.

'Okay, we'll go straight out.' She answered unaware of the desire within her guest. 'Peter said he would see us on board for dinner. He has a lot to do, leaving the ship at such short notice. I'm sorry he can't be here with you.' Her voice went soft and apologetic and then picked up again. 'Still, we can have a good time and see the old workhorse later.' She pointed to Nick's mug. 'When you have finished that I will show you the beauty of rural Hampshire.' Nick took up the mug and drank even though the coffee scalded his lips.

'Let's take my car.' Nick called up the stairs to Carol who had gone to get a jacket.

'All right. You get the car started. I'll be right down.' Her excited voice echoed around the white painted stairwell.

Carol closed the heavy front door and ran to the white sports car that sat with its engine rumbling malevolently. Nick leaned across, opened the door and Carol breezily jumped in.

'It's so low.' She exclaimed as her bottom touched the seat and her legs stretched out under the dash board. 'It takes some time getting used to after the estate. It's great isn't it?' Nick laughed and engaged the gears, the car moved forward and out through the five bar gate.

'Where to first?' He enquired, not caring where he was sent, only happy to be in her company. Carol's voice appeared to bubble as she spoke.

'Turn right at the end of the lane and I will take you over the Downs and passed where your father will soon be working.' The word had escaped as the mind relaxed and became unguarded. Both looked straight ahead and Nick kneaded the steering wheel with his hands. The word had been avoided over the past day. It was always there, but it was unspoken. The noise of the engine and the tyres on the roadway set up a rhythm that enveloped the small cabin of the car.

'I have been wanting to say it, you know?' Nick spoke quietly with an intensity in his voice. Carol glanced at him and then looked back to the road ahead. 'I can see me in him.' Carol remained silent knowing that he did not expect her to reply. 'He is a stranger to me and you have no idea how that hurts.' His right hand struck the steering wheel. 'Why should it bother me? He is not the man who has looked after me all of my life. What is he to me, really?' He went silent before answering his own question. 'He is my father.'

'I can see him in you too.' Carol's voice was soft with compassion. She thought Peter to be cruel and unfeeling to be on his ship, ignoring his only son. At that moment she despised her husband and it frightened her. Nick smiled to think that Carol could also see the resemblance and now spoke as if a weight had been lifted from his shoulders.

'He is just as I imagined him. Just as Mum described him.' Nick went on to tell of the time he found the photograph and learned the truth about his father. 'Ever since that day I wanted to meet him.' Conversation was easier now. 'Mum was not pleased about this visit. She sees it as a betrayal of my step-father, but I know that deep down she would like to see him again.' Silence again and then Nick realised what he had said. 'Oh, I don't mean,' he trailed off and began again. 'I'm sorry, you know what I mean.' He stammered. 'She would not want to be married to him again, just see him, curiosity, you know?' Nick looked helplessly at his passenger.

'Yes I know.' She smiled. 'I bet you will have to report back after this weekend.'

Nick was openly laughing now, enjoying the conversation and he agreed that he was given subtle hints along those lines.

'The telephone will be ringing all tomorrow until I report in.' He spoke conspiratorially knowing his words would go no further. They turned off the winding narrow lane and onto a wider road.

'Take the next left and you will come to a pretty village, we pass through there and the school is on the right. They will not let us in, but we can still get a good view of the place from outside the gate.'

Nick followed the directions and was soon passing picturesque thatched cottages and a quaint village store. The red edged sign stood out against a backdrop of green leafed trees, 'School of Maritime Operations'. Nick wheeled the car passed the main gate and pulled off the road. He turned the engine off and sat forward with his arms across the steering wheel.

'Only buildings really.' Carol commented and continued, 'but it means the world to Peter.' There was resignation in her voice that she no longer tried to hide.

'He was excited, wasn't he?' Nick replied, recalling Peter's news the night before.

'The Navy is his whole world. Did your mother tell you that?' Carol replied. He turned his body to face her, saw the emptiness in her eyes and remembered his mother's expression in her bedroom all those years ago. 'Well, you have seen it, now let's go find a pub.' Carol bounced back.

'Are you nearly ready?' Carol's voice called along the landing.

'I can't find my tie.' Nick called back.

'Use one of Peter's.' The conversation flowed at a distance.

'No, it's okay. I know I packed one. It's here somewhere.' There was silence for a moment. 'I've found it.' Tying the knot loosely about his neck he gave his appearance a final check in the mirror. 'I'm ready.' He called as he left the room.

'I will be with you in a minute. See you downstairs.' Carol's voice echoed from the end of the landing.

Nick walked down the staircase and waited by the front door. He looked down at his shoes and then tugged at the cuffs of his shirt. He studied his watch. They had twenty minutes to be there. They were not going to make it.

The minutes passed as he paced the hallway. With relief he heard Carol's footsteps on the stairs.

'We will go in our car.' Carol announced and quickly disappeared into the kitchen to collect the keys.

Nick opened the door and let Carol pass him as she hurried out of the house. She walked across to the garage and Nick had to run to catch up. As the metal door swung open he was surprised to see the car standing there. Carol unlocked the driver's door and slid behind the wheel. Nick secured the garage door and then got in.

'How did he get to work this morning?' He asked. Carol pulled at the steering wheel guiding the long estate car out into the lane.

'The ship's driver picked him up.'

'You mean someone drove out all this way just to take him to work?' The extent of his father's influence was only now being understood.

The country roads gave way to well lit Portsmouth city streets and soon they were passing the multi storey car park of the Tricorn Centre.

'It's not the prettiest city in England is it?' Nick commented as they passed the brown streaked concrete monolith. Carol laughed.

'It is a funny old place with a character all its own. You have to live here to appreciate it.'

They fell silent once again and Nick became lost in his thoughts. It did not seem possible that he was born in this city twenty one years ago.

'Good evening Mrs. Wells.' The Police Sergeant touched the peak of his cap as he waved her through the dockyard gates.

Nick smiled to himself. He was entering a different world. He caught glimpses of grey warships between gaps in the old red brick buildings. They drove passed HMS Victory standing majestically in her dry-dock, her masts reaching up toward the sparkling night sky.

Carol slowed the car and turned left between two large, square structures that looked to Nick to be some sort of workshops. He was startled when the sleek form of the destroyer rose like a wall before them. Carol drove onto the wharf and stopped by the white painted gangway that connected the warship to the shore.

Nick glanced at the dashboard clock. They were fifteen minutes late. Punctuality did not usually concern him unless it was to do with catching a flight. Tonight he felt irresponsible and embarrassed. He looked to Carol who did not exhibit any signs of concern. Indeed he thought she looked defiant as she leaned forward to switch off the ignition.

He looked out of the window and up at the flared sides of the destroyer. 'It's a big bastard', he thought and then was interrupted by a movement beside him. Carol had opened her door and was getting out into the fresh evening air.

As they ascended the gangway Nick noticed the activity up on the deck. Two heads appeared over the guard rail and then disappeared. By the time Carol was about to step on board a young Sub-Lieutenant and an even younger Ordinary Seaman were lined up to greet her. Nick watched the two men snap a smart salute and heard the officer welcome Carol aboard. The men held their salutes until Nick was also standing on the grey deck. He acknowledged their ceremonial with a self-conscious nod of his head.

Nick knew that he was staring at the officer and the single gold ring on his sleeve. The thought that they were about the same age crossed his mind. Having to wear a uniform himself, Nick did not usually pay much attention to this form of clothing; however, on this occasion his eyes kept returning to the navy blue cloth, gold braid, and the gold thread of the intricately woven cap badge. He had to admit that in these surroundings it did look impressive. It was an acknowledgment that annoyed him.

'Good evening, Sir' The young officer looked at Nick

and back to Carol. 'If you will follow me please, the Captain is waiting in his cabin.'

Carol's eyes were fixed on the back of the Sub-Lieutenant's head while Nick's darted around this new environment, marveling at the spaghetti like run of cables and pipes, the mixture of machinery and the many signs denoting things he did not understand.

They entered a long passageway with doors leading off at regular intervals on either side. Nick read the signs on each as he passed: Engineer Officer – CMDR R.H.Thomas; Supply Officer – CMDR I.P.Jacks. Nick followed in Carol's footsteps as she turned right and there before them appeared a highly polished door on which was fixed a shining brass plaque. Nick read the ship's motto, Always First. He smiled. 'Perfect', he thought.

The Sub-Lieutenant knocked twice and then turned to Carol.

'It is nice to see you again Mrs. Wells.' The door opened and the young Officer of the Day returned along the passageway. For a moment Nick watched him go and then looked back to the doorway. He was surprised to see another unknown face greeting them when he expected to see his father.

'Good evening Mrs. Wells.' The sailor's round and florid face broke into a broad smile of genuine warmth. Nick saw that Carol was now smiling for the first time since leaving home.

'Hello Kevin. It's good to see you again. He has not been working you too hard has he?' They laughed together in their understanding.

Carol had first met Leading Steward Hawkes when Peter was the Executive Officer of the Navigation School. As Leading Stewards went in the service, Hawkes was of advanced years for his rate. He had found his niche and his years of experience taught him how to exploit it.

'Good evening, sir.' Hawkes formerly greeted Nick and led the way into the centre of the cabin. Peter was nowhere to be seen.

'Cinzano and lemonade, Mrs. Wells?' The Steward asked in mock formality. Carol smiled, acknowledging their private joke.

'I have tried to be more trendy. No luck, I'm afraid.' Hawkes laughed, shrugged his shoulders and poured the cocktail.

'For you, sir?'

Nick turned towards the balding man in the white top and blue bell bottom trousers, but, did not answer immediately.

'Nick.' Carol said his name and brought him back to reality.

'Beer, please.'

'Very good, sir.' The steward pulled the ring on the top of the can and poured the cold contents into a pewter tankard. Placing them on a silver tray he brought them over to the two guests.

'The Captain will be out presently.' Hawkes could read the look on Carol's face. 'He is just changing.'

Nick looked round the cabin not thinking there would be more than one room behind that polished door. His eyes landed on a second door, this one made of grey metal and faced with wooden lattices.

'Won't you please sit down?' Hawkes was playing the perfect surrogate host.

Nick followed Carol's lead and walked over to a small three seater settee, covered in navy blue cotton and trimmed with white piping. Nick continued to look around the cabin.

There were photographs of the ship above the functional electric fireplace, silver trophies sat in a cabinet on another wall and on a large dining table a silver candelabra dominated the mirror like surface. Only the circular scuttles and grey trunking on the deckhead told him that he was in a warship. Hawkes retired through another door situated by the far end of the dining table. Nick tried to crane his neck to see what was inside.

'That is the pantry.' Carol answered his unspoken question. He laughed.

'Thanks. I bet I look like a real tourist.' They smiled together and sat quietly for a moment.

'I am sorry.' Peter's voice echoed around the metallic cabin as he strode from behind the louvered door. 'Gin and Tonic please Kevin.' He called into the pantry as he passed by. The reply was immediate;

'It's on the bar top, sir.' Peter smiled,

'I have got to get rid of old Hawkes, he is getting too many steps ahead of me.' Nick laughed. He had got out of his seat when Peter had entered. They shook hands. 'Have you had a good day?' Peter asked and bent down to kiss Carol on the cheek.

'After a late start.' Nick admitted and went on to tell of the day's events. Peter took his seat in one of the arm chairs that was placed adjacent to the settee. He was dressed in a charcoal grey suit, white shirt and naval tie. His black shoes were highly polished and prompted Nick to steal a glance at his own. Peter listened while Nick recounted his story. As soon as it was told he spoke up;

'Well, I have spent a very profitable day. Squared away a lot of loose ends in the paperwork and worked on a plan for a family's day before I leave the ship.'

Nick looked puzzled, not knowing what Peter was talking about.

'What do you think of the idea Carol?' The question was meant to draw her into the conversation rather than for an opinion. She looked at her husband but only said,

'Good.'

'Good!' Peter exclaimed. 'Is that all you can say? What do you say Nick?'

Nick looked blank and felt stupid. He had to admit that he did not know what they were talking about. Peter explained the concept of the day when the ship went to sea with the families of the crew embarked. It was an opportunity for those who are normally left at home to share in the life of their men folk. Nick was enthusiastic and Peter was openly pleased.

'When could you make it?' He asked.

Nick looked into Peter's eyes,

'Me!' He replied in amazement.

'Yes. When are you free next?' Nick was amazed and elated at the same time. For the first time this man had openly acknowledged him. In his happy confusion Nick blurted out a poor reply.

'Ah well, I don't know.' He was missing his chance

and he knew he must explain or miss the opportunity altogether. 'I have my trips for the next month written in my diary and I have left that back at my flat. I can't give you a definite date without checking the trips.'

Peter's face was impassive throughout and then relaxed as Nick finished the explanation.

'That is not a problem.' He replied. 'If you give me a date when you get home I will work around that.' He smiled and called out to his steward, 'Leading Steward Hawkes, how is dinner coming along?'

The round steward appeared in the pantry door.

'If you would take your seats sir I will be right with you.' Peter turned to his guests and led the way to the table.

Hawkes kept the food and wine flowing with an uninterrupted and discreet rhythm. Peter kept the conversation alive with stories of passed incidents in the ships in which he had served. Carol said very little, except for occasional comments to Hawkes that made both of them smile. Nick kept an ear on Peter's conversation and an eye on the steward's manner. In his mind visions of the officer on the gangway and the steward now serving him mingled to form disturbing implications. As if reading his thoughts Peter asked;

'Have you given any more thought to a naval career?' Carol saw Nick's discomfort register in his expression and posture. He was now sitting upright with shoulders squared to face his inquisitor. She was quick to come between them.

'Oh Peter, what sort of question is that? We talked about that last night.'

Hawkes moved away from the table and unobtrusively disappeared into his pantry. Peter, continued unabashed.

'I know we discussed it, and Nick has had a day to think about it.'

For an instant no one spoke. Nick did not want to discuss the thoughts and images that had unsettled him throughout the evening.

'I can't say that I have.' The lie did not come easily and he felt certain Peter saw through the deception.

'I do not want to keep on,' Peter continued, 'but, you could do well in the service. You are the right age, you have the qualifications.'

'He has the connections.' Carol's voice was sharp and cynical, but, Peter was not going to be put on the defensive;

'You are right, he does have the right connections. An advantage no one should take lightly no matter what the profession.' For the moment Nick was out of the conversation and then Peter pulled him in. 'After dinner I will show you round the ship. It will give you a feel of the life and when we have the day at sea you will really see what it is all about. Don't forget to give me that date when you can make it.' Nick reassured him and they finished the meal with Peter outlining his plans for the weeks ahead.

Nick's shoes echoed on the steel deck. A slight breeze whined through the aerials atop the destroyer's masts. Forty minutes earlier they had left Carol in the wardroom and begun their tour.

They walked along spotless painted passageways,

through head threatening hatches, up and down metal ladders that clattered with the fall of feet on their shining surfaces. The only areas in which they did not venture were the mess decks where the sailors remaining on board would have been surprised by a sudden visit of the Captain. From the few men they did encounter Nick could feel the deference towards the Captain and he could not suppress a feeling of pride in the reflected glory of being with this man. However, as they walked back along the upper deck Nick could not help thinking that no one in this ship knew who he was. He felt like the family skeleton being let out of the closet.

'You are quiet.' Peter had been giving a running commentary as they walked together and came to notice there was no response, Nick turned to face him and Peter took this as a cue to continue, 'What do you think of her?'

Nick summoned a smile. This man would never understand how he was feeling and he did not want to spoil his fantasy.

'I have never seen anything like it.' He answered.

'I know that,' Peter quickly replied, 'isn't she beautiful?' In the dim orange lights of the dockyard Nick could just make out the expectant look on Peter's face. There was only one answer that he wanted to hear and Nick felt obliged to give it.

'Yes. She is beautiful. You are very lucky.' There, it had been said. Nick did not feel the attachment to the ship that his father did. How could he? Nick found it interesting, but it did not excite him. He envied this man for his total commitment to his ship and his way of life, but, he knew he could not make it his. The Captain's reply startled and angered him.

'Luck has nothing to do with it.' Nick's eyes narrowed and he felt his stomach tighten as Peter went on. 'Hard work and dedication,' he paused, 'you must never let anything stand in your way. You must know what you want and go after it.' There was another pause and then the question came. 'What do you want Nick?'

Nick breathed deeply in an attempt to control his emotions while his mind screamed, 'How dare this man keep on mounting his high horse and deliver his high and mighty speeches. What did he want? He wanted to scream at this pompous man and tell him that he wanted a father he never had. He wanted to say that having two fathers was no substitute for not having known and been acknowledged by his true father. Quantity was not better than quality and he now felt that he had missed out on both.' He wanted to say all this but knew that he could not, instead, he answered,

'I want to live my life on my own terms without being accountable to anyone. I want happiness before wealth, and do you know what I would do if I had the money?' His voice was edged with defiance and he did not wait for an answer, 'I would buy a house in the middle of nowhere and drop out.'

For the first time that evening Peter was speechless. They walked on in silence until Peter could contain himself no longer.

'Drop out!' Peter stopped walking and looked at his son. 'You have not even started life and you want to drop out?' Nick was surprised to hear no anger in the voice, only amazement and frustration. 'I do not understand you Nick.' Without waiting for more Nick replied.

'You will never understand me. You don't know me. You do not really know anyone.'

The words had been said. There was no going back. Peter thought for a moment and then went back on the attack.

'How can you say that? You have been here two days.'

Nick interrupted,

'That is how I know. I have only been here for two days and I have seen you for about five hours.' The emotions he had tried to suppress now came easily to his lips. The sound of traffic carried on the breeze was all that could be heard at that moment. Both men stood motionless and then Peter stood back and drew his left hand across his face.

'You just don't understand. I don't know what your mother has been filling your head with but…'

Nick sprang to his mother's defence;

'Hold it right there. Don't go bringing Mum into this.'

Peter tried to retake the initiative without success,

'I only meant.' He began to say but was quickly interrupted,

'I know what you meant. It is not me who does not understand, you don't even know that Mum still loves you.' There was complete silence as the world seemed to stand still. He had not meant to say that. Peter stood looking at him and then spoke,

'Don't talk rubbish,' he sneered, betraying his own emotions for the first time. Anger welled within Nick again, the arrogance of this man spurred him into another attack,

'Mum has never said a bad word about you. She still has your picture in her bedroom,' he waited for this revelation to register, 'it is you who does not understand. You don't know anything about people.' Peter was visibly stunned and did not rally for a few seconds.

'This is not the time nor the place to talk about this. We had better get back to Carol.' He looked at his watch even though he could not see the face clearly in the dim light. 'It's getting late.' Nick shrugged his shoulders and turned to walk back to the hatch that led to the wardroom. He had gone a few paces when Peter spoke again, this time his voice was quiet and controlled. 'I appreciate what you have told me Nick, but, I do not think we should bring this up in front of Carol. What do you say?'

Nick shook his head knowing that his father had only taken from their conversation what he saw as important to himself. However, he was glad that the battle was over.

'That's okay by me.' He answered and felt Peter's hand rest on his shoulder.

'Where have you two been?' Carol asked as the door swung open and the men entered. 'I thought you had fallen overboard and was just going to get Kevin to run off with me.' The steward blushed visibly and sought the refuge of his pantry.

'We have had an extensive tour.' Peter replied breezily and smiled at his wife.

'Has he made a sailor out of you?' She asked Nick and could not help but notice that the younger man was not so exuberant. She continued to talk so as to give him a chance to settle down. 'I wouldn't like to spend months on end in this floating prison even if it does have over two hundred bored men in it.'

'Carol!' Peter scolded in an attempt to curb his wife's mischievousness. She did succeed in bringing a smile to Nick's face.

'If it was full of bored women I would certainly consider it.' He replied.

'You should join the Wrens.' Carol quipped and caused Nick to laugh out loud. 'What's so funny?' She asked. Through tears of laughter Nick replied,

'There are a lot of guys in my job who could probably get in.' Carol laughed along with him while Peter remained aloof from their conversation.

'We had better make a move,' he suggested. 'Give the Leading Steward a few hours off.'

Hawkes smiled and went to collect Carol's coat.

'Thank you for a lovely meal Kevin.' Carol said as the steward held her coat for her to put on. She knew that Peter did not really like the informal manner she adopted with his steward, but she refused to change.

'My pleasure Mrs. Wells. It was good to see you again.' His eyes reflected true affection for the Captain's wife. He then turned away to open the door for their departure. Nick thanked him and saw himself standing at the open doorway of an aircraft bidding the passengers farewell.

'Thank you Hawkes,' Peter spoke formally, 'see you on Monday. Have a good weekend.'

'Thank you Sir.' The Leading Steward closed the

door and ran to the telephone to warn the gangway staff that the Captain was on his way.

'Good morning Nick. Sleep well?' Peter was standing in the far corner of the kitchen pouring himself a cup of black coffee. 'Tea or coffee?' There was no hint in his voice or manner to betray any feelings he might be harbouring from the night before. 'How about some toast?' It was a new day and it appeared yesterday had been forgotten.

'Just coffee please.' Nick answered quietly, wanting to say more.

'Carol is out getting the horses ready. You two are off riding I understand.' Peter poured the coffee. 'Have you ridden before?' He handed Nick the mug.

'Not very much, but I have seen lots of westerns.' It was a poor joke and Nick was surprised to see Peter smile. It made him feel more confident. 'Do you ride?' He asked.

Two pieces of toast popped up from the toaster and Peter retrieved them and laid them on a plate. He took the butter and answered as he spread a thin layer over the golden brown slices.

'Horses and I do not get on. There isn't one horse that I have got on that hasn't thrown me off.'

'That's because you can't control them.' The back door slammed shut and Carol strode into the room her face radiant from the morning air. 'He can boss men about but he can't boss horses.' Peter did not reply except for raising his eyebrows and then bent down to get a jar of marmalade from the low cupboard. Carol turned her attention to Nick. 'Have you had anything to eat?' She asked. Nick raised his mug of coffee. 'You will need more than that inside you.' Nick grew concerned.

'How long are we going out for?' His voice reflected his concern.

'A couple of hours. We'll be back for lunch.'

'A couple of hours!' Nick exclaimed. Carol gave a resigned smile,

'You men.' Was all she said.

Nick turned to Peter,

'I think I'll have that toast now.' He said

'We will take it easy for the first half hour and let you get the feel of the horse and let him get used to you. Okay?' Carol called back over her shoulder as she led the way out of the paddock and onto the green rolling hills of the downs. Nick just nodded. Concentration was etched deeply in his furrowed brow and in his hands that held the reins as if they were lifelines that may slip away without warning.

The countryside looked enchanting with the early flowers of Spring adding their brilliant colours to the many shades of green. The sun's rays had warmed the earth, transforming the early morning dew into swirling white mist that rose from the ground like the smoking traces of a spent fire.

At first Nick sat uneasily astride the swaying saddle as the horse picked his way through the tall grass. As the minutes passed so his confidence grew until it was he who suggested they quicken the pace. Carol laughed at his bravado.

'Remember this was your idea.' She shouted and gently spurred on her mount. Nick, who was rapidly losing himself in the adventure, shook the reins and jiggled his feet against the horse's flanks in an attempt to elicit a faster response. Eventually, and probably because he saw his equine friend disappearing into the distance, the horse broke into a trot and then a cantor. Forgetting all Carol had told him Nick held on with every part of his body that was in contact with the horse. The gyrations of his body defied both the laws of motion and gravity until there came that magical time when his buttocks were in unison with the movement of his mount. With each successive rise and fall of his body Nick's confidence grew.

'Very good.' Carol called as she rode toward him, admiring his style. He looked at her, his face beaming with pride and achievement.

'What now?' He asked as they rode side by side along the brow of a hill that gave a panoramic view across miles of green quilted countryside.

'Now we walk.' Carol announced and slowed her horse's pace.

'Walk?' Echoed Nick, drawing in on the reins in true cowboy style and expending a lot of effort for little result. Once again it appeared his horse was following the lead of the other more than obeying the commands of its rider. 'Why do we have to walk?' Carol laughed at his enthusiasm and drew near to him so they could talk more easily,

'Because we have only just left home and we have another couple of hours riding ahead of us, and because there is a gate up ahead that I don't think you are quite up to taking at the gallop.' She was teasing him, but he did not mind. He could not remember feeling so free and happy at just being alive.

Carol held the metal gate open as Nick passed through and then deftly shut it behind her. The latch rattled in the lock. Nick waited for her to catch up and they continued a gentle amble across the unspoiled countryside.

'You live in a lovely spot.' Nick commented as he looked around and then returned to a joking mood. 'It's certainly a good view from up here.' Carol laughed at him trying to stand in the stirrups.

'You won't be admiring it for long if you keep that up.' He quickly sat down and adjusted his position in the saddle. The novelty of horse riding was just making itself felt on his backside. 'Are you ready for a gallop?' Carol asked with a gleam in her eye. 'Remember what I told you and follow me.' With those challenging words she was off and running, her brown hair trailing behind her in the wind. Without command Nick's horse set off in pursuit. The rocking motion of the gallop and the exhilaration of speed filled him with pure joy and excitement. They rode like two dispatch riders over the flat surface of the ground. The grass was shorter there and the ground felt firmer, echoing the tread of the horses hoofs as they pounded out their rhythm.

'That was fantastic.' Nick's voice croaked with excitement when Carol finally slowed down and turned to meet him.

'How about a rest?' She asked and was instantly howled down.

'Rest! How about another Charge of the Light Brigade?'

Carol had not felt so relaxed and happy for a very long time.

'Oh Nick, you are mad.' Her face lit up as she spoke, 'you will feel your bottom tomorrow. Come on, we'll go and sit down under those trees.' She pointed to a small copse of trees about two hundred yards in front of them.

'What kept you and Peter away for so long last night?' Carol was rolling a long blade of grass in her fingers and then put it between her lips. They were lying in thick, lush grass at the base of a towering oak. Nick was propped up on one arm. Although he had agreed with Peter not to discuss last night's events he now interpreted that to mean their references to his mother. He was only too willing to talk about last night with a sympathetic audience.

'Peter.' He stammered. 'Dad.' He paused and then in exasperation cried out, 'Oh! I just don't know what to call him.' Carol put out her hand to comfort him,

'It must be hard for you.' She said, almost in a whisper. Nick breathed heavily,

'No. Not really. It's just bloody awkward.' He stopped and looked at Carol for a long time. 'I just don't know if I like him! I'm not even sure, now that I have met him, that I want him to be my father. It's so bloody confusing?' Carol was silent, thinking. This outburst did not surprise her. Nick went on. 'You're great. A lot of fun. If it wasn't for you I would have gone home on Saturday morning.' Now it was going too far and Carol thought that she had to put it back in perspective.

'You are very sweet, Nick, but don't forget that your father has had a lot of adjusting to do over the past weeks.' She sat upright to lend weight to her words. 'You don't know what it took for him to have you on his ship yesterday.' She stopped, not sure how to put what she wanted to say next. 'No one knows about you down here.'

Nick laughed without humour.

'Don't you think I know that? How do you think it feels to be the man who never was?' Nick placed his head in his hands and ran his fingers through his hair. Carol moved closer and put her arm around his shoulders.

'Give it time Nick. It will be worth it in the end, believe me.' Her voice soothed him, her arm felt comforting about him and he knew it was time to change the subject.

'You are right about the old rear end. I don't know about feeling it tomorrow, right now I've got a numb bum.' Carol laughed, the moment had passed. She had not found out what she wanted to know but she now knew the fears and frustrations of Nick Wells. She also knew that the time had come to move on.

'Come on, let's see if you have forgotten all I've taught you.' Carol rose to her feet and walked over to the horses. Nick followed, a bit more stiff legged than an hour or so before.

They rode around the copse of trees and back in the direction they had come.

Peter was in the yard as they entered,

'Welcome back,' he waved and strode over to shut the gate behind them. 'Well, how did you like it?' He asked, looking up at Nick who relaxed his hold on the reins. The reply was full of feeling,

'Don't ask.' Nick slid from the saddle, stretched and rubbed his backside with both hands.

'Now you know why I don't indulge.' Peter joked. Nick acknowledged the comment with a smile and a nod of his head. He then turned to Carol.

'What next?'

He was amazed to see that she had already removed the saddle from her horse and was leading him to the stable.

'You go inside and make a pot of tea. I'll take care of the horses.' He did not have to be told twice.

Carol rejoined the men in the kitchen.

'Well you two certainly have one thing in common… your command of horses.' Both looked at each other across the table and all three disintegrated into laughter.

'It has been good seeing you Nick.' Peter clasped his son's hand in his own. 'Remember to give me that date. I want you to be there.'

'I'll let you know as soon as I get home.' Nick assured him and turned to Carol. 'Thank you for a wonderful time.' She shook his hand and smiled,

'Thank you for coming to see us and make sure you do it again soon.'

'I will.' Nick's voice trailed away full of emotions he was unable to express. Reluctantly he let go of her hand and to disguise his feelings returned his attention to Peter. 'All the best with your new command and thanks again. I am glad to have met you at last.'

'Don't leave it so long next time.' His father replied.

Chapter 16

Nick lay staring at the pink plastic telephone only inches from his right hand. He willed it to ring, to hear the shrill sound of its alarm that would release him from the torment of sleep that would not come. Two hours ago he had drawn the heavy blinds to hide the afternoon sun and tell his brain what his body already knew, in London it was midnight. He wanted to get some rest before working through the night to cover the miles from Chicago to London.

Every Atlantic night stop was the same, a vain attempt to snatch a few hours sleep in the afternoon before the long night flight home. Nick's thoughts returned to the telephone. His eyes darted across to the black face of the clock that sat on the bedside table. 'Only five more minutes and the phone should ring.' It then occurred to him that the flight might be delayed. He glanced across to the message light on the wall. It was not glowing red.

'Thank God for that.' Nick said aloud and kicked the bedclothes from his body. Rolling his legs off the side of the bed he stood up and walked across to the aluminium stand that supported his suitcase. Casually he threw a pair of jeans and a tee shirt into the open space.

'Ring ring ring…' even though he was expecting the call the shrill sound of the telephone alarm made him jump. In two steps he reached the offending machine and spoke to the computerised answering machine. Nick cursed himself,

'I always do that.' He felt foolish for talking to a machine that neither heard nor cared about his polite reply. He firmly set the receiver down in its cradle and went to take a shower.

Under the pulsating spray he prepared himself for the night ahead. 'You had to be ready for it. Psych yourself up otherwise the night would be a long, hard failure. Without the right preparation, the right attitude of mind, the demands of so many people would drain the body and the mind.' Nick had told these thoughts to Carol. He had explained to her what he could not tell his father. She had listened and understood. It was to her his spirit now went as he turned the silver taps to stop the flow of water. He would not be seeing her for two weeks and the thought of those empty days depressed him. He could not get her out of his mind.

The aircraft was not full and in the upper deck cabin, where Nick was working, five of the eighteen seats were empty. The first round of drinks had been given out and he prepared to distribute the plastic meal trays. He worked mechanically through the routine he knew so well from months of repetition. He tried to keep a smile on his lips but knew that sometimes his eyes betrayed him. A call bell rang and a white light illuminated over one of the passenger seats and Nick went to answer it.

'Yes sir,' he opened the encounter with a smile. A grim face with features that resembled the weathered remains of roughly hewn granite stared back at him.

'What do you call this fish … Steward?' There was a long interval between the question and the title. Nick could not fail to recognise the intimidation in the man's tone. He adopted a breezy attitude and answered genially,

'Phillip, Sir.' His face was composed not betraying any indication that his answer was anything but the truth. In stark contrast the eyes glinted on the rock face and the voice deepened with suspicion. 'Could he have heard correctly?' His eyes were piercing in their stare, searching for an answer. Eventually he spoke,

'What did you say?' It was both a question and a threat. Nick was not about to be shaken,

'Fillet, Sir. Fillet of Salmon.' He spoke respectfully. 'Probably caught in your own Lake Michigan.' Nick smiled and the man appeared to mellow with the reference to his homeland.

'Thank you.' He said and continued, appearing to forget what he was going to complain about. 'May I have a glass of white wine?' The tone was now pleasant and submissive. Nick had won.

'One against a thousand.' He said to himself as he went to get the bottle from the iced wine drawer.

The meal was over and the in-flight movie was flickering on the screen suspended from the ceiling. Nick pulled out one of the meal trolleys from its garage like stowage and placed himself upon it. Soon he would have to feed the two pilots and the engineer but that could wait while he had a quiet cup of coffee. Perched on the cold aluminium surface he sipped the hot liquid and peered out into the cabin's blackness. A bell sounded in the galley and a small light appeared over one of the aisle seats.

'Bugger, it!' Nick cursed and dismounted the trolley. Pushing aside the maroon curtain that separated the galley from the passenger cabin, he walked forward along the aisle. As he neared the seat he knew who had pushed the button. The woman was in her late forties. Nick had noticed her as she came up the spiral staircase at the beginning of the flight. Her hair was fashioned into a tight, curly perm that gave her face a whorish attractiveness. Since the wheels had left the runway she had been doing her best to deplete the aircraft's stock of Drambuie. Nick had followed her progress and even considered refusing her another miniature bottle. On reflection he rationalised that she was not causing any trouble and appeared to be handling the intake of the liquor very well.

Nick approached the seat and knelt down so as to be out of the white beam of the film projector that was playing the in-flight movie. Leaning over he cancelled the light by pressing the call button a second time. Suddenly and without warning a hand came up and drew him down until his head was pressed against the firm, wired swell of the lady's breast. His ear was assailed by wet lips and an exploring tongue that both bore fragrant traces of the Highland spirit. There followed a moment of inaction until his mind cleared, then, placing his free hand on the arm of the chair he levered his body upright until his head was clear of the danger. He remained kneeling and glanced around to see if any of the passengers had witnessed his plight. An older man sat beaming across the darkness, his smile illuminated by the projector's jumping light. Nick raised his eyes in recognition and fought to gain his composure. He returned his attention to the woman,

'Yes madam, what can I do for you?'

As soon as the words left his lips he knew his mistake. He had walked into it with both eyes open and now, nervously, awaited her reply.

'There are two things I need.' She said in a low meaningful tone.

'Here it comes' Nick thought and prepared himself... The lady continued,

'I would like another Drambuie and one of your in-flight magazines.' Nick was relieved and a little disappointed.

'Yes Madam, I will get them for you.' The conversation had assumed a completely different nature and Nick started to relax. The lady spoke again,

'Oh yes, and one more thing.' She stopped for a moment and then continued, her voice still matter of fact, 'when you want to make love I'm ready.'

Nick rocked on his knees. Having expected it he still could not believe what he had heard. Guiltily he looked about him and was thankful for the darkness. His reply was almost a reflex and he spoke as if the last words had never been said,

'Certainly Madam. I will get those things for you right away.' Quickly he rose to his feet and retreated to the safety of the galley. Behind the protection of the curtain he stood and marvelled at what he had just heard.

He poured the drink, collected the magazine from the rack and then peered through the curtain. He could not see her head. He felt panic once again. 'Where was she?' His eyes scanned the gloom. There was no sign of her and so he decided to venture outside his sanctuary. With unsteady steps he approached the seat. As he stood on his tip toe to look over the back of the chair he saw the woman slumped down in her seat. Not daring to kneel down this time he walked in front of her and presented the glass and magazine on a silver tray. Relief swept over him and his whole body relaxed.

'Thank God for that.' He said under his breath as he looked down at the temptress who was now fast asleep.

The remainder of the night was uneventful and the dawn heralded their arrival in London. Nick had served the continental breakfast to all except his admirer, who remained asleep throughout the meal.

Twenty minutes from the airport the aircraft's nose dipped as it started its descent. The seat belt and no smoking signs lit up and the soft Scottish lilt of the stewardess gave the landing briefing over the public address system. Nick went through the cabin to ensure that all the passengers were secure in their seats. He was determined not to be intimidated by his suitor who was now awake.

'Where were you last night?' He asked boldly. 'I was waiting for you.' His eyes sparkled, enjoying the advantage.

'I'm sorry. I fell asleep.' Her apology was sincere and then her tongue moistened her lips. 'I have twelve hours in London before my next flight. We could get a hotel room.'

'Shit!' Nick's mind exploded. 'Why didn't I quit when I was behind!' He felt as if the whole aircraft cabin must have heard the invitation. 'Now what?' He had to think fast.

'I can't do that,' he replied in feigned surprise. 'I'm married.' The lie came easily. She did not take her eyes from his face.

'So am I.' She answered and flashed the gold ring on her left hand. Nick gave a weak smile, coughed and retreated once again.

By eight o'clock Nick was clear of the airport perimeter road and thinking of his plan for the day ahead. He would get home, freshen up and have a few hours' sleep before going to see his mother. He had promised her the visit as one of the conditions for not opposing the meeting with his father.

It was late afternoon when he left his flat, not quite refreshed but feeling a lot better than when he arrived. No matter how deep the sleep it never fully compensated for the ever present jet lag. The eyes never felt clear, the mind was always a little slow and the body easy to tire. 'You never get used to it, you just put up with it.' He often told himself and thought about it now as he pressed his right foot on the accelerator pedal and eased the car out into the middle lane.

The motorway was a hectic melee of cars heading out

of the city. Another day's work over, the wheels pounded the black tar macadam surface transporting their driver's home for a few hours rest before the commuter treadmill would start all over again. It was a lifestyle Nick was glad not to be a part of, jet lag or no jet lag.

'Basingstoke 7.' The road sign displayed the distance to travel. He would soon be at his parent's house. His foot eased off the accelerator pedal and slowed the car's advance. The questions would start soon enough. They will not come blatantly and there will be no hint of prying. They will be there in his mother's eyes.

The house in which he grew up was a neat four bedroom detached property with Georgian style windows and an imposing, panelled, front door. Everything from the lace net curtains to the trimmed edges of the manicured lawn was exact. The black wrought iron gates were open and Nick drove into the driveway, coming to a stop in front of the garage door. He knew that his step-father would be home by this time and his car safely tucked away behind the protection of those black gloss doors. He had never known the man to be late for anything, whether it be going to work or arriving home. That punctuality had allowed Nick to perpetrate many a boyhood prank and be home before it was discovered.

Nick opened the car door and leaned over to the back seat to collect a sports bag whose zip was straining under the pressure of its load of dirty laundry. The front door opened before he had a chance to press the bell. His mother held out her arms and kissed him gently on both cheeks. She then hugged him to her as if he was the prodigal son returned.

'It is so good to see you.' Her eyes endowed the words with love and happiness. Since leaving to live in his own flat every homecoming was the same. Nick looked into her face, 'she is still an attractive woman,' he thought. She had kept her figure and her face betrayed no signs of ageing, only a maturing beauty and an awareness of life.

'Come on in.' She said. With her arm enfolding him she led Nick into the sitting room where his step-father sat crossed legged in a deep chair of burgundy leather. He did not get up as his son entered, but simply looked over the top of the newspaper he was reading.

'Hello son. Good trip?'

Nick looked into the older man's face. The sharp line of the pencil moustache and the slicked back hair receding from the forehead gave him an appearance that always daunted his step-son.

'Yes thanks.' Nick answered. 'I don't know where they get the money to fly all over the world.' Before his father could comment he continued, 'it keeps me in a job I guess.'

'Don't you ever forget it.' The tone was stern and emphatic. 'Too many of your generation think the world owes them a living.' Nick's stomach tightened as his step father went on, 'at least you do have a job, and a good one.' Nick was relieved when his mother came into the room carrying a tray laden with tea cups and biscuits. She set them down on the coffee table in the centre of the room and spoke to Nick,

'You will have the house to yourself while you are here, your brothers have gone camping.' She always referred to Steve and Terry as his brothers, as if saying it strengthened the bonds of blood.

'You can help me lay the concrete for the back shed I am going to build.' His father said.

'Arthur!' His mother protested but was cut short.

'You won't mind, will you son?'

His mother spoke up again,

'He has just come home.' This time it was Nick who interrupted her.

'It's alright Mum.' He said. 'I'll be glad to help. What else am I going to do?' He then smiled and continued. 'First though, I need a big meal inside me, what's for dinner?' The tension was broken.

The evening passed as it always did when Nick came home. The television dominated the corner of the room and his step-father's eyes darted between the images on the screen and the black print of his evening paper. Every now and again he would comment on one of the articles, at times becoming aroused, never asking for the opinion of those around him. The longer Nick lived away the more he felt a stranger in his own home. As he sat at the end of the sofa he could feel his mother's eyes rest upon him. He turned toward her and saw those questions he knew were there. No longer able to stand the tension he made the excuse of feeling exhausted and retired early. As he walked up the curved staircase he expected to hear his mother's footsteps behind him. That night he went to sleep thinking of that house in the other part of Hampshire.

The sky looked threatening all day and the men worked fast to lay the concrete. Angela kept them supplied with cups of tea and on each occasion warned her husband not to overdo things. It was as she was returning to the house after one of these refreshment calls that his step-father spoke, his voice low so as not to be overheard.

'Nick, I am worried about your mother.' Nick took the cup from his lips and stared into his step-father's eyes. The clink of the cup making contact with the saucer seemed to echo around the garden. His step-father continued. 'I know you went down to see your father last week and I do not expect you to tell me about that,' he paused, 'that is between you and him; but, I am concerned about what you have told your mother.' There was an ominous silence and for the first time in his life Nick saw the age etched in his step-father's face. He was eleven years older than his wife and it now occurred to Nick that the age difference had always worried him. He had kept Angela on a tight rein and Nick recalled they had never done anything apart. He had thought it was through a mutual desire to be together, now, he wondered if it was through a fear of being apart. This vulnerability touched a chord of sympathy in his step-son and Nick knew he had to reassure this man who had been his father for so long,

'I have not spoken to Mum.' Nick's voice faltered on the opening words, making them sound unconvincing. His step father was quick to respond.

'Don't hide things from me, aye boy. I won't have it!' Nick was not going to allow himself to be provoked into a fight. He took a deep breath before answering.

'Honest Dad. Mum has not asked me about the visit and I have not mentioned it.' The hawk like eyes scrutinised Nick's face looking for confirmation of the words. Nick had called him 'Dad' and that reassured him. The muscles in his jaw relaxed and an embarrassed smile curled the ends of his lips. He came and placed a hand on Nick's shoulder;

'Sorry Son.' He apologised and went on. 'Your mother has been acting strangely these past weeks,' he stopped to think, 'it is like she is not here for a great deal of the time.' His voice then grew stern, 'and it all started with that visit of yours.' Nick tried to answer but was silenced with a raised hand and his step-father continued, 'when you do speak to her be careful what you say.' Nick could keep silent no longer.

'What is that supposed to mean?' Anger gave a razor edge to his words and then he felt ashamed of his temper.

'I don't know.' The worry and torment were crying out in the voice and the upright body now slumped under the burden of doubt and uncertainty. Nick wanted to change the subject and run away from this potentially explosive situation.

'I'll get another bag of cement.' He said and walked away.

They finished the job in virtual silence, punctuated only by instructions and requests. It was as they were cleaning the tools and tidying the site that his step-father re-opened the subject.

'Nick, I do not want you to misunderstand what I am going to say.' He stopped and looked at his step-son. The silence seemed endless and Nick was about to ask what he meant when the words came. 'I think it would be best if you cut short your stay this time.'

'What!' Nick exclaimed and was silenced.

'Listen to me.' His step-father held up a restraining hand and continued. 'I didn't want you to pay that visit. I knew it would upset your mother, and I was right. Your being here is a reminder of a time that has passed. A time I wanted to stay in the past.' He stopped to gauge Nick's reaction and when there was no outcry went on. 'All this upset will pass but not while you are here. I am sorry Nick. You do understand, don't you?'

Nick stood before him, his face a passive mask of the rage within him. Eventually he could hold back no longer,

'I think I do.' He hissed, 'and I won't have to be asked twice. I do have time to wash up first don't I?'

'Now you are being stupid.' His step-father snapped. 'I am not asking you to go away forever, just until all this blows over.'

'This will never blow over.' Nick said vehemently and walked away. As he walked through the kitchen his mother saw the fire in his eyes.

'Whatever is wrong Nick?' She asked as he disappeared through the door and went into the hallway. She ran after him calling. 'What's the matter? What has happened?' Nick stopped on the stairs and turned toward her. His expression was now one of calm.

'Nothing Mum, forget it.' He continued up the stairs and went into his bedroom.

The door opened and his mother stepped inside. Concern took the colour from her cheeks and the light from her eyes. She shut the door behind her and leaned against it.

'Now what have you two been saying to each other?'

Nick cradled his face in his hands and slowly drew them down until he was looking over the top of his fingers toward his mother. His heart went out to her as he saw the anguish in her face.

'Dad thinks it would be better if I left early.'

His mother was stunned for an instant and then asked why? She walked over to her son and they sat together on the bed. Nick explained the conversation he had with his step-father. A long sigh escaped his mother's lips and she closed her eyes as if to shut out the world. Nick took hold of her hand.

'He could be right, Mum.'

Anger flashed from her tongue. 'What do you mean? What do you know?'

Nick did not flinch from the attack but moved his hand and placed his arm around her shoulders. The bond between them was very close, closer than that between herself and her other two sons, she knew that. Nick spoke softly to her.

'You have been dying to know about my time with Dad.' As soon as the word was said he knew it was the first time he had referred to the man as his father without having to think about it. It now served to confuse him more. 'How many fathers can one person have?' He asked himself as his mother spoke again.

'You are partly right.' Her voice was almost a whisper and she went on. 'I want to know what you did and I want more than that.' She stopped and moved her position on the end of the bed. She was now facing her son. 'I want to see him too.'

A distant clap of thunder proclaimed the arrival of

the storm. Dense droplets of rain fell, at first individually and then in torrents as the clouds hid the afternoon sun.

Nick stared into his mother's eyes and saw the misty signs of suppressed tears hidden there. Another clap of thunder and it was nearer now.

'Do you know what you are saying, Mum?' Nick asked, gripping her hands in his. She nodded her head and dislodged the first tear. Nick followed its watery progress down her cheek.

'I just want to do what you have done.' She said, her voice quivering with emotion. 'I would just like to see him again…that's all.'

Nick brushed the tear from her face and leant forward to kiss the spot where it had been.

'I am seeing him next week.' Nick said softly, 'I'll ask him then.' His mother's voice became more resolute.

'I don't want his wife to know. I just want to see him.' Nick sat back surprised by the words and their meaning.

'I can't do that.' He protested and his mother became more assertive.

'I did not stand in your way and I am just doing the same as you.' She argued.

'But what about Carol?' As Nick said her name he knew he had betrayed himself.

'Don't tell her.' His mother's voice was now surprisingly hard. 'Why does she need to know?'

The room suddenly lit up in a kaleidoscope of brilliant colour as a lightning bolt shot between the clouds. The thunder that followed echoed throughout the house.

Chapter 17

The white tower of St Catherine's Lighthouse stood out against the green fields that rose on the hills behind. The destroyer's bow rose and fell in a regular arc of motion as the warship sliced through the low Channel swell. The wind was fresh without being cold and it felt good on Nick's face as he leant on the grey ironwork of the ship's bridge wing. He looked down to where the white water met the ship's side and raced along its surging length. His thoughts went out as if drawn by the turbulent white foam of the disturbed sea. He could not erase or mask the words of his step-father that had banished him from home. He had taken them with him on a flight to Boston, and both passengers and crew had suffered. The Flight Purser had threatened to report him if he did not improve his attitude. Nick's reply had been direct and a more aggressive man would have carried out his threat.

The metal deck moved under his feet and the ship heeled to starboard. Nick was caught unawares by the maneuver and looked up in surprise. He glanced into the crowded bridge and saw the Captain talking to the Officer of the Watch. Nick recognised him as the young Sub-Lieutenant who welcomed him aboard on the night of his last visit. The ship's bow moved to the left, gathering way as the destroyer's superstructure heeled further to the right. Nick looked toward the stern. The ship's wake was like a white scar on the sea's lazy blueness. His eye caught a woman in a bright red dress run out and take hold of a young boy who was tottering towards the metal guard rail. As his eyes traversed the length of the ship Nick noticed the vivid smatterings of colour against the grey dullness of the ship's superstructure. His thoughts mellowed as he watched men pointing out the different parts of their ship to wives, children or parents. It was one day when families could experience a little of the life their men had made their own. A life that took them away to a ship that demanded total commitment.

Nick's eyes returned to the bridge. It looked dark against the sunlit brilliance of the wing. He smiled to see a small boy talking into the microphone under the proud stare of his father. Nick walked toward the open hatchway.

'There you are.' Peter's smile showed the joy at having Nick there with him. 'I lost you for a moment,' he said and then asked, 'we are going to practise a man overboard drill, how would you like to handle the ship?' Nick's smile left his lips and uncertainty gripped him. His father saw the change in expression.

'I'll talk you through it. Come on, you will enjoy it.' They walked inside and Nick's eyes focused on the compass at the centre of the bridge. The Officer of the

Watch leaned against it as he held a telephone handset to his ear. The officer turned to the Captain,

'The quarterdeck is ready for the man overboard drill sir.'

'Very good.' Peter acknowledged...

Peter walked to a communications console and took a small black microphone from its securing bracket. He placed the plastic mouthpiece to his lips. Nick listened as the commanding voice echoed around the ship telling everybody about the exercise that was about to take place. Nick flinched when he heard his name coming from the loud speaker.

'My son, Nick, will be doing the first run, anyone else who would like to have a go would you please make your way to the bridge.' The metallic click of the microphone's button being released signalled the end of the broadcast.

Nick felt his stomach turn over and felt as if all eyes were upon him in the enclosed area. It was a great relief when he saw Carol come through the hatchway at the back of the bridge. She smiled and Nick's heart went out to her. Earlier that day she said she would stay below and chat to Leading Steward Hawkes. Now she was with him and his confidence returned.

'Right, Nick.' Peter's voice brought him back to the job in hand. Peter explained the use of the microphone, the engine revolutions that governed the speed of the ship, and, the amount of wheel required to turn the destroyer quickly yet safely. Nick did not see him give the signal to the sailor standing on the port bridge wing, but, he did hear the ensuing cry from the port lookout.

'Man overboard. Port side!'

'All right Nick, bring her round, port twenty,' his father quietly advised, 'revolutions two one zero.'

Nick repeated the order into the microphone and heard it repeated back to him by the quartermaster on the wheel.

The mass of steel and aluminium appeared to hang in space as the bow swung like a pendulum around to the left.

'Right, Nick.' Peter called. 'Look out for it. It's a red can with a red and white flag tied to a staff.' Nick's eyes strained to see the tell-tale splash of colour against the blue swell of the sea.

'Man overboard – red nine zero.' A lookout's voice called and all eyes turned to see it. Nick flashed a questioning glance to the Captain, but caught the Officer of the Watch's eye instead.

'Keep the wheel on.' He mouthed and indicated a circular pattern with his finger. Nick then realised that the ship would pass the danbuoy and eventually come around behind it. Indeed, that was now happening although to Nick time felt as if it was standing still.

'Ease your helm Nick.' The order was given as if his son was one of the ship's company.

'Port ten.' Nick passed the order to the helmsman.

'Good lad.' Peter acknowledged the correct use of the wheel and continued. 'You better get ready to slow down.' He advised and went on to explain how the ship should be lined up with the flag and the quartermaster given a course to steer.

Nick took a bearing of the flag and brought the handset to his lips. He depressed the button to speak,

'Steer two six zero.' He said and the order was repeated back to him.

'Watch your speed Nick. You will fly right passed. Bring the engines to slow ahead.' Peter spoke quickly.

Nick spoke again to the quartermaster. In contrast to the initial maneuver everything now appeared to be happening too fast. The red metal of the danbuoy could now be seen along with the flag and its mast.

'Which side do you want to pick it up?' The question took Nick unawares. Here was something else to think about. He looked along the bearing. The buoy was drifting to the left.

'Port side.' He answered, trying to sound confident.

'Good. Don't lose it.' Peter's voice was matter of fact. 'Use five degrees of port wheel and stay on it. Be prepared to stop both engines. You will be surprised how long it takes one of these beasts to slow down.'

Nick gave the appropriate orders and felt the plastic of the handset slip in his perspiring hands. He no longer considered the eyes that were on him. It was as much as he could think about to stay in line with the buoy.

'I must not let it go down the wrong side.' He told himself. He felt the destroyer slowing down and watched the flag threatening to cross the bows to the starboard side. It was then that he remembered the previous wheel order. He spoke into the mouthpiece;

'Midships. Starboard five.'

'Now you've got it.' Peter exclaimed.

The buoy could be clearly seen only one hundred yards ahead of the ship.

'Midships.' Nick ordered

The destroyer settled in the water and the danbuoy drifted towards it as if they were drawn together by magnetism.

'It's too fast! We're going too fast!' Nick's mind screamed out, unable to think of a way to slow the relentless advance.

'You will need to go slow astern.' Peter said as he strode towards the port bridge wing. Nick gave the command and watched as the flag disappeared from sight under the sharp rake of the destroyer's bow. Hurriedly he followed his father's footsteps and took the microphone as it was handed to him. The buoy was passing fast down the ship's side and it was not going to stop.

'Stop both engines.' Peter gave the order and Nick blindly repeated it into the handset. 'Too fast.' Peter said, as all eyes watched the red buoy pass along the grey length of the ship's side. 'Leave it in the water and we'll give the next man a go.'

Nick stood transfixed, looking down into the water. The chequered flag waved triumphantly as it bobbed in the tumbled wake.

'Who's next?' Peter asked as he re-entered the bridge. Another young man stepped forward and Nick saw that it was the Executive Officer's son. He looked younger than Nick and Nick secretly hoped that he too would fail.

'Good try, Nick.' The caring voice of Carol bathed him in comforting warmth. Self-consciously he looked around and was thankful that attention was now focused on the new contestant.

'Thanks.' He answered and then added. 'Thanks for

coming up.' Carol smiled and in her eyes was more than a step-mother's affection.

'That was a good show, Nick.' Peter's voice interrupted them. 'Not many people get it on the first attempt.' Instantly Nick thought, 'I bet you did.'

'Come on, let's go below and have lunch.' Peter suggested and led the way down into the panelled passageways of the ship's interior. He turned to Carol. 'I have invited a couple of department heads and their wives to join us. We don't get much opportunity to meet socially.'

Nick, who was walking alongside, could see by the flash of annoyance that passed across Peter's face and he knew that the news had not been well received.

They were soon at the door to Peter's cabin and he stood to one side to allow Carol and Nick to enter before him.

The sound of talk ceased as the door opened and in respectful silence those inside waited for their commanding officer to enter. Nick scanned the room. There were three couples and a lot of gold braid standing to disciplined attention.

Peter entered smiling and introduced Carol and Nick to his guests. Formality was relaxed and Hawkes circulated with a tray of wine and sherry. The Captain had given permission for his officers to drink as they would not be standing a watch during this day at sea. He was also confident that none of them would take more than one.

'It is lovely to see you again Mrs. Wells.' A middle aged woman with hair speckled by undisguised grey strands approached them.

Nick noticed the overweight figure framed in an obviously expensive but matronly suit. He smiled as he compared the two wives. The lady then turned her attention to him.

'So you are the Captain's son. I am very pleased to meet you.' She presented her hand and Nick gently clasped it. 'What do you do Nick?'

He answered, saying only that he worked for an airline.

'Are you a pilot?' Shifting his weight uneasily Nick answered,

'No.' He paused. 'I'm a steward.'

The conversation faltered and only Carol's quick thinking saved an embarrassing impasse.

'There are not many cities in the world you haven't seen, are there Nick?' He looked at her, the gratitude showing on his face and she continued. 'Where is it you have just come back from?'

The way was now open for him to get into the conversation on his own terms. He proved so entertaining that when it was time to be seated for lunch the Supply Officer's wife, as Nick found her to be, insisted on sitting next to him so she could hear more of his stories. The Supply Officer was quick to take the opportunity to seat himself next to Carol.

Nick stole glances around the table and noted that the officers present all appeared older than their Captain. He could not fail to notice the pedestal on which his father was placed. It then occurred to him, the irony in the fact that this respect was paid by everyone except his wife. Nick looked at Carol and admired her natural beauty. 'He must be mad.' He thought. It was then he remembered the promise made to his mother. The realisation made him go cold. Once again he looked at Carol. 'Betrayal', the word resounded inside his brain. He could not do it.

After the service of sweet and cheese Nick noticed Hawkes speaking to the Captain.

'Excuse me ladies and gentlemen.' Peter spoke. 'We are about to commence the helicopter display. So, if you would like to see this I suggest we adjourn to the upper deck.' No sooner had he finished speaking and the guests began to move.

'I will stay here if you don't mind Peter.' Carol spoke from her chair and all eyes looked down upon her. The annoyance in Peter's manner was thinly disguised and Nick did feel sympathy for him. 'Carol did seem to go out of her way to frustrate him,' he thought, 'perhaps she would be happier married to someone else?' He could not pursue this line of thought as his father called to him.

'Come on Nick, being a kind of 'wafu' you should find this interesting.' Nick joined him and they left the cabin at the head of the group.

The helicopter's thrashing blades clawed at the air, lifting the small aircraft up and away from its floating platform. Nick looked at the sailors sitting in the open doorway. One dressed in a black wetsuit, the other, in a flying suit and dome like helmet. The destroyer slowed its advance until it sat rolling gently in the swell. The voice of the flight deck officer crackled over the intercom;

'Ladies and Gentlemen, boys and girls, we are about

to demonstrate the technique of air-sea rescue. Please keep your eyes on the helicopter.'

While the crowd on the destroyer's upper deck were all looking at the helicopter Nick looked at his father. He swallowed hard and then spoke.

'Dad.' It was the first time he used the title to his face and even though his father had now openly acknowledged him, the word still did not come easily to his lips. Nick made himself repeat it. 'Dad. There's something I have to talk to you about.' Peter looked round and saw the concern in the set of his son's jaw and the hardness in his eyes.

'What is it?' He asked, concern now registering in his own voice.

Nick looked about him and saw there was no one standing by the ladder to their left. Taking hold of his father's arm he led him to this quiet place.

'This is difficult,' he began and then stopped. Peter was about to ask what was wrong when Nick summoned his resolve and continued. 'Mum wants to see you.'

Peter stared in disbelief. It felt a lifetime before he spoke and when he did, anger and uncertainty were coupled in his voice,

'That's impossible. What are you trying to do?'

Nick reeled under the attack. He turned away and held onto the guardrail. The knuckles on both hands began to turn white under the pressure of his grasp. Out at sea the clattering form of the helicopter was rising into the air having lifted a diver from the sea. Peter looked at his son's stooped shoulders and regret replaced anger.

'I'm sorry Nick.' He placed his hand on his son's shoulder. 'It's impossible. You will have to explain that to your mother.' There was no reply and Peter erupted again. 'What do you want from me?' Nick turned to face his father, his eyes were now hard and empty.

'Nothing!' He sighed. 'There is nothing you can do for me and I don't think you are capable of doing anything for anyone but yourself.' The words now said, Nick braced himself for the reply. Peter remained quiet and lost in his thoughts. The words had struck home. He had been hurt. It was Nick's turn to feel guilty and it was he who spoke first. 'All I did was deliver a message.' His voice was low and calm. At that moment he despised his mother for placing him in this situation. When Peter did speak Nick could hardly believe what was being said.

'All right, when does she want to see me and where? I assume you have a plan.' The insinuation niggled Nick and it showed in his voice.

'As I said before, I am only the messenger, but if you want to have a meeting I told Mum that you could use my place.'

Peter was momentarily lost in his thoughts. A man of instant decisions he was now in uncertain territory.

'When?'

'I'm going away next week.' Nick remembered his mother's words; 'If there was to be a meeting then there was no point in wasting any more time.' He looked his father in the eye. 'I leave on Sunday for seven days.'

'What day does your mother suggest?' Peter asked.

'Monday.'

'What time?'

'Eleven o'clock.'

'I'll be there. I'll tell Carol that I have a meeting at the MOD. Leave me a map of your area and let me know where you keep the key. I don't want to carry out this meeting on your doorstep.'

The noise from the returning helicopter drowned out further conversation. Peter pointed to the hatch that led back inside the ship and they walked toward it.

It had been a long and busy day for the ship's company. It had also been a success. Wives normally accustomed to waving farewell to their men from the dockside now went ashore with them. Small children worn out by the unusual motion of the ship and the sea air were cradled, fast asleep, in their fathers' arms. Nick looked down from the bridge wing where he had gone to allow Carol and his father to be alone. Peter had announced that he would not be going home that evening and Carol took the news badly. Nick walked out, preferring his own company to the battleground of the Captain's cabin. It surprised him to see Carol walking along the deck below him. He wanted to call to her but felt too self-conscious in his exposed position. He then realised that she was leaving the ship. Pushing himself off the metal rail he ran for the ladder, clattered down the steps and hurried along the deck.

'Carol, wait.' He called.

She stopped and turned around. For a moment her face did not register any recognition.

'Don't say he told her!' The thought that she knew of the meeting and his part in setting it up alarmed him so much that he felt his stomach turn and his whole body drain of its life's blood. He stopped and his hand went out to grasp the metal rail that ran along the ship's superstructure.

'Nick, are you alright?' Carol's arm went about his shoulders. He glanced at her and the look in her eyes told him that she did not know. In a moment of confusing torment he wanted to tell her everything, to apologise and beg her forgiveness. The words died in his throat.

'No sea legs.' He lied and smiled weakly.

'Come on we'll get you to a pub in the country where you can't even smell the sea.'

Taking her arm from about his neck she repositioned it around his waist and they walked together to the gangway.

'Good evening Mrs Wells.' The Officer of the Day said and saluted. 'I hope you enjoyed your day.' Realising the position of her arm Carol thought quickly.

'I did, thank you, but my step-son will be glad to be on dry land again.' The lieutenant smiled and looked condescendingly at Nick.

Carol led the way down the wooden gangway with Nick feeling foolish close behind. The car was parked at the end of the jetty. They reached it and Carol slipped behind the wheel. Turning to Nick she explained that Peter wanted to stay on board as the ship was due to sail early the next morning.

'It did not stop all these others going home.' She said bitterly, pointing to the men and their families heading toward the dockyard gate.

'How long will he be away?' Nick asked.

'Only for the day.' Carol replied in a flat disinterested

tone. 'He would stay on that bloody ship even if it never went anywhere.'

Talking of leaving the ship, Nick remembered that he had left without any word of goodbye or thanks to his father. He told Carol and she laughed.

'I would not lose any sleep over it,' she replied, 'when I left his head was buried in reams of paper and he was mumbling something about unexpected events interrupting the ship's plans. I think you and I were the last things on his mind at that time. That bloody ship.' She swore again.

Carol was silent for a long while and then her mood changed.

'Ah well, where shall we go for dinner?' Nick remained silent, still unable to speak and Carol continued. 'I promised you a country pub away from all this salt air didn't I?'

Nick was thankful she had not waited for him to reply. Turning the heavy estate car away from the wharf she drove slowly passed the flowing mass of people emptying from the dockyard.

'We were lucky to get away with that.' Carol sighed as she switched off the car's ignition, leaving them surrounded by silence and the night.

'You didn't drink that much.' Nick came to her defence.

'You don't have to drink that much to be over the top these days.' She replied and opened the door. 'Come on let's go inside and have a nightcap.'

Nick had not been honest. Carol was drinking heavily

in the pub and had refused his offer to drive home. 'His father was a bastard.' He thought.

The lounge was bathed in the soft light from two table lamps, set in opposite ends of the room. Carol came in carrying two Irish Coffees brimming over the lip of their glasses in creamy promise. She handed one to Nick and then flopped down in the arm chair opposite him.

'Do you have to go tomorrow?' She asked while sipping at the ivory liquid at the rim of the glass. At that moment, with the subtle light highlighting the fullness of her lips and the line of her neck to the swelling of her breasts, Nick wanted to say that he would stay with her forever. He knew it was impossible and ached with frustration and futility. They drank their coffee in isolated silence, locked in thoughts that could not be shared.

His glass empty Nick could find no excuse to remain downstairs. Reluctantly he excused himself and left Carol draped in her chair, staring vacantly into the dying embers of the fire.

In bed he lay listening for the sound of her footsteps on the stairs. He fell asleep with his mind full of visions and forbidden dreams.

Knowing he had been used as an instrument of deception and realising the feelings that now dominated every moment spent in her company, Nick knew he could no longer be alone with her. Next morning he packed and loaded his car before Carol came downstairs. She asked what he was doing up so early. He made his excuses sound as convincing as a reluctant heart and troubled mind could. They were accepted without question, but Nick told himself there was disappointment in her eyes. As he drove through the wooden gates at the end of the driveway he looked in the mirror. Carol had gone inside. The courtyard in front of the house was empty. It was a vision that stayed with him.

Chapter 18

Peter looked about him as he entered the stairwell that gave access to the twelve flats on Orchard Row. The building was neat and functional. It rose three floors with the main entrance being built in the centre of the structure. Outside, the grounds were laid to lawn with a short access road to the highway. Small balconies at each unit overlooked this major road that was only partly screened by a row of billowing green conifers. Peter checked the residents list that was secured to the wall. The building had a caretaker and Nick's note told him to collect the key from this man. It was not an arrangement Peter liked.

'Oh yes. The young man told me you would be staying.' The turtle rimmed glasses gave the caretaker an older appearance than his years deserved. Peter wanted to correct him and say that he was not staying, but, the wish to leave this prying presence was even greater. As he climbed the stairs to the second floor he could feel the eyes on his back. The key slid easily into the lock and turned silently. As the door swung open and he walked inside

Peter felt like an intruder. Quietly he closed the door and the metallic click of the lock shattered the silence. He walked to the middle of the room and looked about him. On one wall hung a modern print in an aluminium frame that subtly showed a naked woman draped across the bonnet of a red Porsche coupe. Peter stood admiring the lines of both before seeking out the kitchen.

It had been a long drive. The morning traffic was heavy and his thoughts and uncertainty drained him. Without question Carol had believed his story about an appointment with the Ministry of Defence. As he drove along the busy road he wondered if she would care if she knew the truth. They were almost strangers now and he could not say when the alienation began. He told himself she would be happier when he was ashore and wondered why it was his deception that now triggered thoughts of reconciliation. He did not know. Nor did he know what he was going to say to a woman he had not seen for over twenty years. A woman he had once loved, although he was not certain of that either.

The hot, black coffee felt reassuring. It was a drink associated with long night watches, operational exercises, and command decisions. His eyes went back to the curves and shadows of the glossy picture. He was not sure how long he had been staring at the wall when his thoughts were interrupted by the noise of the handle turning on the front door. He stood, staring at the revolving knob. Slowly the door swung open. Peter rose to his feet. The door completed its arcing movement and Angela stood framed in the entrance. A pink summer dress highlighted the blondness of her hair and caused Peter to think if it had always been so. Had she changed? They studied each other, neither wanting to see that twenty years had passed.

'Hello Peter.' Angela spoke first. She entered the room and closed the door carefully so as not to make a sound. Peter moved to meet her. Taking her hands in his he studied her at arm's length and then spoke, his voice at first faltering.

'It's good to see you again. You look very well.'
Angela smiled and replied.
'Only very well. I was hoping that I hadn't changed.'
Peter laughed.
'No really. You do look lovely. You haven't changed.'
Angela was now smiling, revealing beautiful white teeth and a discreet dimple in her left cheek that shed the years and made Peter think that she really had not changed.

'Come on Peter you are digging yourself further and further into that hole, but thank you anyway.' Leaning forward she gently kissed him on the cheek and then withdrew. Peter felt the uncertainty in the embrace.

'Come sit over here and tell me what you have been up to since I saw you last.' He said and raised his right hand in the direction of the settee. It was the only seat in the almost empty room. Angela placed her handbag on the small telephone table by the door and walked to the sofa.

'He doesn't spend much of his hard earned cash on furniture and decoration does he?' She commented.

'He doesn't spend much of it on food either.' Peter answered from the kitchen where he had gone to switch on the kettle. 'Old Mother Hubbard ran a catering business compared to this kitchen.' They both laughed and a little of the tension was lost.

Peter returned with two full cups of coffee.

'No biscuits I'm afraid, and certainly no food for lunch so how about I take you out? There must be some good restaurants around here. I hope you are still a coffee drinker. White and one?' Angela accepted the coffee.

'You remembered.' She said and smiled up at him and answered his question. 'I really can't stay away that long.' She said. The thought of flaunting the rendezvous in public scared her. That morning, as she kissed and saw her husband off to work, the thrill of intrigue stirred within her. From that moment guilt became the dominant emotion. It was ironic, but, being alone with this man in a borrowed flat seemed more innocent than sitting in a crowded restaurant. Peter accepted the decision and settled himself back on the sofa.

'Well then, what have you been up to?' He asked again. Angela relaxed and told a condensed history of the past years. As she spoke only half her thoughts were on her words. The others were looking, comparing and appraising the man she had once married.

Peter sat beside her, diverting his eyes only when he placed his empty cup onto the floor. A lot of what Angela was saying Peter had heard from Nick. He did not let on, happy for the excuse to look at her, to study the blueness of her eyes, the classic line of her face. She was still a beautiful woman he decided. He thought of Carol and compared Angela's manicured beauty to that of his wife. It was something he missed. The realisation hurt and annoyed him. Carol was a rebel, a personification of the anti-spirit he suppressed in himself. It had been exciting, but, it was not enough. She had not compromised and he could not change. Angela was the ideal, he had seen it once and he saw it now. His reflections were halted by a question.

'Now you've heard my life story, what about you? Nick tells me you are a Captain of a destroyer and soon to take command of some school. Has life been good to you, Peter?'

He waited before answering. His fingers toyed with the gold cufflinks on his left wrist. He remembered being presented with them at the Naval College, a time uncluttered by women and family. He smiled as he spoke, but, there was no humour in his eyes.

'That's a broad question.' He answered and stopped to reflect again before continuing. 'I suppose it has.' He then turned the question on Angela. 'Is life good to anybody? We reap what we sow and all those other clichés. I believe I've done well. This school you referred to is the School of Maritime Operations and should lead to my flag. I am one of the youngest Captains in the Navy today, and I will be the youngest Admiral.' He knew that his voice had become raised and he was speaking too fast. He stood up and walked over to the artificial stone fireplace that was set against the wall. He looked back at Angela and said; 'There has been a price. There is always a price.' His voice was once again controlled. Angela moved her position on the settee. Her fingers intertwined and her knuckles reddened from the pressure of her grip. She felt compelled to speak and there was a question she had to ask.

'What do you think of Nick?' It was plainly put and Peter took time to answer.

'He is a nice boy.'

'A nice boy!' Angela erupted. 'Is that all you can say about your son? He's a nice boy!' Exasperation gave a sharp edge to her voice. 'Flowers are nice, sweets are nice, even the weather can be nice, but you cannot describe your son as nice!'

Peter reeled under the attack until anger provoked a response.

'What do you want me to say? He's my son by birthright only. I don't know the boy.'

Angela was quick to pick up on the loose word.

'He is not a boy. He's a young man. Why do all you middle aged men,' she gave weight to the adjective, 'always think of young men as boys, lads. You are all the same.'

Peter placed his hands behind his head and arched his back. The stretching of his tall frame calmed him and he took a deep breath.

'I'm sorry.' He paused and quietly continued, 'You asked me what I thought of Nick and I will tell you.' Peter returned to the settee and sat down facing Angela. 'I think he is bright, strong, and handsome. He has everything going for him except,' he stopped and waited until he could see the question and uncertainty in Angela's eyes before proceeding. 'He lacks drive, ambition. He has no direction, no purpose about his life and I find this disappointing.' The silence, when he stopped speaking, made the small room feel very bare of cover and there was to be no hiding place. Angela sprang to her son's defence.

'Direction! What is direction? Where are you going Peter?' Her eyes sparked with fire and vengeance, 'and when you get there what will you have gained?' For an instant her eyes glistened with unfallen tears before she concluded; 'and what will you have lost?'

Peter would not be put on the defensive.

'I have got whatever I have gone after in the sure knowledge that nobody is going to give you anything in this world. There are a lot of others who will take what you have already got. If they can.'

With those words the ghost that had haunted her for the past twenty years was finally laid to rest. She understood clearer then than she did all those years ago why she had left him.

'I think we have said it all, don't you?' She asked, getting to her feet. The action startled Peter who looked up at Angela unaware that anything he said would have offended her. He felt uncomfortable and stood himself.

'What about lunch?' He asked in genuine amazement. Angela was quick to answer.

'I don't think so Peter. I must be getting back.' Having said that she walked across to pick up her handbag and turned before opening the door. 'I am glad we had this chance to talk. I feel that I know you now. I don't think I ever really did before.' He remained standing across the room from her and before he could move she turned the door handle and stepped outside. 'I don't think we will be seeing each other again so I will say goodbye.' The door closed with a quiet finality.

Chapter 19

The aircraft cabin was in darkness except for the isolated yellow glow of an illuminated seat light. Nick sat on the hard cushioned surface of his crew seat and stared down the cylindrical tube. The movie had just finished and Nick prayed that the passengers would sit quietly, or preferably, go to sleep. The orange rays of dawn were already appearing low on the clear horizon and one raised window blind would ruin his well laid plan. Their departure from Bombay had been delayed due to technical difficulties with the aircraft. The Captain ordered a free round of drinks as a means of calming the passengers. Nick and Jim Sanderson, the steward on the other end of the bar trolley, saw it as a way of ensuring a quiet night. By leaving two miniature bottles of whatever drink the passenger asked for they hoped to lull their passengers to sleep in an alcoholic haze. Now, in the peace of the dark cabin, it appeared their tactics had worked.

Nick looked at his watch. It certainly looked genuine. He shook his wrist to convince himself that the hands would not fall off. He shook his head admiringly and wondered how they did it. He smiled thinking that nearly all the crew had at least one fake watch to match the imitation shirts and jeans they had also bought in Hong Kong. Nick almost laughed aloud when he recalled Jim's comments about buying his watch. The red haired Yorkshireman exclaimed that he could not resist a bargain, especially when it meant a saving of two and a half thousand pounds.

'Is nothing genuine?' Nick thought as he sat in the darkness, his ears filled with the droning of the aircraft's four engines. His mind continued to wander, to relive the last eight days that had taken him from London to Abu Dhabi, Hong Kong and Bombay. It had been a good trip with a good crew. They had hired a sailing ship in Hong Kong and spent the day cruising the waters around the island, stopping for lunch and a swim off the beach at Repulse Bay. The serenity on that side of the island was almost unbelievable when considering what lay on the other side of those jagged, green peaks. In Bombay he had done his shopping, leather handbags and wallets for his family and a gift for Carol. He hoped she would like the beaten silver bracelet. It was one purchase where he had not haggled to the point of walking out of the shop. On that occasion it did not seem right. His train of thought was broken by the staccato sound of the telephone that sat in its cradle adjacent to the crew seat.

'Four left, Nick.' He spoke into the handset, giving the position of the crew seat at which he was sat.

'Nick, this is the Flight Purser. We have a problem.' The words were coming in short bursts and Nick knew there was something very wrong. 'We have had a message from the ground that a bomb threat has been made against this flight. I don't want the passengers to know, but I want the crew to do a search of the aircraft. We will be diverting to Bahrain. I will be making an announcement saying that we are diverting because of those mechanical faults that delayed us in Bombay. I want you to alert the crew down there and call me back when you've done so.' The line went silent for an instant and then crackled back to life. 'Remember Nick, we don't want a panic. Discretion and vigilance, all right?'

'You've got it.' Nick answered, returned the telephone to its cradle and went off to carry out the instructions.

Three of the crew were in the rest seats at the rear of the aircraft. They received the news with shocked disbelief. Nick told them to get back to the galley as casually as possible.

'Don't let it look like someone just threw a bomb in here.' He said with a half smile.

'Sick Nick. Very sick.' Jim Sanderson spoke for all of them.

When the four crew members were assembled in the galley Nick telephoned the Flight Purser.

'Very good, Nick. Now stand by for my briefing and when I begin to speak turn the cabin lights up one notch.' Nick repeated the instruction and for the first time felt an emptiness in his stomach. He told himself that this was just another false alarm. He once took a flight to Kuwait that was supposed to have a bomb on board. That had been a false alarm and so was this, he told himself again, but was only half convinced.

Nick stood near the panel that housed the light controls for the rear cabins. The public address system was activated and Nick's fingers went to the round dial. From a darkness punctuated only by a single white call light and the faint hint of dawn at the bottom of each window blind, the aircraft's interior was awakened by the yellow brilliance of the cabin lights. As if activated by light, people stirred, disbelieving eyes opened, squinted and then looked around. Others tried to ignore the transformation and turned their faces away and hid their eyes in caverns created by their distorted bodies. It was the deep and deliberate voice of the Flight Purser that defeated the most determined sleepers.

'Ladies and Gentlemen. I apologise for disturbing you but I thought I had better tell you as early as possible that due to a slight technical difficulty we are having to divert to Bahrain. We will be landing there in about one hour and ten minutes from now. The Captain will be speaking to you as soon as we are established on our new course. Members of the cabin crew will be passing through the aircraft to answer any questions you may have. Once again I apologise for this unexpected change of plan and assure you that there is nothing to worry about. We will keep you informed of further developments. As you are awake the cabin crew will shortly be serving a refreshment. Thank you for your attention.'

A groundswell of voices filled the aircraft and white lights flashed to life above many passenger seats. Nick looked up and down the cabin watching the annoyance, anger and resignation.

'Nick, come in here.' He looked toward the galley

where the command had originated. The other three crew members were now joined by the Senior Steward. It was he who was calling. Nick moved inside out of the inquisitive stare of the passengers. The Senior Steward outlined the action they were to take to try and locate any suspicious objects.

The lights would remain on until the descent into Bahrain and throughout the flight the search would be carried out. Half the crew would go through the cabin with the refreshments while the other half would carry out the search. Nick asked the question that was on each of their minds.

'What do we do if we find it?'

Jim was quick to answer, in his broad Yorkshire brogue,

'Put your head between your legs and kiss your ass good-bye.' It was an old joke but they all laughed to release the tension each was feeling. The Senior Steward brought them back to reality.

'If anyone finds any package that looks suspicious let the Flight Purser know and he will tell the Captain. Do not touch it.' A sombre silence now reflected the mood in the galley. The Senior Steward spoke again. 'Okay Nick, you and Jim go out into the cabin. Start at the centre and work your way back. Be subtle, but be thorough.'

Nick's eyes, scanned the floor, skimmed over faces and looked into shadows. He stopped to answer questions and listen to complaints. At such times he took the opportunity to bend low over his inquisitor and search around the seats. Each piece of hand luggage now looked suspicious. Nick smiled remembering what a constant source of aggravation hand luggage was. Now there was the unbelievable situation where one, or more, of those bags may be housing a bomb that could tear the aircraft and its two hundred occupants apart.

'It can't be true.' Nick told himself over and over again as he made his way methodically along the rows of seats

Looking at his watch the hands did not appear to move. After the initial search and the service of refreshments Nick went out again. It was harder to do nothing than to patrol the cabin. 'It was funny', he thought, 'he always avoided going out in the cabin on a night sector. There was always someone who would ask for something and those around would see what was being served and ask in turn. So it would go on. Boredom requiring attention, so he used to think. Now Nick was out in the cabin and no one spoke. People just watched and wondered. Nick was sure that sooner or later someone would work out what was going on and then all hell would break loose. Or more worrying, someone would find something.

Daylight was now streaming through open, window blinds. Most of the passengers had given up trying to sleep and sat, reading, talking or flicking their way through the entertainment channels on the armrest of their chair. The crew continued to search but without knowing exactly what they were looking for, saw many suspicious objects without finding a bomb.

The minutes passed, a tense, nervous time for those who knew what might be hidden, somewhere in the aluminium shell of the 747 jetliner.

'It has to be a hoax.' One of the stewardesses had

come down from the forward galley and now stood with Nick and Jim. Her voice was asking more than telling. 'If there was a bomb it would have gone off when we took off and were full of fuel, or else when we were over the sea.'

'We are over the sea.' Nick said dryly.

'Oh, you know what I mean.'

'Yes sure, we have all gone over those possibilities.' Nick was smiling now. 'I agree with you. I think it is just a hoax and all that will happen is that we will get home a couple of days late.'

While they guessed at what might happen the nose of the aircraft went down sharply and the pitch of the engines changed.

'Thank God we are on descent.' Nick said and then added with mock gravity. 'What if they calibrated it to go off on landing?'

'You had to say that didn't you?' Jim smiled and shook his head in despair at his friend's sense of humour.

'Come on, let's go and prepare the cabin.' Nick led the way.

'Jim, Nick.' The Flight Purser's voice stopped them and they looked around. 'Find the two girls and get in here.' He ordered, and stepped into the galley. Nick went to carry out the instruction.

When they were all gathered together the Purser looked at each in turn and then spoke,

'We are going to evacuate the aircraft.' He waited for his words to register on his crew and then continued. 'The Captain has received further messages and it looks very much as if there is a bomb on this aeroplane somewhere. Naturally the airport authorities in Bahrain are not going to let us go anywhere near the terminal and they don't have enough steps to bring to the aircraft for a rapid enough evacuation. So it is down the slides for everybody.' He went on to outline the plan and the preparation required and ended with the words. 'I know you checked your safety equipment when you got on board, but, do it again. It looks like you will need it.'

'Good morning Ladies and Gentlemen.' The Captain's voice filled the cabin, 'I have an update on the situation and as you have no doubt noticed we have started our descent into Bahrain.' There was a faint click as he took his finger from the transmission switch. It was only a brief pause but served to get the attention of everybody on board the aircraft. 'Ground Services has advised that due to the nature of our fault it may be necessary to evacuate the aircraft immediately after we land. I want to stress that this is merely a safety precaution and no cause for alarm.' He stopped again. The passengers took the news in a stunned silence. 'I would like you now to pay close attention to the landing announcement and follow the instructions of the cabin crew.' Another short break and then he concluded. 'Once again I do stress that this is only a precaution and there is no cause for alarm. Thank you for your attention.'

The crew stood at the front of their cabins looking over the worried faces of their passengers. No one spoke while the emergency landing announcement was playing. Once it stopped voices both raised and soft, nervous and scared filled the air. For the first time Nick thought how small and enclosed was the interior of the aircraft.

Quickly he pushed unnerving visions to the back of his mind and began preparing the cabin. He briefed passengers on the brace position to be adopted on landing, checking that all cigarettes were extinguished, seat belts secured, tables stowed, seat backs upright and armrests down. There was so much to do that further fears did not have a chance to assail him as the aircraft continued its descent.

'Cabin Crew take your seats for landing.' The co-pilot's voice echoed through the cabin.

'One thousand feet.' Nick thought and the figure stuck and played in his brain. Instinctively he sat down and adjusted his safety harness. Opposite him sat two men who he had placed there earlier. He had explained that it was their job to get out first and remain at the bottom of the slide to help the other passengers clear the area. He also told them how to open the aircraft door in case he was not able to do it. That thought played on his mind. The three of them sat looking at each other in an unspoken bond of duty and fear.

'Brace! Brace!' The order was called over the public address from the flight deck and Nick watched as heads bent low behind seat backs and arms came over to protect vulnerable sculls. He hoped everyone had got the position right, a consideration that reminded him to adopt the brace position himself. Placing his knees together he put his feet as far forward as he could and pressed down firmly. Interlocking his fingers behind his head he drew his elbows together.

Through the small window on the door Nick could just see the azure blue waters of the Persian Gulf giving way to the sands of the island of Bahrain. Small, square, stone buildings were dispersed among the tall, glass structures of the new Bahrain. A financial center of the Middle East and now a haven for two hundred people descending to its shores with hearts and minds full of fear.

Nick heard the engines flare. He glanced out of the window. The runway was beneath them now, flashing passed like the visions in his mind's eye. It felt as if they were gliding. Downward, downward towards the hard, black coated surface. Nick prayed for a gentle union of the aircraft with the ground.

In his imagination he saw the wheels touch the runway and the aeroplane disappear in a noiseless cloud of smoke and flame. It was a chilling vision that consumed him as he saw the plane engulfed by death. Then he realised they were down. They were on the runway. The engines screamed in reverse thrust that halted their advance. On the outside the rocky ground at the edge of the black and shimmering runway flashed passed the window. Straining at his harness Nick leaned forward to get a better view. 'They were down,' he sighed under his breath.

Relief was to be short lived. Nick saw the vivid red paintwork of the fire engines and the pulsating blue lights on their roofs as they sped alongside the aircraft. Nick sat back in his seat. He looked at the red knob of the door's mode selector handle. It was in 'automatic.' 'Good.' Nick continued to talk to himself. That was the correct setting for the landing and the taxi along the runway and would mean that, barring faults, when the heavy door opened the escape slide would fall from its housing on the door to the ground, sixteen feet below.

The aircraft lurched onto its nose as the Captain applied the final pressure to the brakes. They had stopped. It took Nick a few seconds to understand what had happened. He had to mentally shake himself to break away from the state of limbo he felt himself to be in. His eyes surveyed the cabin, no one was moving. There was no sound, at least no human sound, only the high pitched scream of the engines as their blades circled noisily in the hot desert sun. Slipping his arms free of the shoulder harness he unfastened the metal buckle of his seat belt. He looked out of the small window on the door and was relieved to see no trace of fire.

'Thank God!' This time his words carried to the two men seated in front of him. He looked at them, their faces expectant, wanting to be told what to do. The evacuation signal shrieked out its alarm.

'Get on your feet!' Nick screamed. 'Come this way!' He lifted his hands above his head and signalled like a possessed policeman on traffic duty. He then turned to the men by the door. 'Right. You two know what to do?' They nodded their assent. 'Good.' Nick's reply was lost in his actions. Quickly he grasped the silver handle protruding from the door and rotated it toward the rear of the aircraft. As the heavy weight swung open Nick was relieved to feel the power assist mechanism come into action. The door was opening faster now and the stabbing rays of the Arabian sun streamed into the cabin. Nick could sense movement behind him and without taking his eyes from the inflating rubber slide placed his arms across the open doorway. 'You two ready?' He called over his shoulder. The pressure from the advancing crowd that was now moving as one forced him to strengthen his hold. The slide was almost inflated. Nick waited for its twin runways to become rigid and then stepped to the right and clear of the exit. 'Jump, Jump, Jump!' He yelled and pushed the two men out with a forceful hand between their shoulder blades.

'Jump, Jump.' The commands were simple and direct, and delivered at the top of his voice. A stream of people passed before him like lemmings leaping from a cliff. One lady sat down at the top of the slide. The line halted. Nick placed his foot under the woman's ample back side and tipped her out.

'Jump, Jump!' He ordered and became more physical, ejecting anyone who slowed the line with either his hand, knee or foot.

The world dissolved into a blurred mass of humanity. His head reeled from his own commands and the thinly veiled impulse to panic. Time was lost, it stood still, it raced away, it meant nothing to anyone unless it stopped for all.

'Get the passengers out. How they leave the aircraft does not matter. Do not allow anyone to stop the line.' The training, the drills were paying off, the aircraft was emptying and Nick realised he was consciously thinking again.

The arrival of more passengers running, pushing and shoving along the aisle from the rear of the aircraft told Nick that one of the slides had not worked. 'How many more had failed?' The question crossed his mind and was then blotted out by his own commands.

'Jump, Jump, Jump!' He called over and over again until the tide of frightened people began to slow down and Nick had time to think and look about him.

'Jim!' He called, seeing the steward hurrying down the empty cabin.

'All clear in 'E' Zone.' The Yorkshireman called. His eyes were glazed by fear. He then shook his head and said; 'My bloody slide failed to deploy, fucking useless.' He swore again, 'fucking useless.'

Nick placed his hand on Jim's shoulder,

'Okay mate let's get out of here. I'll just check my zone and see you at the bottom.' Nick hurried off along the baggage strewn aisle. He could see that a lot of people had initially taken their hand baggage before realising their folly. He tripped over a briefcase and kicked it under a seat. 'Bastard!' He cursed and continued the search. 'Nothing. Let's get the hell out of here.' He commanded himself. He was now free to escape. Turning back to the door he ran towards it. The sun's rays illuminated the exit with a corridor of light. Nick launched himself through the door and hit the slide halfway along its sloping length. He slithered rapidly down until he hit the deceleration pads at the bottom and came to a sudden halt. Nick looked and saw one of the men he had earlier delegated to be a 'catcher.' 'You still here?' He asked, smiling broadly with relief at being out in the open.

'Not for much longer.' The man replied with a nervous grin.

'You and me both.' Nick said, and they ran to join

the rest of the passengers who were gathered together up wind about one hundred yards from the aircraft. 'Am I the last?' Nick asked Jim, who was the first crew member he came to.

'Yes, what's wrong? Couldn't you drag yourself away?' Jim was smiling but the tension still showed in his eyes and the unsure tone of his voice. Not having an exit had hit him badly. Nick then thought to look back to see if any other slides had failed.

The huge form of the jumbo jet sat stranded on the taxiway with a cordon of security and fire vehicles around it. It resembled a craft from another world, lifeless yet threatening.

Nick's eyes studied the fuselage, picking out the yellow tongues of rubber that were the escape slides. He tried to focus his vision, to look at each in turn, but found himself staring at the door through which he had just left. His eyes began to fill with tears and he could see no further than his memories.

Chapter 20

Carol sat at the foot of the bed staring out of the small window to the rising ground and hedgerows that concealed the lane running along the ridge. She often sat there, not seeing the beauty of the late spring blossoms, lost in her thoughts, creating and re-living fantasies.

An open letter lay on the pale blue counterpane. Carol had read it many times. It had both frightened and thrilled her. Nick had written to tell of his adventure and explain that he would be late in arriving. This would be his third visit and she wondered if it was all too much too soon.

In his letter Nick described the investigation into the incident that had kept him and his crew in Bahrain for six days. The newspapers had given brief coverage to the drama and Carol smiled every time she read the line, 'You may not hear about this. The company tries to keep this sort of thing as quiet as possible. Bad for business.'

She picked up the two page letter and re-read the date he said he would be arriving. 'It was today. The start of another working week for some. Just another week for her.' She thought, but she was glad it was starting this way. The realisation disturbed her. She thought of Peter who had been away ten days without a word. 'He could have at least telephoned,' she told herself, as the days went by. He was only off the West Coast of Scotland, visiting a small town that had adopted the ship when it was first commissioned. 'Bloody jolly.' She sneered in her mind. 'Probably screwing the mayor's wife.' She then laughed. 'No, no.' The thoughts continued, 'that would be the last thing he would be doing. Sex was dead, buried. Killed by gold braid and grey ships.' A feeling of hopelessness consumed her. The white paper slipped from her fingers and dropped to the floor. Once more her eyes returned to the world outside the window.

She had no idea how long she sat there before becoming aware of the deep, laboured sound of a car's engine. Her eyes searched the gaps in the hedge for a glimpse of the vehicle. She glanced at the bedside clock, it read ten to twelve. 'That's too early.' Her thoughts told her and she looked outside again. She could not disguise her excitement and wanted to run down stairs to greet him as he drove through the gate, but something held her back. The engine sound grew louder until she could see the black paintwork of a car through the green leaves of the hedgerow.

'That's not right.' She said aloud and hid behind the white net curtain. The driveway was still visible and she felt secure in her hiding place.

The black car wheeled through the gate and swept along the stoney driveway. Carol saw the name written across the top of the car's front window and recognised it as the local taxi firm. Her brow furrowed as she tried to work out what was going on. 'Peter was not due home for another four days and the ship's car would have brought him not the local taxi firm,' she reasoned and thought on. 'It was too early for Nick and he would have driven down.' She then thought of the train, 'he must have decided not to bring his car'. A smile lit up her face and she pulled the curtain back.

The car below stopped suddenly disturbing the loose stones around its tyres. Carol saw the passenger door open and was about to run from the room and down the stairs to the front door when an image caught her eye. Standing away from the window she looked again. The car door shut and the taxi pulled away. Carol approached a little closer. Craning her neck she looked down into the courtyard. 'Who is it?' She wondered, as uncertainty replaced joy. The figure was dressed in a cream sports jacket and tan trousers. The back was turned to her. The stranger was looking towards the stables. Carol jumped when he eventually moved and turned around. She noticed that he walked unsteadily and was now facing the house. Carol's heart felt as if it had stopped pumping blood throughout her body. She stood paralysed with disbelief. The thick shock of blond hair had receded from the temple and Carol noticed the dark line of a scar running from the exposed scalp to the middle of the forehead.

'It can't be.' She told herself, but, could not deny the tanned features and the carriage of the body. The visitor moved toward the house and was hidden from view by the slanting roof of the porch. Carol waited for the chime of the doorbell.

Once and then again it sounded. She knew it must be answered. Again it chimed as she slowly walked from the room. At the top of the stairs she stopped and looked at the white door below her. One by one her feet passed over each step until she stood with her hand on the brass latch. The bell sounded again. Carol's hand released the lock and drew the door toward her. The midday sun cast its rays across the floor. The visitor now stood before her, his tall outline traced by the light. Their eyes met, searching each other's faces, neither believing the other was really standing in front of them

'G'day Carol.' The visitor spoke first. There was silence from inside the house. Eventually Carol spoke,

'I thought you were dead.'

The man laughed and Carol's eyes were drawn to the scar that appeared to grow more vivid on the slope of his exposed forehead.

'What sort of welcome is that for an old mate?' He smiled warmly, a stranger no more.

'Phil. I am sorry, come on in.' Carol stood aside and let him pass. It was then she noticed the limp in his right leg and the effort it took to move one foot in front of the other. She said nothing. He stopped at the entrance to the lounge. 'Go on in,' she said, 'can I get you anything. How about a cup of tea? I won't be a minute.' All this was said without giving the visitor a chance to reply. Carol hurried to the kitchen and filled the kettle. As the water heated and bubbled in the stainless steel container she returned to her guest.

Phil was sat on the edge of the sofa, his left leg bent, the right extended straight out in front of him.

'I can't believe it's you and that you are here.' Carol smiled nervously.

'I hope you don't mind me coming to see you.' Phil spoke quietly, his eyes never leaving Carol's face.

Carol could not hold his stare.

'Of course not.' She replied. 'It's... it's just a shock.'

His smile broadened and Carol became annoyed.

'Well it is! How long has it been? Eleven, twelve years? And not a word.' The whistling of the kettle interrupted her speech. She left the room and returned a few minutes later with the tea and a plate of biscuits. She handed both to Phil. He thanked her and placed the cup and saucer on the small table alongside his chair.

'I am sorry for not writing,' he hesitated, 'you know how it was.' He smiled knowingly. Carol understood his meaning and softened her approach.

'Well what have you been doing all this time?'

He was quick to reply, looking about the room as he did so.

'Not as good as you by the look of things.' Carol followed his eyes but did not answer. He noted the silence and continued. 'Where's your husband? Away sailing the seven seas?' He felt childish as soon as the words were out, but knew he was powerless to stop them. He was annoyed with himself for letting his feelings show so soon. He had not come to open old wounds, he knew that, although what he expected to gain from the months of searching and this meeting, he was not sure. It was more of a quest. He was in England and had to find her. He now waited to see if his opening words had harmed him.

Carol's voice was evenly pitched, she refused to be drawn again and wanted to know how he had found her and why? She gave him a resume of Peter's career and his plans for the future. Phil nodded, answered where appropriate and analysed every word and nuance.

It was by no means a one sided encounter. As she spoke Carol looked at her visitor, examining every feature; the scar, the leg, and the eyes that never rested. He was no longer the uncomplicated man she knew from all those years ago. As if reading her thoughts he looked at her and asked.

'I suppose you would like to know how I got these.' He quickly pointed to his forehead and tapped his leg. Carol looked away. 'Was she really so transparent?' She asked herself and apologised.

'I am sorry Phil. I didn't mean to stare.'

He laughed without humour and his eyes became hard and staring. As he spoke Carol grew uneasy, she thought she could almost see the mind leaving the confines of the body, going back in time, while its battered shell stayed in the room with her.

'Do you remember how keen I was to go to Vietnam?' Carol nodded her head but remained silent. He did not expect an answer and gave little time for one. 'I had only been there three weeks when this happened.' He stopped and stared long and hard at his immobile leg. 'I was on what was supposed to be a routine sweep just outside our base perimeter. I was not even at the front.' The story was now coming in bursts and Carol could see that he was now back in that frightening time. 'The other guys must have walked around it, over it. I had to tread on it.' He went silent again and screwed his eyelids tightly together.

'Phil.' Carol sighed and knelt down in front of him. She took his hands in hers. 'You don't have to go through it all again.'

'Oh, I do!' He barked and his voice was full of hate. 'I always have to go through it. I have to live with it.' As he spoke he struck his leg and the sound echoed about the room. Carol stayed still not knowing what she should do or say. She was thankful when Phil spoke again. His voice was once more controlled. 'I was the one who trod on it.' He repeated. 'They must have come the night before and laid new mines all around. I was not the only poor bastard to cop one. I lost one of my mates that day.' For the first time since the conversation began his eyes focused on Carol and he saw her before him. He placed his hands on her head and stroked her hair. 'Why do you think one of those things should kill one man and leave me alive?' Carol shook her head from side to side and felt the tears welling inside her. 'I asked that question for years,' he continued. 'At first I thought that I was the one who was hard done by. I did not want to live. Not like this.' He touched the artificial leg as he spoke. 'Every time I got undressed all I saw was half a man. It wasn't me...you know?'

Carol got to her feet and kissed him gently on the forehead.

'I'm so sorry Phil.' The tears were now rolling in single tracks down her face. A drop of the tender moisture touched his face and brought him out of his melancholy.

'Hey what are you crying for? I've come a long way.' He then laughed. 'I'm more worried about losing my hair now.'

Carol wiped her tears away, smiled and quickly kissed him on the lips.

'You look fine to me.' She said softly. He smiled and kissed her back.

'I did miss you.' His voice was now serious again and charged with pent up emotion. 'I have never blamed you.'

The frankness with which the words were delivered had a stunning effect. Carol was unguarded.

'I could have done it better.' She admitted.

'If we knew then what we know now, ay?' Phil answered.

'No.' She replied. 'I knew enough then. I just did it badly.'

Phil shook his head and replied,

'Let me tell you, there is no good way.'

Carol raised her eyes, smiled and replied.

'I think you are right.' Carol saw the chance to escape from a conversation that hurt her with every word and she took it. 'So what brings you to England?'

Phil's reply was quick and sure.

'Apart from seeing you, you mean.' Carol felt her cheeks redden. She rarely blushed and it was not a feeling she liked. She hoped Phil had not noticed but knew that he had. He continued. 'My leg gave me an out, and not only from the Army. I dropped right out, bummed round Australia drinking anything I could lay my hands on. I was pretty bad.' He smirked at the understatement.

'What happened?' Carol felt responsible and wanted

to move on, 'what brought you back?'

Phil waited before answering. Carol could see that he was back in those dark days again.

'It was ironic really,' he paused, 'the cause of my problem turned out to be my salvation.' Carol moved uneasily. 'The war that took my leg, scared my face and took my self-respect proved to be the best thing that ever happened to me.' Carol looked puzzled and he continued. 'I was cleaning floors in the offices of an outback newspaper in Queensland, anything to pay for the booze,' he added as an aside, 'when I heard that they were running stories on the Vietnam War. Well, I didn't think there was anyone in that little town better qualified than me. So I submitted a piece. They liked it and I was given a temporary contract to write a series of articles. It turned out to be good timing because it was a few years after the war ended, people had gotten over the guilt and wanted to know the facts. Those that took part wanted their story told and the rest wanted to listen. A big paper in Brisbane got hold of the series and hired me. I went to Uni part time and studied Journalism. Being a returned serviceman the government paid my fees. You can see the irony now.' Carol nodded and thought that it was quite a story.

'So what brings you here?' She asked.

'Oh yes, to cut a long story short, I was sent to the States to cover the Vietnam Veterans Revival. That done, I decided to go home the other way round the world.

'The long way.' Carol smiled and asked. 'How did you find me?'

'Never underestimate the power of the press.' His

smile broadened and Carol did not pursue it. It was now Phil's turn to ask the questions.

'What about you? Do you have any little Wells' running around?'

Carol's smile was more polite than happy and she did not answer directly.

'Before we get into my life story can I get you anything to eat?' She asked. He declined. 'Something to drink then? More tea? A beer?'

'Now you're talking like the sheila I used to know.' For the first time in their meeting Carol noted his accent and the memories flooded back.

'You sound like the boozer I used to know.' She quipped. They both laughed and felt easier. Carol left the room, leaving Phil to look around and ponder the purpose of his visit. He was not alone for long. 'Here you are sport, an ice cold tube of the amber nectar.' She laid the accent on thickly as she presented the can and a glass. He smiled up at her, his eyes the mirror and voice of his heart.

'You always were a bloody good bar maid.' He joked.

'Bar maid.' She retorted in mock horror, 'wine bar hostess please.' They laughed once again and Phil took a draw at his glass without taking his eyes from her. He drank long and hard, the level of the glass decreasing steadily until he suddenly stopped and wiped his moist lips with the fingers of his left hand.

'For Pommie beer that's not too bad.' The appreciation was genuine. 'I must have talked myself dry, do you know that didn't even touch the sides.'

Carol looked with affection as he spoke. She recalled

how much he liked a beer on those hot days in Sydney and she was prepared now.

'Lucky I brought two then wasn't it?' She said, handing him a second can.

'You're a little beauty.' He said and touched her hand as he reached out to take the can. It was an intentional act and one that Carol did not miss.

'You wanted to know if I had produced.' She said breezily. 'Well, I have to confess I have been a little lax in that regard.' She smiled, hoping that he would believe it was of little concern. Then her face straightened and her tone became matter of fact. 'I do have a step-son.' Carol was unable to tell if the look that registered on Phil's face was one of disbelief or disappointment When she went on to say that he was nearly twenty one years old the expression was unmistakably amazement.

'How can you have a step-son of that age? You are about the same age as me.' The question exploded from Phil's lips and made Carol laugh. The Cinzano and Lemonade she had made for herself, when Phil opened his second can of beer, splashed over the rim of her glass. 'What about this step-son then?' He was not going to let her get away without an explanation.

'Peter had a son by his previous marriage.' Phil looked blank and Carol continued. 'Peter is older than me.'

Realisation dawned.

'Of course.' Phil exclaimed. 'In praise of older men ay?' The comment was barbed and passed unchallenged but not unnoticed. Phil drained his glass. 'Do you mind if I pour myself a little Scotch?' Carol was surprised by the request but soon recovered.

'I'll get it for you.' She offered but Phil was already on his feet and heading toward the bar.

'No, you stay there, just tell me where it is.' He did not need directions and soon found the bottle.

'Would you like me to get some ice?' Carol offered. That too was declined. Phil poured himself a large measure and returned to the sofa.

'Tell me about your step-son.' He said as he sat down. Carol spoke easily, telling how Nick had tracked his father down and how they met after so many years.

'A bit like you and me.' She said and went on to tell of Nick's job and recent adventure, omitting to mention his father's disapproval of the career. She concluded by saying that he would be arriving that afternoon. 'You will have a chance to meet him.' She said.

At this news Phil looked concerned and then spoke.

'Doesn't Peter mind his twenty one year old son staying in his house alone with his thirty year old step-mother?'

Silence enveloped the room. Carol could hardly believe what had been said and did not trust herself to answer. Phil took a long drink at his whisky and stared into the golden liquid. It was he who spoke first. Apologies flowed from his lips as he swore he did not mean it as it sounded. Carol remained silent. He drained his glass and then rose to recharge it. Carol watched him walk across and pour an even larger measure than the last. Still she said nothing and he became annoyed.

'Come on. I've apologised.' He said and paused before adding, 'you must admit that it could look a bit funny to outsiders.' He offered in his own defence, and, then his emotions overwhelmed him. 'You don't love your husband. That's obvious. It is equally obvious that you do like his son. I don't blame you. Your old man sounds like a real asshole. You do need someone younger, more your own age. You've been cloistered up here in the wilds of the English countryside for too long. You need a new life. You need me.'

Carol was struck dumb. She could not fully take in all that was said, but, she felt a rage grow inside her. Soon the explosion came.

'How dare you say that! How dare you tell me what I should or should not do! Who do you think you are coming into my life after all these years and then telling me how I should live it? If you know me so well then why do you think I left you all those years ago?' She did not wait for an answer. 'I did not love you, that's why. I did not love you then and I certainly don't love you now. My life may not have come straight out of a young girl's story book, but it will do me, thank you very much.' Carol fell silent and her body slumped in the seat. Waves of emotion passed over her and when she spoke again her voice was quieter and more resigned. She repeated her question and each word was stressed in slow deliberate speech. 'Just who do you think you are?'

Phil had finished the second glass of scotch and manipulated the empty tumbler on his fingertips. As if realising his show of nerves he suddenly stopped and placed the glass on the floor. He sat upright and began to speak, his voice no longer one of confidence and drive. Instead, he faltered and, at times, whispered, putting his right hand to his eyes. He could no longer look at her for more than a few seconds.

'You say you never loved me. If that is true then we lived many lies while we were together; but, if you say it then it must be true. I don't know.' He coughed and cleared his throat. 'What I do know is that I loved you and have never stopped loving you.' He now looked into Carol's eyes and held her stare until it was she who looked away. 'Even when I read your letter I still loved you. Shit.' His voice faltered. 'Even when I wanted to hate you I still loved you. You really screwed me up.' He stopped to remove a tear before it could fall and compromise him. 'I went to the war not wanting to come back. My mates didn't like going on patrols with me because I didn't care what happened to me, or them.' He stopped talking and looked down at the leg that was set rigid in front of him. 'I should be dead. Those that saw it don't know how I wasn't blown away with the smoke. The time John Tyson stepped on one of those things there wasn't enough of him to put in his violin case.' Phil's mind travelled back. 'He was a bloody awful violin player but we listened to him play all through basic training, jungle training and then on the ship. He really was a bloody terrible musician but a bloody good bloke.' The tears were now rolling unchecked down his face. His thoughts consumed by images of flame, pain and death. Carol sat in stunned silence, frightened by the raw emotion she saw in front of her.

'I'm sorry.' She whispered and reached out to touch his hand that rested on the blue floral cushion he was now holding. The feeling of a human touch caused him to flinch. He looked down at the intruding hand and pulled his own away. Carol recoiled at the rejection and clasped her hands to her lips. Phil's eyes raged as he stared at her.

'You're sorry!' His lips curled into what was almost a snarl as he spoke. 'What have you got to be sorry about?' He raised his arms to embrace the room. 'You are set up for life, happy in a world of your own making.' He hesitated and his voice grew more bitter when he spoke again. 'Perhaps you are sorry because you know that it is you who is responsible for this.' He traced the line of the jagged scar down the ridge of his forehead and then let his hand drop to his immobile leg.

'How could you Phil?' Carol's voice echoed the horror of the accusation. She grew frightened at being alone with a man she no longer knew and who looked at her with unblinking eyes that were now blind with hatred. 'You don't believe that.' It was both a question and a statement. 'I didn't know that would happen. How could I?' He made no answer and she continued. 'I could have said goodbye better. I have admitted that. I was young. I didn't know what to do for the best. It wasn't my fault.'

'Everything you do follows a plan.' Phil's voice grew more resigned. 'Now.., then.., it is all the same. You do what you like and let the rest of us pick up the pieces.' He then looked at her with that piercing stare she now dreaded. 'Who are you going to play with next?'

Carol understood the implication in the words.

'You bastard!' She swore and rose to her feet. 'You are crippled more than you know and I don't think we have anything more to say to each other. I'll telephone for a taxi.' She hurried from the room thankful for the excuse to be alone. Anger, uncertainty, even guilt, all these emotions caused her to nearly drop the telephone receiver as she removed it from its cradle. Concentrating hard to find the number she dialled it with an unsteady hand.

'Oh!' She exclaimed, having put the receiver down and turned to re-enter the room. Phil was standing before her.

'I'll wait out in the drive.' His head dropped and he looked to the floor. 'I don't know what went wrong. This is not what I had planned for us.'

Carol held her ground.

'We have both changed. We can't go back. No one can.' She walked towards him. 'Come on let's go back and sit down, the taxi will be a while.'

Phil did not move.

'No. I want to go outside.' He answered and walked passed her toward the front door. As it swung open and the sun fell on the carpeted floor he turned. 'I will never see you again but I want you to know that you are never out of my thoughts. I know I said some stupid things in there' he nodded toward the lounge, 'I really don't know how I am going to live without you.'

The hatred and anger fell away to be replaced by a sad affection as Carol drew close to him and kissed his cheek. Her feelings stemmed the flow of words telling her that enough had been said.

They walked outside and stood in the bright sunlight. The minutes passed in silence until Phil spoke again.

'I really didn't mean all those things I said in there.'

Phil broke down again as he looked back at the house. Carol followed his gaze and then looked at him.

'I don't know what to believe anymore Phil, but, I do know that whatever we had, is gone. Perhaps it is just as well we had this meeting. I thought you were dead all those years ago and now it is your turn to lay my ghost to rest and get on with the rest of your life.' The sound of an approaching car silenced them. They listened and waited for it to come into view.

'I really thought you would be going back with me. I must have been mad.' Phil appeared to be talking to himself as the black taxi pulled into the drive. He turned to face Carol and held out his hands to take hers. 'Forgive me for what happened here today.' His voice was sad and this was reflected in his stance. His shoulders were slumped and his head low on his chest. The car drove up to the house and stopped before them. The driver remained in his seat affording them a last moment of privacy. Phil spoke again,

'Remember me as I was.' He said and squeezed her hands. Carol looked into his lined face and went on her toes to kiss him tenderly on the lips. It had been an afternoon of intense emotion and now she felt the tears on her cheeks. Concentrating her powers to control her voice she spoke,

'Have a good journey back to Australia,' and, forcing herself to smile, added, 'I'll look for your name in print.'

'Thanks a lot.' He said quietly and let go of her hands. 'Goodbye Carol.'

The finality of the words was disarming. Carol watched as he limped to the waiting car, his lameness touching a chord of sadness within her. He looked back as he opened the door. His eyes looked hollow and his face held no expression. Carol brought her hand up to wave but checked it. The car pulled away and he did not look back.

The tears ran in uncontrolled rivers down Carol's face. Alone and uncertain she stood looking for the car long after it had disappeared from view. She suddenly felt exposed and ran to the house. The front door slammed behind her. Hurrying upstairs to her room she threw herself onto the bed and buried her face in the pillows.

For a few moments Carol did not know where she was. It was dark outside. She had been asleep, but, for how long? She had no idea. The doorbell rang and she realised that it was this high pitched sound that had brought her from the darkness and dreams of sleep.

'Oh no!' She cried and leapt from the bed. The bell sounded again. Quickly she glanced into the dressing table mirror and attempted to straighten her hair with her fingers. Again the bell rang. 'Shit!' She exclaimed and hurried from the room.

The house was in darkness. She flicked the switch at the top of the stairs and descended to the door. The bell rang again.

'Who is it?' Carol called through the thick door. Living in the country and often alone had made her sensitive to callers.

'It's me, Nick. Are you alright?' Carol opened the door and held out her arms to embrace him.

'Oh Nick, it is so good to see you.'

'Are you okay?' Nick repeated the question. He could feel the tension in her body and the welcome was out of character. He often wished it would be like this and always dismissed such thoughts as fantasy. Now he was in her arms and it worried him.

'What time is it?' Carol answered his question with a question as she released her embrace and stood aside to allow him to enter the house. Nick looked at his watch,

'Twenty past nine.' His tone was puzzled.

'I must have dozed off. I didn't hear your car.'

'Carol.' Nick was more determined now. 'Is there anything wrong?'

Carol answered but could not look at him as she spoke.

'No, No of course not.' She fought to change the subject. 'It's lovely to see you again. I read about your trip. How are your family? Did you have a good drive down?' The comments and questions reeled from her lips and all the time she knew she was making a fool of herself. Nick grew more concerned. He knew he would have to take his time if he was to find out what was wrong. He went out to the car to fetch his suitcase certain that whatever was upsetting Carol had to involve his father.

When he returned to the house Carol was in the lounge room pouring herself a long drink.

'Would you like one, Nick?' She asked as he entered.

'Beer would be good.'

'There's some cold ones in the fridge. Do you mind?' Nick went off to the kitchen but soon returned. 'Here's a glass.' Carol held out a dimpled tankard.

'Thanks.' Nick answered and asked. 'Where's Dad?'

Carol walked over to the settee and was about to sit down when the images of the day flooded back. She stood up.

'Can I get you anything to eat?' Without waiting for an answer she left the room. Nick followed.

'Is Dad home?' He asked again, certain that he was the reason for Carol's nervous state.

The harsh brightness of the kitchen light highlighted every tired line of her face and the redness in Carol's eyes. Pretending to be looking for something in one of the cupboards she did not turn to him when she answered.

'No. He's off the coast of Scotland somewhere. The last official visit he will be making as Captain of his ship. He will be back on Monday.' Nick was confused. There was something very wrong. He wanted to know what it was. Carol stopped scrambling around in the cupboards and turned. Her face was ashen and wet with tears. Her eyes burned red and lost. Finally, unable to contain her feelings any longer her body heaved as she gave vent to her pain and cried out;

'Nick it's been awful.' She sobbed and came to him. Shyly he placed his arms about her, unsure of how to comfort her and ignorant of what was wrong. Holding her close he cradled her head on his shoulder. 'It wasn't my fault you know?' The words were murmured and their sadness overwhelming. Nick remained silent and drew her closer. They stood in the bright light of the kitchen holding onto each other for many minutes before Nick could find words to say.

'Let's go and sit down in the other room and you can tell me what's wrong.'

'No I can't go in there.' Carol pleaded.

'But you have got to sit down and unwind.' He thought quickly, knowing that Carol was in no state to think for herself. 'You go upstairs, lie down and I'll bring you a cup of tea.' Carol offered no argument and moved out of his arms. She left the room and Nick set about preparing the hot drink. He thought about tea always being the answer for the British in distress and smiled thinly. The kettle appeared to take a lifetime to boil and afforded time for Nick to think and worry.

He placed the cups on a tray and carried them out into the oak beamed hall and up the stairs to the bedroom. Carol had draped herself along the bed and was hiding her head in her hands when Nick walked in. He placed the tray on the bedside table and looked uneasily around him. On hearing his approach Carol took her hands away from her face. The tears had stopped and dried on her cheeks. She thanked him as he put the tray down and handed her a cup. He waited while she drank and then asked.

'What happened here today?' He sat perched on the edge of the bed. Carol just stared at him before answering.

'I had a visit from a ghost. A man I knew in Australia years ago. I thought he was dead.' Nick looked blank and quietly asked.

'How did he find you? Why did you think he was dead?' Carol sat up and propped two pillows behind her head.

'This is one of those long stories you always hear about.' She tried to joke to prepare herself for the telling. She started where it all began, on an aeroplane twelve years ago. As the story unfolded she felt her spirit being lifted. It was as if she was being set free. Nick listened and said nothing. He was hearing a story but not getting any answers. Carol's tone then changed and she became agitated once again. 'Look at this.' She said, jumping from the bed and going to the bottom drawer of her dressing table. Quickly her fingers sought out what she wanted, a brown piece of newspaper, discoloured through time. She walked the few paces back to the bed and handed it to Nick. He read the article and checked the date. 'You see?' Carol asked, as if the paper told everything. 'You see why I thought he was dead? A friend of mine sent that to me and after that no further news came.' Nick re-read the article.

'But it doesn't give any names.' He said flatly. Carol's mood became tearful once more.

'It didn't have to. Don't you see? It was the end. I knew it was.' The tears were flowing freely once more and Nick moved close to comfort her. 'Oh Nick, it was awful.' She sobbed. 'Today he returned. He only had one leg. His face was scarred. He said it was all my fault.' Having said the words that damned her she flopped into Nick's arms and cried like a child.

He rocked her body back and forwards, kissing away the tears as they fell.

'It wasn't your fault.' He whispered over and over again.

Slowly she settled, the sobs that rent her body eased and then stopped. She felt his lips on her face and turned towards him. Their eyes met, his full of pity and fear, hers of gratitude and uncertainty. Their faces drew together and their lips met in a quivering, tender embrace. They kissed once, drew apart and then kissed again. Their lips fused in a union of fire.

Carol moved her hands to cradle Nick's face. His followed the contours of her body, moving beneath her arms until they found the soft tender flesh of her breasts.

'Carol.' He sighed in anguished ecstasy and then she felt his hands fall away.

'Don't.' She pleaded and guided them to the buttons that held the front of her blouse. Together they unfastened each one until she lay exposed before him and powerless to stop. His whole body shuddered.

'You are beautiful.' He whispered and placed his lips on the taut, pinkness of her nipples.

'So are you.' She responded and began to remove his shirt. Her fingers worked deftly with the light touch of a butterfly on his skin.

Their lips did not part and they caressed as each garment that separated their bodies, was discarded to the floor. Naked they clung together, the line of each body fitting that of the other. There were no words of love, instead, their bodies spoke in a language that would not betray them to the world outside their embrace.

The early morning sun sent shafts of light through the small squared window panes and lit up the room in a haze of yellow light. The sound of the birds nesting under the eaves was the clarion call of the new day. Nick stirred and turned onto his side. He opened his eyes and looked at the smooth brown skin of Carol's back. The auburn hair falling across her shoulders accentuated her nakedness. His whole being felt as if it would explode.

Never had he known such an all-consuming passion. He moved closer to Carol's sleeping body. As their skin touched she moved and lazily turned to face him.

'Good morning.' He said with mock formality. Carol stared as if her brain did not believe what her eyes were looking at.

'Oh, Nick!' She exclaimed in a low frightened voice. 'What have we done?' In her eyes fear replaced disbelief. Nick moved closer and touched her temple with the back of his hand as his mother used to do to him when he was young and afraid.

'We made love.' He whispered and looked into her frightened face to assure and be assured.

'What have I done?' Carol rephrased the question but her voice still sounded desolate. She pulled away from his touch. 'Oh Nick!' She cried.

'You haven't done anything wrong.' The words were no consolation and only served to fuel Carol's guilt. Her voice became more shrill.

'I haven't done anything wrong.' She repeated his words and then sighed. 'I have slept with the son of my husband and you think that is not wrong?' Carol left the bed and pulled the dressing gown about her. Nick tried to calm her.

'It wasn't your fault. You didn't seduce me. It just happened.' He said and Carol laughed

'Nothing just happens, Nick. As you get older you will find that out.'

Nick recoiled at the reference to his age. She had hurt him. She attacked him where he felt most vulnerable, but he would not be put off.

'So what if we did plan it? What if we knew it was going to happen all along?' He waited before he said what his heart was aching to say. 'God knows I have dreamt of nothing else almost from the day I met you.' His voice softened. 'I love you. I want to look after you. I have seen the way my father treats you and I think he is a fool. I would never do anything to hurt you. If you want me to leave I will, but, before you say that, what have we done? We comforted one another at a time when we both needed it.' Carol would not be calmed

'What if I become pregnant? What then?'

The question threw Nick into confusion. It was an outcome he had not considered.

'You won't, you can't.' He stammered, now completely on the defensive. 'You're married.'

The naivety of his words made Carol laugh and her anxiety subsided enough for her to think rationally again.

'You have got to go Nick. Whether we planned it, desired it, dreamt it. It doesn't matter. There is no excuse for what I have done. I don't blame you. What I do ask is that you forget it, forget me and get out before any more damage is done.'

Nick could see only too clearly that further argument was pointless. His disappointment gave way to bitterness.

'I've got time to get my pants on, have I?' Carol did not answer. She turned away and left the bedroom.

Dressing quickly Nick hurried downstairs expecting to find Carol sitting at the old pine table in the kitchen. She was not there. He walked through the house looking in every room. It was not until he returned to the kitchen that he saw her outside, leaning on the five bar gate and looking over the green paddock to the copse of trees beyond. He crossed the room and opened the door. He was careful not to let it slam behind him. He approached quietly, each step shortening as he neared her. She did not turn around. Her hands grasped the wooden rail. She said nothing and it was left to Nick to begin. He began nervously.

'I love you.' Carol did not move and he continued. 'I do. I'm not just saying it because of last night.'

Carol laughed, an abrupt, disbelieving exclamation.

'You are not old enough to know what you are talking about.' She turned her body to face him. Nick squared his shoulders.

'You are, I suppose.' He sneered. 'How old are you? Thirty? That's old is it?' The tension mounted menacingly and Carol fueled the fire.

'It's old enough.' She snapped and continued. 'Now why don't you leave me alone? Get in your car and get out of my life.'

Nick's body went rigid with pent up anger and then he erupted.

'You've got it!' He barked, turned and strode off to where his car was parked.

Carol did not follow. She returned her hands to the rail and listened to the sound of the engine start up and then fade away in the stillness of the country morning. Tears filled her eyes.

Chapter 21

Carol leaned against the Victorian brickwork of a dockyard storehouse. The mild mid-morning breeze off the water tossed the hair about her face. It annoyed her as she thought of the time it had taken to get it just right. She wanted to look perfect when Peter's eye first caught her. He would not be expecting to be met. It was something they had not done for many years. Part of the old life that had died along the way.

The sharp bow of the destroyer appeared at the end of the jetty and glided wide to maintain the channel for its turn and run in to its birth. No other family members were present. It had only been a short cruise and did not warrant a great homecoming. However, for Peter, it was his last stretch of sea time in command and Carol wanted to mark the occasion.

The destroyer turned and headed slowly towards the marker flag positioned on the jetty. From being just part of the harbour scenery the grey mass of the ship soon dominated its surroundings. Carol watched as the first lines were passed between ship and shore. The heavy ropes appearing to be symbols of both security and bondage.

On the starboard bridge wing Carol could see the sun reflecting off the gold leaves that adorned the black peak of the Captain's cap. She stood away from the wall and began walking towards the ship. The gangway was being hoisted into place as the ship's sheer sides towered above her. She looked up but Peter had left his position on the wing of the bridge. Carol wondered if he had seen her and then smiled. She knew how intently he concentrated on his work and that she would have gone unnoticed.

Two sailors were carrying a varnished wooden cross down the narrow gangway. Carol stood back. Following close behind was another sailor carrying a white life preserver on which was written the ship's name in bold gold lettering. The two pieces of equipment were placed together at the foot of the gangway. The job done, the three men hurried back on board and Carol followed.

The gangway staff were busily organising their area of operation and the appearance of the Captain's wife on board the ship caused great concern. Carol was stopped by a very young sailor who she knew by the crispness of his uniform was both new to the ship and the service. When she introduced herself he completely went to pieces. The confidence with which he challenged her presence on board deserted him. He looked about for assistance and found it in the form of a Leading Seaman who instantly recognised the visitor, took over and escorted Carol to the Captain's cabin.

The Leading Seaman knocked twice and then excused himself from her company. The friendly face of

Leading Steward Hawkes greeted her. Carol could see a hint of surprise in his round smiling face.

'Mrs. Wells. It is so good to see you again.' He stood aside to let her enter the cabin. His tone became a little more formal. 'The Captain is changing. I will tell him you are here.' Carol was quick to seize her opportunity.

'That will not be necessary. I will tell him myself.' Hawkes was stunned. This was most irregular. While on board he considered the Captain to be his responsibility. It was his duty to protect him from any unbidden interruptions, even from the Captain's wife.

Carol sailed passed him to the door that led to Peter's sleeping quarters. She did not knock but bowled straight in. The surprise was total. Peter was standing beside his small bunk wearing only a pair of uniform trousers, his hair was still wet from the shower. His expression was one of complete disbelief. For a moment he could not speak.

'What are you doing here?' Where is Hawkes?'

'Would you rather see him?' Carol smiled disarmingly. It took a moment but eventually Peter saw the humour. They laughed together and Carol approached, placing her arms around his waist. She looked up at him.

'I thought you might need cheering up as this was your last trip in command.'

'Thanks.' He said softly and lowered his head to kiss her. He had been feeling unsettled since being woken early that morning. Carol then noticed him becoming the Captain once again.

'You can't stay here.' His voice was matter of fact. Carol expected this response. She moved closer to him and placed her hands on his chest, catching the thick mat of black hairs between her fingers.

'Why not?' Her voice deepened and the pupils of her eyes dilated to form inviting black pools. Peter moved awkwardly but maintained the pressure of his thighs against her.

'Carol what is going on?' He asked in confused frustration. She smiled back at him.

'I've missed you and now you are back and are not going away again for a long time.' She cooed, moving her hands down to the waistband of his trousers. 'I haven't had you at home for two years and I thought you might like to see what it is going to be like.'

Peter moved his hands to restrain her as she began unfastening his belt.

'But, Carol.' He protested. 'It is the middle of the day, what if somebody comes in?'

Refusing to be stopped Carol's hands returned to the buckle and dexterously unfastened the metal clip.

'You are the Captain,' she sighed, 'you can do as you like, and, if you like, you can do me.'

Her task complete she placed her arms about his neck and drew him to her. For a moment he hesitated, nervously holding back. Then, he let his hands travel over Carol's body and through the sheer material of her dress discovered something that released him from the bonds of uncertainty.

'Oh my God.' He sighed.

'I didn't think we would have much time.' Carol whispered.

Stepping out of his own clothes Peter slid the dress

above Carol's head and lifted her onto the bunk. The unusual and potentially dangerous situation excited them both and heightened the urgency of their embrace. Peter held Carol to him and took her with deep, demanding strokes. There was little tenderness in his lovemaking, only a need for quick gratification. The lust that had been aroused so rapidly was as equally satisfied. He rolled from her.

'That is what I call a sailor's homecoming.'

Carol smiled and playfully placed a kiss on the end of his nose.

'Glad you liked it, sailor.' She said, pressing herself against him.

Peter sat up and looked at the clock on the bulkhead,

'If you have any ideas of a repeat performance save them until tonight. Right now the Captain has a ship to run.'

Carol smiled up at him.

'I'll hold you to that Captain.'

He patted the firm flesh of her exposed thigh.

'You do that.' He kissed her again and then, taking his weight on his arms, propelled himself from the bunk. He pulled on his trousers and went to the white shirt draped across the back of a chair. 'I just took a shower and now I need another one. If I have one now, old Hawkes will really know what went on here.'

Carol would not be suppressed.

'Let's take one together and really give the ship something to talk about.' She smiled impishly. Peter looked at her, alarmed at first and then laughed.

'You would have us do it too.' He fastened his shirt and

looked about the floor for his shoes. 'Save that thought for tonight.' He looked at her lying on his bunk, her head supported by one hand, the other draped between her naked legs. She fluttered her fingers and stared back at him. He refused to weaken. 'Come on Carol, get out of here.' He finished knotting his tie.

'Aye Aye Captain.' She saluted, exposing her body to him. She lifted her legs high and over the side of the bunk. Her dress slipped down her body and she smoothed the material with her hands. 'You look dashing.' She said admiringly as he put on his blue jacket and fastened the brass buttons. 'You look too young to be a Captain.'

'Thank you.' He smiled. 'Now put a brush through your hair and take that, 'guess what we've been doing' expression off your face. You are too young to be a Captain's wife and I have a ship full of sailors who do not need any clues as to what a young wife could do to the 'Old Man'.

'Spoil sport.' She pouted, kissed him and reached in her handbag for her hair brush and make up. 'I thought I would spend the day in town and after you are finished here we could go for dinner. What do you say?' She said while putting her hair back in place and retouching the smudged edges of her face.

Peter was waiting with his hand on the door knob. Now dressed, he thought of Hawkes and checked his watch. Carol had been in the cabin for nearly half an hour.

'Sounds good.' He replied, a little impatiently. 'Now we had better get out and show ourselves.' He made a final check to see that Carol was ready and then opened the door.

Leading Steward Hawkes was in the galley and on hearing the Captain enter the cabin went out to meet him.

'Tea or coffee, sir?' He asked. Peter's eyes flashed.

'No thank you. Mrs. Wells has to be going and I have duties ashore.' He concentrated on sounding matter of fact.

'Very good, sir.' Hawkes replied and retired once more to his galley.

Peter looked at Carol, who was fighting to suppress a laugh. 'I could have just done with a cup of tea.' She whispered. Peter smiled and shook his head.

'I bet he knows that. Now, let's go before you ruin my reputation.

Nick sat in the darkened crew area, his mind alight with images in a catalogue of pain. The maroon curtain was swept aside and Bob Hayward, the Senior Steward, swung himself into the seat beside him. He rummaged in his pocket and withdrew a crumpled packet of cigarettes and a gold plated lighter. The ignited flame briefly illuminated the area and then only the red glowing tip of the cigarette stood out against the darkness. The Senior inhaled deeply. Nick had glanced at him when the curtain was opened but was soon lost again in his own thoughts. The two men sat in silence. After exhaling a long ribbon of smoke Hayward spoke;

'Okay Nick. What's wrong?' There was no response. 'Come on Nick, while it's just the two of us tell me what is bothering you.' This time the reaction was instant and sharp.

'Nothing is wrong and if there was it would not be any of your business.' The gauntlet had been dropped. The Senior Steward raised his voice.

'Don't be stupid. I've flown with you before. I know what you're like and it's not the bloody minded idiot that you have been on this trip.'

'Forget it.' Nick acted unconcerned which only served to annoy his supervisor more.

'No I will not forget it. How can I when I get passengers commenting on the boot faced steward and it's me who has to go into the office to answer the complaints. It's not good enough.' Hayward took a long draw on his cigarette.

Nick turned to face him,

'Look. We only have four more hours to London, then we can all go home and forget this trip ever happened.'

'Oh great!' The Senior scoffed. 'You can forget it, but, as I said, it is me who is called in to explain why certain passengers have written in complaining about the service... and it isn't just this flight.' He waited for the meaning of these words to register before continuing. 'The Flight Purser has a notice from the office to keep an eye on you. Apparently this sort of thing is becoming a regular feature with you.' He paused again. 'You are not helping yourself Nick, I'm not kidding. If another bad report goes in you could be on your bike.'

Nick had heard enough. His tolerance, was now so easily eroded and he stood up to leave.

'If you'll excuse me I'll get back to my passengers and if you, the Purser or the office don't like the way I do my job then you all know what you can do about it.' Nick pulled back the curtain and stepped into the cabin aisle. Turning left he headed for the toilets at the rear of the aircraft. Hayward sat back and drained his cigarette of its last ounce of nicotine.

Nick closed the toilet door behind him and squinted as the bright light came on. Staring at his reflection in the mirror he asked himself, 'what the hell do you think you're doing?' As he stared into the glass he thought of Lynda Swan. 'You are a bastard.' He said to his image in the mirror.

They had met again on this trip. Lynda was as passionate and exciting as she had been in Barbados but, she was not Carol. There was not the subtle tenderness. There was not the fire. Eventually he could live the lie no longer. He made excuses. He did everything to escape from the relationship except tell Lynda the truth.

Two months had passed and no answer had come to the letters he wrote to Carol. Now, as he stood in the fluorescent light, looking into the mirror marked by dry water splashes, he knew what must be done. For the first time in those long months he laughed as he regarded his surroundings. On arrival in London he would go home, rest and then drive down to see Carol. He would give no warning, nor ask for permission. The decision was made. He returned to the crew seats, put his head through the curtain and was relieved to see Bob Hayward still there. The Senior Steward looked up.

'Sorry Bob.' Nick apologised. 'I'll get things sorted out.' The older steward smiled and nodded his head.

'That's good news. I'll have a word with the Purser

and get you a stay of execution. Don't let me down, Nick.'

Nick smiled,

'Okay.' He said and closed the curtain.

It had been a long night but it would soon be over. As the cabin crew brought the dirty breakfast trays back into the galley the aircraft's nose dipped at the start of its descent.

'Watch your backs!' Nick called as he entered the galley with an arm full of small plastic trays that threatened to spill their sticky contents over everything and everyone in the area. His arms embraced the tottering pile and his chin wedged the uppermost tray in place. As his hands touched the shining work surface the bottom tray slid from his grasp causing all the others to follow in a crescendo of falling plastic.

'Shit!' Nick exclaimed as he bent down to pick up the pile of plastic. As he stood up and slid the trays into their box like stowage he turned to the two girls working with him. 'Cabin Service is like making love,' he said, 'no matter how long it takes there is always a mad rush at the end.' All three laughed, relieved at being in the final stages of a long night flight. Lynda was particularly happy to see Nick laughing again.

The trip had been a nightmare for her. It began with Nick being attentive, caring, sexually demanding and then it all went wrong. He became silent and moody. He would not touch her, he made excuses to be away and finally would not even acknowledge her. No explanation was given and the more she insisted on one, the more distant he became. Now, as they approached London she saw him reverting to his usual behavior, and, although still hurt by his rejection hoped he was not lost to her forever. While they were laughing together in the galley she moved closer to him. Nick smiled at her but said nothing.

'Could someone start collecting headsets?' The Senior Steward called into the galley. Without hesitation Nick pulled a large plastic bag from a drawer and left to carry out the instruction. Lynda watched him leave, annoyed and frustrated by the Senior's timing.

The aircraft disgorged its passengers leaving only those requiring assistance from the crew and ground staff. Nick moved to help an old lady with her hand baggage when Lynda came up behind him.

'I'll take her off Nick. Would you collect my cabin bag and bring it to the front door?'

Nick did as he was asked and moved forward passed the rows of seats strewn with rubbish and the reminders of a long night's work.

Nick followed Lynda onto the crew bus and sat beside her for the journey to the Customs Hall. In a hushed voice he apologised.

'I'm sorry it hasn't worked out.' Lynda shrugged her shoulders and smiled helplessly and Nick continued. 'I have had a lot on my mind and I let it get on top of me.'

'That's okay.' She replied, wanting to say more but not finding the words in the confines of the crowded bus.

Having had their baggage checked they walked outside the Customs building and along the pavement that led to the Cabin Crew Reporting Centre. Cars and people hurried passed them in the hectic world that was London's busiest airport. Inside the Crew Centre the activity was no less hurried. Uniformed figures crowded the cream paneled offices and corridors. Crews filed in and out of the briefing rooms, individuals checked their 'pigeon holes' for mail while others lined up in front of the cashier's windows to pay in cash boxes that contained currencies taken from all parts of the globe. At the end of the main reception area was a long corridor that led to the management offices. In those small rooms, decorated with photographs of the company's aeroplanes, sat the suited men and women responsible for the administration, training, welfare and discipline of all those at the other end of the corridor. As Nick crossed the crowded floor he looked at the row of offices and recalled Bob Hayward's warning. They were checking up on him. He knew that now and could stay one jump ahead. Bob had given him a break, he knew that and would not let him down.

'Nick.' The feminine voice drew his attention away from the corridor. He looked around and saw Lynda standing beside him. 'Will I be seeing you this stand-off?'

'I'm surprised you would want to after the way I have been acting.'

'That's all right.' Lynda tried to dismiss the incidents as if they were already forgotten. Nick took her arm and led her to a more secluded part of the room. When he spoke his voice was serious.

'I don't think it is a good idea for us to see each other for a while.' He saw Lynda's expression harden but he had to go on. 'I have told you there is a lot on my mind and right now I have to be left alone to sort everything out.' He did not have to explain further. Lynda pulled away and faced him squarely.

'You can have all the time you need.' She snapped. 'Just don't expect me to be around when you have finally sorted yourself out!' She turned and retreated into the mingling crowd.

Nick watched her go with mixed feelings of relief and sadness. He had not wanted to hurt her, but, if that was the price for restoring his life with Carol then he would gladly pay it.

It was eleven o'clock by the time he parked his car and walked up to his flat. He felt exhausted but hated the thought of wasting precious time when he could be on the road to Carol. As he threw his suitcase onto the bed he thought again. He could not arrive in the evening and expect to be given a room for the night. A more subtle approach was needed. He would have to arrive in the morning with the option of returning home that same day. He opened the lid of the case and the thought of waiting another day tormented him. He knew he could not stand to do nothing. Emptying the old clothes onto the bed he set about re-packing. He had a quick shower, dressed, picked up the case and left the flat. He was back on the road one hour after arriving home. His eyes felt heavy but the adrenaline coursing through his veins kept his mind active as he considered the plan of action. He would drive to Meonstoke and find accommodation for the night. Tomorrow, he would go and see her.

Chapter 22

Carol put the book on the white wrought iron patio table and slid her sunglasses to rest on the top of her head. It was a beautiful morning with cloudless blue sky and the sun pouring its warmth over the land. She heard the car pull into the driveway but did not get up. She was expecting her cleaning lady to call. The front door bell rang.

'That's odd,' she thought, 'Mrs. Cotes always comes to the back door.'

'I'm around the back!' She called and waited in her seat expecting to see the spherical figure and jovial face of the village cleaning lady. When her visitor finally appeared Carol was gripped with disbelief and panic. She sat rigidly in her chair as Nick approached. His smile was a combination of uncertainty and embarrassment

'Hi.' He greeted her and put up his right hand as if to wave and drew it back down to his side. 'I've come to say sorry. I said it in my letters but I don't know if you read them.'

Carol stood up and walked toward him. Putting out

her hands she held his and kissed him gently on each cheek.

'You don't have to apologise.' She said softly. 'Come and sit down. Can I get you a drink?' Nick declined and took a seat. He was both surprised and relieved by his reception. In anticipation of this meeting he had not slept well that night.

'You are looking good.' Carol lied, noticing the dark shadows under his eyes. He smiled at her diplomacy.

'Thanks.' He replied and returned the compliment, only this time, he meant it. He was amazed at just how fresh and vibrant she looked. The pink blush in her cheeks made her look vivacious and alive.

'How is the Captain enjoying his new job?' Nick found it easier to address his father in this abstract way. He had hoped they would become close but now abandoned that wish as impossible. Carol smiled,

'He's fine. Lost in his work. Same old story.' The smile left her lips. She recalled the days between leaving his ship and assuming his new command when the years seemed to slip away. The love that brought them together was regenerated and with it came laughter and friendship. Without a ship the Navy appeared to relax its hold over him. Carol had prayed that this rediscovered love would survive. Two things were to happen that dashed these hopes and made a mockery of her feelings. The first was his new command. The second was more shattering.

Nick noticed the smile vanish from Carol's lips and the laughter from her eyes. He had all the answers he needed but still could not let the subject drop.

'He does live at home doesn't he? No more sea time.'

Carol rose to her feet.

'Let's say he sleeps here.' A silence fell between them until Carol spoke again. 'Now, what about that drink?' Nick was happy now to let it rest.

'I could murder a beer.'

Carol went into the kitchen and returned with an iced tankard glistening under a canopy of white foam.

'You really know how to serve a beer.' He joked as he accepted the drink.

'That comes from living in Australia for three months.' She smiled and realised that the meeting she had been dreading was a relief rather than a torture. She had not felt so relaxed for a long time. It was good to have someone lively to talk to. The village women were either preoccupied with their children, their husband's career or their own fantasies. She kept in touch with her mother who was a support when needed, but, there is no absolution without honesty and Carol always carried the secret burden in her heart. She took a seat and placed a glass of orange juice on the table. 'Peter will be home at midday. We are going to a Fleet Reception in the dockyard. Something to do with NATO exercises that have just finished.' Nick felt uncomfortable and reached for his beer. He thought fast,

'Will I have a chance to meet him before I go? I have to get back to London this evening. I'm off on a trip tomorrow.' He hoped the lie sounded convincing.

Time passed quickly. It was not until Carol heard the sound of Peter's car that she realised the cleaning lady had not come.

'That will be Peter.' She said, getting to her feet. 'It is handy for him just working down the road.' She left Nick sitting at the table and went into the house.

Carol opened the front door just as Peter was about to insert his key in the lock. They kissed on the cheek.

'Nick is here.' Carol said brightly. Peter hung his cap on the peg by the door and took off his jacket.

'Good. We haven't seen much of him lately.' He said and led the way through the house and out into the garden.

'Can I get you a drink?' Carol called after him.

'No thanks. We'll have more than enough at the reception.' Carol just nodded her head.

Nick stood up as Peter stepped onto the patio. They shook hands.

'Good to see you Nick. It's been a long time. Have they been keeping you busy?' Nick waited for Peter to sit before doing so himself. His father continued. 'I'm afraid we will not be able to hang around. We have to attend a 'do' in the dockyard.'

'Nick knows.' Carol interjected. 'He has to get back for a trip tomorrow.'

'No rest for the wicked Ay?' Peter commented and Nick blushed. Without waiting for an answer Peter continued excitedly. 'What about our news then?' Nick looked blank. 'Hasn't she told you?' This time he waited for a response. Nick shook his head. 'I'm going to be a father.' The words landed like the repeated blows of a sledge hammer. Nick looked up at Carol with questions in his eyes. She looked away. Peter was puzzled by the silence. 'Isn't that great news?' He was almost begging for recognition. Nick shifted his gaze to rest on his father.

'Yes, congratulations.' He was stunned and sounded less than enthusiastic. Peter did not appear to notice.

'I was not too happy at first. You know, in my forties and already being a father.' He spoke as if Nick was an acquaintance. 'Then I realised that this was a second chance.'

Nick was still too stunned to react. His eyes shot back to rest on Carol's face. He searched her expression for an answer but she would not look at him. Peter was still speaking,

'It is due in February. We'll see you again before then I expect.' Nick did not answer and Peter turned his attention to Carol. 'We better start getting ready.' He stood up and turned to Nick. 'Sorry we have to rush off. Let us know when you are next free and we'll arrange a meeting.' He walked off the patio and into the house. Carol did not follow.

'Is that my child?' Nick's eyes bored into her. His voice trembled. Carol stood her ground.

'No.' She replied firmly. 'No, it is not.'

'How do you know? How can you be so sure?'

'Because you are not the only man I have been to bed with! Peter and I have been trying for a child for a long time now. He would not admit that up until now we had failed. I think he believed that it was his fault. You know how he is. Anyway, now we have finally made it and he thinks he is going to have the son that you never were.' It was a harsh lie she hoped would stop further questions. Nick stood back and fought to hold back his tears.

'I don't believe you, but I don't want to hurt you. I'll

go now. You have my number if you want to talk.' He turned and disappeared around the corner of the house, leaving Carol staring after him. She knew that the only ally she could count on had just left her.

She remained outside reliving her lies and remembering the scenes when she broke the news of her pregnancy to Peter. For the first time in their marriage she had been scared of him. Frightened by his rage and saddened by his abuse. He called her irresponsible, stupid, selfish but never questioned how such a mistake could happen.

Throughout the weeks that followed she grew to love the baby growing within her. It was her liberation from playing the supporting role. It had been something she had done and right or wrong it would be her child. There were times when she wanted to scream her independence and silence her tormentor with the knowledge that the child was not his. For the child's sake she could not do it. At other times she would plunge to the depths of despair, torturing herself over the events that led to her baby's conception and the knowledge that even she was not sure if it was Peter or his son who was the father of her child. Now, standing alone she felt depressed, trapped by the lie she created and which she now had to live with forever.

'Are you coming to get ready?'

Peter called from an upstairs window. His tone impatient. Carol looked down at her stomach, not yet showing the signs of the life developing within. She placed her hands on the bump as if caressing her unborn child and assuring herself of the life that she controlled.

Nick spent the days of the stand-off in his apartment, alone with his thoughts, questions and images. A calendar lay at the foot of his bed, the days of the past months obliterated by pen strokes. No matter how many times he checked the dates the conclusion was always the same. The child had to be his. It was a fact that both scared and thrilled him. No matter what Carol said or how fiercely she argued, he had to be the father. Then her words would echo back at him, 'You are not the only man I have been to bed with.' He hated the words that cheapened the love he felt for her. The child had to be his. A baby born of love, not the designs of a calculating plan struck between two married strangers. She had to protect her marriage, her stability and him. It was the easy way out, but, it was not right. A child should be brought into a world of love, not convenience. He was the father and Carol did love him. The more he thought the greater became his passion. He saw in his vision a love that Carol did not feel for her husband and which he now claimed for himself.

Chapter 23

Nick cursed his scheduler for making his next trip three weeks long and sending him to the other side of the world. He felt the separation keenly but reasoned that the time away would allow Carol time to realise how much she needed his love and support.

On arriving back home he parked his car and ran to the bank of mailboxes set in the wall by the main entrance to the flats. The key was in his hand as he stood before the black metal opening praying that it held some word from Carol. His desolation was total as the small door swung open to reveal a buff envelope from the council and a colourful circular from a pizza fast food restaurant. He slammed the door shut and struggled to remove the key. Disappointment choked in his throat and his stomach cramped with a stabbing pain. He pulled at the key and it eventually came free in his hand. He turned and ran back to the car. The wheels spun on the black asphalt surface. He drove out into the late morning traffic having no idea where he was going, only that he could not return to an empty flat.

In contrast, Carol's life became very full with events in which she took little pleasure.

'That is the second one of those you have had.' Peter sounded alarmed as Carol slid the spoon between her lips. A drop of white cream settled on the corner of her mouth and she discreetly removed it with a stroke of her finger.

'It's delicious.' She replied, unconcerned.

'I don't care.' Peter retorted, 'Remember what the doctor said about putting on extra weight.'

'Oh Peter, give me a break, it's only a bowl of strawberries.'

'It's not only the strawberries.' Peter was not going to be put off. 'The cream and that glass of champagne will not be good for you or the baby.' Carol let the comment pass.

The late summer sun reflected off the white canvass surface of the marquee. In the corner of the giant tent the Royal Marines Band sat behind their music stands and entertained the crowd.

'Captain Wells, congratulations on your appointment.' Peter looked round and into the smiling face of a Royal Air Force Wing Commander. The officers shook hands.

'Thank you very much, John.' Peter replied and returned the smile.

'Congratulations to you Mrs. Wells.' The airman continued. 'I understand you are soon to be a mother.' Carol smiled an embarrassed smile.

'Not until February.' She replied.

'Well, I wish you both the best of health.' He smiled and walked on. Carol spoke through her smile.

'Who was that?'

'John Morrison, he's in charge of the Air Force section here.'

'How did he know about the baby? I hardly show.'

'You can't keep secrets in a small community like this.' Peter hoped Carol would let the subject drop.

'You can if you don't let it out in the first place.' She replied through clenched teeth. 'You've only been here a few weeks and everybody knows our business.'

Peter took Carol's arm and guided her out of the marquee and onto the open lawn.

'What is wrong with people knowing that you are pregnant?' He looked about them as he spoke. Carol's answer was on her tongue awaiting the chance to be heard.

'This is a small place and I don't want to be the centre of everyone's petty gossip.' She adopted a mocking tone in her voice, 'did you hear the Captain's wife is pregnant? When is it due? They have left it a bit late haven't they? Oh, he already has a son in his twenties, this is his second wife.'

'All right. That's enough.' Peter's anger unfurled like a battle ensign and Carol knew that she had gone too far. 'I am going to be a father for the second time and I am proud of that fact. I know, at first, I was not too keen on the idea, but, now I am. I do not see why it should be such a big secret.' He waited to see if his words were getting home before continuing. 'I am the commanding officer of this establishment and these people are my second family.' As if by way of illustration he looked around. 'I wanted them to know. Not all one thousand of them. Just a select few. I do not see anything wrong with that.' He looked into Carol's eyes and commanded her attention. 'I would like you to remember that you are a part of this world. That is why you are here now. On a ship the Captain's wife can keep a low profile, ashore, she is an integral part of the social structure of the establishment. I want, and I expect you, to play your part.'

Carol's brown eyes narrowed and she breathed deeply to suppress her displeasure. She knew this was not the place to pursue the argument and it frustrated her to remain silent. She looked about at the uniformed officers and their ladies. She had always enjoyed these, 'strawberry and cream 'do's' because the champagne flowed and the food was deliciously decadent. However, she was not going to be used as a walking, talking symbol of the Captain's power. She would not say so now. That would be a waste of breath. Peter would learn soon enough.

'Captain Wells, Mrs. Wells, how good to see you.'

The high pitched feminine voice startled them both. They looked to see a woman in her late forties, dressed in a high necked, navy blue dress that gave her thin neck the look of a tortoise extending its head to explore the world outside of its shell. Her hair, which had been left to turn its natural colour, was neatly set in a French pleat. She spoke to Carol.

'Will you be joining the riding club, Mrs. Wells? We have a very good stable here.' She pointed with her bird like hand towards the trees that bordered the establishment's main gate. 'They are down there.'

Peter wondered how such a frail looking woman

could control a horse, let alone be the exceptional horsewoman he knew her to be. She was the wife of the First Lieutenant, an officer who had risen through the ranks to be the third in command of this large establishment. Peter answered for Carol;

'I'm afraid Carol has some very special cargo aboard and we cannot risk damaging it. We have agreed no more horses until after the baby is born.'

Carol tried to hide her annoyance and surprise. She could not recall any such agreement and resented having words spoken on her behalf. A smile veiled her lips, but, could not conceal the annoyance in her eyes. Peter's interjection also stunned the First Lieutenant's wife who fumbled for words to say next.

'Oh very well,' she finally spoke, 'perhaps we could meet for coffee?'

Carol cringed inside but continued to smile;

'That would be nice.' She lied.

'Yes, well, I must find my husband. It was good talking to you.' She looked at Carol. 'I will call you then?'

'That would be nice.' Carol replied and could have kicked herself for her lack of originality. Peter placed his arm around Carol's shoulders and gave her a hug.

'That's my girl.'

'Oh Peter, you know how I hate coffee mornings.' She whined like a petulant school girl.

'We serve where we can.' He squeezed her again. 'Come on, we'll have one more champagne and then that is it.'

'Party pooper.' Carol scoffed and walked with him back into the marquee.

As the long weeks of pregnancy passed Carol became more bored, restless and resentful. Peter refused to let her do anything for herself. Mrs. Cotes came every day to do the housework and it was getting so Carol could not stand the sight of the woman and dreaded the sound of her voice when she announced her arrival at the back door. If Carol wanted to go anywhere Peter insisted she use a taxi rather than get behind a steering wheel. He even tried to ban road journeys altogether. Carol longed for the day when she would be rid of the bump that went before her, draining her energy and chaining her to the house. However, she also knew that when the baby was born her unique position would disappear. Behind her desire for freedom was also the fear of what it would bring.

Letters from Nick kept arriving through the dying days of summer and into the golden hues of autumn. In the evening twilight Carol would bring out the letters and read them. Nick always mentioned the baby and always as an extension of herself.

Chapter 24

In the short days of November Peter announced that he had to attend a meeting in London. Carol insisted on going along. In a state of high excitement she telephoned Nick and arranged for them to meet for lunch.

'Are you sure he said he would be here to meet you?' Peter asked as he steered the Volvo off of the Embankment and into the car park of the Ministry of Defence.

'I told him I would be standing by the statue of Montgomery at eleven thirty.' She answered.

Peter looked at his watch,

'Well you have ten minutes to wait. I'll stay with you.'

Carol laughed.

'No you won't. You have a meeting to go to and naval Captains are never late. I'll be alright. No one is going to molest me in this condition.' For a split second the irony of this meeting struck her. Peter had only agreed to the outing because Nick would be looking after her. Her body trembled.

'Are you warm enough?' Peter was concerned and protective. 'It is pretty chilly today.'

Carol touched his arm.

'Don't fuss. I'm fine and the baby is centrally heated.'

'You look after him in the big city.' Peter got out and walked round the car to open the passenger door. Carol moved sideways and placed her feet on the ground. Placing her hands on the leather seat she pushed herself upright. Peter walked her to the pavement, kissed her on the cheek, warned her once again to be careful and returned to the car.

Carol watched as he slowly drove away. She then turned and walked around the side of the white building until she reached the grassed area on which stood the statue of the military leader. Her heart jumped when she saw Nick's broad back resting against the statue's solid plinth. She crossed the damp grass, keeping out of sight until she stood directly behind him.

'Boo!' She called and laughed. Nick leaped from the statue in faked alarm and placed a hand over his heart.

'Don't you know you can kill a man that way?' He smiled with eyes alight with pleasure. 'You look lovely.' As he admired her he noticed her blush under his gaze.

'Don't be stupid.' She was flattered but shy. 'The last time London saw a shape like this,' she looked down at her stomach, 'they were flying in the sky protecting the city from air raids.'

'Rubbish.' Nick scoffed and smiled. 'You look great.'

'Where are we going then?' Carol said and changed the subject.

'There is a restaurant down by the Embankment that I've heard is very good. I thought we would go there.'

'Sounds good to me.' Carol answered eagerly,

enjoying her freedom. They hailed a taxi and were soon in the bustling traffic passing alongside the Thames. 'I love these taxis. They are London for me. I don't come here enough.' Carol spoke like a young girl on a special outing.

'You are here now and it's so very good to see you.' The close proximity of their bodies made his words more intimate. 'Did you get my letters?' He asked.

Carol felt ashamed. She would not admit that, although she had not answered any, all were hidden at the back of her lingerie drawer.

'You know why I couldn't answer them.' She spoke quietly and they sat in silence for a few minutes staring out of opposite sides of the taxi.

'It looks delightful.' Carol exclaimed as they walked through the heavily framed dark oak doorway. 'How did you find this place?'

'I haven't actually been here before, but I have heard it's good.' Nick owned up.

'Well, it looks lovely.' Carol smiled up at him as they walked to the bar.

Time had made them intimate strangers and conversation did not come easily. Nick felt exposed on the high bar stool and as soon as the first drink was finished suggested they find their table. The menu afforded a small measure of protection and Nick was grateful for having something in common to talk about. It was not until they finished the second glass of wine that either felt at ease. It was Nick who spoke first.

'Only three months to the big day. How's it going?' It was a very open question to which Carol offered a guarded reply. Nick was not satisfied. 'How's my father taking the waiting?'

It was a question Carol could not ignore. The alcohol relaxed her inhibitions and the frustrations of the past six months weakened her loyalty.

'He is looking forward to having a son.' Nick knew exactly what she meant and stayed silent. 'Peter will not let me do a thing for myself in case I harm the boy.' Carol fell silent for a moment. 'I suppose I should be grateful for the attention.' Her voice trailed away as she became lost in her thoughts. Nick tried to bring her back.

'I'm glad he's looking after you.'

Carol's eyes flashed,

'He is looking after the baby.' She replied and said no more. The meal arrived and released them from immediate conversation. They ate in silence and then Nick spoke again,

'Why don't we do this again?'

Carol looked up from the table and into his eyes.

'Nick, you are priceless.' She said and he moved uneasily in his seat. 'Here we are hardly saying a word to each other and you want to do it again.' Nick dropped his head and stared at the food in front of him. Carol knew she had gone too far. 'No, wait a minute, you're right. We haven't seen very much of each other for a long time. You have seen even less of Peter. We should all get together.' This was not what Nick had meant.

'I don't want a family reunion. I have had one of those. I want to see you. We could have lunch, dinner, a walk in the country, anything. I just want to be with you.'

Slowly and deliberately Carol pushed the plate away from her. She glanced out of the window at the brown water of the Thames. Nick sat motionless, not taking his eyes from her face. Eventually she spoke;

'We both know why that is not possible.' Nick was about to object when Carol raised her hand to stop him. 'I am not going to argue with you Nick and if you make things difficult I can't see how we can be together at all.' The words came easily to her lips but tore at her heart as they were said. Nick remained silent. The mere hint of losing her caused a flutter of panic in the pit of his stomach. His face mirrored his fears and Carol reached out across the table to rest her hand on his. She smiled to reassure him. 'What are you doing for Christmas?'

'Christmas!' Nick exclaimed, caught off guard by the question.

'Yes. Christmas. It's not far away. How about spending it with us?' Nick shook his head. His face had not relaxed its frown and Carol became annoyed. 'Well, do you want to come or not?'

The waiter interrupted Nick's answer as he cleared the table and asked if they wanted coffee. They ordered and when Nick judged that the waiter was out of earshot answered,

'I will have to spend Christmas Day at home. I can't get out of that.' His voice lacked enthusiasm.

'What about Boxing Day?' Carol asked, now becoming concerned. Nick thought for a moment.

'Yes. I can do that.' He answered, although there was still hesitation in his voice. Carol found herself becoming agitated. Nick was lost in his thoughts and just as her quota of patience had almost run its course he spoke again. 'I have a trip on the twenty seventh and there is no way I can go sick for that if I want leave in February when the baby is born.' The mention of the birth made Carol's heart skip a number of beats. 'I could come for the day.'

Carol nodded her head and told him that would be fine. Their coffee arrived and Nick suggested they have a liqueur with it. Carol remembered the baby inside her and refused.

Outside the restaurant the street lamps flickered into life and bathed the afternoon gloom in a sickly orange glow.

'I hate November. The short days and bleak, long nights and nothing to look forward to.' Carol looked out of the window as she spoke. 'At least in December there is Christmas and the New Year. November gives nothing except fog, rain and hours of lonely darkness.' The words trailed off as Carol looked away from the world outside the restaurant and into the bottom of her empty coffee cup. 'I better be going. Peter said he would be finished by four thirty. He wants to get out of London before the exodus.' Nick smiled knowingly and signalled for the bill.

As they walked out into the gathering gloom, the evening's cold, damp veil settled upon them. Nick buttoned the top of his coat and looked along the congested road for the rounded, black shape of a taxi. He caught sight of one cutting across the lanes and it was empty. Instantly, his arm shot out and he ran to the curbside. As if homing in on an electronic signal the cab pulled out of the traffic and halted without appearing to slow down at all.

'Where to guv?' A flat and sweat stained cap sat squarely on the cabbies head and a pencil was wedged behind his right ear.

'The lady will be going to the Ministry of Defence.' Carol looked surprised.

'Where are you going?' She asked in alarm. Nick looked at her with uncertain eyes.

'I came by train. My station is just down there.' He pointed.

'Aren't you coming to see Peter?' She asked and felt suddenly exposed. Nick had opened the door and she could see the driver listening to their conversation. 'Come on Nick. The driver's waiting.'

'I can't.' He confessed and Carol could see how vulnerable he was. 'I'll see him on Boxing Day. Tell him I had a night departure and had to get back to pack my case.' He stepped forward and gently kissed her on the cheek. Carol smiled and kissed him back.

'Hurry up lady. I'll be done for parking if I stay much longer.' The cab driver called through the open door.

'You better go and thanks for coming. Thanks for everything.' Nick said and smiled.

Impulsively Carol leaned forward and kissed his lips.

'Thanks for lunch, see you soon.' She turned and got into the cab. Nick closed the door and the car pulled away before he could say anything more.

Carol looked back through the rear window to see Nick walking away. She hoped he would look round so that their eyes would meet just one more time. He did not and she sat back against the black seat, disappointed and alone.

Chapter 25

On a cold and clear Christmas Eve Carol and Peter attended the Midnight Mass in the village church. In her present condition Carol felt the Christian message more than she had ever in the past. The circumstances of motherhood seemed to bring the birth of Christ closer. She sat in her pew looking up at the white haired vicar. His old face was lined and his soulful eyes reflected a life spent shouldering the burdens of others. Carol let his voice flow over her, soothing and calming the fears that had arisen as the days of the birth drew nearer. Boredom had provided the time for thought and thought brought trepidation. Fear of the unknown, fear of pain, fear of a child that was not 'normal'. Peter's breezy confidence did nothing to allay her anxiety. He was already playing the part of the proud father and would not listen to any suggestion that even hinted that his son would be anything but a healthy and intelligent boy who would make a superb naval officer.

Carol was trotted out to all the Christmas affairs and hated every one of them. She was not a woman to take pride in her condition. She hated her distended abdomen and pleaded with Peter to let her stay home and get fat in peace. He laughed off every request and protest, citing the doctor's praise about her not having put on an ounce over the baby's weight. For Carol, that weight and her shape were more than enough.

At these functions the conversation invariably centred on the maternal and Carol soon tired of the clichés and the horror stories about the trauma of childbirth. She invariably sat down. Peter insisted she not tire herself. While looking at the legs of those around her she told herself that there had to be a way out.

Christmas Day passed in almost total silence. In the morning, as always, Peter rose early and despite the chilling wind went for his two mile run across the field. On his return he brought a cup of tea to Carol's bedside. Both activities had now become a ritual. The former Peter had always done when he was ashore, the latter was added when Carol started carrying his 'son'.

Even on Christmas Day, and, in the privacy of their bedroom, Peter's naval cravat did not look out of place. Carol had known him too long for that. However, on this day it appeared to fly from his neck like a battle ensign. It was the symbol of the service that would take her son away and Peter was the instrument of its will. Such was the conviction that Peter wrought in her. The unborn child must indeed be a boy. A son she would bear but would never know. Peter would take him for his own and cast her out as an instrument unbending to his will and no longer required.

Carol dressed and went downstairs. Breakfast was simple. A bowl of cereal and a glass of orange juice. Peter had gone outside to secure the paddock gate that had blown open by the strong winds that rose with the dawn. Carol ate in silence and then walked into the darkened sitting room. Crossing to the heavy velvet curtains she glanced at the small green tree that stood forlornly in the corner. Five coloured baubles hung from its spiky branches and a silver star perched precariously on its summit. Around its potted base and stacked with parade ground precision were eight boxes wrapped in colourful paper of red and green. Carol was excited and surprised at the sight of so many parcels and intrigued to know what was in the largest that lay at the bottom and supported the pile. Like a young girl she looked over her shoulder before going to check the names on each wrapped box. At first she toyed with the labels, looking at festive scenes on each and marveling that Peter should have taken so much trouble over each one. Then, when she felt completely alone, she read the writing, in Peter's hand, on the largest parcel. *'To my Son with All My Love from Dad.'*

Disbelief, hatred, panic, all these emotions tore at her. Her heart pounded within her breast and she felt the passage of bile in the back of her throat. Grasping the swelling of her body she fought to calm herself. She swallowed and closed her eyes. As her breathing became more regular so the coldness on her skin gradually disappeared until she felt sufficiently recovered to look at the cards on the other packages. All but two had the same message. She saw her present to Peter and soon found the one labelled for her. Taking it in her hands she hurled the parcel across the room. It landed and tumbled to a halt at Peter's feet.

He stood in the doorway, tall and dominating. His face wore an expression of annoyed, curiosity.

'What are you doing?' The question demanded an answer. Carol sat on her haunches and buried her head in her hands.

'You really don't know, do you?'

The desperation in her voice brought him nearer. Kneeling, he placed his arms about her shoulders and rested his lips on her forehead. He increased the pressure of his arms and drew her body to him.

'I know this must be an emotional time for you.' He chose his words carefully. 'We do not have long to wait now and I will be with you all the way.' Carol broke down and cried and her body shook in his arms.

'Oh Peter.' She sobbed, unable to say more.

He held her until her body stopped convulsing with each new flow of tears, and, when she had been still for a few minutes he judged that it was time to move.

'Come on let's open the presents.' He got to his feet and held out his hands. Carol wiped her eyes with the back of her hands and allowed herself to be lifted to her feet. They walked over to the tree and Peter discreetly placed the wayward present back among the other parcels.

Carol's hands went mechanically through the motions of removing the layers of wrapping paper while Peter waited expectantly to witness her surprise. His disappointment and hurt was etched in the lines of his face. Eventually he had to say something,

'Don't you like it?'

Carol was opening the fourth package and sat among piles of torn paper, cardboard, toys and blue baby clothes. She put down the half opened parcel and picked up a navy blue track suit of the minutest proportions. Holding the soft material to her cheek she raised her head to look at her husband,

'It's bad luck.' She sighed, unable to truly express the fear and despair she felt so painfully in her heart.

Peter dismissed the words with a laugh.

'Don't be silly. How can it be bad luck' He scoffed. Carol felt herself rising to the bait and could not stop from taking it.

'What if it's a girl?' She wanted to goad him. Upset his well-formed plan. Place doubt where there was certainty. Instead, he knelt before her, his face full of confidence.

'Come on, you know better than that.' He smiled, but there was no trace of it in his eyes. 'It wouldn't dare.'

'That's a lovely ring.' Carol's mother held her daughter's left hand and admired the band of diamonds that encircled her finger. Carol's parents had come for Christmas dinner and ended up as the table and kitchen staff. Peter refused to allow Carol to either carry a plate or use a tea towel. Carol followed her mother's eyes to rest on the eternity ring.

'He is a little premature isn't he?' The comment delivered in complete innocence caused Carol to laugh aloud.

'I am getting used to it.' She replied.

That night the events of the day swirled around

behind Carol's eyes and collided with the dull, persistent throbbing of a sick headache that would not go away. She opened her eyes to look at the sleeping face of her husband. He was secure in his own world, a world that owned him and was now asking for another sacrifice. An unborn child was to be taken and fashioned in its image. Carol screwed her eyes shut and wanted to cry out. To scream for the pain to go away and to tell the alien force that it would not triumph. It would not triumph because she, the mother, would not allow it. She wanted to fight but even more than that she wanted the dancing world behind her eyes to settle and the head splitting ache to leave her.

The final weeks of pregnancy brought with them the return of the dizziness and headaches she thought had gone with her youth. In the first years of marriage she bore the distressing attacks as the price she had to pay for abandoning Philip Sewel and adapting to life as Mrs. Peter Wells. Time had appeared to prove her right as the frequency of the headaches became less with the passing years. Prior to pregnancy, if she reached for a sedative it was because she could not adapt to the situations life presented her. At that time she convinced herself that all women thought the same. As if as payment for those times of weakness she now had to accept the pain knowing that she would not risk harming her baby by taking any form of drug. Her only recourse was to close her eyes and pray that she would find relief and salvation in childbirth.

'Why do you want to go there? You've only been home two days. Who invited you? Your father or her?' Nick relived the inquisition over and over again. As his finger touched the doorbell those last words swept over him. The reference to Carol was like an obscenity expelled from his mother's lips. The metallic chime echoed in the hall and his mind went back to the answer he had given.

'Carol invited me if you must know.' He would never forget his mother's sneering look and knowing reply.

'Infatuation. I thought boys got over crushes in school.'

'Nick, it's good to see you. Merry Christmas.' Peter grasped his son's hand in a vice like grip. 'Come on in, come on in, and get out of this freezing weather. Christmas is all very well but why does it have to be so damn cold?' He shut the door and led the way into the warm house. 'Carol, Nick's here.' He called into the lounge room. Carol lifted herself out of the arm chair and walked heavily over to greet him. They kissed formally but held onto each other's hands long after their lips parted.

'I am so glad you could make it.' Carol's voice was almost a whisper. A shy smile crossed Nick's lips.

'I wouldn't have missed it for the world.'

'All right you two, break it up. Just remember she's your step-mother Nick. I knew I should never have married a woman ten years younger than myself. They attract too much attention.' While Peter joked Nick and Carol separated. He did not notice their discomfort. 'Where did we put Nick's present?' He asked Carol.

Carol was thankful for having something to do and went to the tree to collect the parcel. Unwrapping the folds of paper Nick exposed a black box hinged along one edge. Expectantly he raised the small lid to reveal a silver fountain pen with his initials engraved along its shaft. He took it out and felt its balanced weight between his fingers. His face was alight with joy.

'No excuse for not staying in touch.' Carol said and her eyes smiled up at him.

Presents had been exchanged and they settled down in front of the blazing log fire to drink sherry and eat mince pies and Christmas cake. Nick placed his empty plate on the low table in the centre of the room and turned to ask Carol when she had time to bake? As he watched a light went out behind Carol's eyes.

'I didn't. Mrs. Cotes made it all.'

Nick understood and said no more. Peter was oblivious to the meaning behind the words and asked;

'Nick, I have to go down to the school to check up on a few things. Do you want to come along?' The expression on Nick's face said more than words ever could. Peter smiled. 'I know it's Boxing Day but there is no rest for the wicked.'

Nick thought fast. He had not driven down for the day to spend it in a deserted naval establishment where he suspected his father only wanted to press his case for Nick to enter the service. He looked to Carol and asked if she would be going along. She shook her head and answered.

'No. I have dinner to prepare.' She quickly corrected herself. 'I mean, to put on the table.'

Nick felt momentarily lost and then inspiration came. He looked to his father;

'If you don't mind I will stay and give Carol a hand.' He knew Peter could not argue after all he had said about Carol not over doing it. However, he did notice the disappointment in the set of the mouth and the hardness behind his father's eyes.

Peter got to his feet and went to collect his overcoat from the porch at the rear of the house. As he returned and passed the doorway he looked in.

'I won't be long. See you both later.'

Nick and Carol sat in silence while they waited for the front door to close.

'Do you think I should have gone?' Nick asked. Carol heard the need for reassurance in his voice.

'Did you want to go?' Her abruptness caught Nick off guard.

'No.' He answered and shrugged his shoulders.

'Well then. You did the right thing.'

The barrier was going up. Carol knew that Nick was trying to take over that part of her life he felt his father had forfeited. She had already decided that no one was required in that role.

Nick was persistent.

'Why does he have to go to work on Boxing Day?' Carol smiled, seeing the purpose behind the question.

'I thought you would know your father better than that by now. He never leaves work. I despise him for it, but, even I have to admit that it is that kind of determination that has got him this far, and will get him to the top.'

Nick continued to probe.

'Why did you marry him?'

Carol's eyes narrowed as she looked into his open face. 'The time has come,' she thought.

'I think we have had this discussion before.' She said. Nick moved uncomfortably in his chair as Carol answered his question. 'I married Peter because I loved him. I was foolish enough to think that he could love me as well as the Navy.' She paused to reflect on her words. 'In his own way I expect he does.' With difficulty Carol got to her feet. 'I respect Peter for what he stands for, and for his success; but, I can no longer live with him.' Nick sat upright as if struck between the shoulder blades. He had instigated this conversation to enhance his position in Carol's eyes at the expense of his father. He did not expect such an easy victory. His heart was beating so hard he thought she must surely hear it. Carol paced the room, cradling the unborn baby in her intertwined fingers. She did not look at him while she spoke. 'As soon as the baby is born I am going to leave him.' Her voice was resolute. Nick's reply was tactlessly blurted out;

'Why don't you leave him now? You can come and stay with me. I would look after you and the baby.'

Carol's expression did not change. Her face remained impassive, her voice unchanged.

'I want my child to have a name. The poor thing will have a hard enough time as it is without being a bastard.' The word and the way it was delivered stung Nick into replying and saying words he did not want to contemplate.

'He won't let you go.'

'What if it's a girl?' Carol's reply was quick and revealed a truth they both knew. 'If Peter knew that I was going to bear him a daughter, do you think he would hang onto me then?

Nick replied sharply.

'That's a stupid thing to say. He is not likely to let it be seen that he is the sort of man that kicks his wife out because she is giving him a baby girl.'

'Damn you men!' Carol exploded. 'I am not giving him a baby. It is my baby!' Nick felt his gut tighten as Carol continued. 'You say that he wouldn't throw me out. Okay, you're probably right, but, I don't know that for sure. That is not the point. How do you think I feel knowing that if he thought I was carrying a girl he would drop me like the proverbial hot potato? I want to be the one to say I have had enough. I am not going to hang around and watch him take my son away from me, or worse still, ignore my daughter. Can you imagine what will happen if I don't provide him with a son?'

Nick had not considered the prospect, caught up as he was in his father's certainty of having a son and heir. Carol was not waiting for answers from anyone. She knew what must be done and had already formulated her plan. When she spoke again, her voice was charged with bitterness and disappointment.

'Either way I lose and I'm not staying around to see my own life and the life of my child destroyed by the ambitions of a …' She stopped suddenly. The words that entered her mind were not for the world to hear. Silence once more enveloped the dimly lit room.

Carol ambled across to the window and stared out at the misty grey sky that shrouded the barren trees so thickly that it looked like falling rain.

Nick stared after her. He knew then that not only his father but he too was losing her. He had to say something. To remain silent was to admit defeat.

'I would look after you and the baby.' Carol turned away from the window. Nick continued defensively; 'no strings, honest. I'm only saying that, if you need somewhere to go, then come to me.'

Carol placed her hands behind her and leaned back on the window sill. Her face had lost its anger and her voice was tender now.

'You must know that this is not your baby.' She took one hand away from the window and patted her bulging stomach. 'I appreciate your kindness and I value your friendship, but, I am not looking for a relationship to replace the one that has died... and I do not want to come between you and your father.' She reflected for a moment and then added, 'perhaps I should have thought about that a little sooner.' Nick flinched at her honesty and Carol saw his anguish. 'I want us to be friends, close friends. I would like to see you...but, I'll never come and live with you.' She moved away from the window and came to stand in front of him. She leaned forward and her lips brushed his forehead. He looked in her eyes in hopeful expectation but she moved away once more. In the middle of the room she turned and her voice was lowered in a tone of intimate conspiracy.

'There is one favour I must ask of you. It's a big one and I would not ask if I didn't think my future, and the future of my baby, depended upon it.'

Nick held out his open hands to her.

'Anything. You name it.' Carol came to him once again and sat beside him on the settee.

'I don't want Peter to know anything of what we have said here today.'

Nick smiled. He could not fail to miss the hypocrisy in what Carol asked and what she had said about not coming between father and son. He could not ignore it, but he could overlook it. He would do as she asked.

'Thanks Nick.' She kissed and leaned against him, resting her head on his shoulder. He enjoyed the pressure of her body against his and stayed motionless in case any movement should scare her away. 'Oh Nick.' Her voice was muffled in the breadth of his chest. 'Sometimes I feel completely alone.'

At that moment she appeared so helpless that Nick wanted to take her in his arms and hold her until her fears were gone. Before he could act she pulled away and was gone.

'I'll go and see about dinner... You stay here. I'll be right back.'

Obediently Nick stayed in his seat and tried to understand the two personalities he had been with in those precious minutes. She had been scared and he could not help her. Then, she had been so full of confidence he wondered if she needed him at all.

Peter returned as the sky was turning to the darker hue of approaching night. Nick had helped Carol lay the table and now they sat eating cold turkey and re-heated Christmas pudding. The conversation was about the world, its cities, customs, adventures and experiences. If the others did see the direction in which the conversation was being guided they acted too late. Peter adroitly transformed an anecdote about a New Year run ashore in Singapore to a commentary on what the coming year had in store for him, and then to what it could mean for Nick. He spoke of his afternoon visit to the school.

'You should have come with me Nick. I could have shown you what the Navy of today is capable of doing. We have a big job to do and not everybody is up to it.' He stopped and looked into Nick's face. 'I believe you are.' He saw Nick's lips move and raised his right hand to stop him. 'Don't say anything just yet. I am not saying this because you are my son. You are a very bright young man and you have a great deal to offer any employer, but, you have an even greater responsibility to use your ability for the benefit of someone other than yourself. This year you can do something about that.'

Nick resented having to defend himself to a man who had forsaken him so many years before.

'I have a career that I enjoy. I agree that it doesn't extend me but who needs artificial responsibilities? The only responsibilities that I feel are worthwhile are those to do with the family.' The barb had been thrown and he saw by the set of Peter's jaw that it had struck home. Nick saw victory in his grasp and abandoned caution. 'What has your career responsibilities cost you? Do you know what it cost me? It cost me a father I never knew, just a faded photograph hidden away in the back of a disused drawer.' He stopped abruptly. He had gone too far. Surely victory was not worth this? 'Sorry I should not have said that. It wasn't fair.'

Carol took the opportunity to step in and separate father and son.

'I think enough has been said on both sides and we all know that nothing in this world comes easily and nothing is free. What is important is that we are together now and who knows, it may be the last Christmas where we are all gathered around this table.'

Peter was quick to stop her.

'Don't be so maudlin. If that is how these father and son discussions affect you then I for one am only too pleased to let the subject drop. What do you say Nick?' His son's attention was focused on Carol and Peter had to repeat the question, 'well Nick how about it?'

The words filtered through to Nick's consciousness where they mingled with Carol's declaration and his own troubled thoughts. He could not ignore how easily she spun her web. She knew they would not be together next year and was revelling in her deceit. He had been used but could not betray her. He agreed to the truce. They returned to their dinner and finished the meal in a silence that shielded them all.

After the coffee cups were cleared away Nick looked at his watch. It was eight o'clock and he still had to pack for his flight the following day.

'I feel bad about leaving you with the dishes.' He apologised.

'I bet you do.' Carol grinned and went to collect his coat. She soon returned and he put it on.

'Remember me at New Year somewhere in the heart of Africa.' He joked.

'You enjoy the sunshine and think of us freezing in

the heart of Hampshire.' Carol smiled and he looked into the sensuous depth of her eyes, losing himself in their beauty and willing her not to forget him in the months ahead. It was Peter who broke the spell.

'Yes, you enjoy the celebrations wherever you are and come and see us in the New Year.'

The indifference in his voice caused concern for Nick and he spoke hurriedly,

'I will be here when the baby is born.' It was more a question than a statement and Nick was relieved when Carol spoke up.

'Of course you will.' She was smiling and once more Nick saw the intrigue in her eyes. 'Peter will call you as soon as I go into hospital.' Nick was smiling openly now.

'Thanks. It means a lot to me. I have got leave over that time so please, be punctual.' Carol smiled and he turned to Peter. 'I look forward to your call.' The men shook hands firmly and Nick returned his attention to Carol. 'Look after yourself and the baby.' He held her hands and kissed her gently on either cheek. He was stopped from expressing what his heart cried out to say by the powerful presence of his father.

The cold north wind tore at their warmed bodies as it blew through the open doorway. A fine covering of snow lay over the ground.

'Don't keep the door open. It's bitter out here.' Nick called back as he ran to the car. Each footfall crackled on the icy ground.

'You drive carefully.' Carol called after him.

Nick opened the car door and waved as he swung himself into the driver's seat. The engine turned over twice before coming to life. The penetrating beam from the headlights illuminated the thin blanket of falling snow. The tyres made their mark on the virgin covering as the car slowly moved away. Nick sounded two parting blasts on the horn as he drove out onto the country road, now glistening in shimmering whiteness.

Carol waved, closed the front door and turned to Peter, who was already walking back inside the house.

'You will call him when the baby is due, won't you Peter?' He stopped and faced her.

'I don't know why it is so important for him to be there, but, if that is what you want, of course I will.'

She came and wrapped her arms around his waist.

'Thank you.' She said and squeezed him gently.

Chapter 26

Dark clouds scudded across the sky. A watery full moon sat haloed in the heavens, its pale light highlighting the skeletal forms of the winter trees that made menacing images in the night. Peter locked the front door and was on his way to secure the back when Carol called excitedly from the top of the stairs

'Get the car Peter. It's happened!'

For a man trained for action and instant decisions, Captain Peter Wells RN was remarkably slow to react. Carol came down the stairs dressed in a nightgown and carrying a small overnight case to find him still standing in the hallway. For a moment she thought he looked like a little boy, lost in nervous indecision, staring up at her.

'Get a move on Peter or I will give birth right here and you can do the honours.'

The prospect struck a chord of urgency within him and he ran to collect his car keys from the hook in the kitchen. He unlocked the front door that he, only moments before, secured and ran to the garage. Carol heard the garage door open and the heavy throbbing of the car's two litre engine. She wrapped a heavy coat about her shoulders, picked up the case and closed the front door behind her. Peter brought the car to a stop and leant across to open the passenger door. He did not want to leave the driver's seat and so lose valuable seconds.

'Take it easy Peter.' Carol smilingly rebuked him as she positioned her rounded body on the car's front seat. 'We will be going to Casualty rather than Maternity if you are not careful.' Peter was not about to be put in his place.

'You take care of the child bearing and I will take care of the driving.' He replied. 'How long do you think we have got?' His voice was edgy with concern and he spoke quickly without waiting for answers to his question. 'Is the door closed? Good. Here we go.' So saying he placed the car into first gear, depressed the accelerator pedal and took his foot off the clutch. 'At least it's not raining.' Talking as much to himself as to Carol he spun the steering wheel through his hands and pointed the car's bonnet towards the open gate.

As they drove along the top of Portsdown Hill the dark clouds overhead looked close enough to touch. Below, the orange lights of the city traced out the main streets that led away to the Solent and the Isle of Wight beyond. Peter glanced to his right to catch a glimpse of the dockyard in the clear night sky.

'Oohh!' It was the first indication Carol had given that she was in pain. Peter turned to look at her.

'Are you all right? It's not coming is it?'

Carol inhaled noisily,

'I don't know. How long until we get there?'

Peter skirted the roundabout at the top of the hill and joined the road that led down to the hospital.

'We're nearly there. Hold on.' He said through clenched teeth.

It was a four wheel drift of which any rally driver would have been proud as Peter brought the car through the hospital gates. The brakes squealed as the heavy estate halted outside the entrance to the Maternity Department.

'You stay here.' Peter called as he left the car and ran through the swing doors. Carol grimaced again as another contraction passed down her abdomen. She took a deep breath and exhaled slowly through her teeth. Peter soon returned with a nurse, pushing a wheelchair, following close behind. Carol was speedily transferred to the chair and taken up in the lift to the ward on the second floor.

'You stay here Mr. Wells.' The nurse pointed to a small waiting room at the end of the highly polished corridor. He watched as Carol disappeared through a pair of green painted double doors. The title by which he had been addressed played on his mind. 'Why had Carol insisted on a civilian hospital when the naval hospital would have been far more suitable?'

Peter paced the room as earnestly as any father he had seen in countless old Hollywood movies. It then occurred to him that he must look the epitome of the expectant father and so stopped and sat down in one of the green plastic cushioned seats. A pile of outdated magazines lay stacked on a small table in one corner of the room. He walked across and thumbed through them. Finding nothing of interest he started pacing once again.

'Ah, Captain Wells.' To hear his correct title both startled and pleased him. He looked into the smiling face of a young man dressed in black corduroy trousers, a red plaid shirt and a white coat that hung loosely open about his shoulders. 'I am Doctor Jenner. Your wife is changed and in bed, you can go along and see her if you wish.' Peter looked confused.

'Aren't you going to take her to the delivery room?' The young doctor smiled.

'I don't think we will be seeing any action tonight. It has started all right, but, these first births usually drag themselves out. I have given your wife a mild sedative. She could be in for a long session and I want her to have a good night's sleep. Don't stay too long, and, for your own sake I would suggest you go home and get a good night's sleep yourself. We will call you in good time to get back here.'

Peter straightened at the doctor's familiarity and the suggestion that he should go home. He was not accustomed to being advised by a man so many years his junior.

'I will stay if you don't mind. In my career one gets used to long nights out of bed.' The doctor nodded his head.

'I'm sure you do. Well, I'll leave you to it.' He turned to go and then stopped. 'Remember do not stay too long. You will find Mrs. Wells through those doors on the right.' He pointed up the polished corridor and then walked off in the opposite direction.

Peter found Carol propped up against two billowing white pillows, sipping warm milk. She looked radiant, her cheeks flushed, her eyes bright and expectant.

'The doctor says that nothing is going to happen until the morning.' Peter said and checked his watch. It was ten minutes passed midnight, twenty minutes ago they were at home preparing for bed. 'He is very young, isn't he?' Peter continued with concern in his voice.

'Yes he is, and he knows what he is doing. Will you be going home? They will call you when it is time.' Peter shook his head.

'No, I'll stay in the waiting room. I don't think I would sleep even if I was at home.'

'I think I'm going to.' Carol's voice suddenly sounded drowsy. Peter guessed the drug was taking effect. She settled lower in the bed. He bent over to kiss her forehead.

'See you in the morning.' He whispered. She smiled back at him.

'Yes, it's a big day.' He was turning to leave when her soft voice stopped him. 'Don't forget to call Nick. He will want to get down here.' Peter felt the hair rise on the back of his neck but managed to answer in a calm voice.

'I will do that right now. You go to sleep and I'll see you in the morning.'

He walked from the room annoyed at his own pettiness. Stopping a passing orderly he asked the location of the nearest telephone. A few minutes later Nick's confused voice could be heard in the receiver. Peter delivered his message. Nick immediately came awake.

'I'll be there in an hour and a half. Don't let her start without me.'

Peter laughed and relieved some of the tension he had been feeling, but would not admit to.

'I don't think we can do anything about that, but I can tell you how to get here.'

'Good thinking.' Nick's voice was heady with excitement. Peter gave the directions and a warning.

'Drive carefully, there is lots of time.'

He replaced the receiver and returned to pace the waiting room as he had the bridges of so many ships. A nurse entered and asked if he would like some tea. He accepted eagerly and, as she was leaving, asked about Carol. The nurse looked teasingly back at him.

'She is fast asleep and having a far more comfortable night than you. Why don't you go home?'

'I'll stay thanks very much.' Peter answered. The nurse smiled and left him to his vigil.

Peter had resolved not to keep looking at his watch and so when Nick came hurrying up the cream linoleum staircase and into the corridor outside the waiting room he was taken by surprise.

'How did you get here so fast?' Peter asked as Nick entered the waiting room. The men shook hands. 'Did one of your jumbo jets drop you off?' Nick smiled and answered.

'The roads are pretty clear this time of night and there is no rain about.' He paused to catch his breath. The run from the car park and up the two flights of stairs had winded him. When he could speak without panting he continued. 'This is all a bit sudden isn't it? I only got home this morning,' He checked his watch. 'Or should

I say yesterday morning. I thought the baby wasn't due until Wednesday. Any earlier and I would have missed it all together.' Peter's eyebrows raised as he suppressed his thoughts and offered an explanation.

'These first babies are not the most punctual of God's creations.'

'You can say that again.' Nick replied and his eyes fell on the empty cup. 'Where did you get the drink?'

'A nurse brought it for the expectant father.' Peter replied with a smile. Nick looked concerned and then remembered a vending machine he had passed at the bottom of the stairs.

'Would you like a refill?' He asked and Peter accepted. Nick removed his coat, threw it onto one of the chairs and left the room. Peter was happy to be alone once again. He could not deny the feeling of jealousy at having someone else there sharing, what he considered to be, his duty. Left to his thoughts he became more annoyed about his diminishing role. He recalled Carol's wish not to have him present at the birth. She had been adamant. She had insisted that it was her responsibility, and when the baby was born she would present it to him.

'One tea for you and there are also sandwiches. I bought two rounds.' Nick handed a paper cup and one of the sandwiches to Peter. 'When was Carol admitted?' He asked as he sat down. Peter recounted the events while Nick sat with his feet resting on another chair he had positioned in front of him. He had kicked off his trainers. 'Sorry about this, but, it looks like being a long night. I think I better get comfortable.'

They talked for a couple of hours before Nick said he was going to get some sleep. Peter watched him settle down under the cover of his faded leather jacket. He looked at his watch again. It was nearly four thirty. He began pacing once more.

'Arghh. I can't move my neck.' Nick complained as he came round from what appeared to Peter to have been a remarkably sound sleep.

'You certainly slept well.' He commented and Nick laughed.

'I'm good at it. Did you get any shut eye?' Peter shook his head. 'You must be knackered.' Nick exclaimed. 'I'll get some coffee. What time is it?' Peter looked at his watch. It was now a reflex action.

'Half seven.'

'Any action up the corridor?' Nick asked and glanced at the door to Carol's room. Peter shook his head.

'I haven't seen a nurse go in there lately. I expect she's still asleep.'

Nick fastened the laces on his shoes and stood up.

'Well, don't let anything happen until I get back.' He said and ran out of the waiting room. Peter smiled after him, realising he had enjoyed his company during the long night. Even though Nick had deserted him in sleep, it was a support just having him there. Peter felt the beard stubble on his chin as he walked out along the corridor. The pale green doors of Carol's room drew nearer and Peter looked about him like a criminal. Seeing no one he moved toward the door.

'Can I help you?'

The stern face of the ward sister froze him in his

tracks. He turned and looked into the disciplined face. She wore little make up, her brown hair was streaked with grey and tied in a severe bun that perched on top of her head. In an apologetic tone Peter explained that he was hoping to see his wife.

'Mrs. Wells is still sleeping Captain. We will call you as soon as she is ready to accept visitors.'

Peter was pleased to hear his correct title being used. He made a mental note to thank them for their courtesy. He returned to the waiting room and found himself looking forward to the coffee Nick was to bring. It had been a long night.

Another hour passed before Peter was summoned to Carol's bedside. Nick remained in the corridor until Peter told Carol that he was outside.

'Oh let him come in Peter.' Carol said excitedly. She sat up in the bed and quickly played with her hair. Nick walked in, his eyes lighting up when he saw her.

'Hello.' He said warmly. 'You look lovely.' Carol felt herself blush. Nick walked forward and kissed her on the cheek. 'How do you feel?'

'I don't think I will be waiting too much longer.' As if waiting for its cue the baby moved and, for the second time since Peter had been there, Carol's face contorted with pain. 'Ooh, that was a strong one.' She said through gritted teeth. The two men stood by, their faces reflecting their concern and inadequacy. Peter spoke awkwardly. He was well and truly out of his element.

'Isn't there some gas or something they can give you to ease the pain?' The defiant smile that crossed Carol's face said it all.

'They are not going to take this experience away from me, and I do not care how much it hurts.'

The men stood in silence, each admiring her spirit and thankful that it was the woman's lot to endure the trials and tribulations of childbirth.

'All right gentlemen. I will have to ask you to leave now.' Dr. Jenner's voice was friendly but insistent. He looked at Carol. 'Are you ready to do your stuff Mrs. Wells?' Carol smiled back at him. Peter moved close to the bed and their lips touched.

'I will be just outside if you need me.' He whispered and she kissed him back.

Seeing the two so close Nick moved back toward the door. He waved when Carol looked over.

'See you later.' She mouthed the words and returned his wave.

'You really must go now Captain.' The doctor was positioning himself by the side of the bed as two porters entered to push Carol's bed into the delivery room.

Peter left with a backward glance. Carol was in deep conversation with the doctor and then he saw her face contort again as the pain of another contraction took hold of her.

The men watched as Carol and her entourage travelled the short distance to the delivery room.

'She really was in pain, wasn't she?' Nick's voice and worried expression told the world that this was definitely his first time in a maternity ward. Peter smiled smugly to himself until he recalled that at the time of Nick's birth he was somewhere in the North Sea. This was his first time as well.

Now, both men paced the waiting room, their paths crossing the worn blue carpet. Peter forced himself not to look at his watch every few minutes and then cursed the hospital for not having a clock on the wall.

'It's taking a long time, isn't it? Does it always take this long?' Nick's question gave vent to the tension mounting within him. Peter knew this and realised an answer was not really necessary. He was about to speak anyway when the white coated figure of the doctor interrupted him. Peter watched as the doctor came out of the delivery room and walked purposefully down the corridor toward them. Peter left the room to meet the doctor but the younger man took his arm and guided him back inside.

'How is the boy doctor?' The words exploded from Peter's mouth so that even he was unaware of the slip he had made. Jenner looked puzzled but quickly put that out of his mind.

'Captain Wells, perhaps you would like to sit down?' The doctor's voice was grave. It was Peter's turn to look confused.

'Why should I want to sit down?' He asked with innocence tinged with dread. The doctor's eyes narrowed as he began to speak.

'I am afraid that I have some very bad news.'

Nick took two steps forward to stand on Peter's right hand side. His stomach suddenly felt empty.

'What do you mean, Doctor?' Peter assumed his command voice and folded his arms in front of him.

'I am very sorry Captain.' Peter's back arched as he pushed down on his hands. 'Your wife passed away during delivery.' He waited for the words to register, knowing that he had to convey his grim news while the brain was too numb to react to its grief.

'Carol is dead?' Peter's voice echoed his disbelief. His eyes widened and he shook his head to try and clear the mist that was clouding his brain. The doctor nodded his head and Peter spoke again, 'and the baby?'

Jenner's face relaxed but did not smile.

'Mrs. Wells gave birth to a daughter. The baby is doing well... and that is a blessing.'

'A daughter.' Peter repeated the words in a whisper.

'Yes.' Jenner confirmed, and, now having given the news he wanted to get away. However, there was more he had to say and a lot he wanted to know. Peter helped him find the words.

'What happened? What went wrong?' The doctor looked away and then back into Peter's questioning eyes.

'We can not say for sure without an autopsy, but it appears your wife suffered a brain hemorrhage during the delivery.' His voice lost its confidence and he looked away before speaking. 'The pressure of labour could have dislodged a clot that had recently formed. It is unlikely. I have never heard of anything like it happening during childbirth before. It is very unusual for any woman to die in childbirth in this country, and especially in a hospital. It does happen, sometimes if there is a PPH and we can't arrest the bleeding in time.' Realising he was rambling the doctor coughed and returned his attention to Peter. 'That is what I wanted to ask you, Captain.' Before he could say anything further the sound of retching drew his attention to the young man who was doubled up on the floor his mouth discharging the half digested contents of his stomach.

'Nick!' Peter called out and went to his side. Nick was crying openly, his face wet with tears and saliva. His father placed an arm around his son's shoulders and looked up to see a nurse rushing toward them carrying a bowl of water that slopped over the metal rim.

Nick retched again and then slumped to the floor. Peter stood aside as the nurse cradled Nick's head and washed the vomit from his face. An Auxiliary nurse, wearing the distinctive brown checked uniform hurried into the room, she too was carrying a bucket of warm water and set about cleaning the floor. Nick was being helped into a chair and a cold towel rested on his forehead. The nurse was holding his hand and looked, to Peter, to be taking his pulse.

'Would you step out here please Captain?' Dr. Jenner guided Peter into the corridor with a gentle pressure on his elbow. 'I am sorry Captain Wells but could you tell me if your wife had a history of headaches? Had she ever knocked her head badly enough to render herself unconscious? Have you noticed any changes in her personality?'

'No!' Peter was both puzzled and angered by the questioning. 'I thought you said it was a brain hemorrhage?' His grief began to turn to anger and the doctor modulated his tone to try and maintain the fragile aura of normality.

'No Captain.' He began slowly. 'I said we believe it to be a brain hemorrhage. Although, as I said, that in itself is unlikely. Without an autopsy we can't say for sure.'

He waited before asking his next question. 'That is why Captain Wells, I want to ask your permission to carry out such an operation.'

Peter's eyes felt as if they were on fire and his own pulse pounded in his temples. For a moment he thought he would take hold of the young doctor and throw him across the corridor. He did not try and disguise the menace in his voice.

'If you go anywhere near my wife I'll break every bone in your body.' The words were not said loudly, but, their meaning was only too clear. The doctor stood back, waiting for a moment to impose his own will on the conversation.

'Captain Wells, under these circumstances I do not have to ask your permission.' He was about to appeal for understanding when he was interrupted.

'You do what you bloody well have to, but it won't bring her back. You go ahead, just don't come to me with your so called findings, trying to ease your medical conscience. Now, can I see my wife?'

The doctor's head slumped forward. He was not accustomed to delivering such tragic news and he knew he could have done it better. He stood aside and followed Peter back into the delivery room.

Carol was lying on the bed, her face a vision of serene beauty. Tears filled Peter's eyes as he bent down to kiss the lips that once were so full of life. He cradled her head against his chest and his tears fell on the crisp whiteness of the pillow.

Peter did not know how long he had been there when he felt the presence of someone else in the room. He stood back and brushed a hand across his eyes. Nick was standing a few feet away, his face white with grief, his eyes blazed red in their dark sockets.

'Oh Dad.' He exclaimed helplessly. 'What are we going to do?' He started to sob again and Peter moved to his side.

'Come on son. Carol would not like to see you like this.' He placed a hand on Nick's shoulder and led him to the bedside. 'She loved you, you know.' Peter said and forced a smile onto his lips. 'Now say your goodbyes and remember her as she would want you to...laughing and full of life.'

Nick fought back the tears, his chest heaving under suppressed cries. Both men stood like sentries looking down at the sleeping form on the white sheets. They, for whom the passing of the clock's hands had once been so important were now plunged into a timeless void of grief.

'Excuse me, Captain Wells.' A soft voice penetrated the unreal atmosphere and registered in Peter's consciousness as a slight sound from a world miles away. 'Captain Wells, excuse me sir.' This time he realised that he was not in a dream and looked round to see a young nurse standing in the doorway. 'Would you like to see your daughter?' Once again words held no meaning.

'My daughter?' Peter asked bewilderedly.

The nurse walked closer and Peter thought he saw Carol's face smiling out from under the starched white headdress.

'We have your daughter upstairs. She is beautiful. Would you like to come and see her?'

It was Nick who responded first. The words having broken into his grief like a redeeming shaft of light.

'Can we see her now?' He asked, turning his watery eyes towards the nurse. The girl was not very old and confusion showed on her young face. She spoke again to Peter.

'Would you like to meet your daughter, sir?'

This time the question was understood and Peter coughed to clear his throat before answering.

'Yes, yes I would. May my son come along?' The nurse smiled in her new found understanding.

'Of course. Please follow me.'

She led the way out of the room. As Peter and Nick passed through the door they looked back knowing that this was the last chance to see the woman they loved with the fading bloom of life on her face.

Peter held the tiny baby in his big hands. A shock of black hair peeped out from under the blanket that enfolded his daughter. Peter felt strangely embarrassed as he looked down at the miniature girl in his arms. Nick looked on, over his father's shoulder and said;

'She is beautiful, isn't she? Can I hold her?'

Peter handed over the bundle and, as he watched his son holding the child, his emotions became confused with uncertainty and wonder. 'She is pretty.' He thought, 'but, she is not a boy!'

'How am I going to look after a girl?'

The question came as a cry from the wilderness, an appeal for help, an untypical outburst from a man who never asked for anything except obedience.

The nurse smiled as she watched the two ungainly men holding the infant in unsure hands. The inevitable happened. The baby, sensing the insecurity around her gave vent to her fears and rent the air with cries. Quickly the nurse took her and after only a few moments in capable hands the crying stopped. The nurse placed the child back into its Perspex crib and led the men out into the corridor.

'Do not worry about looking after the baby. We will help you. You can see her anytime and when you are ready you may take her home.' She saw the frown appear on Peter's forehead and added; 'we will help you there also.' The assurance did not go a long way in allaying his fears, but, he was not given long to worry about them as the nurse spoke again. 'Dr. Jenner said that he would like to see you before you leave, he will be waiting down at reception. I must go now. Come back and see your daughter as often as you like.' She lowered her voice before continuing. 'I am very sorry for your loss, but, you do have a beautiful daughter. Goodbye.'

Peter and Nick thanked her and watched as she disappeared into a small ward at the end of the corridor. Peter held out his right hand and touched his son's shoulder.

'Well Nick, let's go see the doctor.'

They took the lift to the ground floor and saw the young doctor standing by the glass doors at the entrance to the building. His face still bore the look of a man who did not want to be there. He would be a lot happier when these men were out of his hospital and he could be left to deal with his patients. He was a good technical surgeon, but, he was not confident in ministering to the bereaved. He prepared himself for the last and most difficult encounter.

'Captain Wells.' He spoke evenly and slowly, keeping his voice a low monotone. He nodded his acknowledgement of Nick's presence and then continued; 'you have seen your daughter?' Peter nodded and the doctor spoke again. 'She is a very pretty baby.' The pleasantries over Dr. Jenner steeled himself for the next duty and hoped he was handling the encounter correctly. 'Now Captain, your wife's belongings are with the Registrar. I don't expect you will want to collect them now as there are a few questions you will be asked that will only serve to upset you more at this stage.' He stopped again and coughed to clear his throat. After the interlude of seeing and holding the baby, the horrors of the day returned to cover Peter like a shroud. He wished the doctor would finish so that he could leave this place. 'There is no easy way of saying this.' Jenner began again by apologising. 'If you would come back in the next couple of days, collect your wife's things and tell us what arrangements you have made.' He stopped abruptly, not able to complete the sentence and changed his tack. 'Now what about the two of you?' Peter and Nick looked at each other and then back to the doctor for an explanation. 'Do either of you feel that you need anything to help you cope with what has happened? Would you like me to arrange for a taxi to take you home?' His face now dropped its official facade and became a genuine reflection of his sadness and concern.

Peter replied firmly as if answering an operational question that implied he needed assistance to complete a routine task.

'Neither will be necessary, thank you.' He shook hands with the doctor and as he did so looked into the younger man's eyes. 'I will be in tomorrow to take care of any formalities.'

Jenner nodded his head.

'Very well.' He said and shook both their hands. He watched as they left the building. Peter had his arm around Nick's shoulder.

Nick was crying again as they crossed the road to the car park. He looked back at the tall, blond brick building and its walls full of non-reflecting windows.

'I can't believe it.' He said in a quiet, sorrowful voice, not meaning for anyone to hear. He removed a handkerchief from his jacket pocket and dabbed his eyes. Peter was walking slightly ahead, but, out of the corner of his eye could see the signs of grief on his son's face. They walked up the slight incline to where Peter had left the car only twelve hours before. Without turning to look at Nick he asked;

'Shall we leave your car here? We can collect it tomorrow. I would appreciate some company on the way home.' It was not true. All Peter really wanted was to be alone, to come to terms with what had happened and work out a plan for the future. Looking at his son he knew that he had a more immediate responsibility.

As they drove out into the mid-morning traffic it struck Peter that everyone was at work. It was Monday. Another working week had begun and for millions of people life went on as normal.

The cold formalities of death occupied the rest of the

week. Having returned to the hospital the following day the true weight of what happened finally descended on Peter Wells. He had made himself walk past the ward where Carol had lain so beautiful in anticipation of childbirth, and, in realisation of death. He recalled holding the baby daughter for the first time. She was a child he was not prepared for. It made him feel alone and in his uncertainty that is how he wanted to be.

Under protest, Nick had returned home to stay with his mother until the funeral. Peter was left to stalk the silent house. In his solitude he began to question his own life, until, on the third day he decided to put on his uniform and drive to the school.

The heavy, navy blue cloth, the gold braid on the sleeves, the white cap with its golden crest and peak felt like a suit of protective armour covering his whole body. As he drove through the main gate and returned the salute of the sentry he felt strengthened by the familiarity of the surroundings and the trappings of the service. His officers greeted him warmly, happy to have him back among them.

Once behind his desk Peter felt a surge of confidence flood through his whole being. It was as if the chair itself was magically charged to rejuvenate its occupant. Peter leant forward and pressed the button on the desk intercom. The voice of his secretary crackled on the other end of the line.

'Yes, Sir?'

'John, could you get onto the Senior Medical Officer and see if he is free to come and have a chat?'

'Aye Aye, Sir.'

The line went dead and Peter looked about the room. His eyes passed over the regulation portrait of the Queen, photographs of past ships in which he had served; a chart of the English Channel and then settled on his desk and the photograph of Carol smiling out at him from inside a silver frame. Leaning forward he took the picture in his hands and sat staring into the brown eyes he had neglected and now longed to see. The buzzing alarm of the intercom brought him back to the present. He pushed the receive button.

'Excuse me sir, Commander Graham to see you, sir.'
'Very good, please send him in.'

Peter replaced the photograph on his desk and left his chair so he could greet the Surgeon Commander as he entered the room.

The flowing white hair of the doctor swept over his head like a rough sea, and his eyebrows rose to meet it like two waves bursting against a sea wall.

'Good morning, Sir. It is good to see you back.' Peter thanked him and directed the doctor to a seat in front of his desk.

'What can I do for you, Sir?' Despite the formality the doctor spoke as an old friend. Peter had first met him at Dartmouth when the doctor was responsible for the medical welfare of new entry Midshipmen. He could not remember him looking any different than he did now.

'Geoffrey, I do not know how much the grapevine has picked up, but, you may know that I have a daughter.' The white sea moved forward and back but said nothing. 'What I would like you to do is find out what help I can get to bring up a baby so that I can continue to carry out my duties without too much disruption.' The Surgeon Commander remained silent for a moment longer and then replied.

'I can do that sir, certainly. However, you must know that being a single parent is going to make new demands on you and your time. You will most certainly have to adapt in some ways.'

'Thank you Geoffrey. I know. You never could resist giving advice, and I will say this, it is worth listening to.'

The doctor was smiling now,

'If I recall correctly you never listened to a word I said in any of our previous encounters.' He stopped and then became serious once more. 'I will do what you ask and if there is anything I can do personally, you know you just have to say the word.' Peter rose to his feet and walked around the desk to shake hands with the Surgeon Commander.

'Thank you very much Geoffrey. I may well take you up on that.'

Nick returned to his mother's home. He roamed the house at all hours of the day and night. He could not sleep. His young mind tried to come to terms with death.

He spoke to his mother about the baby and how he did not think Peter wanted to look after a girl. Angela listened and understood only too well the ambitions that Peter would have had for a son. However, she could not believe he would turn his back on any responsibility. She questioned her son more deeply and uncovered in the unguarded moments of his grief how much he loved Carol Wells. She was disturbed to learn how much she dominated his life and how that love was now transferred to the child.

Nick passionately resented being sent home. He told his mother that Peter wanted to keep him away from the child. At that moment he had cried again. Angela had cradled his head to her breast, trying to soothe away the sobs that wracked his body. It hurt her to see him so upset. She began to think of ways to help her son, and Peter, if he would let her.

Chapter 27

The funeral took place at one o'clock on a cold Monday afternoon. For Carol it was in death as it was in life, her family and a few close friends.

Peter stood outside the chapel. His greatcoat kept out the chill February wind. During the service he felt himself shivering and hoped it had not been noticed.

Carol's parents had offered to provide refreshments for the mourners at their home in Old Portsmouth and Peter now looked to them. His heart went out to Mrs. Adison, her face buried in a white handkerchief, as it had been throughout the service. Her husband had steadied her throughout the ordeal, although, he too looked ashen with grief. Peter wondered whether he should have allowed them to talk him into having the gathering at their home. They had argued that after it was all over they could all go and see the baby at the hospital. Peter had relented. Geoffrey Graham had found out many ways by which the Captain could be helped to bring up his child, but, Peter knew his best allies would be his daughter's grandparents. Mrs. Adison was fifty two years old and her husband six years her senior. They were both fit and full of life. They had been thankful when Peter asked for their assistance and outlined his plans for the future.

He would sell the house in the country and move to Old Portsmouth. He would then be close to Carol's parents. He also knew that the old house held too many memories and some reminders that perhaps he was not as good a husband as he might have been. In another house, another location, he could change and ensure that his daughter benefited from the bitter lessons learned in those cold, silent hours, when he walked the lonely rooms at Meonstoke.

Nick stood beside Peter throughout the service. His eyes never left the polished mahogany casket until it disappeared behind the mechanically drawn curtain. At that moment the finality and gravity of his loss descended upon him like a yolk of granite, but he had no more tears left to shed. It would have been easier if there were. Without them the desolation stayed within him and he became the prisoner of his grief.

Standing in the grounds of the crematorium that overlooked Portchester Castle and the waters of Portsmouth Harbour, Nick knew that if he was to have a place in the life of the new born child he would have to act now. He crossed the black surface of the crematorium's driveway and stood before his father. The long coat bedecked with gold buttons, braided epaulettes and black silk armband gave Peter a foreboding air of authority. Nick steeled his nerve to speak.

'Excuse me, Dad.' The word that had come easily in his grief now came reluctantly to his lips.

'Yes Nick, what is it?' As he spoke he rested a heavy arm on his son's shoulder. The familiarity made Nick feel ashamed. For a moment he found it hard to continue,

'There is someone I would like you to meet.'

Peter sensed the uncertainty and intrigue in his son's voice.

'Very well.' He replied. 'Where is this person?'

Nick led the way to the car park and very soon Peter recognised the mystery person sat in the passenger seat of Nick's car. Angela looked up but did not get out of the car. Peter removed his cap and bent down. He rested his forehead against the top of the door and spoke through the open window.

'Hello Angela.' He said guardedly.

'Hello Peter. I am so sorry.' He could tell by her tone and expression that she was upset but he remained silent. He knew she was there for a reason other than to personally deliver her condolences. She began uncertainly. 'Peter, Nick tells me you are concerned about how to bring up your daughter so that she gets a family environment and you can still continue your career.' Peter's eyes became hard and seeing the warning sign Angela wondered if her information was correct. She had gone too far to back down. 'If you were to agree, I would adopt the baby and bring her up. Of course you could see her whenever you like. She would just be part of a greater family.'

Peter could not believe what was being said and so just stared into the car with both hands now resting on the door. His initial anger had subsided behind a screen of disbelief. When the words did come they held more meaning and were delivered with greater conviction than any emotional outburst could possibly have conveyed. Firstly, he looked sideways at Nick, and then back at his mother.

'Angela, I know Nick is concerned for the child and from what you have just said he must think that I am not. That is not true. Even if it were, I would never allow you to take another child away from me.' He paused to let his words sink in and then concluded. 'I am now going to my in-laws house where there will be refreshments for the guests and you are welcome to come along. Nick knows the address.' He stood up and replaced the cap back on his head which added to his height and the illusion of power. 'If I don't see you there, I thank you for your concern.' He turned to Nick. 'I think we should talk.'

'Yes, Sir.' The reply came automatically

The guests spoke quietly as Peter circulated, offering to refill sherry glasses or stopping to accept condolences. When the doorbell rang he broke away and went to answer it.

He opened the door to find Nick standing under the porch. Peter glanced over Nick's shoulder and was relieved to see that he was alone.

'I am glad you're here. Where is your mother?'

'I put her on the train at Portsmouth Harbour.'

'Good.' Peter touched his son's arm and pointed to a quiet study across the hall from the crowded sitting room. Once inside he closed the door and shut out the rest of the world. Nick stood with his hands clasped in front of him. On the drive from the station he had prepared himself for this meeting, but, he was not looking forward to it.

'Now Nick, there are some arrangements I have made that you should know about.' The friendly tone of his father's voice confused him, now, not knowing what to think, Nick just listened. Peter outlined his intentions as he had done with Carol's parents. He then added something extra that caught Nick completely off guard. 'I have my eye on a Georgian house, not unlike this one.' He looked around the high ceilinged room, indicating with his eyes what he was talking about. 'As you can see they are quite spacious, and, for one man and a baby, far too big.' He stopped before putting forward his most important proposal. 'Would you like to come in with me?' Nick felt as if someone had just kicked him in the stomach. The wind was taken from his body and he felt like sitting down. He fought the sensation and held his ground. Peter continued. 'You would be in comfortable commuting distance for the airport and we could lose each other on any floor of one of these places.'

A smile eventually came to Nick's lips and a feeling of warmth replaced the emptiness of the moment before. He crossed the few paces that separated him from his father and threw his arms around his shoulders, hugging him to his chest. He felt Peter's body straighten under the unbidden show of affection and then relax and return the embrace.

They stood in the middle of the quiet room holding each other, each lost in his own private thoughts.

Eventually, Peter moved back but kept his hands on Nick's shoulders, his arms outstretched.

'Good.' He said. 'Welcome home.'

Matador

For exclusive discounts on Matador titles,
sign up to our occasional newsletter at
troubador.co.uk/bookshop

Milton Keynes UK
Ingram Content Group UK Ltd.
UKHW022247191023
430968UK00010B/367